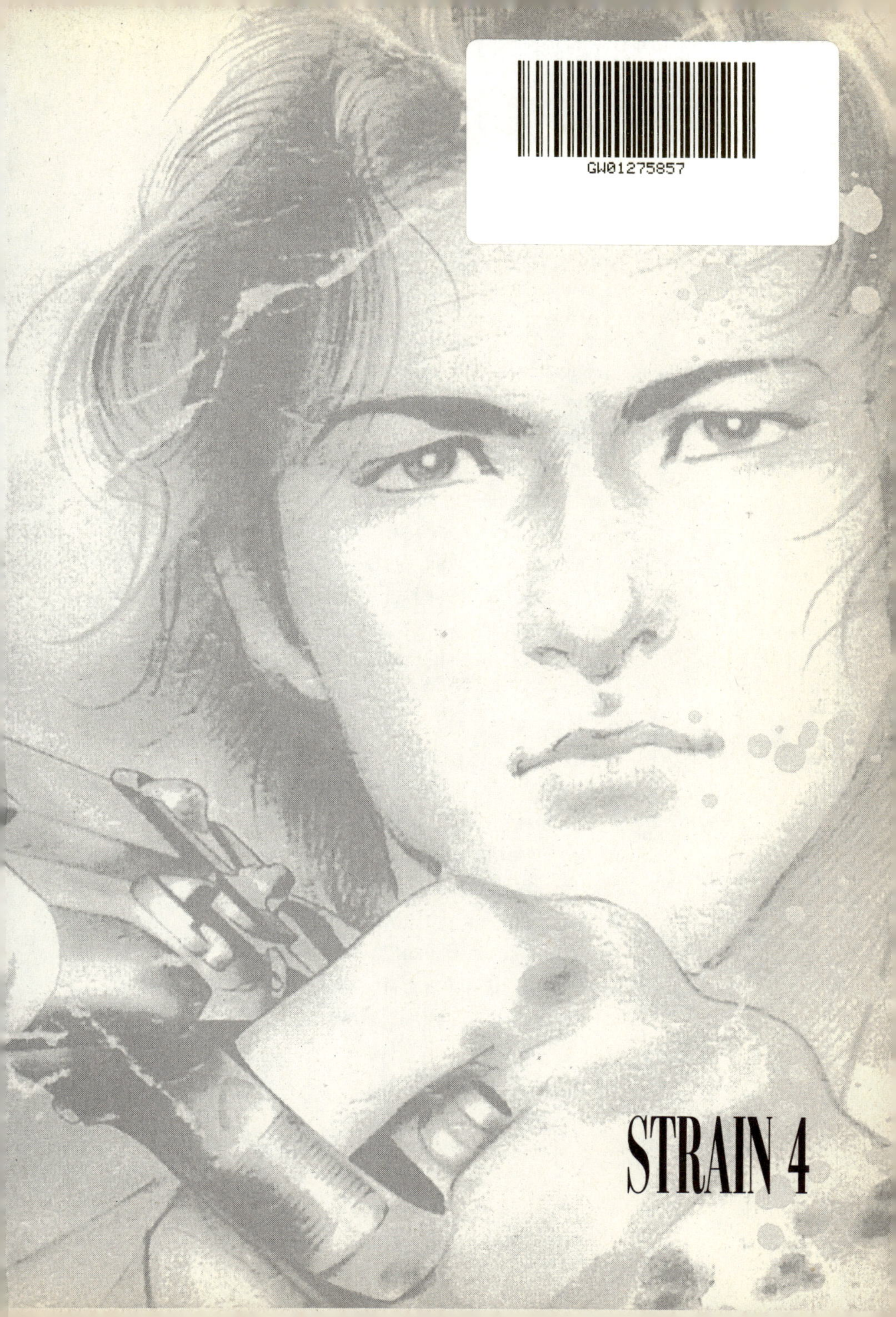
STRAIN 4

THE STORY THUS FAR...

Shunichiro Kusaka's multi-billion dollar gamble has just paid off—a KUSAKA test drill in Borneo has blown out a gusher of oil, proving the possibility of a new Asian power bloc centered around its own petroleum supply. But it's just at this moment of triumph that Shunichiro's crooked partner and old Oxford chum, Chinese mafia lord Shimei Sai, has made a secret deal to buy up Shunichiro's own shares of KUSAKA to form a controlling stake. And now two ruthless men, yakuza Murota and crooked cop Angel, assigned to eliminate Shunichiro's daughter Shion and half-brother Shingo, have instead defected to the side of the hunted. While Murota prepares to whisk Shion and her guardian Kyoko out of the country, Angel introduces Shingo to his heavily-armed friends—bitter Amerasian children of the Vietnam War, just like him...

STRAIN

STORY BY BURONSON, ART BY RYOICHI IKEGAMI

PULP GRAPHIC NOVEL

vol. 4

STORY BY
BURONSON
ART BY
RYOICHI IKEGAMI

**ENGLISH ADAPTATION BY
YUJI ONIKI**

This volume contains the STRAIN installments
from PULP Vol. 3., No. 12 through Vol. 4, No. 7 in
their entirety.

Touch-Up Art & Lettering/Cato
Cover Design/Izumi Evers
Editor/Annette Roman and Carl Gustav Horn

Senior Marketing Manager/Dallas Middaugh
Senior Sales Manager/Ann Ivan
Managing Editor/Annette Roman
Editor-in-Chief/Hyoe Narita
Publisher/Seiji Horibuchi

Printed in Canada

Published by Viz Communications, Inc.
P.O. Box 77010 · San Francisco, CA 94107

10 9 8 7 6 5 4 3 2 1
First printing, Nov 2000

Vizit our web sites at www.viz.com, www.pulp-
mag.com, www.animerica-mag.com, and our
Internet magazine at www.j-pop.com!

PULP GRAPHIC NOVELS TO DATE

BANANA FISH VOL. 1
BANANA FISH VOL. 2
BANANA FISH VOL. 3
BANANA FISH VOL. 4

BAKUNE YOUNG VOL. 1

BLACK & WHITE VOL. 1
BLACK & WHITE VOL. 2
BLACK & WHITE VOL. 3

DANCE TILL TOMORROW VOL. 1
DANCE TILL TOMORROW VOL. 2
DANCE TILL TOMORROW VOL. 3

HEARTBROKEN ANGELS VOL. 1

STRAIN VOL. 1
STRAIN VOL. 2
STRAIN VOL. 3
STRAIN VOL. 4

VOYEUR
VOYEURS, INC. VOL. 1

CONTENTS

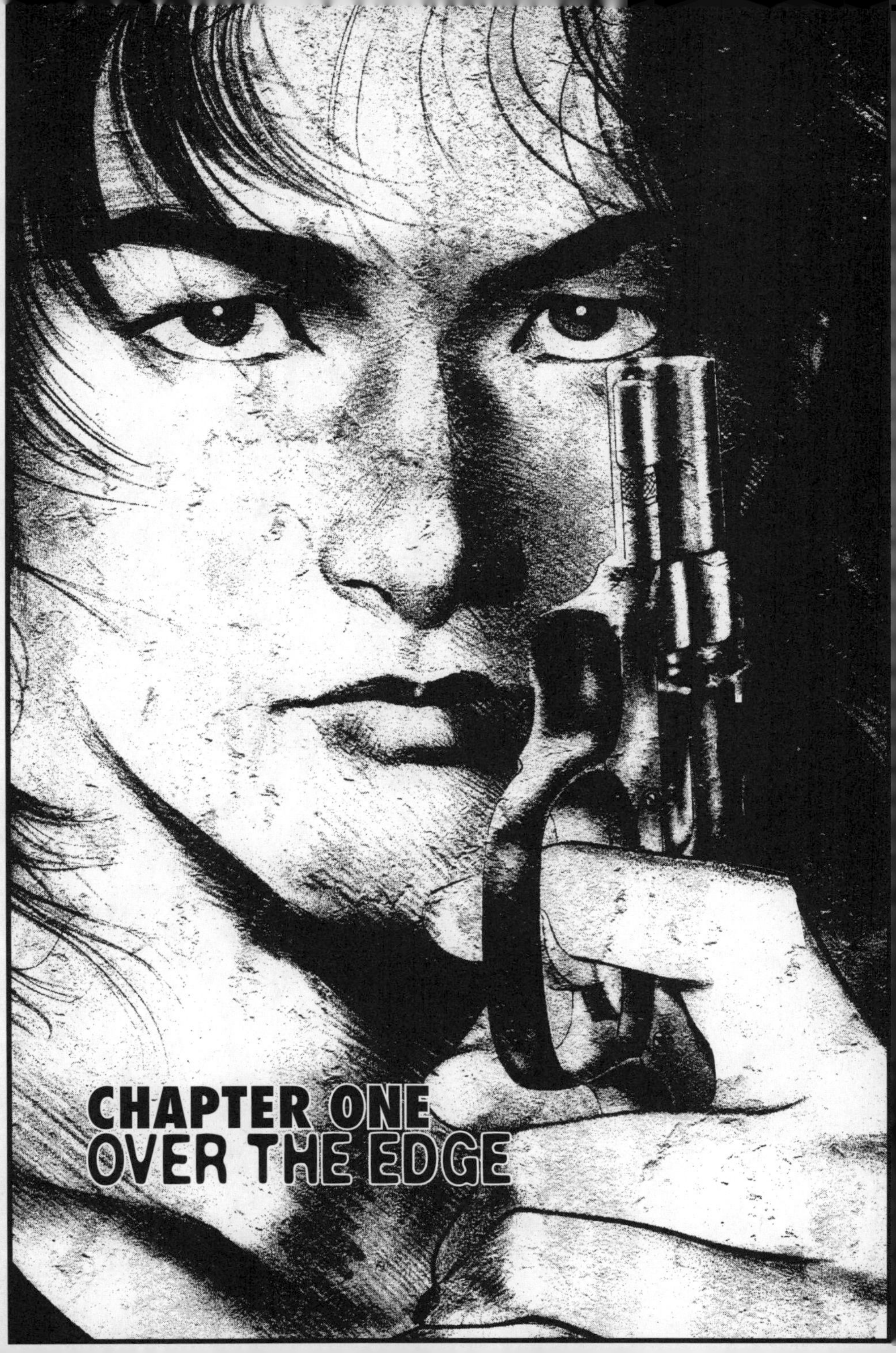
CHAPTER ONE
OVER THE EDGE

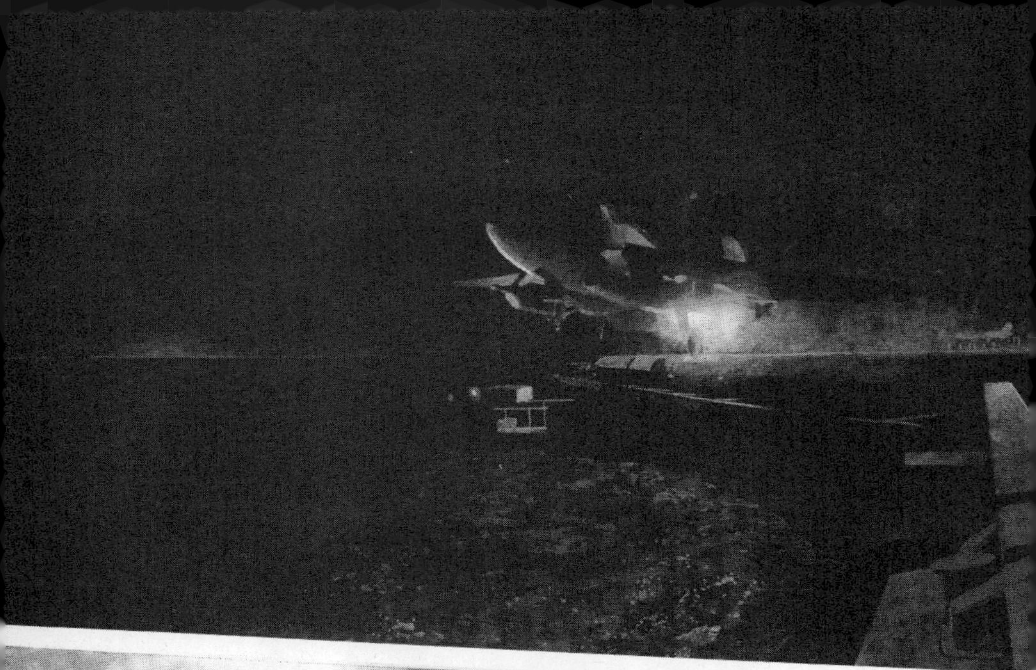

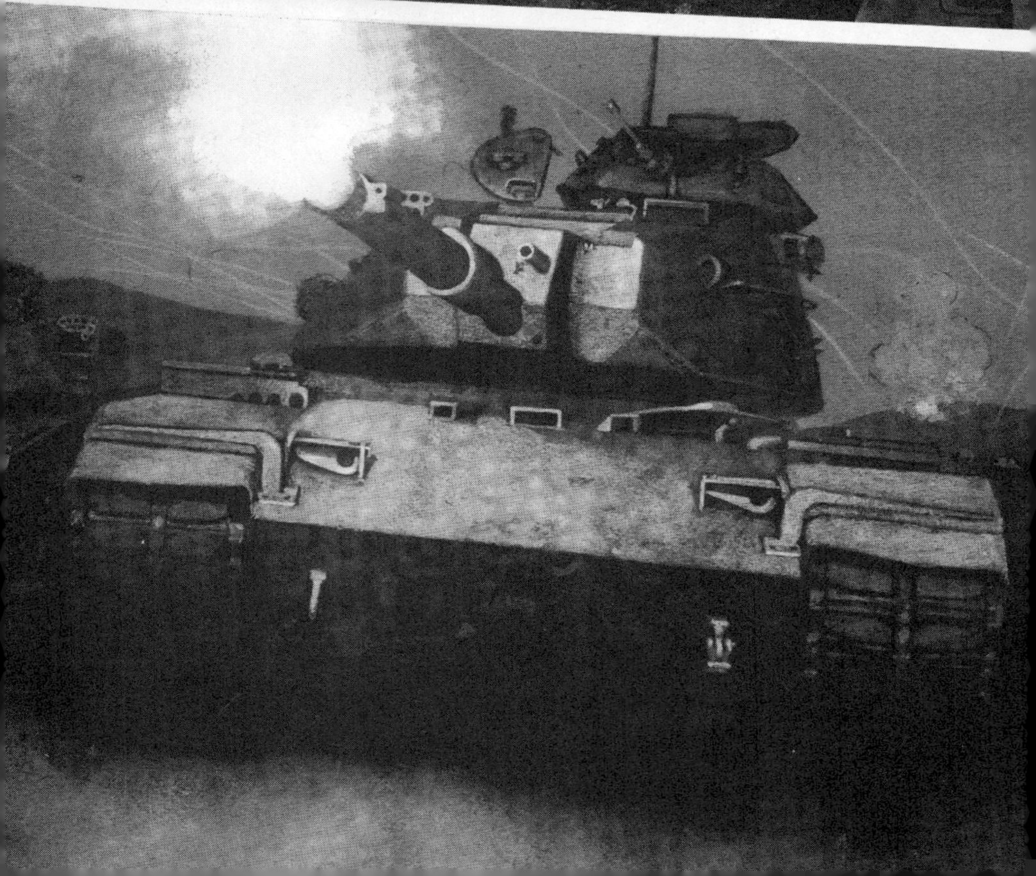

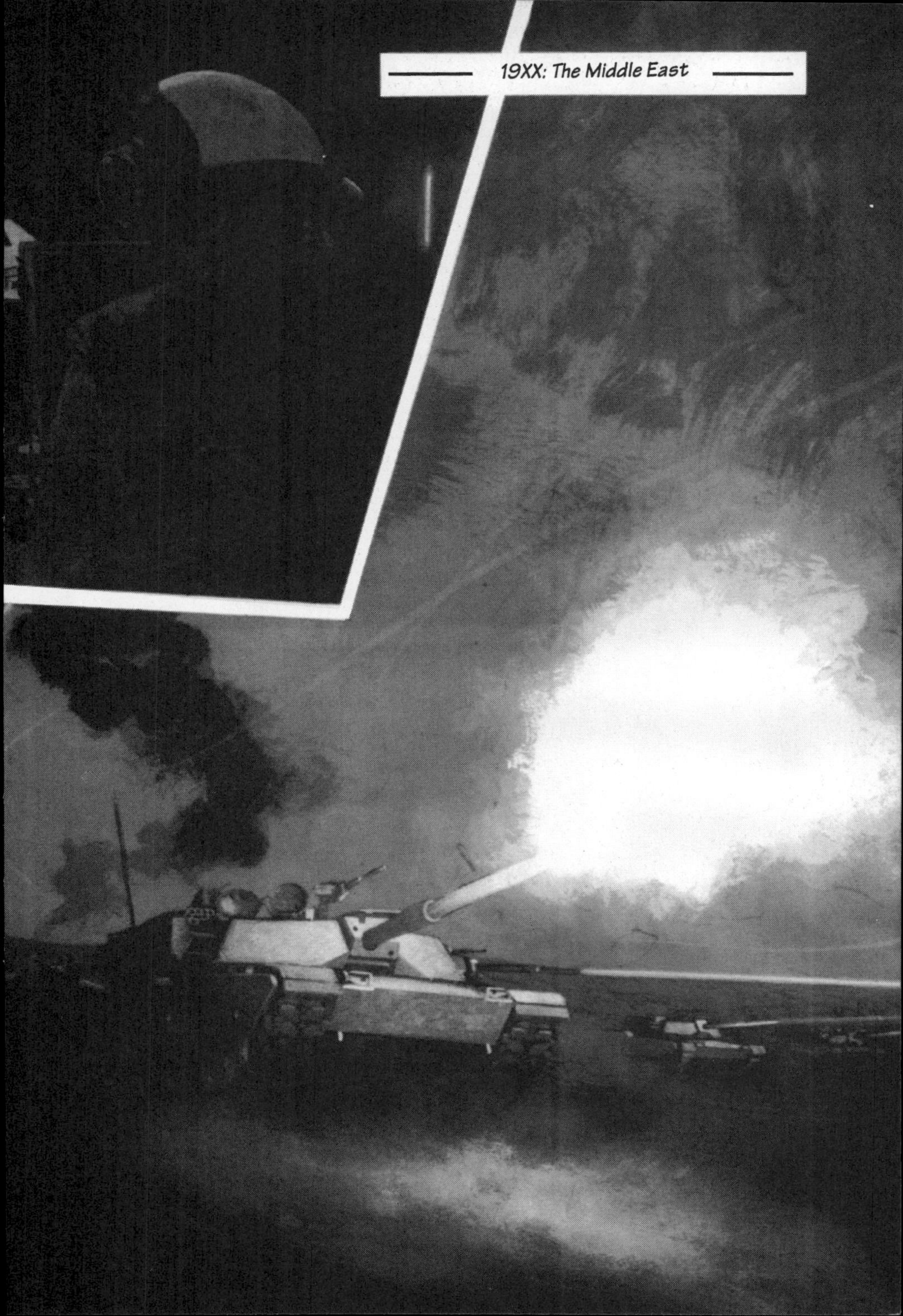
19XX: The Middle East

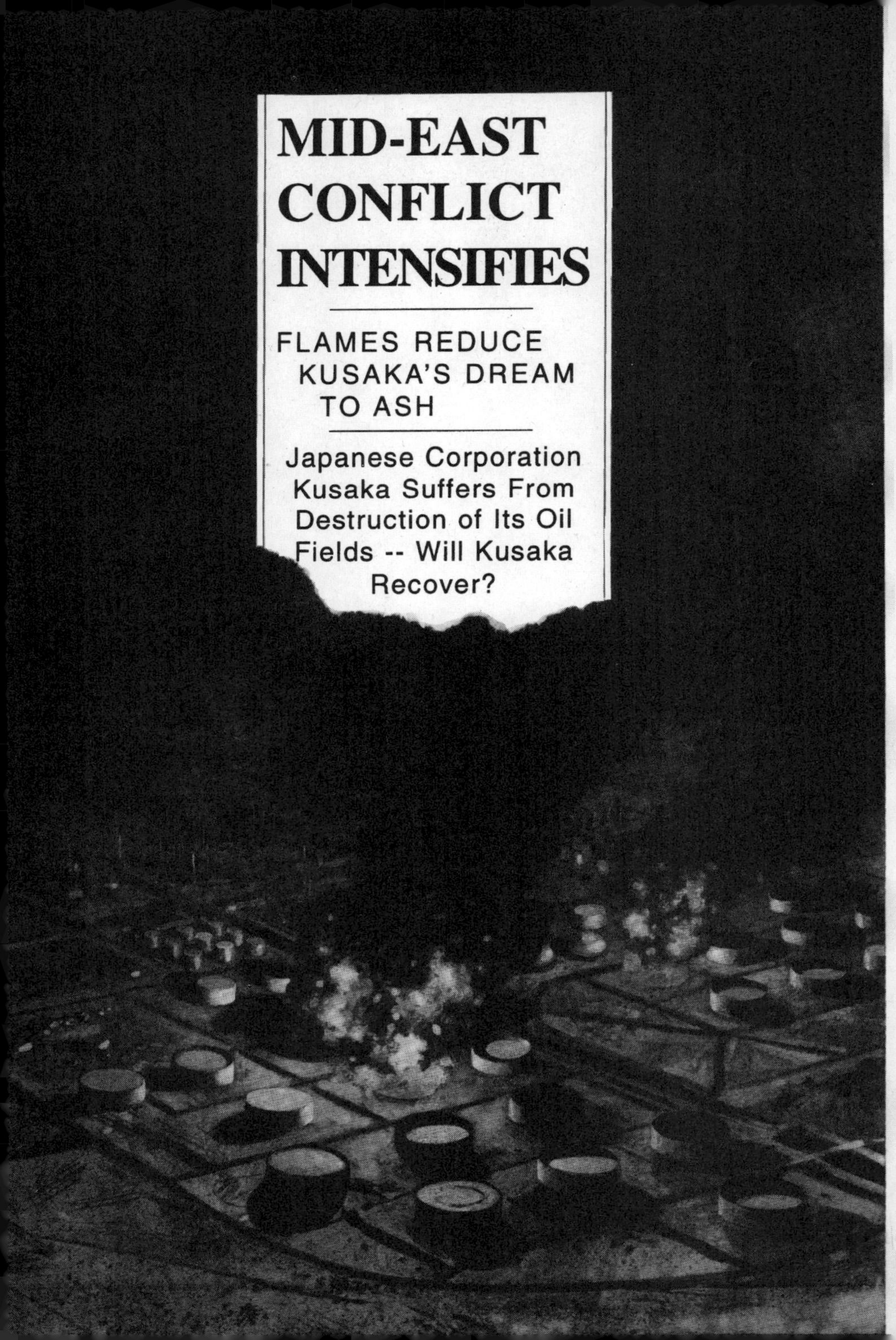
MID-EAST CONFLICT INTENSIFIES
FLAMES REDUCE KUSAKA'S DREAM TO ASH
Japanese Corporation Kusaka Suffers From Destruction of Its Oil Fields -- Will Kusaka Recover?

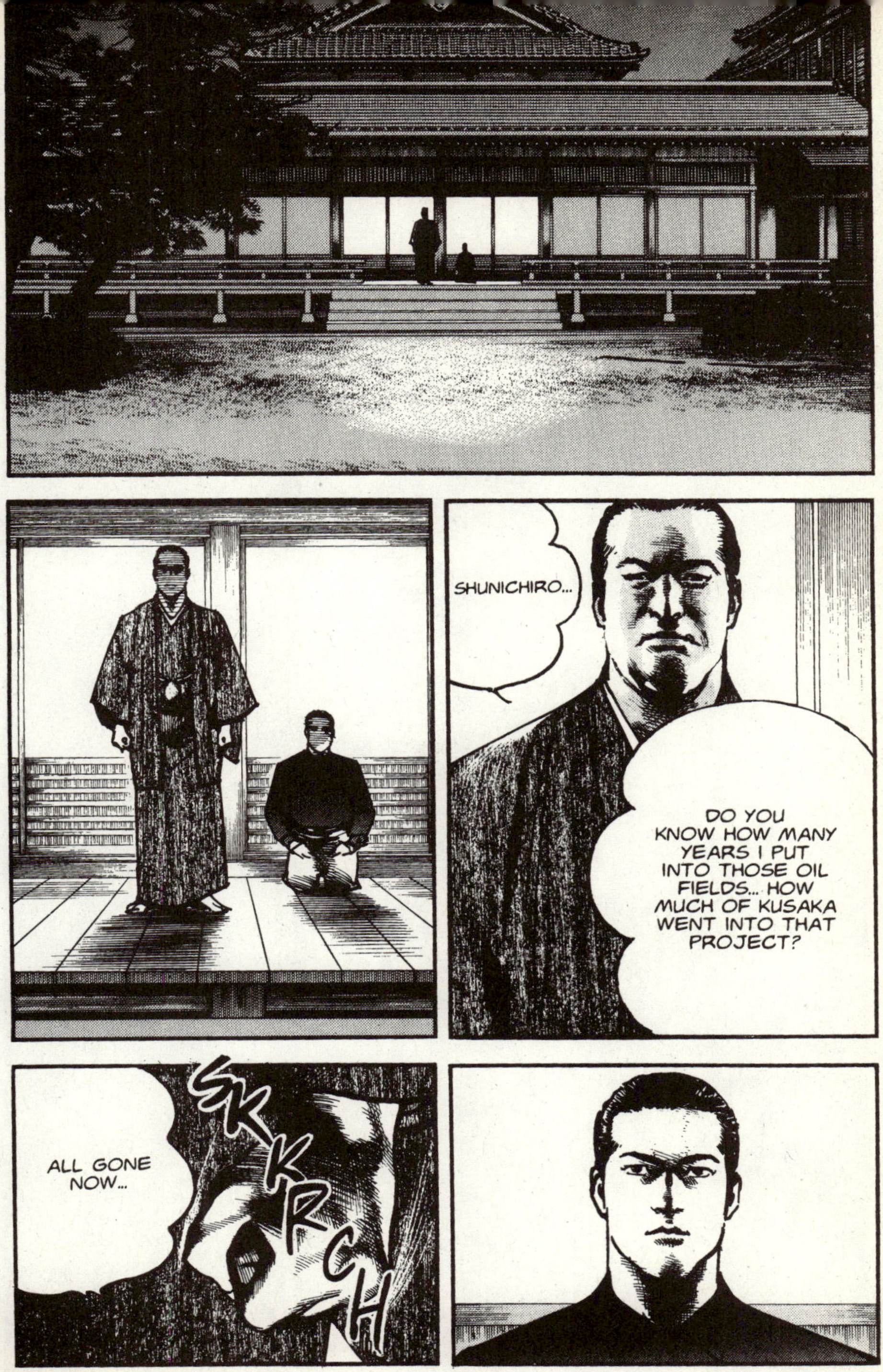
SHUNICHIRO...
DO YOU KNOW HOW MANY YEARS I PUT INTO THOSE OIL FIELDS... HOW MUCH OF KUSAKA WENT INTO THAT PROJECT?
ALL GONE NOW...
SKKRCH

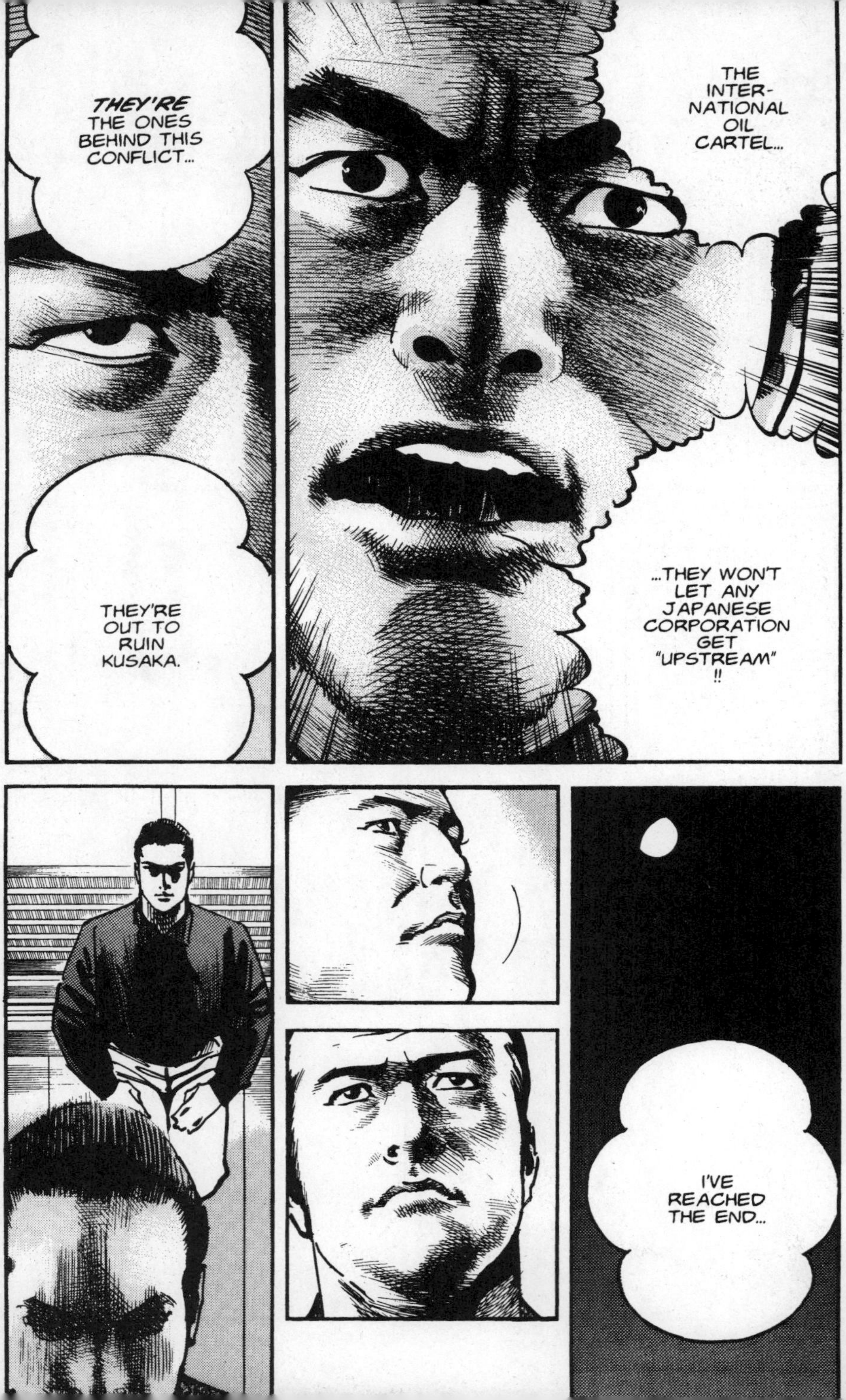
THE INTER-NATIONAL OIL CARTEL...
THEY'RE THE ONES BEHIND THIS CONFLICT...
...THEY WON'T LET ANY JAPANESE CORPORATION GET "UPSTREAM"!!
THEY'RE OUT TO RUIN KUSAKA.
I'VE REACHED THE END...

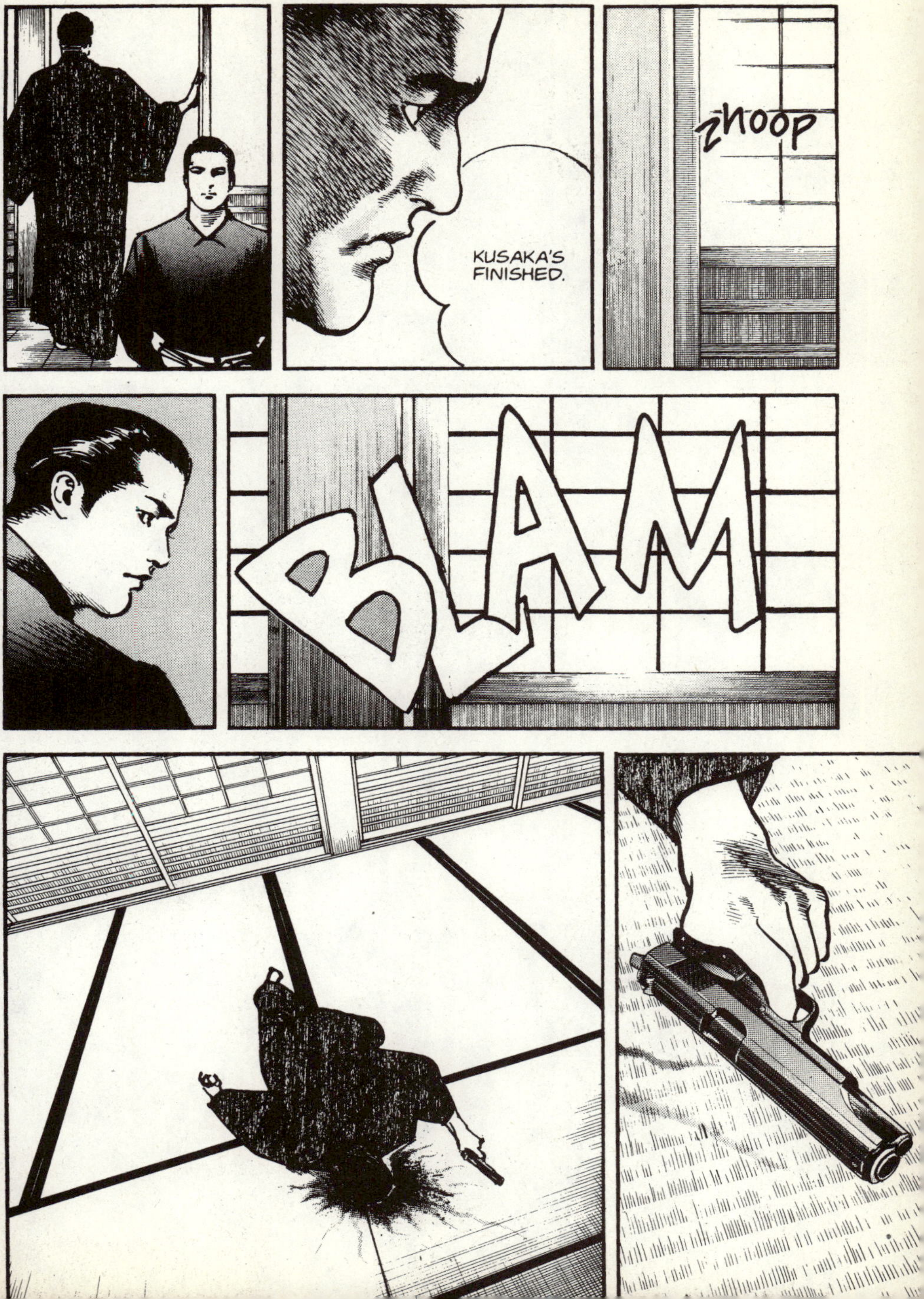
KUSAKA'S FINISHED.
zhoop
BLAM

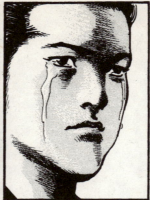

FATHER... YOU ARE WEAK...

THAT MIGHT BE THE END OF YOU...

BUT *MY* KUSAKA IS STILL ALIVE AND KICKING!

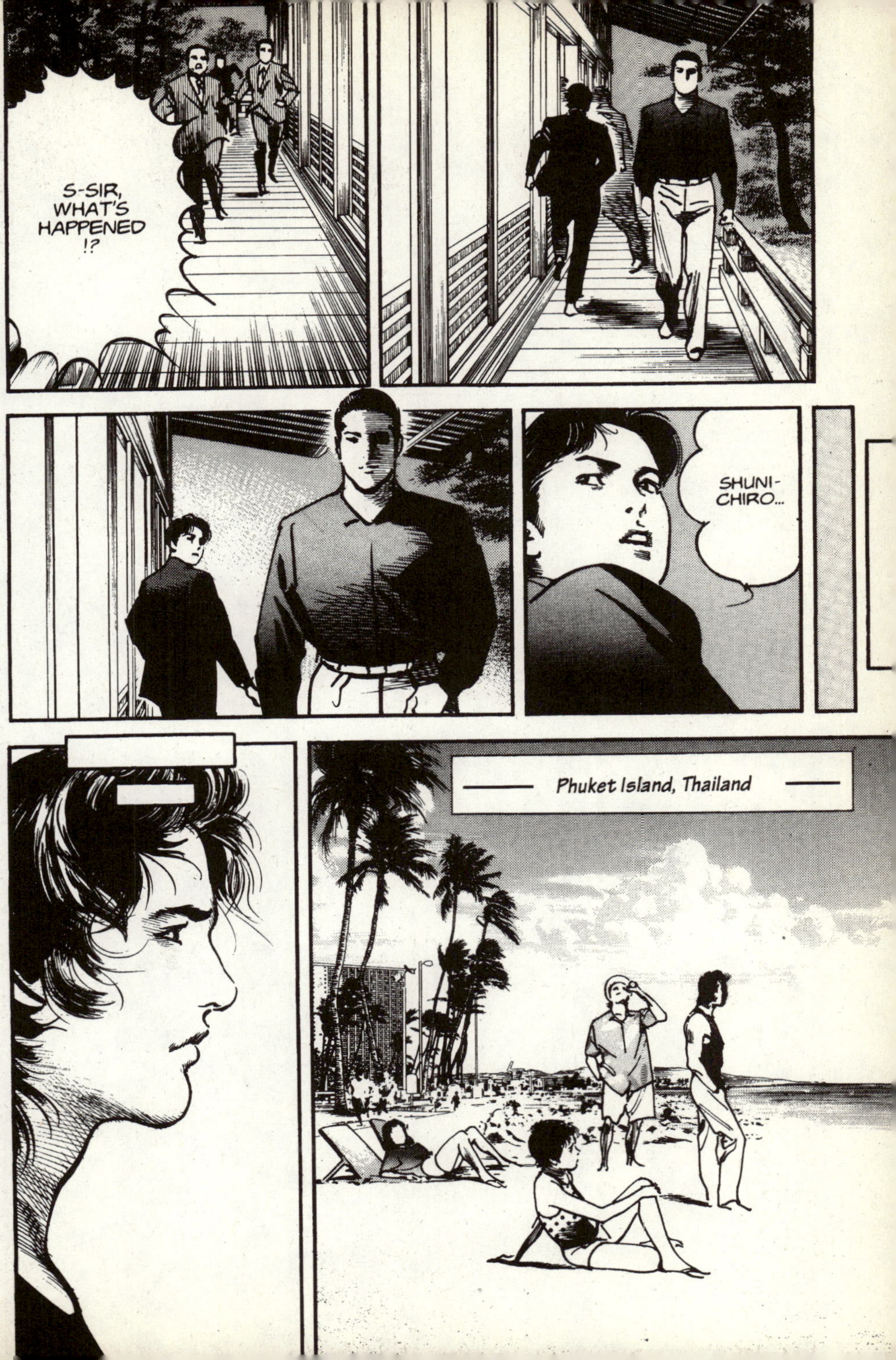
S-SIR, WHAT'S HAPPENED !?
SHUNI-CHIRO...
Phuket Island, Thailand

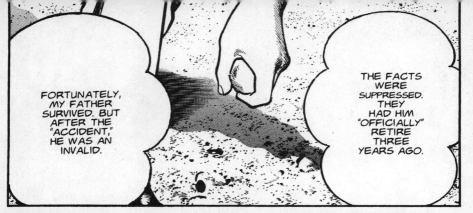

FORTUNATELY, MY FATHER SURVIVED. BUT AFTER THE "ACCIDENT," HE WAS AN INVALID.

THE FACTS WERE SUPPRESSED. THEY HAD HIM "OFFICIALLY" RETIRE THREE YEARS AGO.

THAT'S WHAT REALLY HAPPENED.

FROM THAT DAY ON, SHUNICHIRO WAS A DIFFERENT MAN...

Kusaka Office, Malaysia

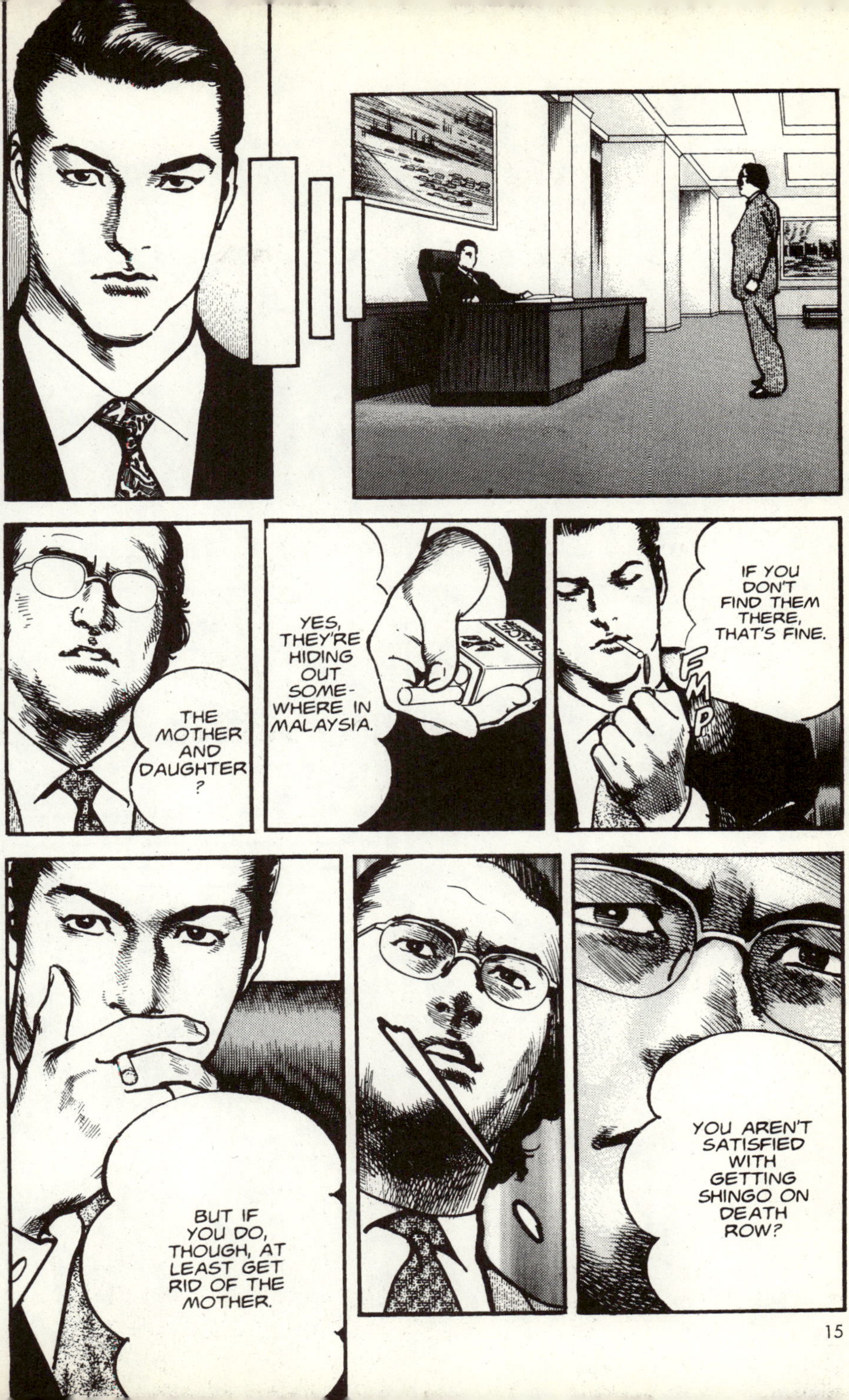
THE MOTHER AND DAUGHTER?
YES, THEY'RE HIDING OUT SOME-WHERE IN MALAYSIA.
FMP
IF YOU DON'T FIND THEM THERE, THAT'S FINE.
BUT IF YOU DO, THOUGH, AT LEAST GET RID OF THE MOTHER.
YOU AREN'T SATISFIED WITH GETTING SHINGO ON DEATH ROW?

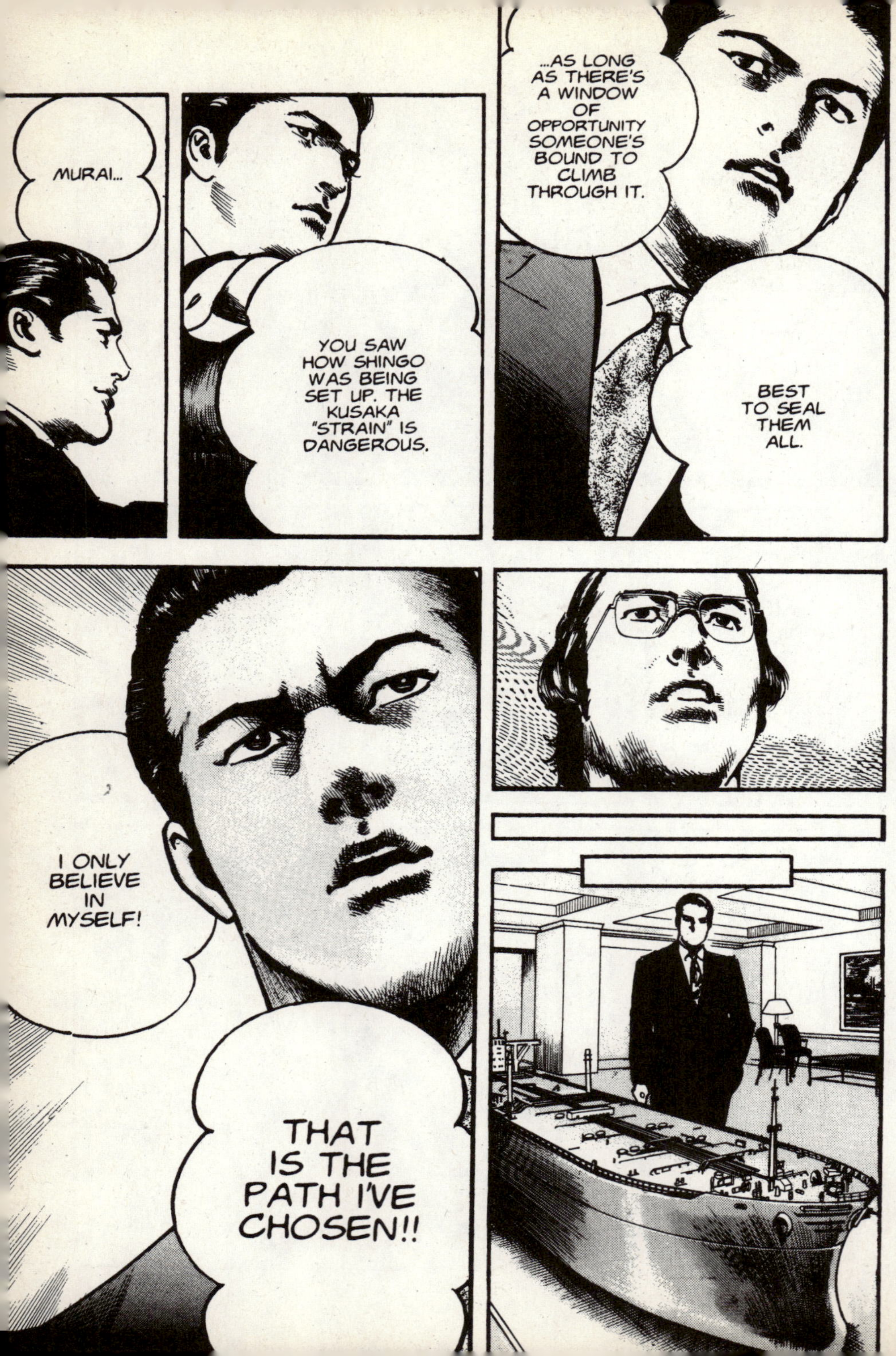

MURAI...
YOU SAW HOW SHINGO WAS BEING SET UP. THE KUSAKA "STRAIN" IS DANGEROUS.
...AS LONG AS THERE'S A WINDOW OF OPPORTUNITY SOMEONE'S BOUND TO CLIMB THROUGH IT.
BEST TO SEAL THEM ALL.
I ONLY BELIEVE IN MYSELF!
THAT IS THE PATH I'VE CHOSEN!!

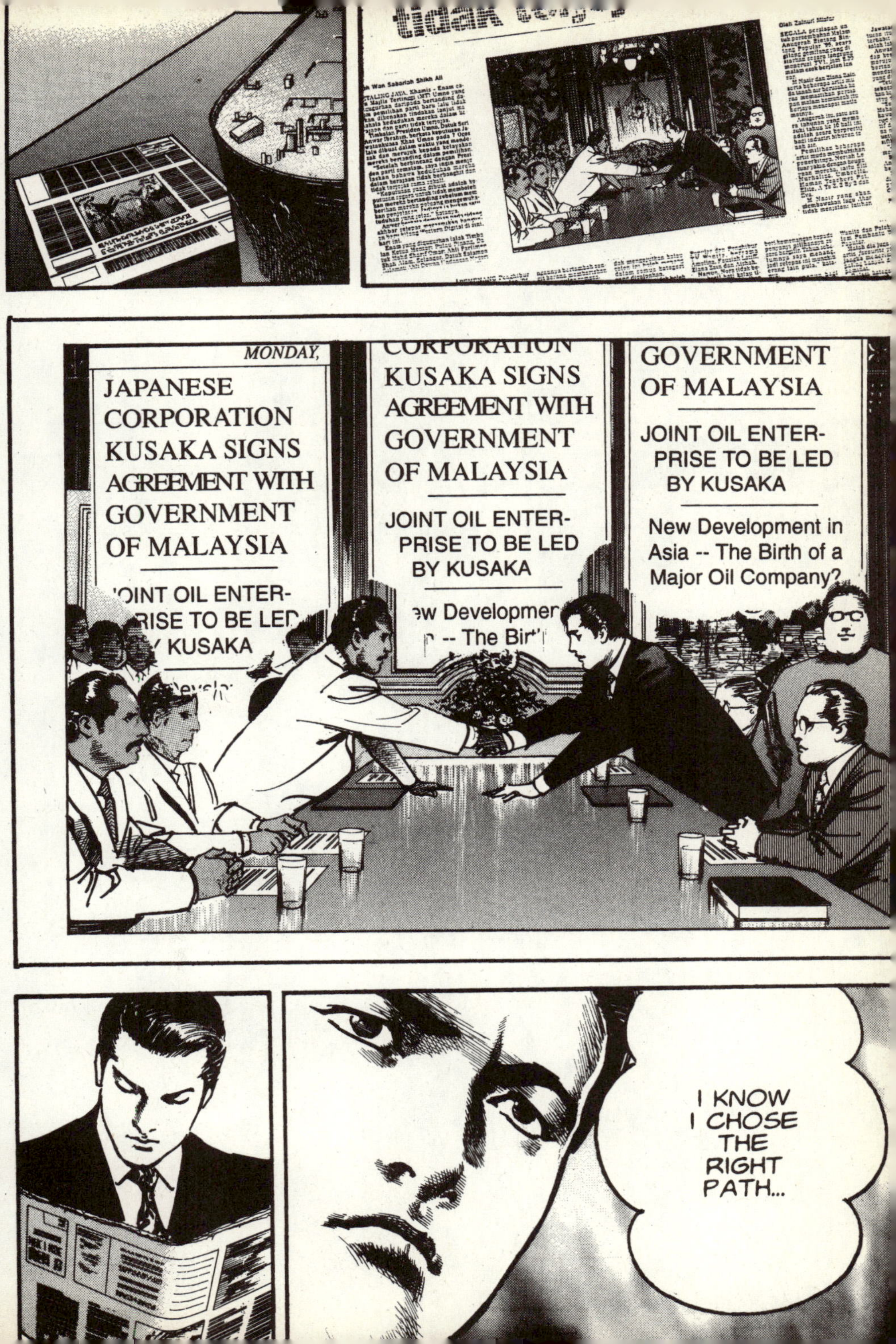

MONDAY,
JAPANESE CORPORATION KUSAKA SIGNS AGREEMENT WITH GOVERNMENT OF MALAYSIA
JOINT OIL ENTERPRISE TO BE LED BY KUSAKA
CORPORATION KUSAKA SIGNS AGREEMENT WITH GOVERNMENT OF MALAYSIA
JOINT OIL ENTERPRISE TO BE LED BY KUSAKA
GOVERNMENT OF MALAYSIA
JOINT OIL ENTERPRISE TO BE LED BY KUSAKA
New Development in Asia -- The Birth of a Major Oil Company?
I KNOW I CHOSE THE RIGHT PATH...

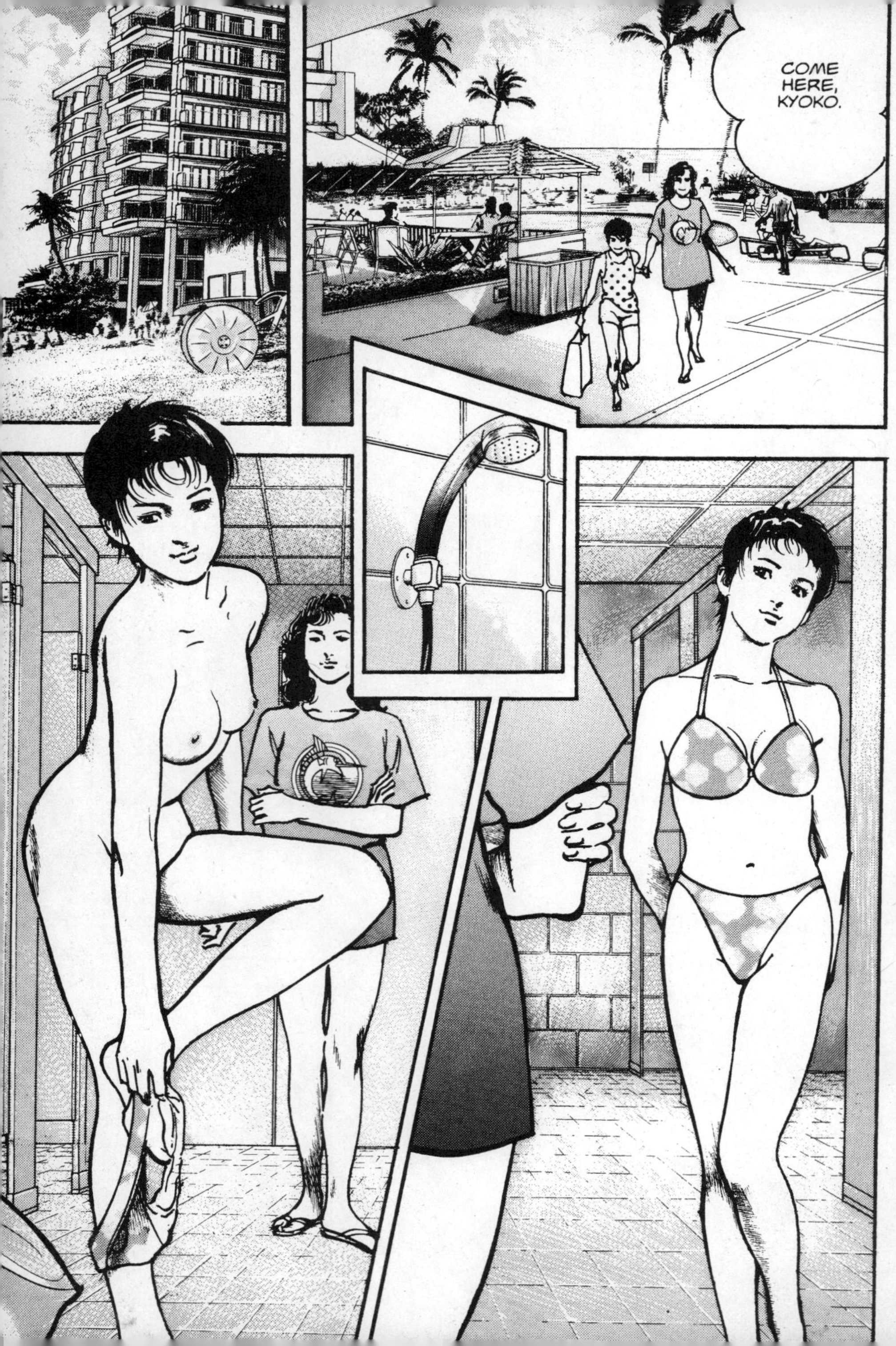
COME HERE, KYOKO.

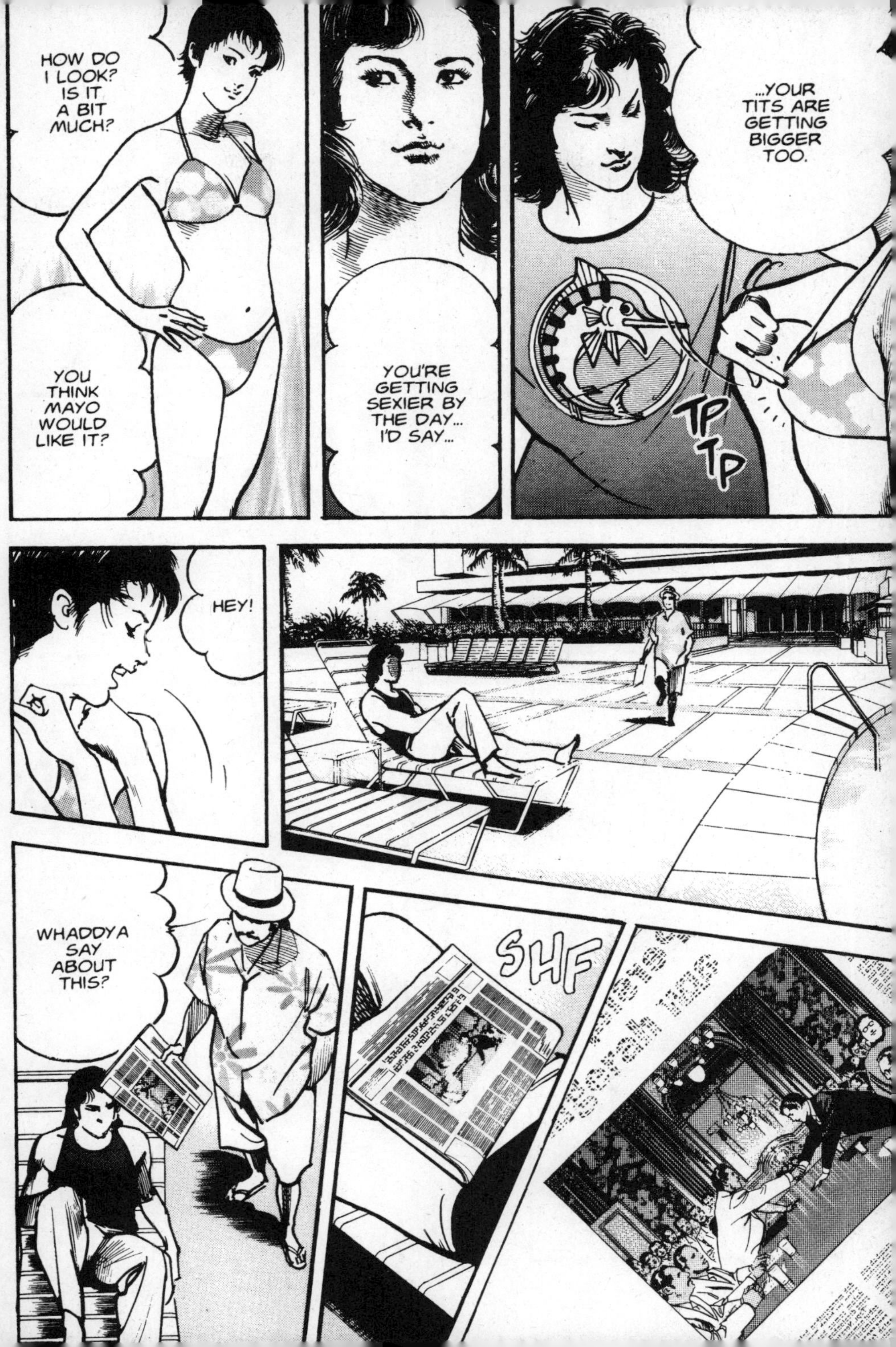
HOW DO I LOOK? IS IT A BIT MUCH?
YOU THINK MAYO WOULD LIKE IT?
YOU'RE GETTING SEXIER BY THE DAY... I'D SAY...
...YOUR TITS ARE GETTING BIGGER TOO.
TP TP
HEY!
WHADDYA SAY ABOUT THIS?
SHF

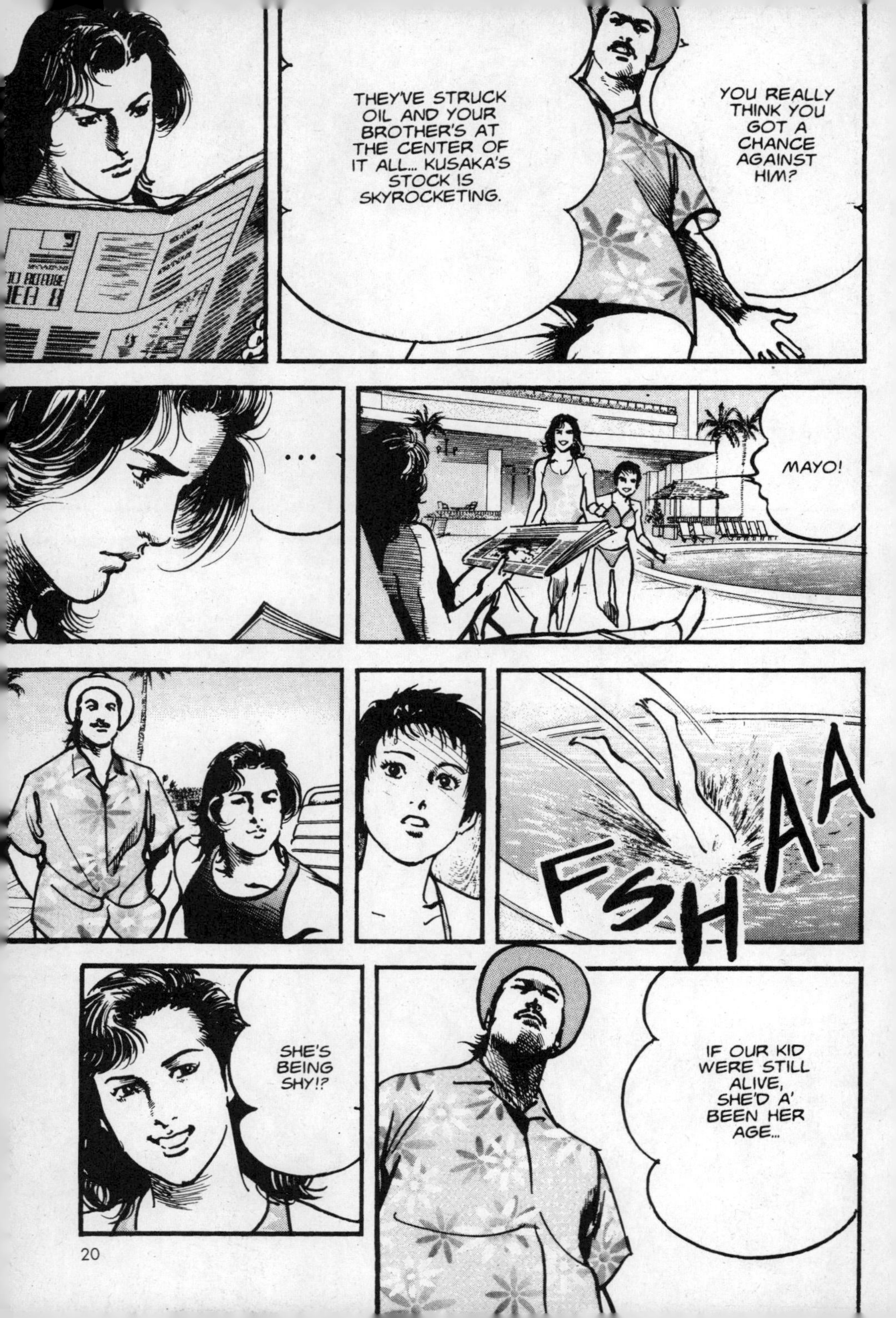
THEY'VE STRUCK OIL AND YOUR BROTHER'S AT THE CENTER OF IT ALL... KUSAKA'S STOCK IS SKYROCKETING.
YOU REALLY THINK YOU GOT A CHANCE AGAINST HIM?
...
MAYO!
FSHAA
SHE'S BEING SHY!?
IF OUR KID WERE STILL ALIVE, SHE'D A' BEEN HER AGE...

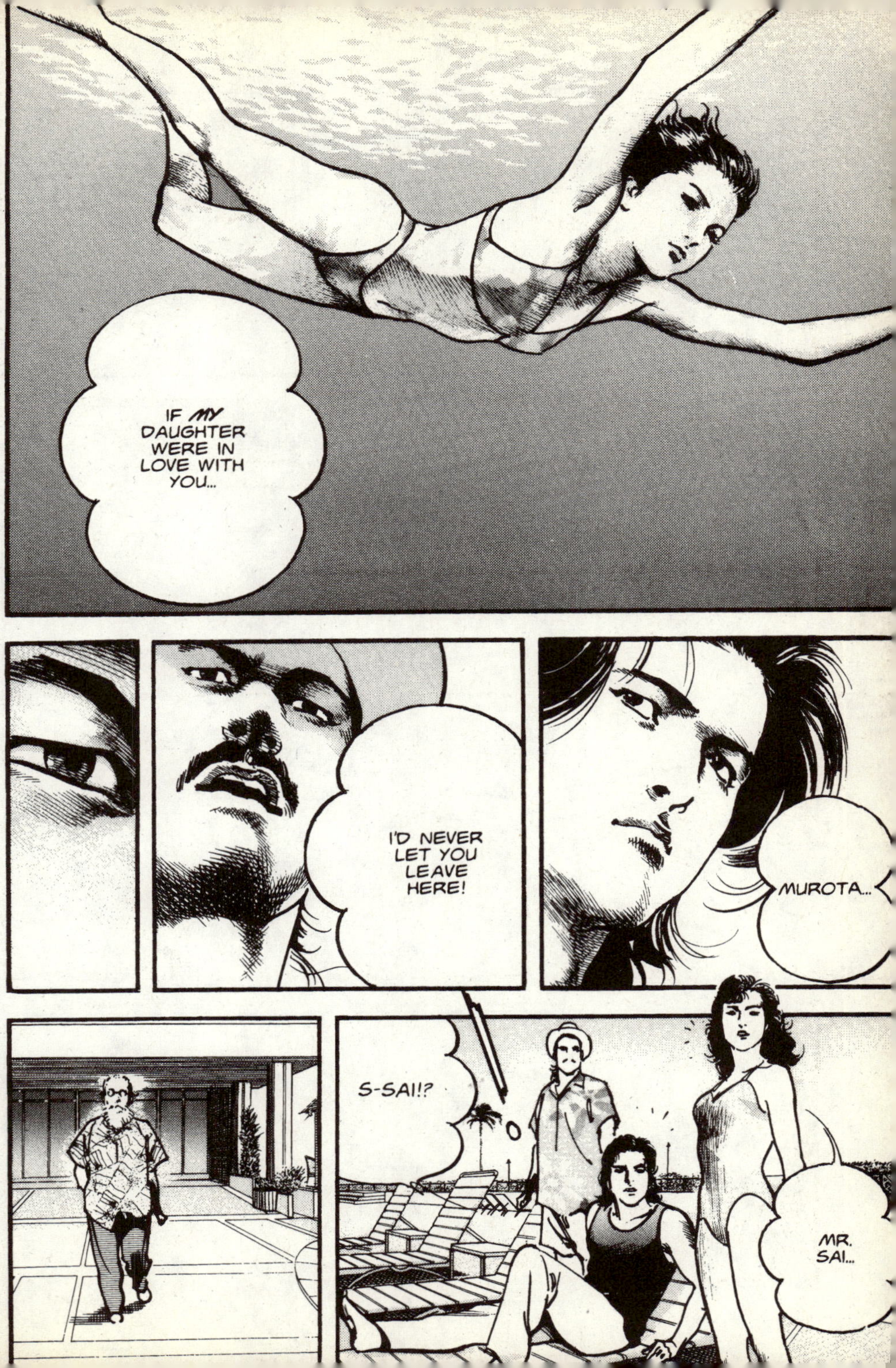
IF *MY* DAUGHTER WERE IN LOVE WITH YOU...
I'D NEVER LET YOU LEAVE HERE!
MUROTA...
S-SAI!?
MR. SAI...

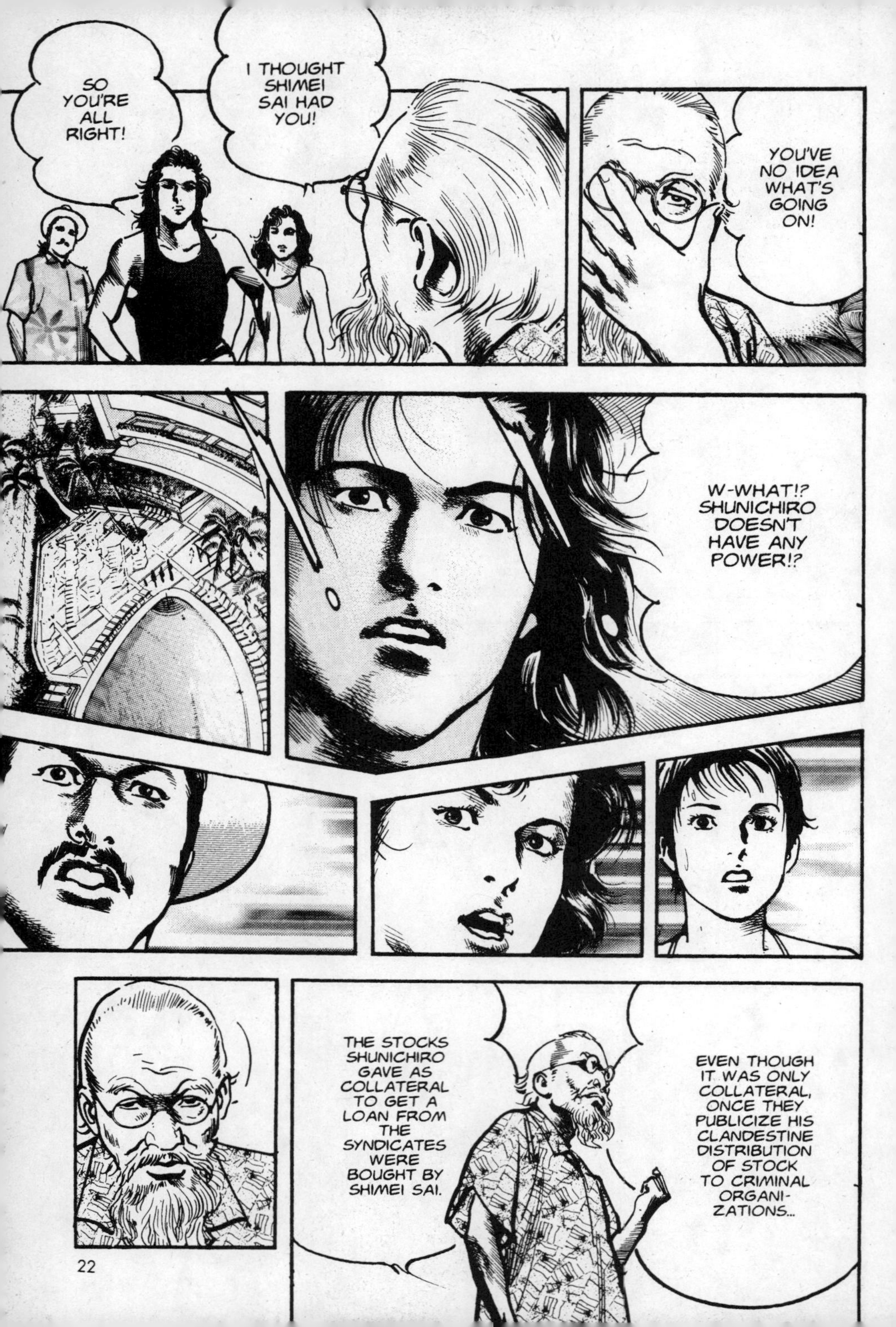

SO YOU'RE ALL RIGHT!
I THOUGHT SHIMEI SAI HAD YOU!
YOU'VE NO IDEA WHAT'S GOING ON!
W-WHAT!? SHUNICHIRO DOESN'T HAVE ANY POWER!?
THE STOCKS SHUNICHIRO GAVE AS COLLATERAL TO GET A LOAN FROM THE SYNDICATES WERE BOUGHT BY SHIMEI SAI.
EVEN THOUGH IT WAS ONLY COLLATERAL, ONCE THEY PUBLICIZE HIS CLANDESTINE DISTRIBUTION OF STOCK TO CRIMINAL ORGANI-ZATIONS...

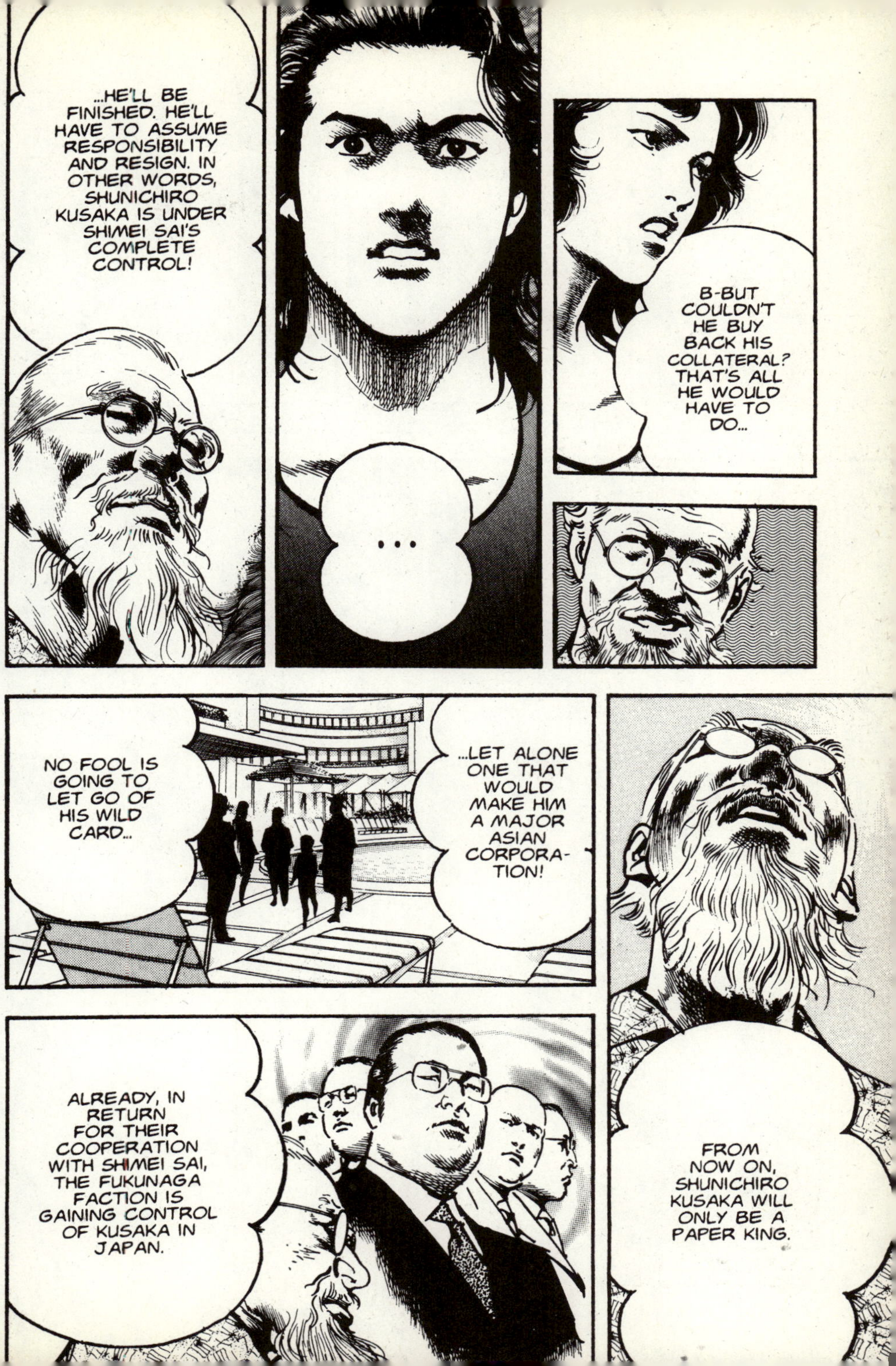

...HE'LL BE FINISHED. HE'LL HAVE TO ASSUME RESPONSIBILITY AND RESIGN. IN OTHER WORDS, SHUNICHIRO KUSAKA IS UNDER SHIMEI SAI'S COMPLETE CONTROL!
...
B-BUT COULDN'T HE BUY BACK HIS COLLATERAL? THAT'S ALL HE WOULD HAVE TO DO...
NO FOOL IS GOING TO LET GO OF HIS WILD CARD...
...LET ALONE ONE THAT WOULD MAKE HIM A MAJOR ASIAN CORPORATION!
ALREADY, IN RETURN FOR THEIR COOPERATION WITH SHIMEI SAI, THE FUKUNAGA FACTION IS GAINING CONTROL OF KUSAKA IN JAPAN.
FROM NOW ON, SHUNICHIRO KUSAKA WILL ONLY BE A PAPER KING.

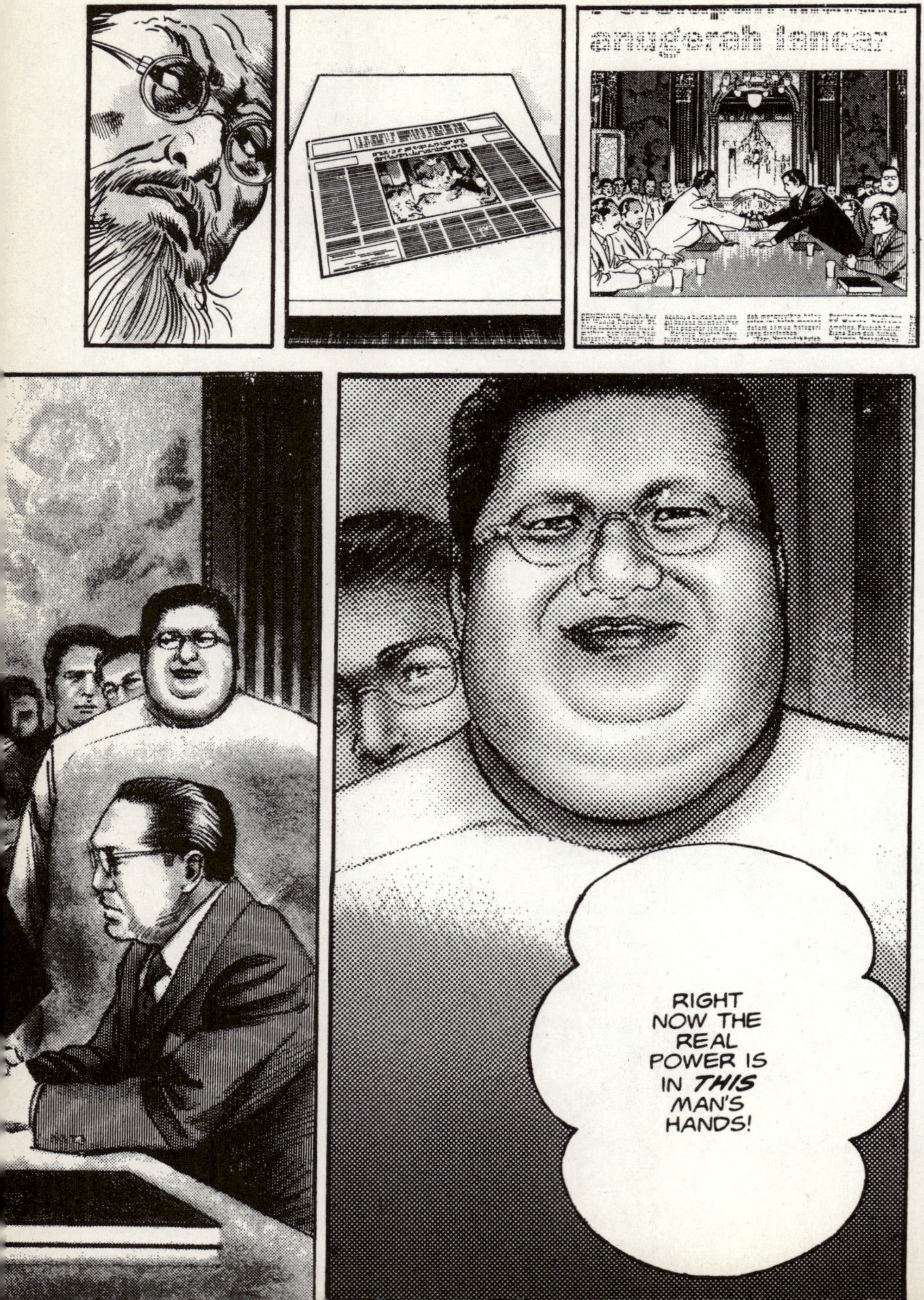
anugerah lancar
RIGHT NOW THE REAL POWER IS IN *THIS* MAN'S HANDS!

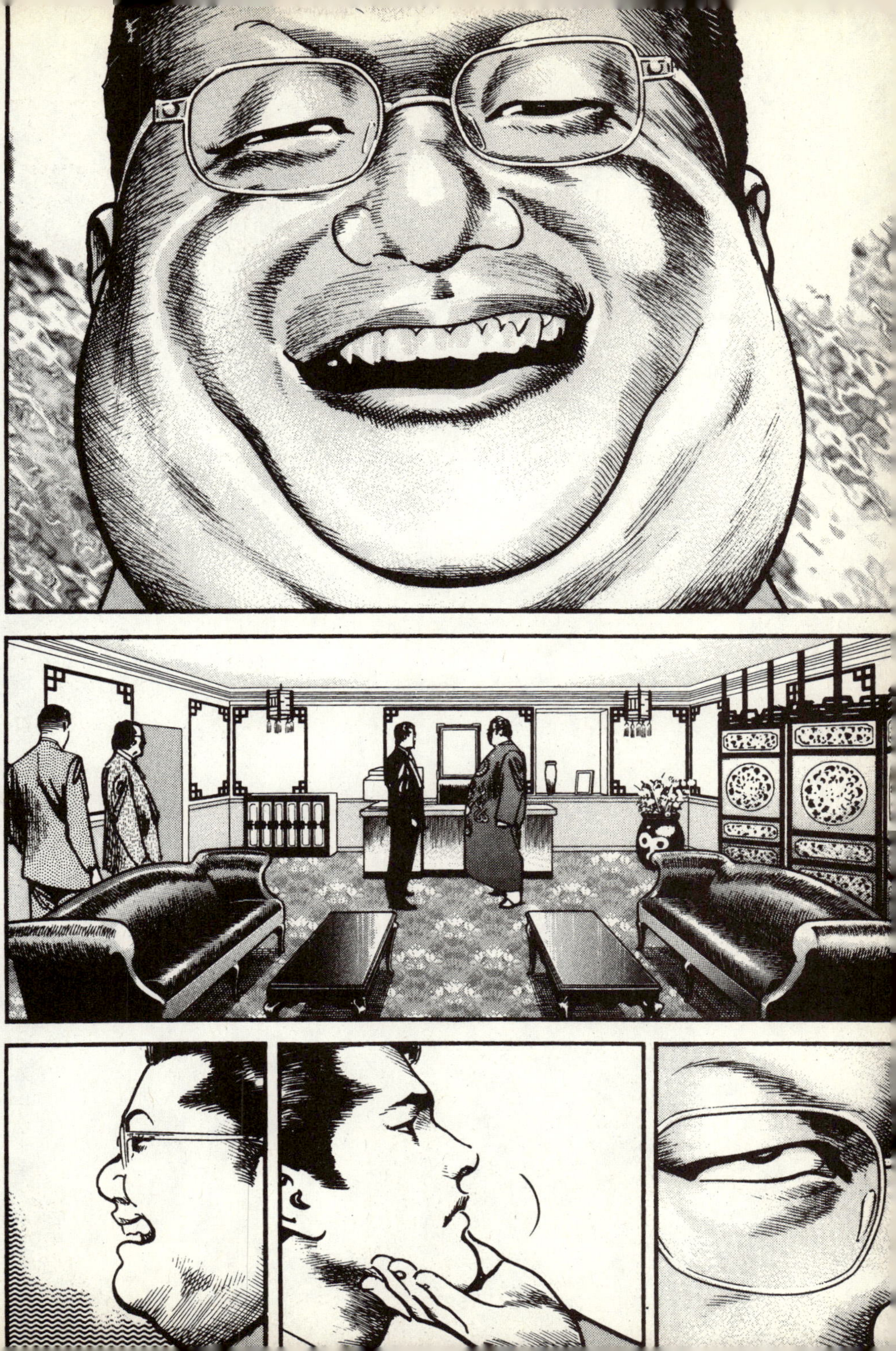

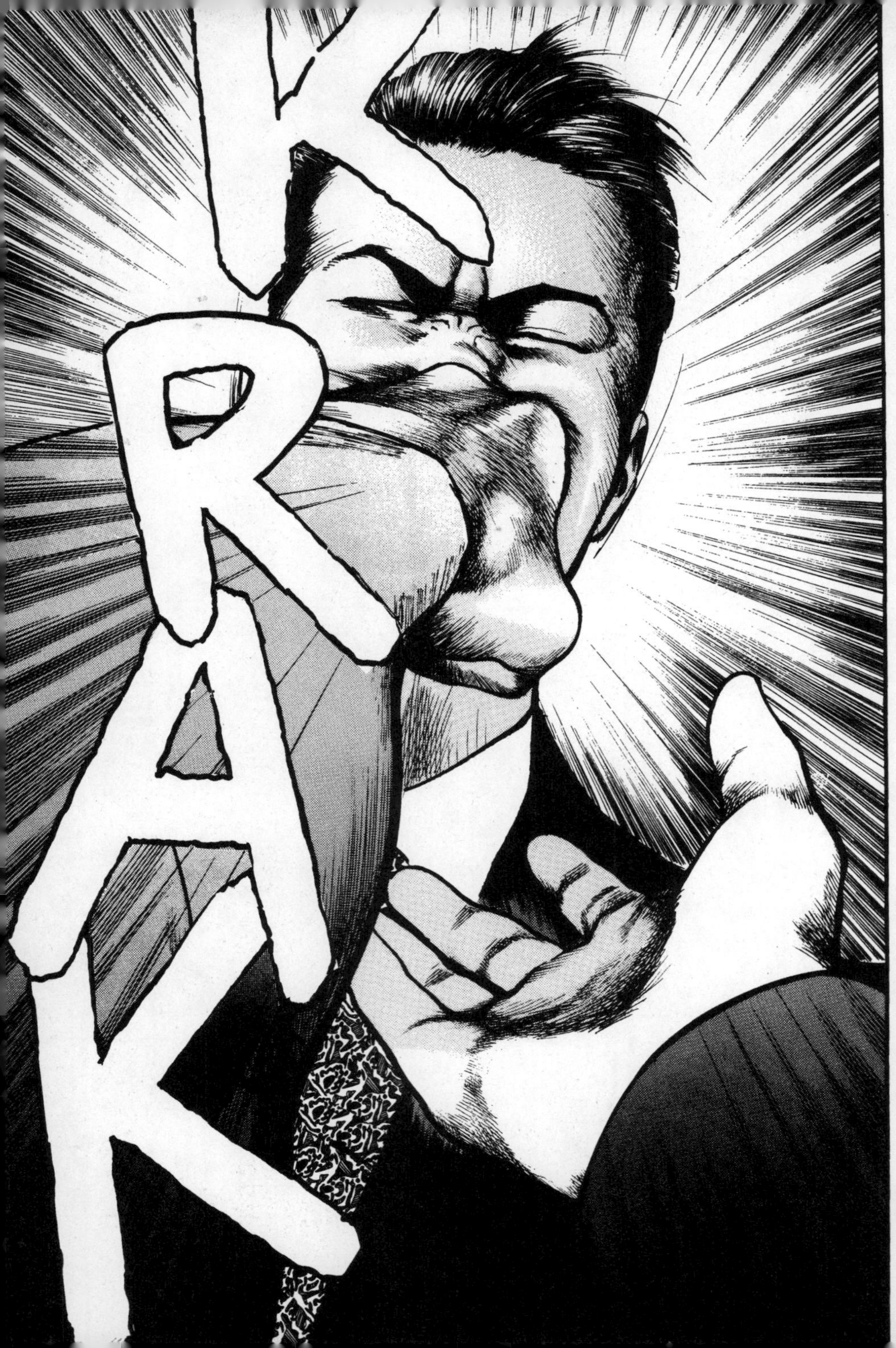
RA

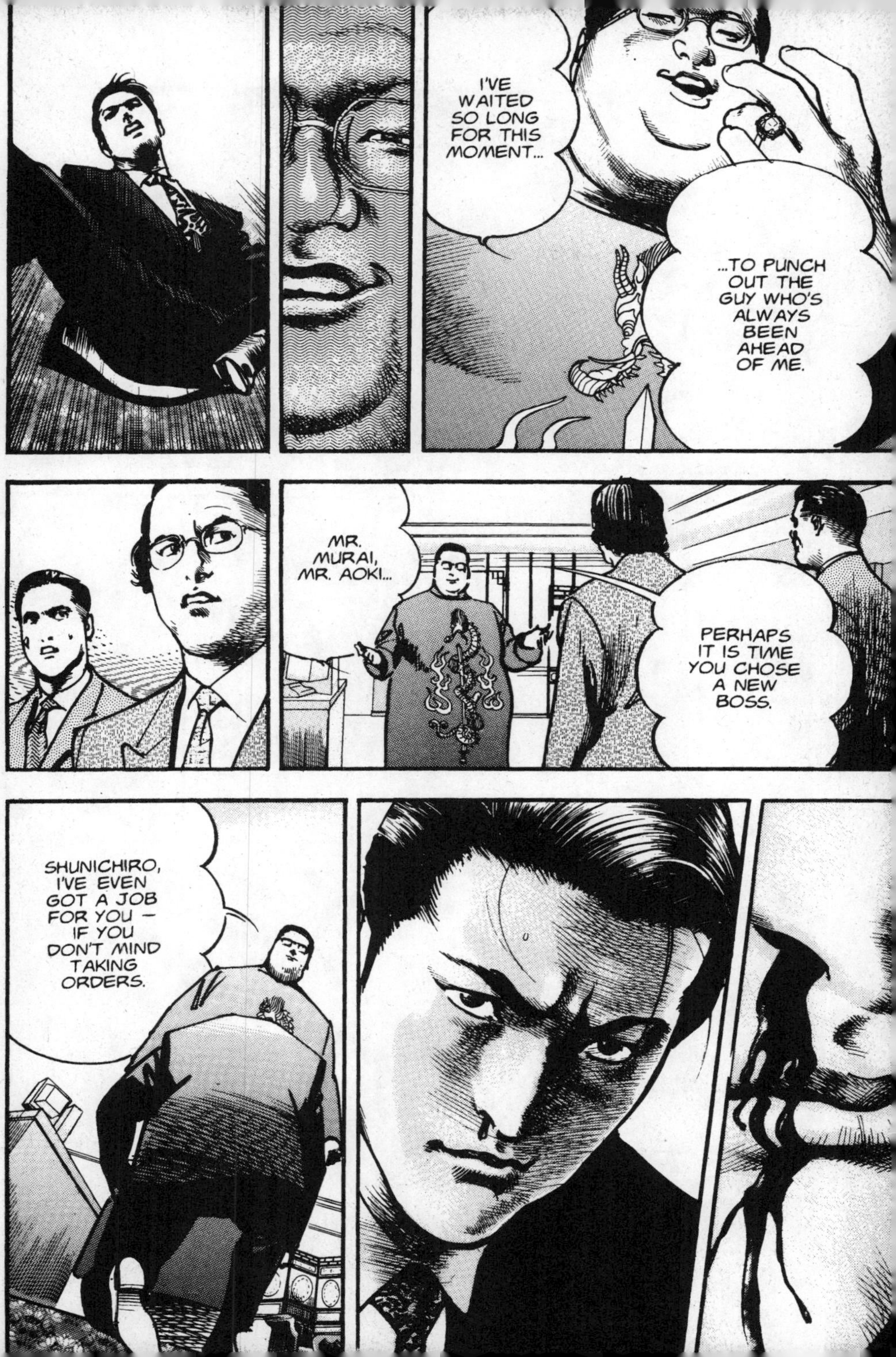
I'VE WAITED SO LONG FOR THIS MOMENT...
...TO PUNCH OUT THE GUY WHO'S ALWAYS BEEN AHEAD OF ME.
MR. MURAI, MR. AOKI...
PERHAPS IT IS TIME YOU CHOSE A NEW BOSS.
SHUNICHIRO, I'VE EVEN GOT A JOB FOR YOU — IF YOU DON'T MIND TAKING ORDERS.

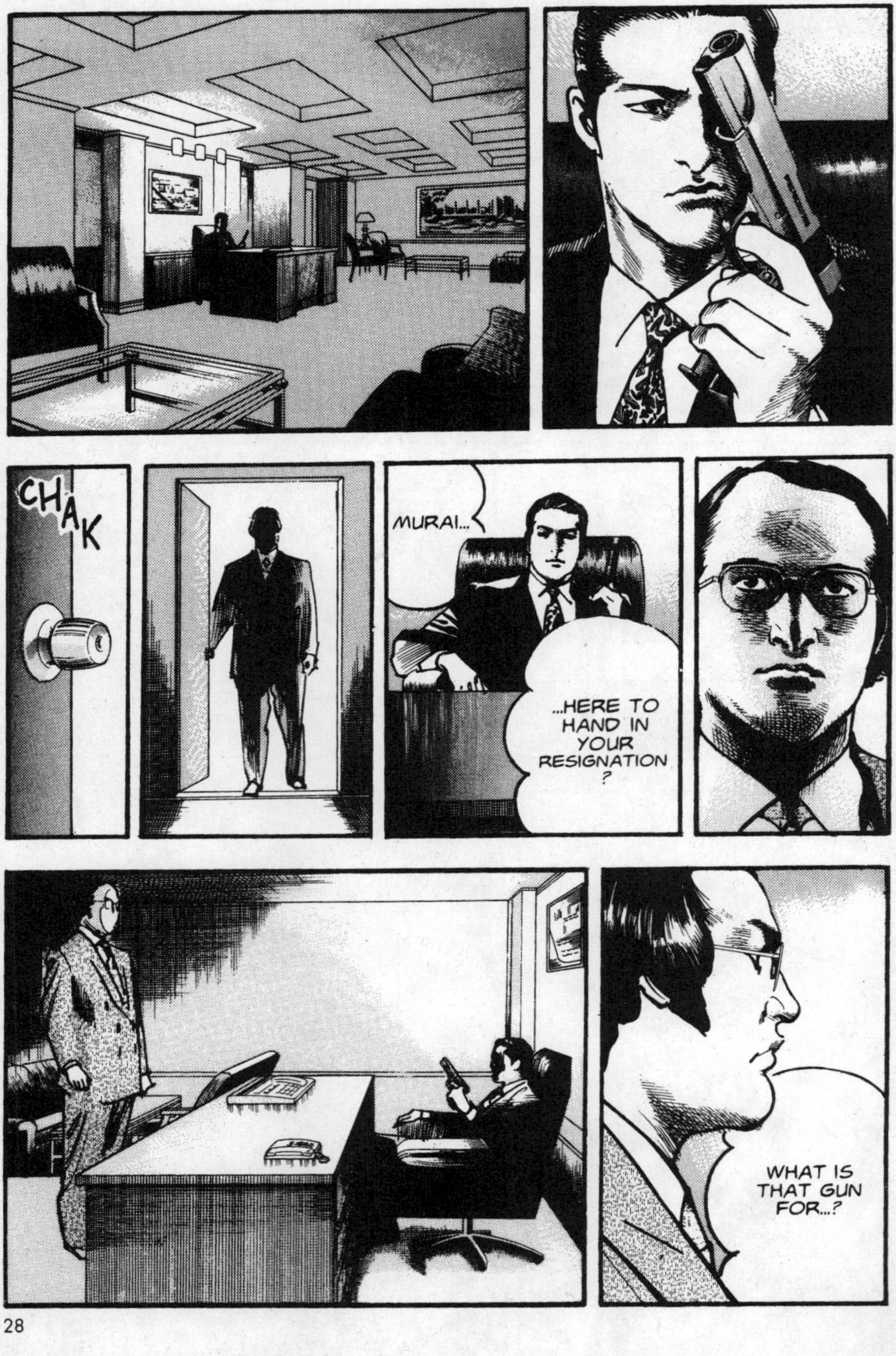
CHAK
MURAI...
...HERE TO HAND IN YOUR RESIGNATION?
WHAT IS THAT GUN FOR...?

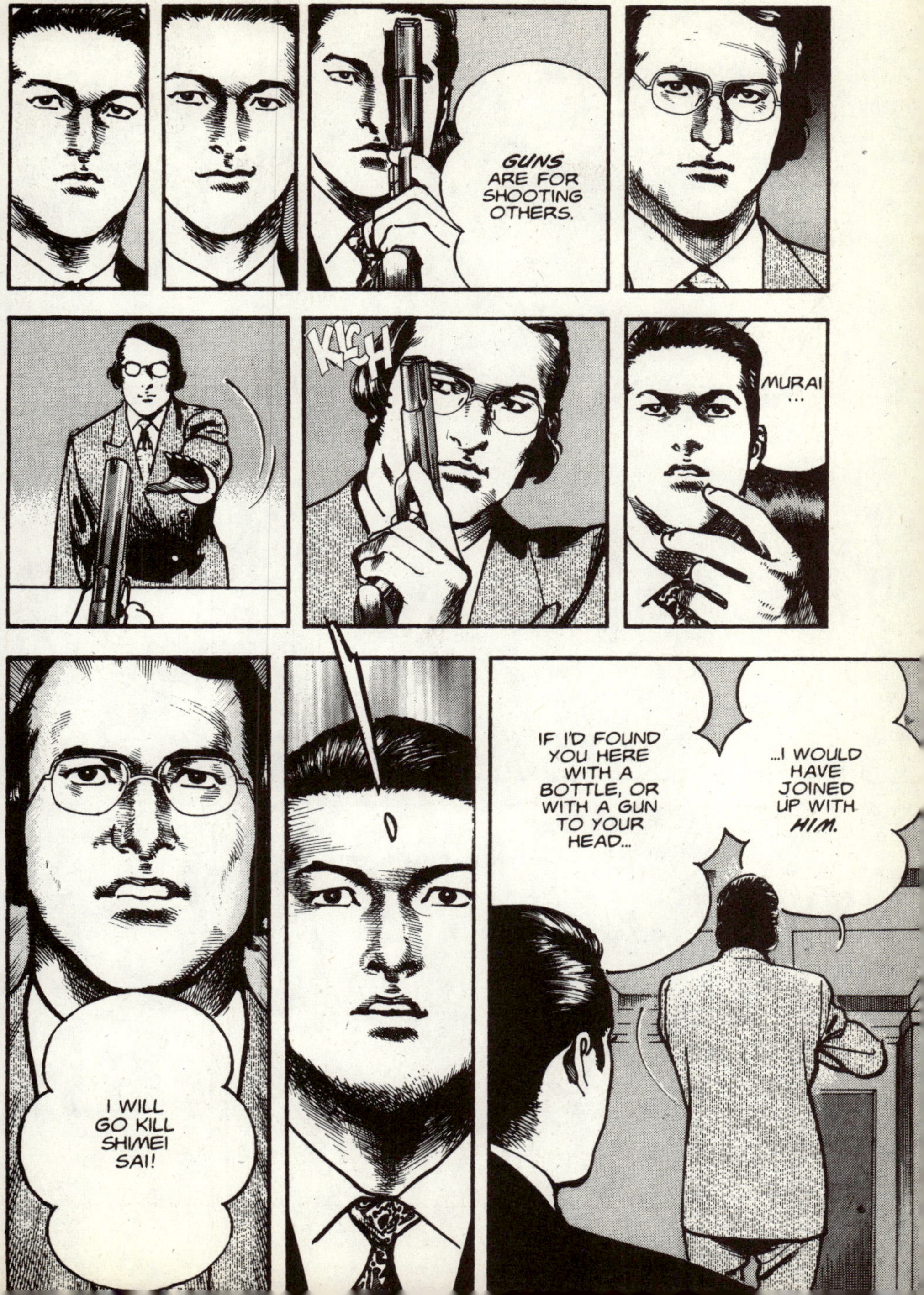
GUNS ARE FOR SHOOTING OTHERS.
KLCH
MURAI ...
I WILL GO KILL SHIMEI SAI!
IF I'D FOUND YOU HERE WITH A BOTTLE, OR WITH A GUN TO YOUR HEAD...
...I WOULD HAVE JOINED UP WITH HIM.

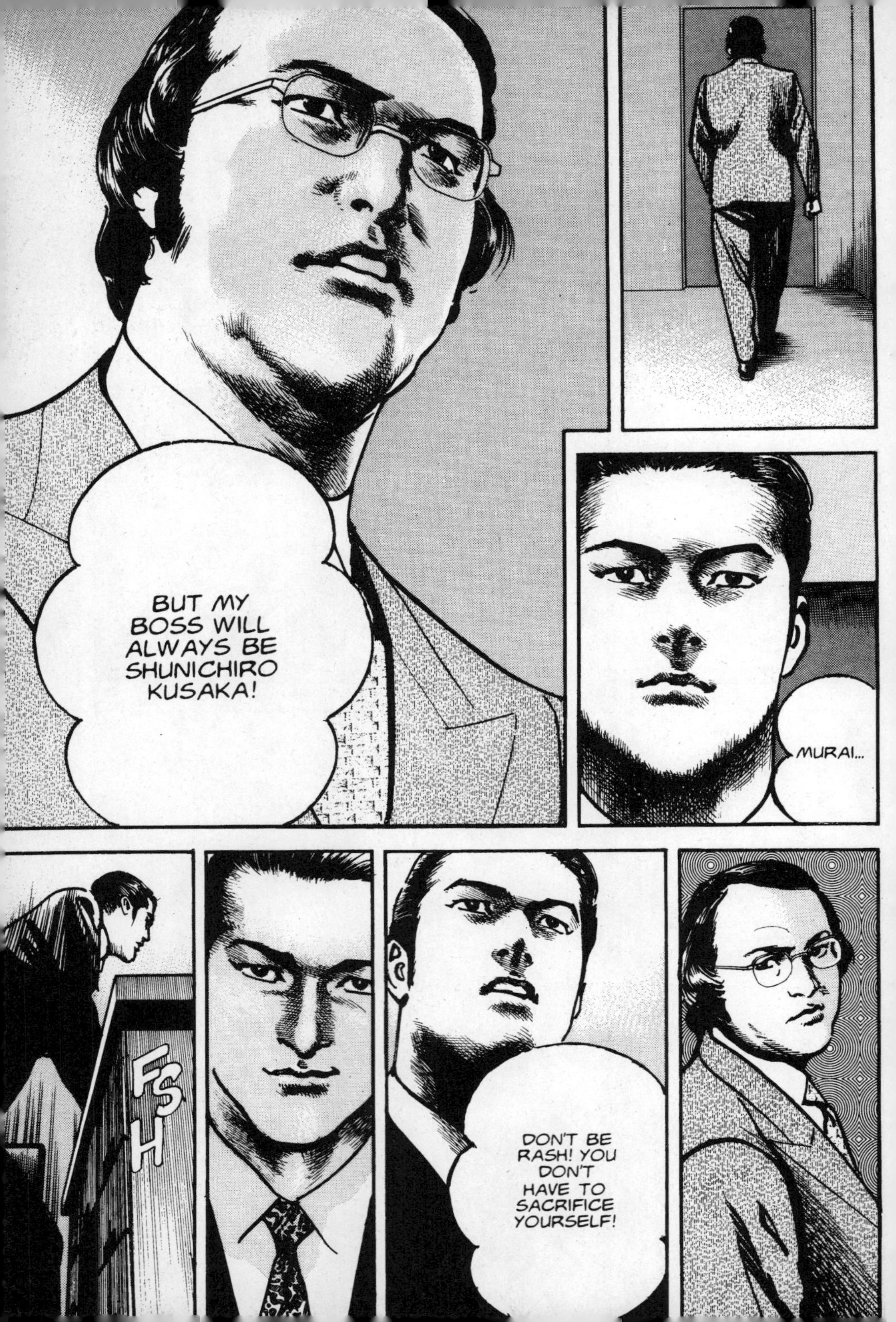
BUT MY BOSS WILL ALWAYS BE SHUNICHIRO KUSAKA!
MURAI...
FSH
DON'T BE RASH! YOU DON'T HAVE TO SACRIFICE YOURSELF!

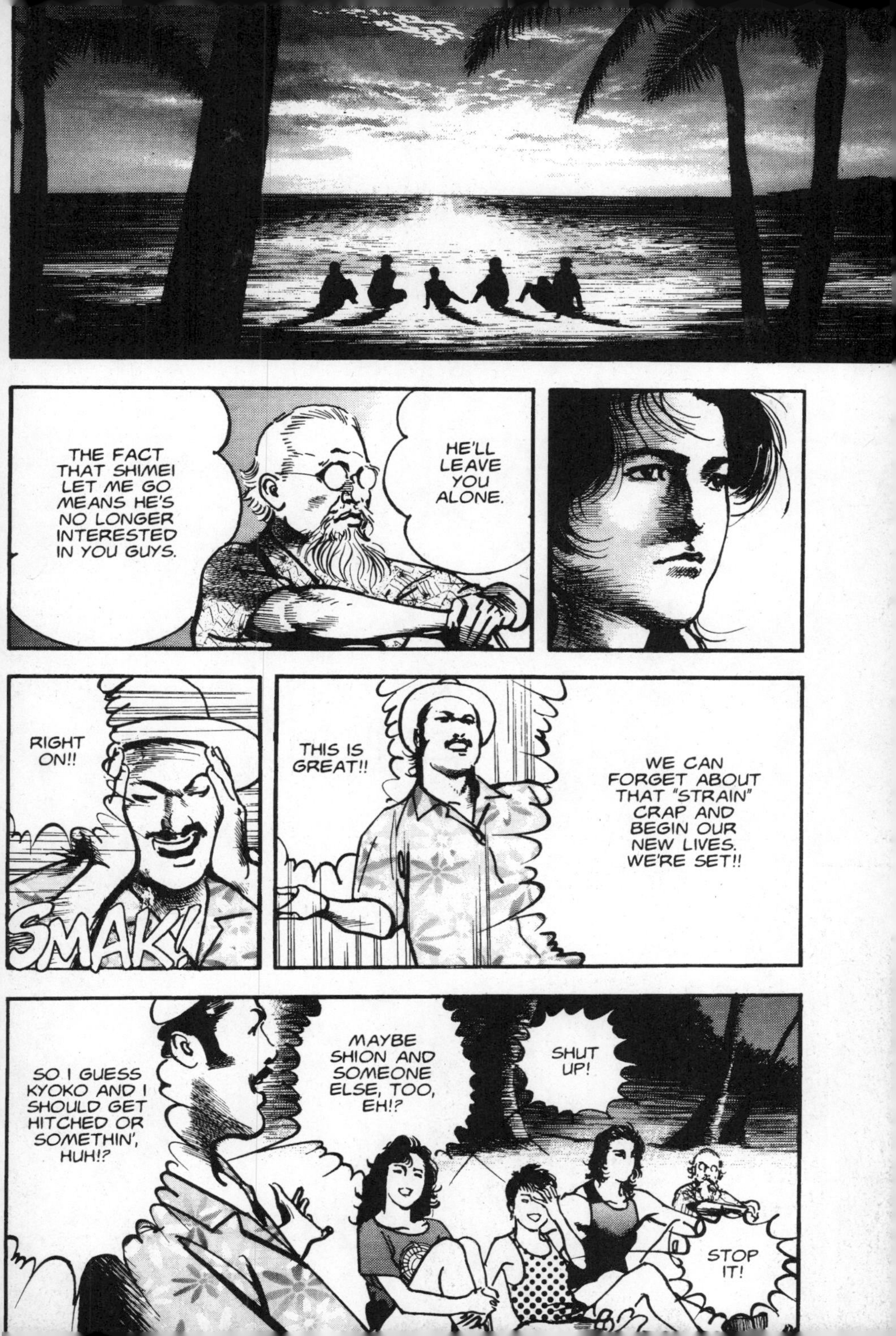
THE FACT THAT SHIMEI LET ME GO MEANS HE'S NO LONGER INTERESTED IN YOU GUYS.
HE'LL LEAVE YOU ALONE.
RIGHT ON!!
SMAK!
THIS IS GREAT!!
WE CAN FORGET ABOUT THAT "STRAIN" CRAP AND BEGIN OUR NEW LIVES. WE'RE SET!!
SO I GUESS KYOKO AND I SHOULD GET HITCHED OR SOMETHIN', HUH!?
MAYBE SHION AND SOMEONE ELSE, TOO, EH!?
SHUT UP!
STOP IT!

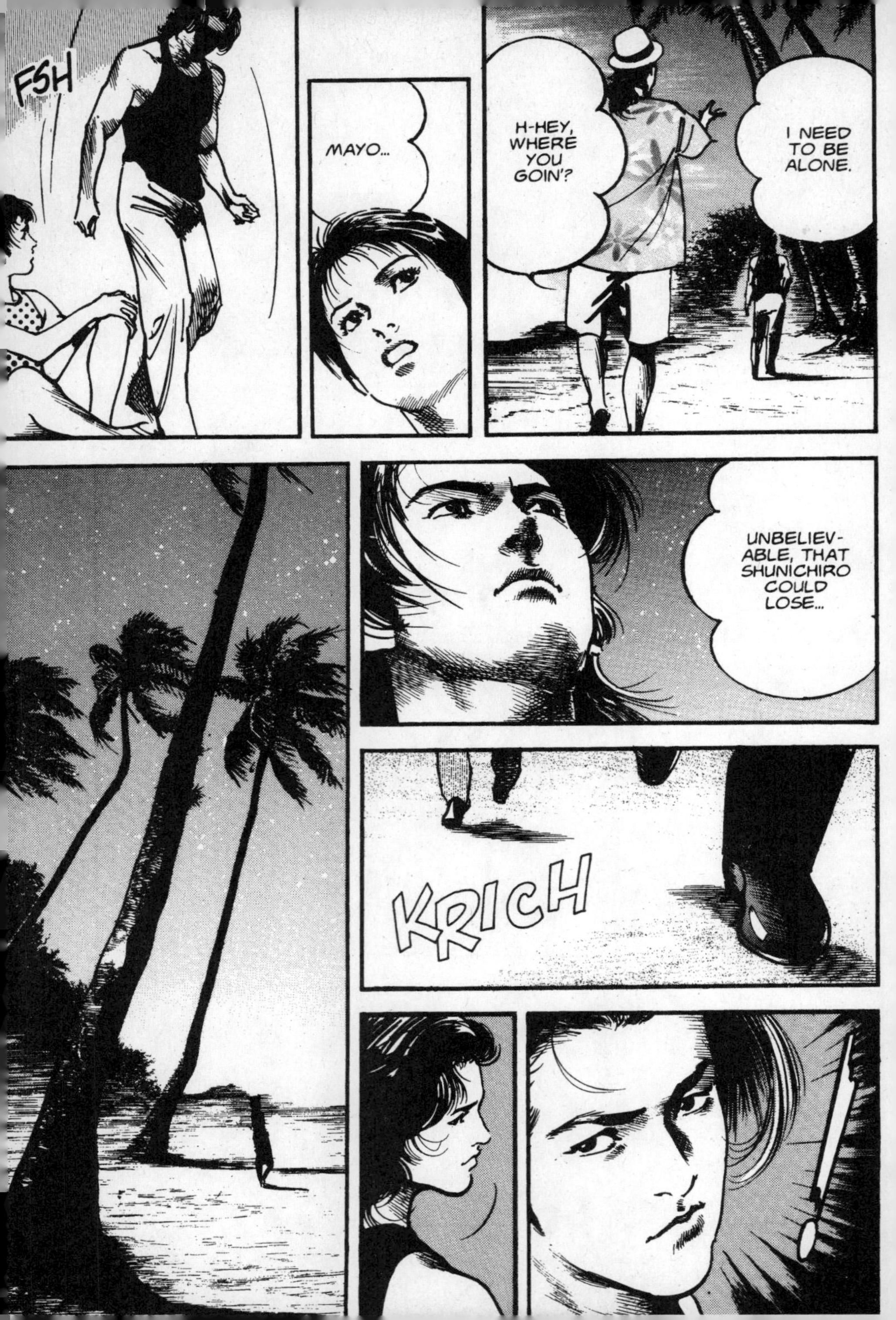
FSH
MAYO...
H-HEY, WHERE YOU GOIN'?
I NEED TO BE ALONE.
UNBELIEVABLE, THAT SHUNICHIRO COULD LOSE...
KRICH

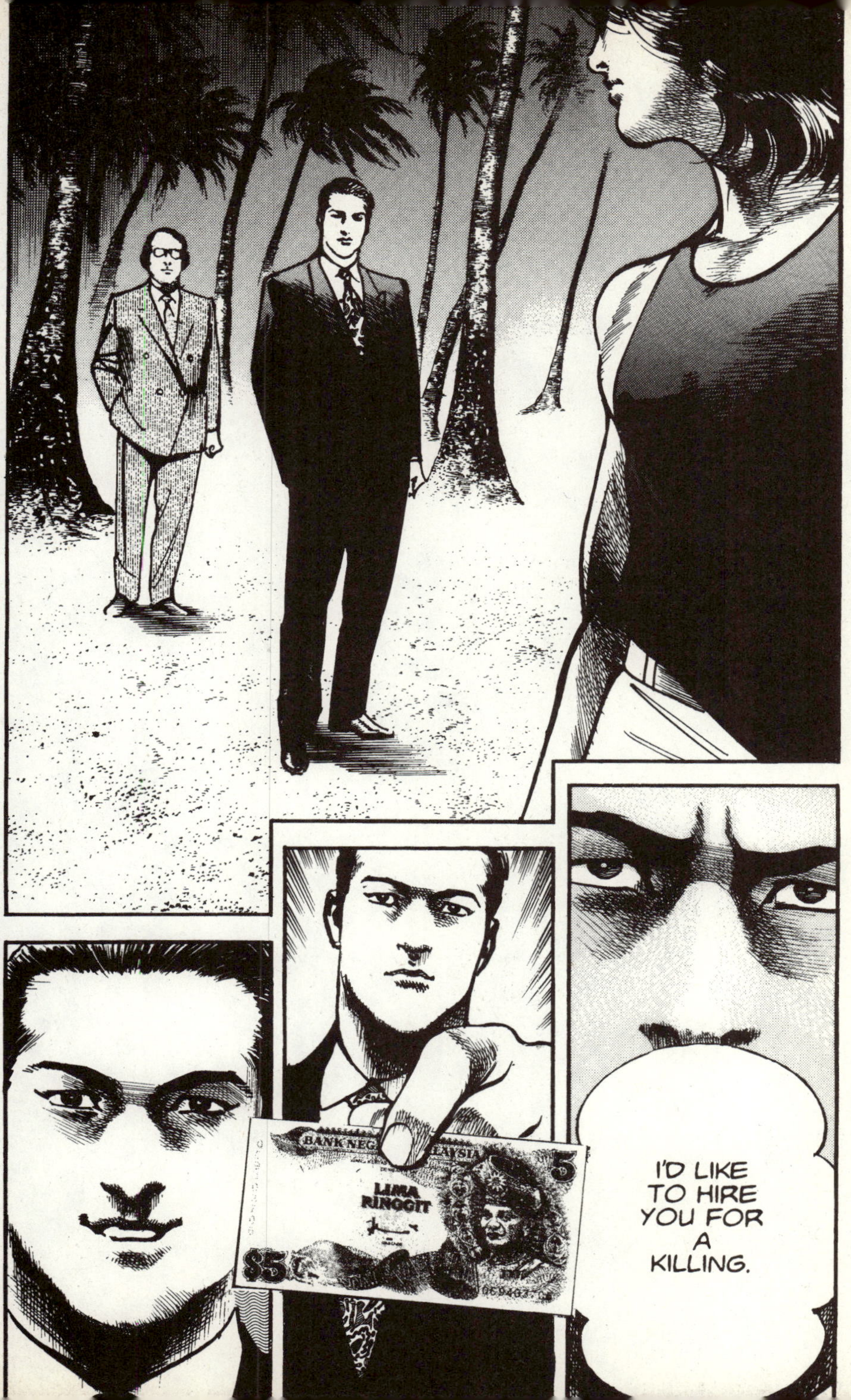
I'D LIKE TO HIRE YOU FOR A KILLING.

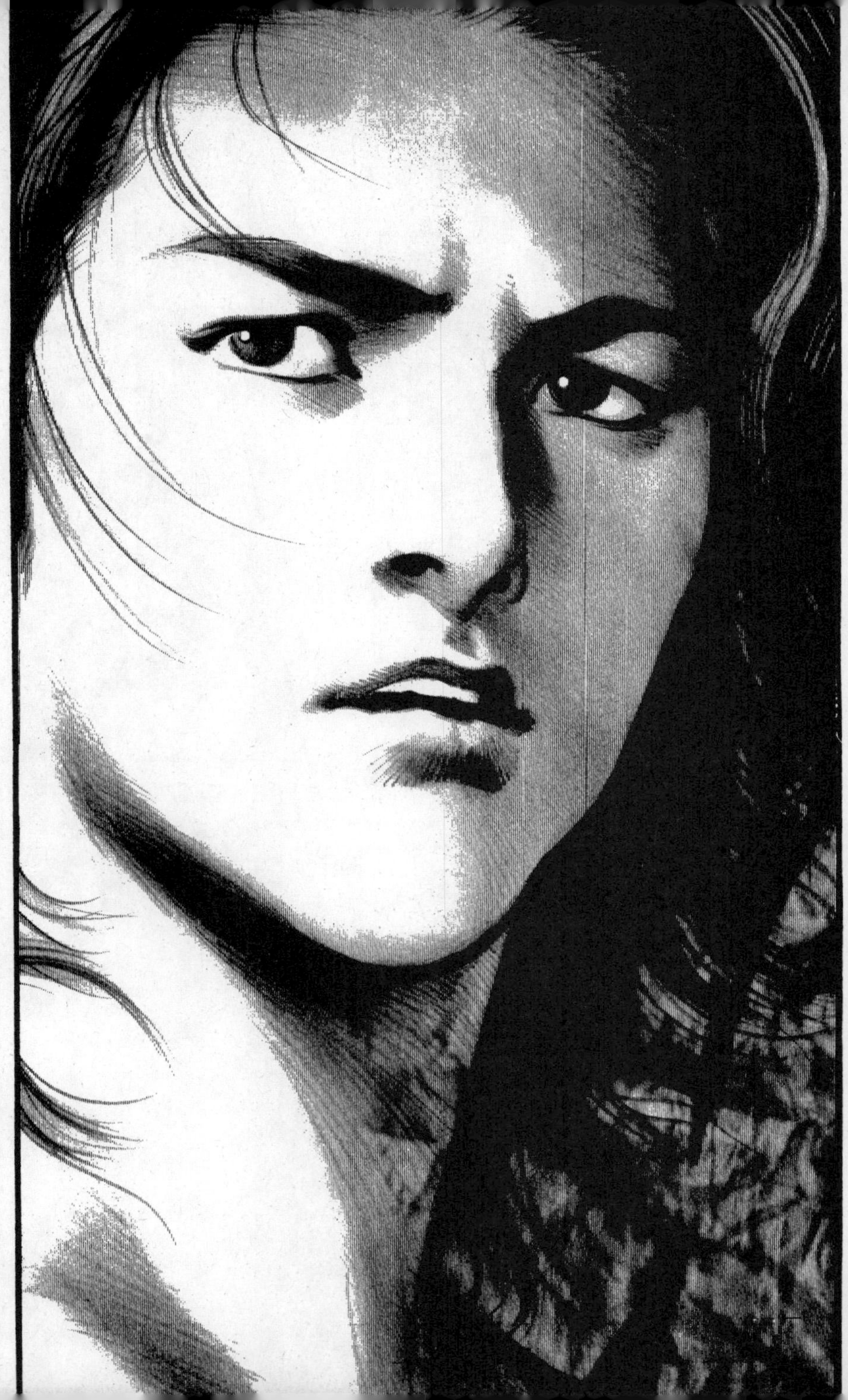

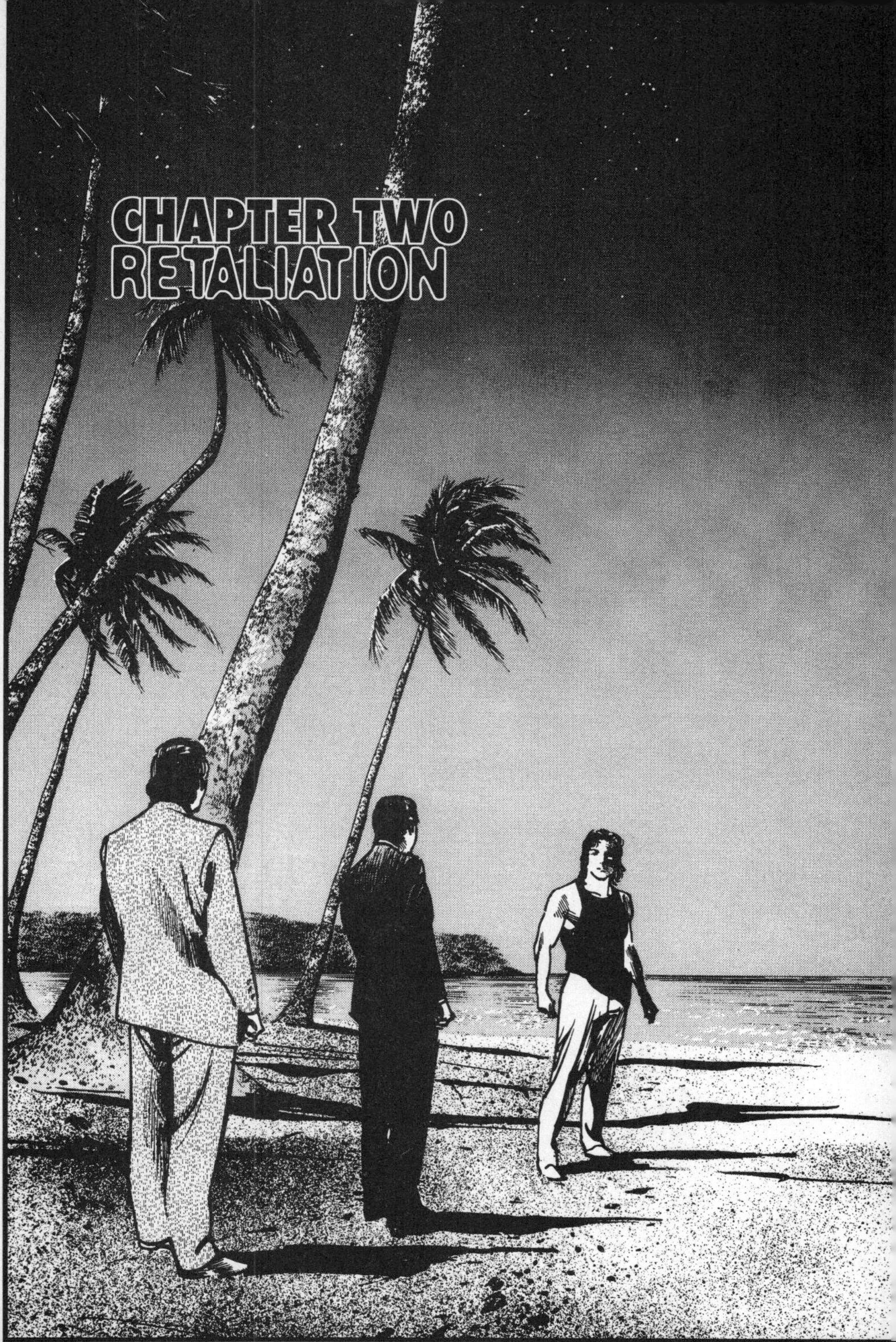
CHAPTER TWO
RETALIATION

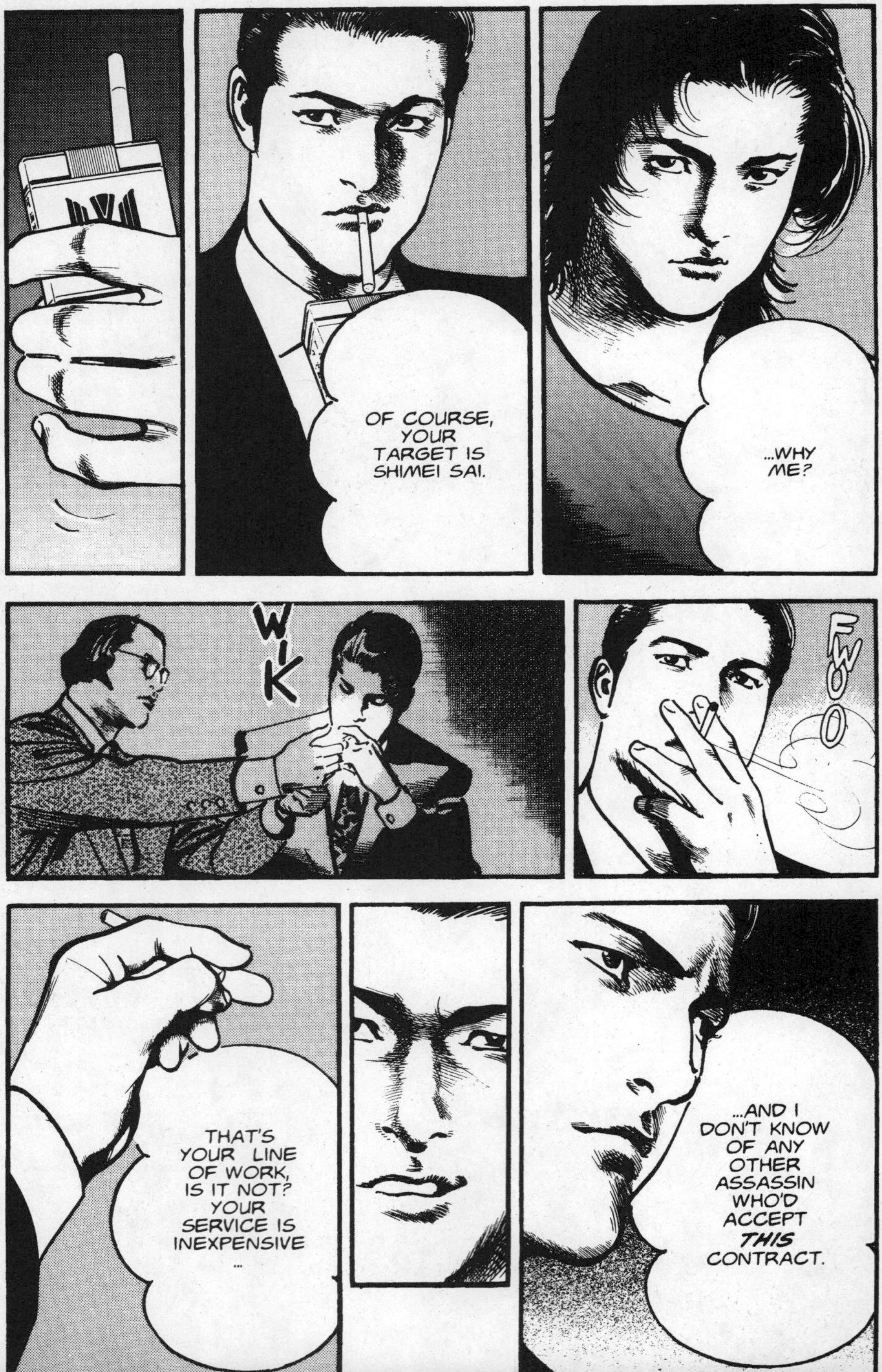
OF COURSE, YOUR TARGET IS SHIMEI SAI.
...WHY ME?
WIK
FWOO
THAT'S YOUR LINE OF WORK, IS IT NOT? YOUR SERVICE IS INEXPENSIVE ...
...AND I DON'T KNOW OF ANY OTHER ASSASSIN WHO'D ACCEPT *THIS* CONTRACT.

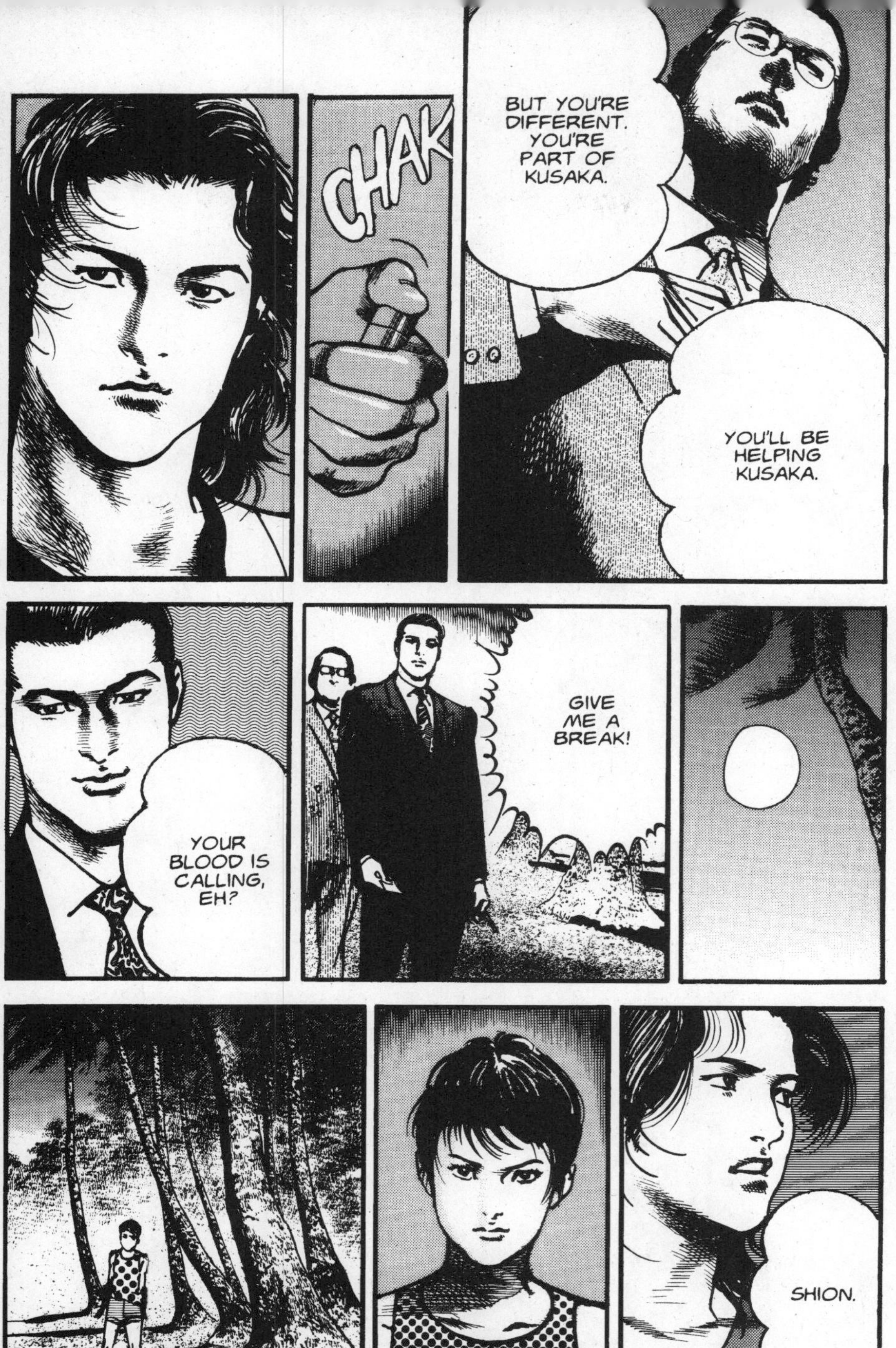
BUT YOU'RE DIFFERENT. YOU'RE PART OF KUSAKA.
YOU'LL BE HELPING KUSAKA.
CHAK
GIVE ME A BREAK!
YOUR BLOOD IS CALLING, EH?
SHION.

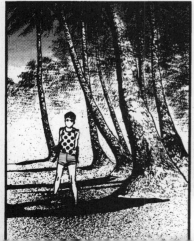

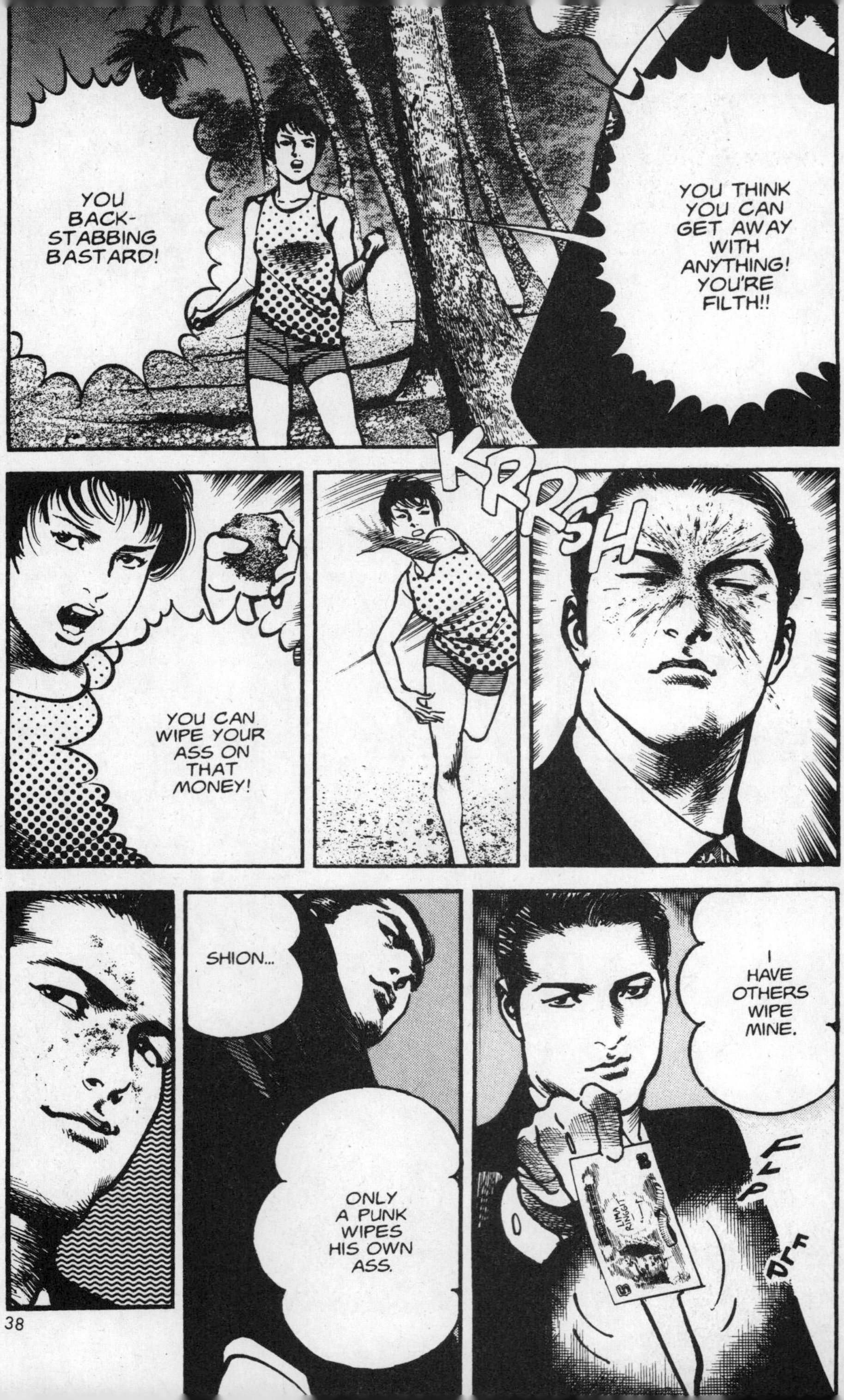
YOU BACK-STABBING BASTARD!
YOU THINK YOU CAN GET AWAY WITH ANYTHING! YOU'RE FILTH!!
YOU CAN WIPE YOUR ASS ON THAT MONEY!
KRRSH
SHION...
ONLY A PUNK WIPES HIS OWN ASS.
I HAVE OTHERS WIPE MINE.
LIMA RINGGIT
FLIP
FLIP

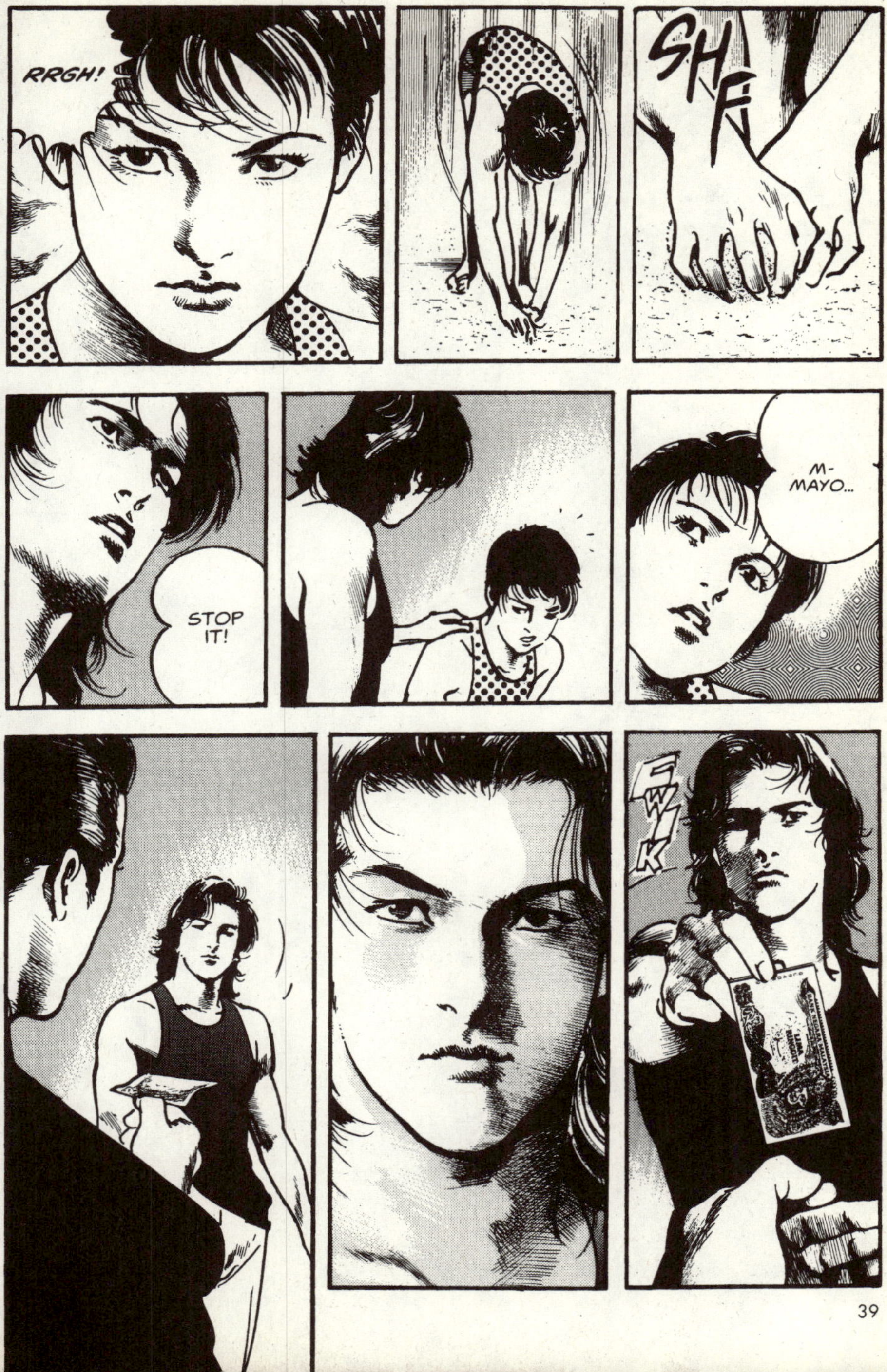
RRGH!
SH F
M-MAYO...
STOP IT!
FWIK

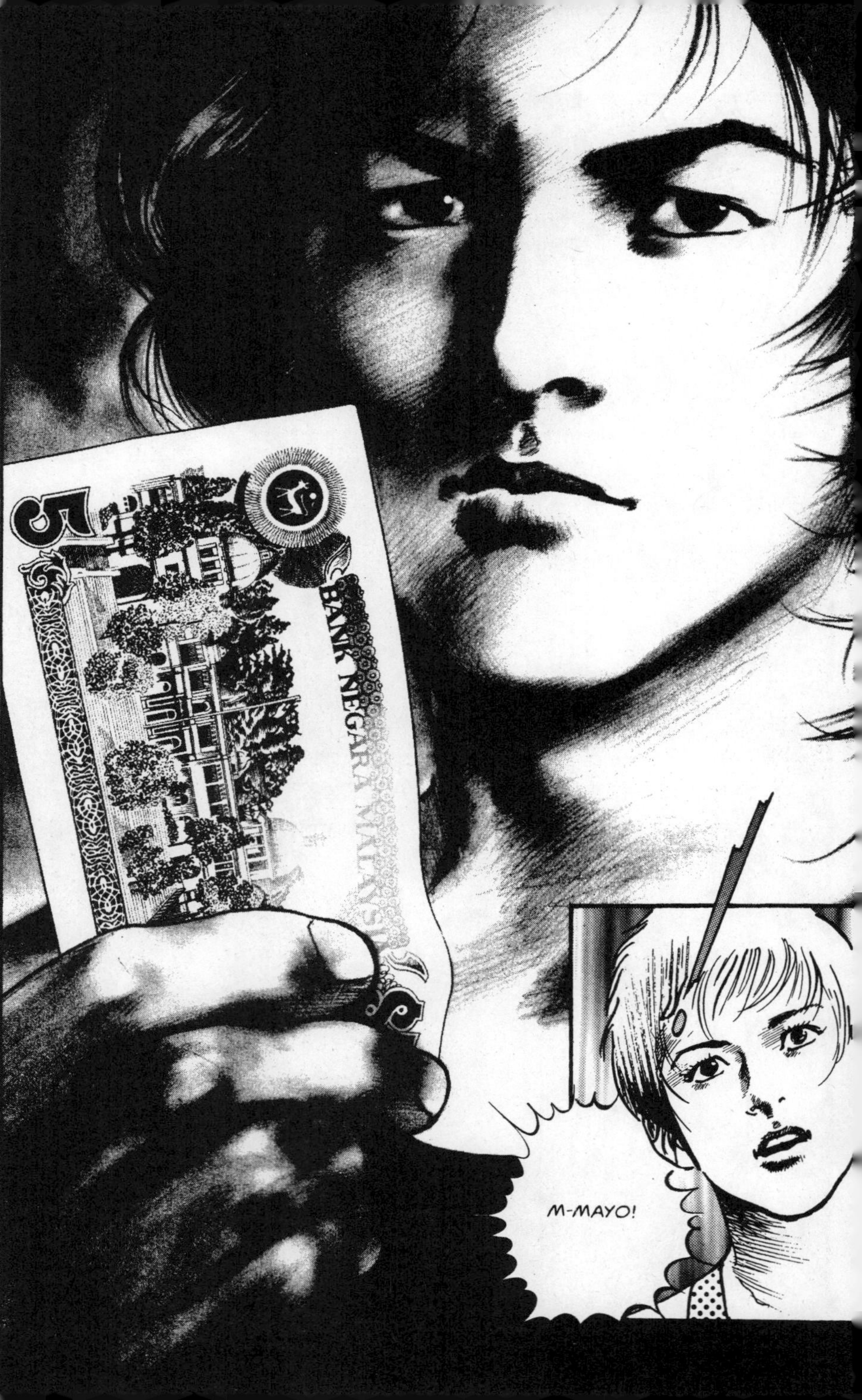
BANK NEGARA
M-MAYO!

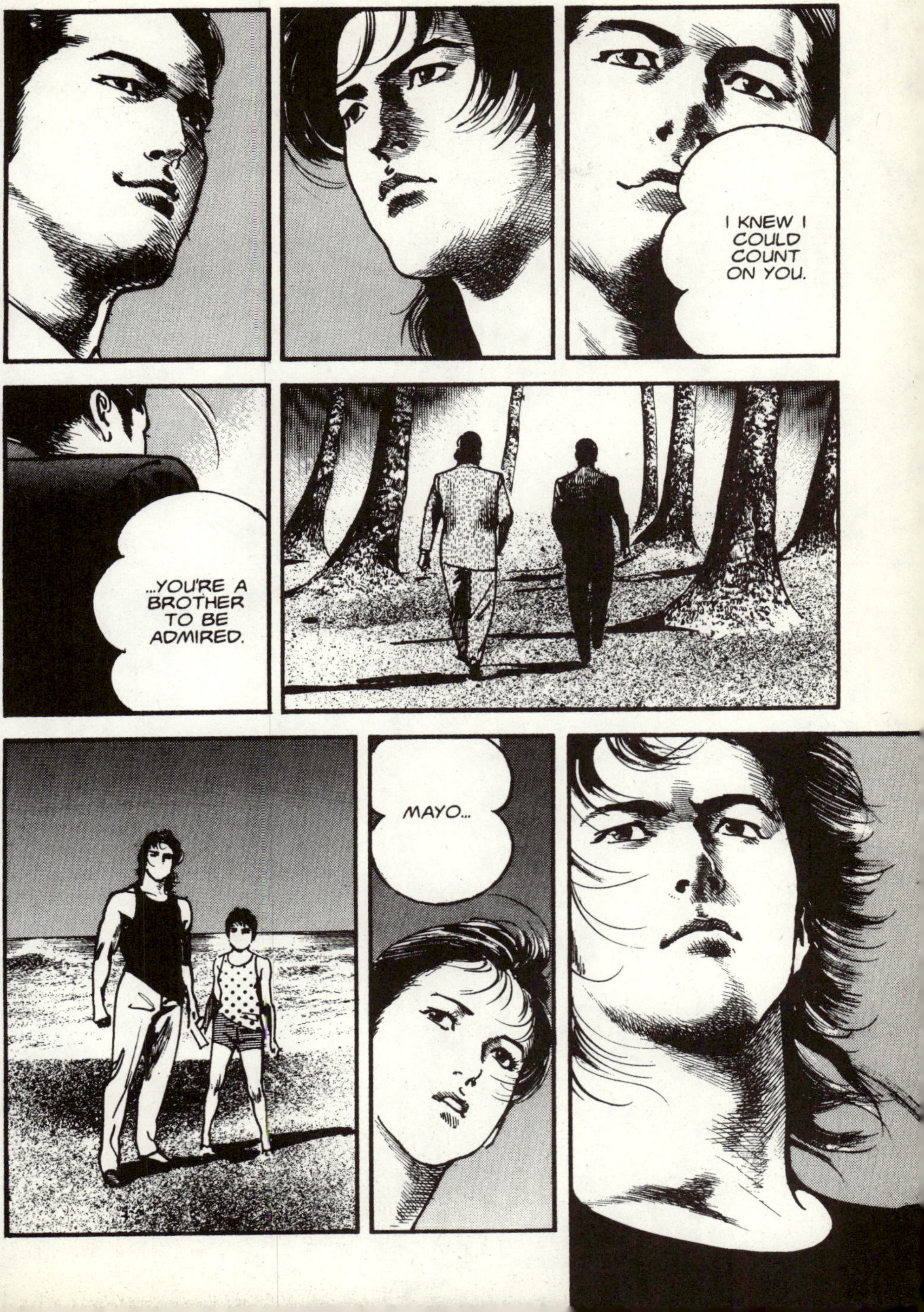
I KNEW I COULD COUNT ON YOU.
...YOU'RE A BROTHER TO BE ADMIRED.
MAYO...

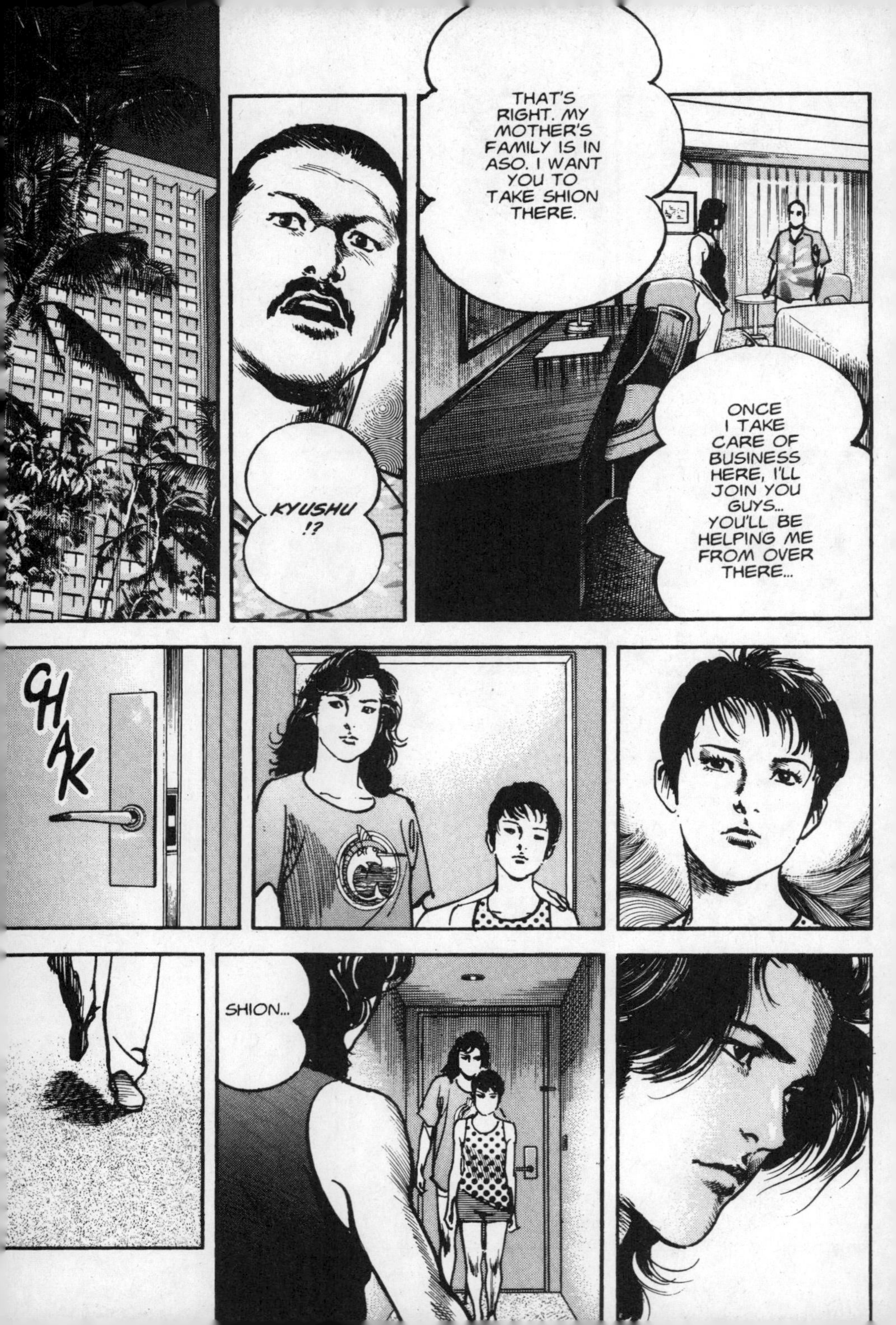

KYUSHU !?
THAT'S RIGHT. MY MOTHER'S FAMILY IS IN ASO. I WANT YOU TO TAKE SHION THERE.
ONCE I TAKE CARE OF BUSINESS HERE, I'LL JOIN YOU GUYS... YOU'LL BE HELPING ME FROM OVER THERE...
CHAK
SHION...

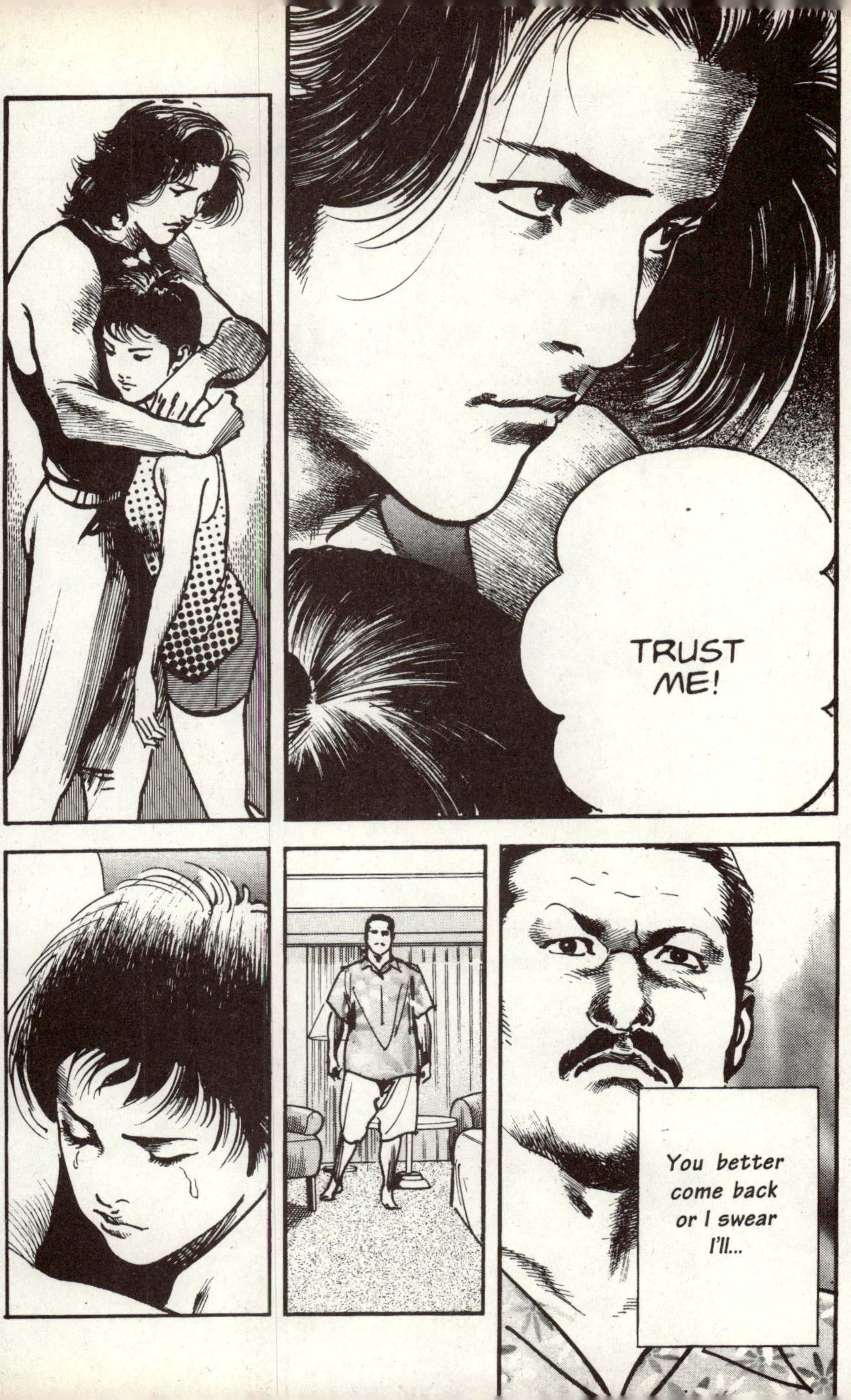
TRUST ME!
You better come back or I swear I'll...

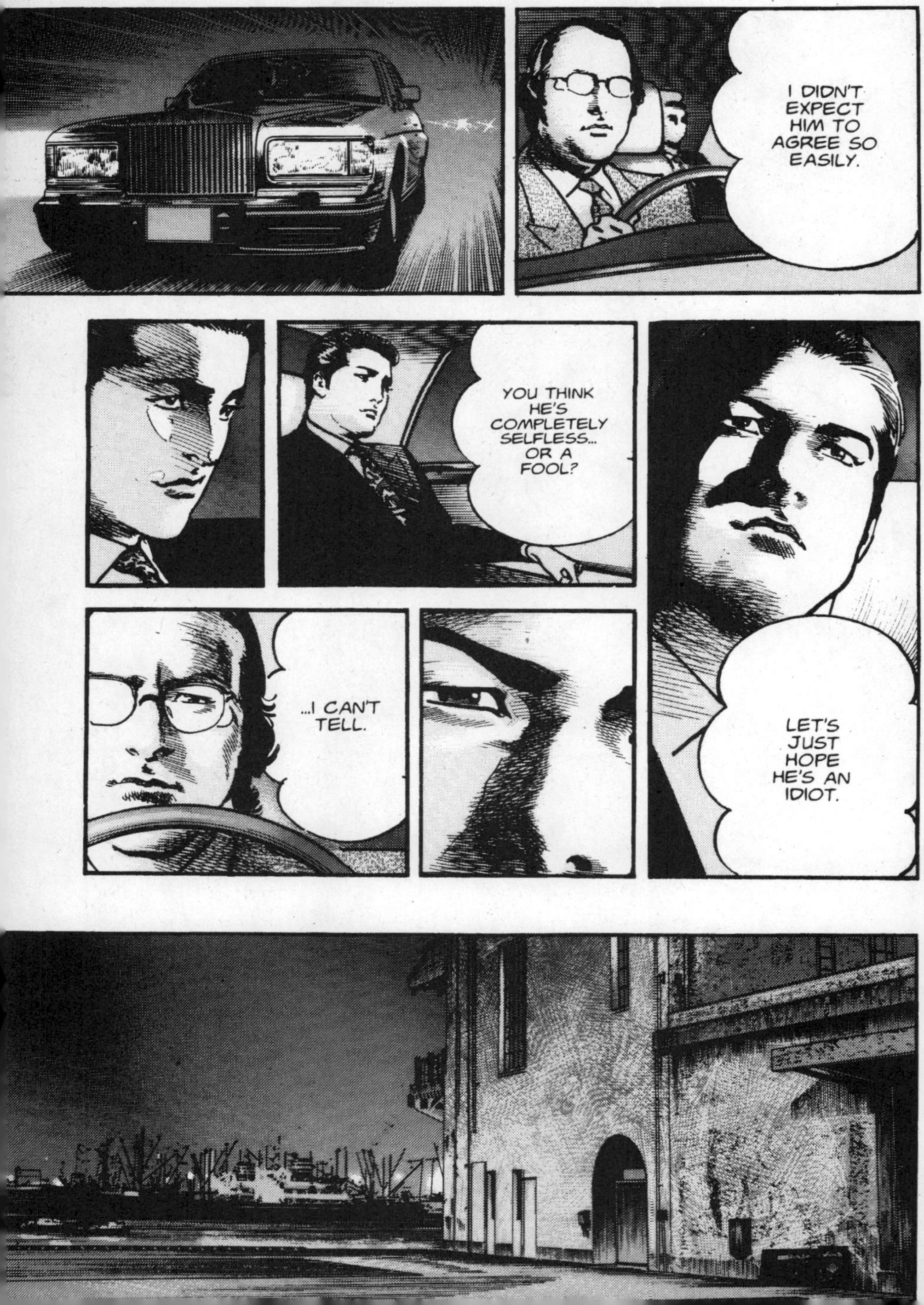
I DIDN'T EXPECT HIM TO AGREE SO EASILY.
YOU THINK HE'S COMPLETELY SELFLESS... OR A FOOL?
...I CAN'T TELL.
LET'S JUST HOPE HE'S AN IDIOT.

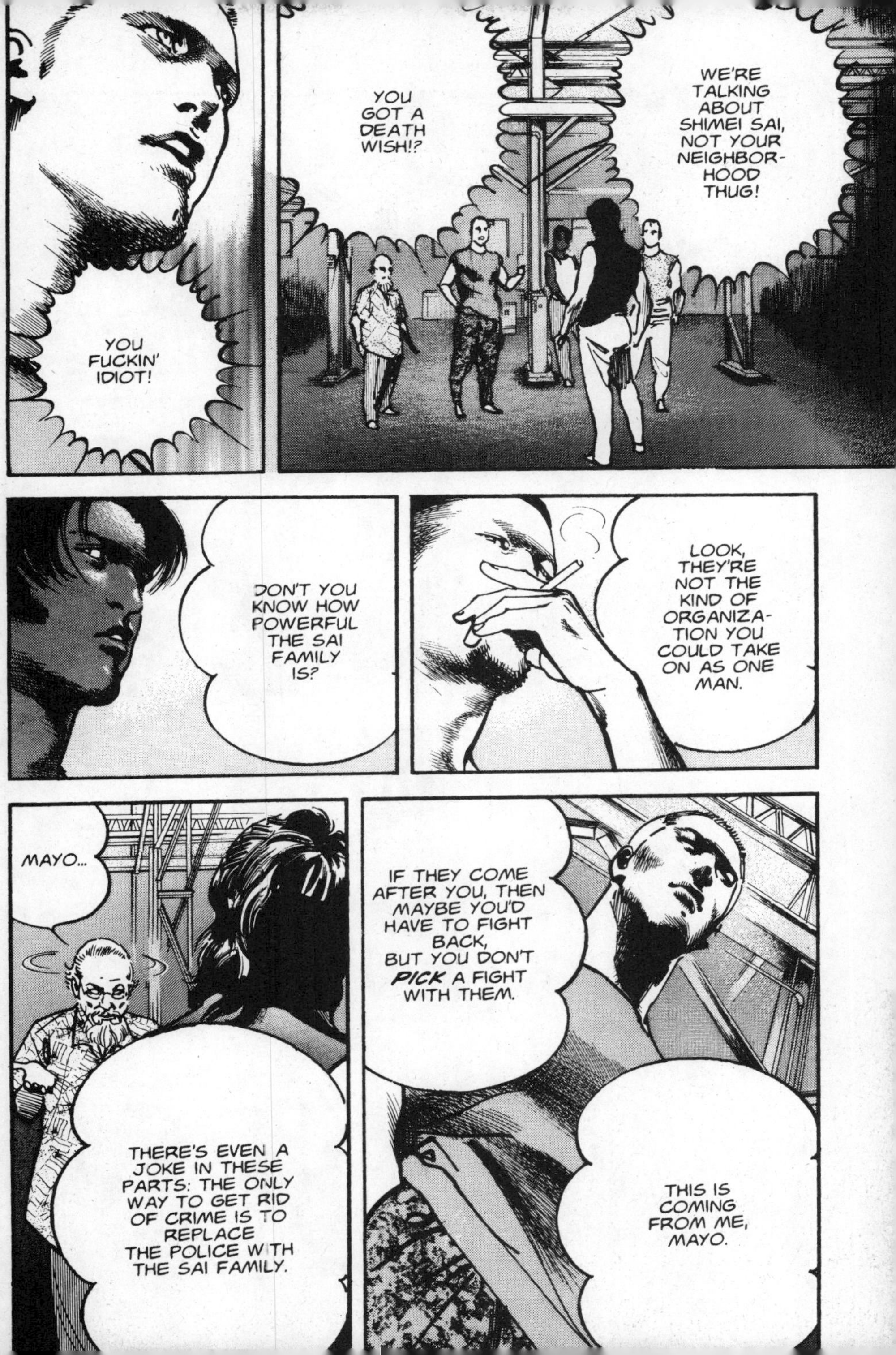
YOU FUCKIN' IDIOT!
WE'RE TALKING ABOUT SHIMEI SAI, NOT YOUR NEIGHBOR-HOOD THUG!
YOU GOT A DEATH WISH!?
DON'T YOU KNOW HOW POWERFUL THE SAI FAMILY IS?
LOOK, THEY'RE NOT THE KIND OF ORGANIZA-TION YOU COULD TAKE ON AS ONE MAN.
MAYO...
THERE'S EVEN A JOKE IN THESE PARTS: THE ONLY WAY TO GET RID OF CRIME IS TO REPLACE THE POLICE WITH THE SAI FAMILY.
IF THEY COME AFTER YOU, THEN MAYBE YOU'D HAVE TO FIGHT BACK, BUT YOU DON'T *PICK* A FIGHT WITH THEM.
THIS IS COMING FROM ME, MAYO.

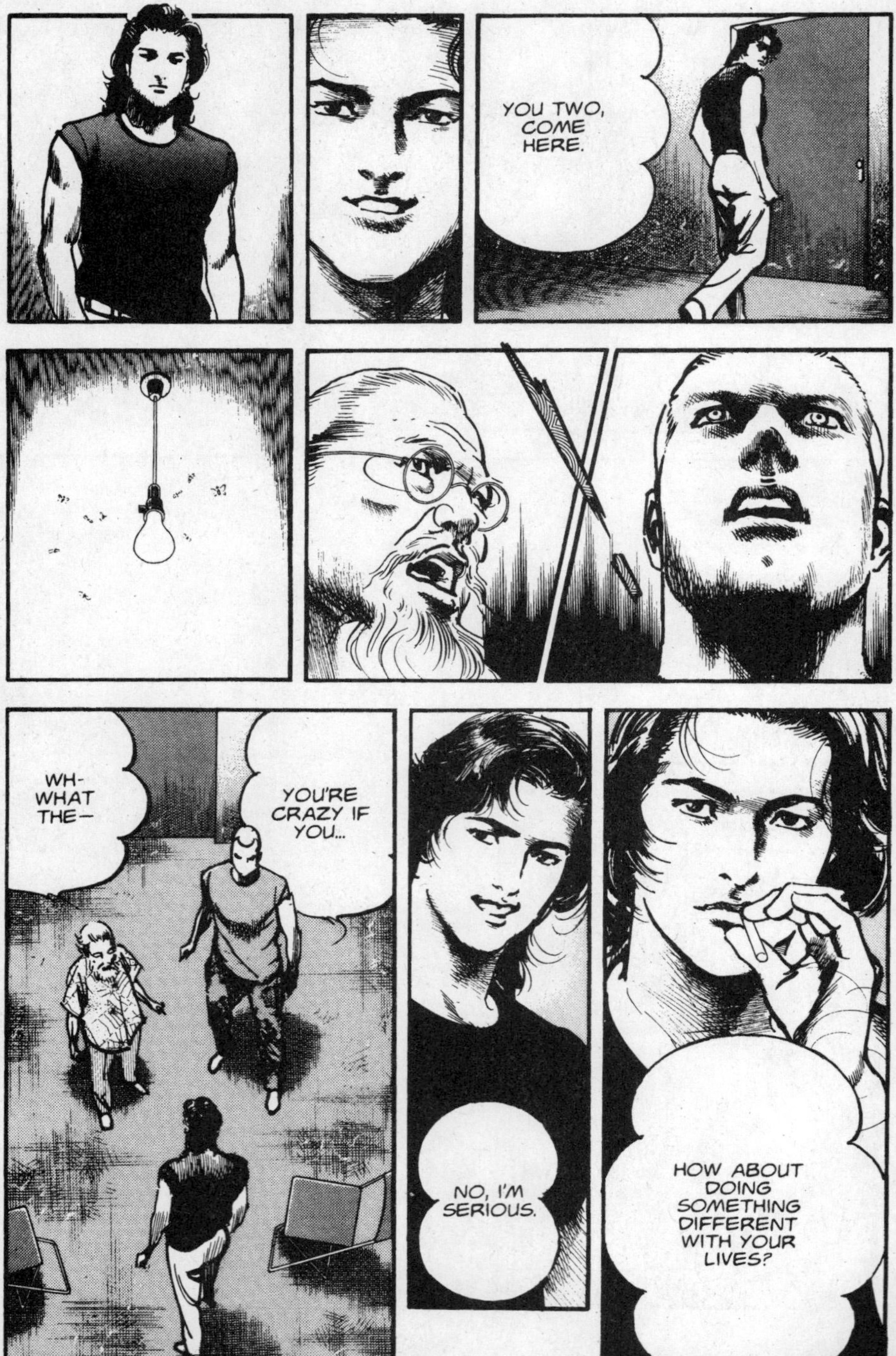
YOU TWO, COME HERE.
WH- WHAT THE—
YOU'RE CRAZY IF YOU...
NO, I'M SERIOUS.
HOW ABOUT DOING SOMETHING DIFFERENT WITH YOUR LIVES?

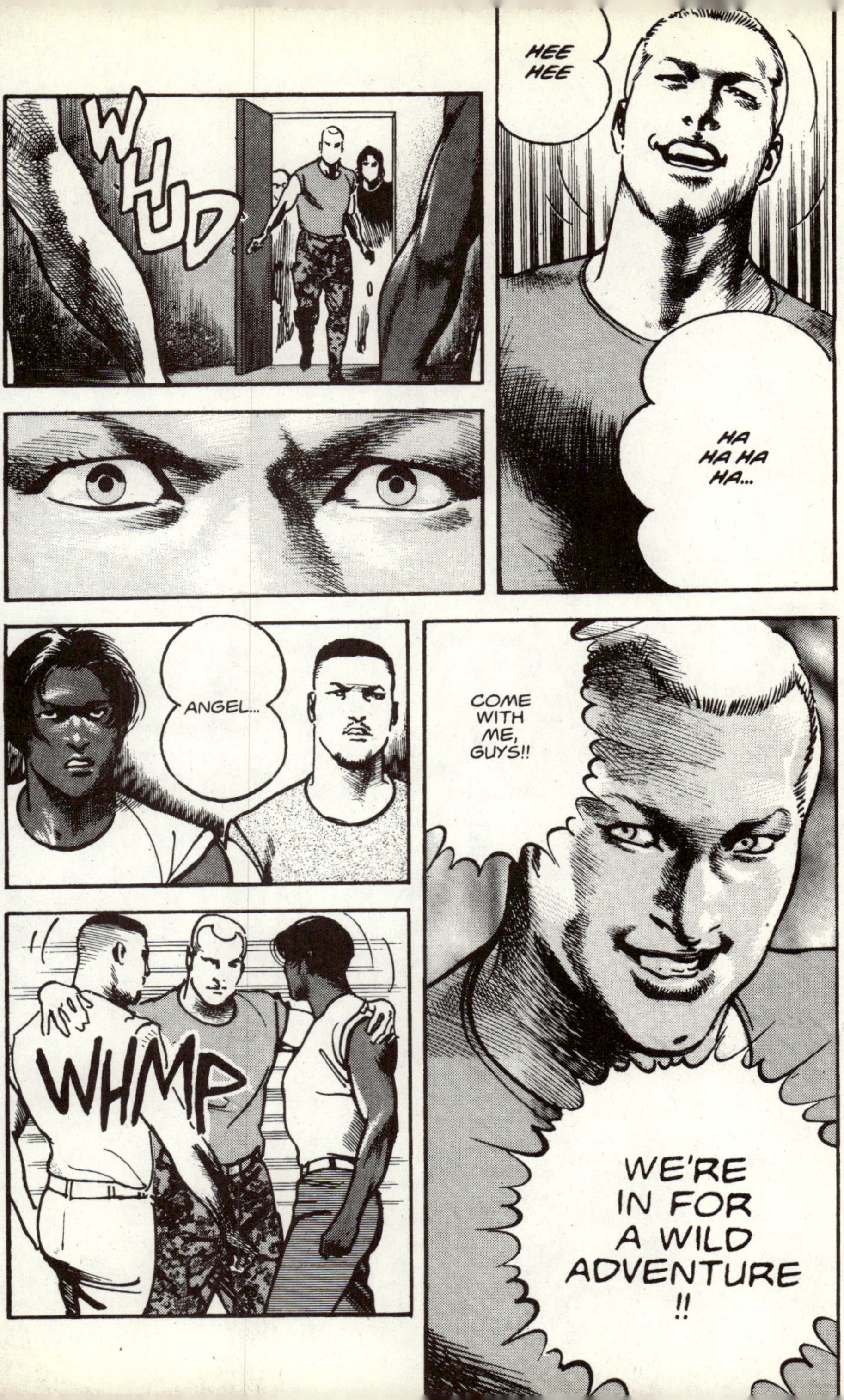
WHUD
HEE HEE
HA HA HA HA...
ANGEL...
WHMP
COME WITH ME, GUYS!!
WE'RE IN FOR A WILD ADVENTURE !!

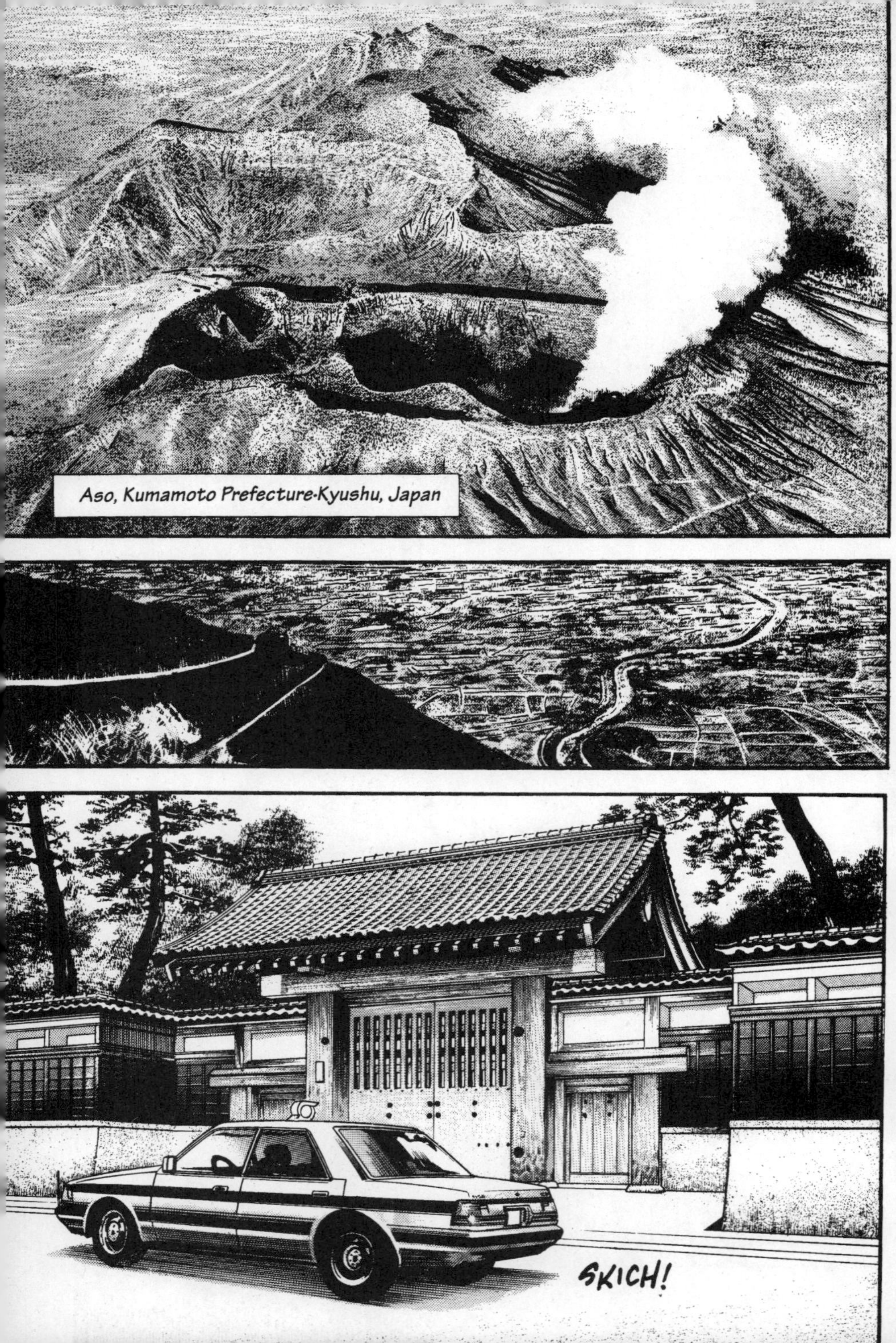
Aso, Kumamoto Prefecture-Kyushu, Japan
SKICH!

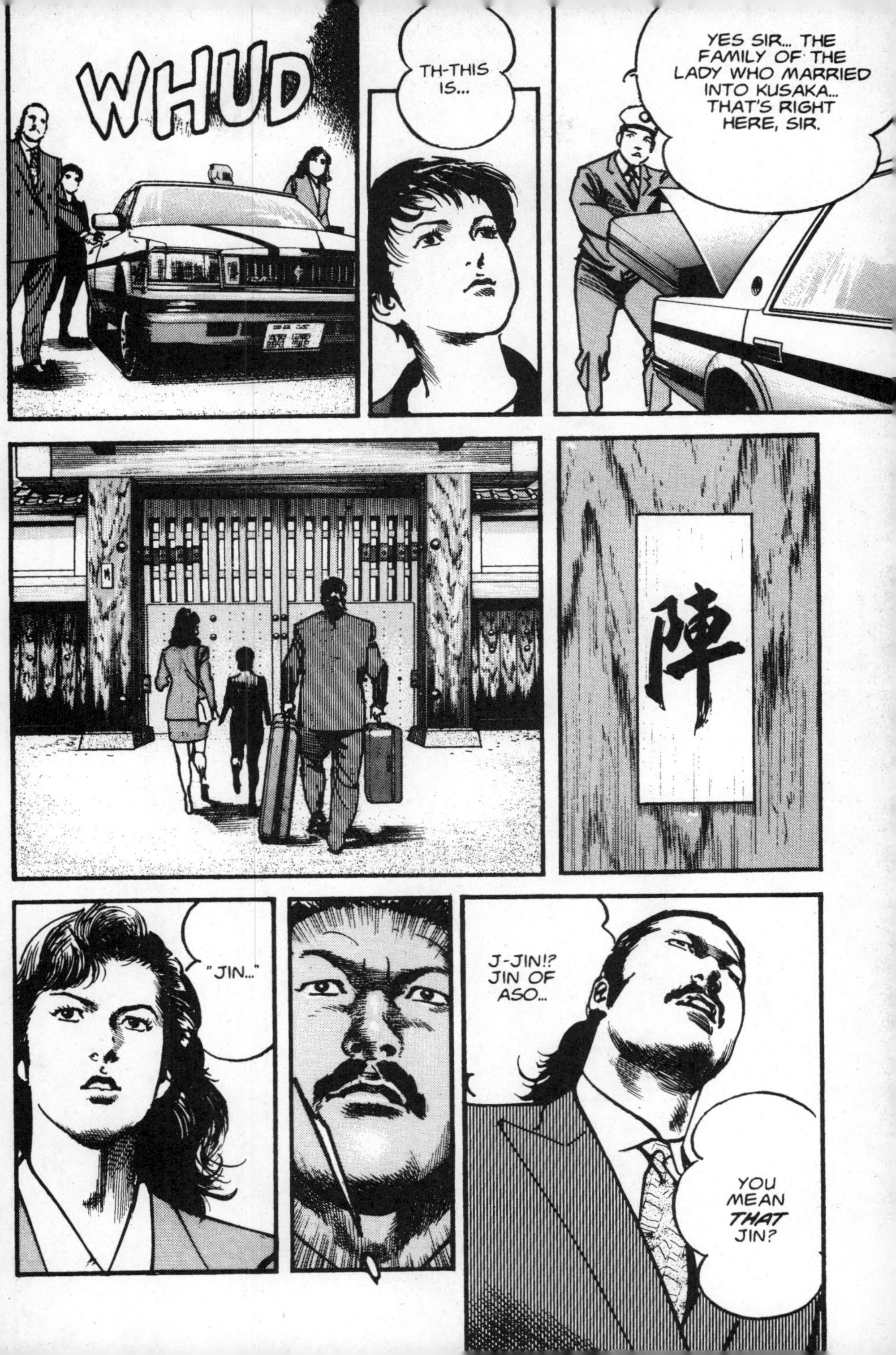
WHUD
TH-THIS IS...
YES SIR... THE FAMILY OF THE LADY WHO MARRIED INTO KUSAKA... THAT'S RIGHT HERE, SIR.
陣
"JIN..."
J-JIN!? JIN OF ASO...
YOU MEAN *THAT* JIN?

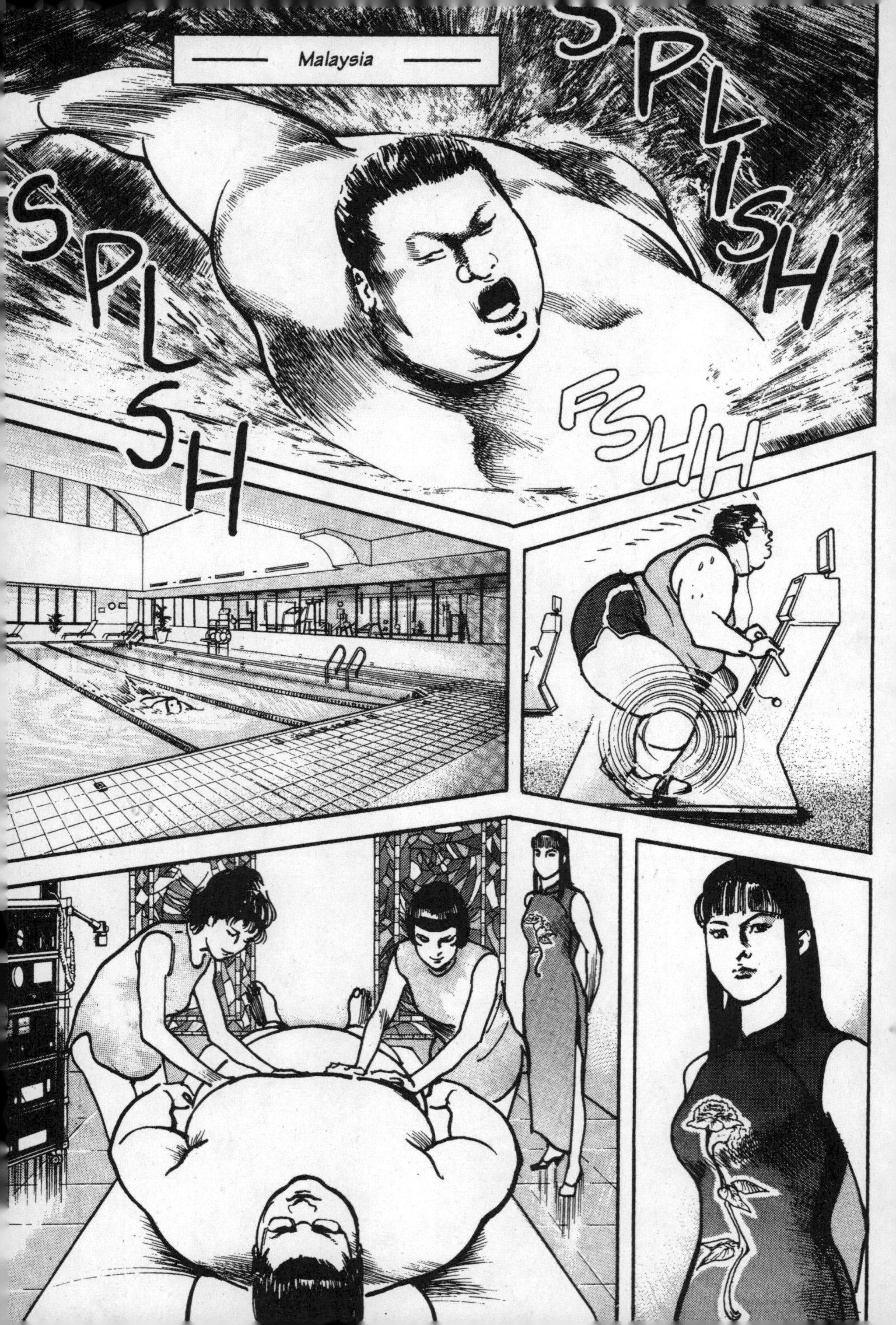

Malaysia
SPLISH
SPLSH
FSHH

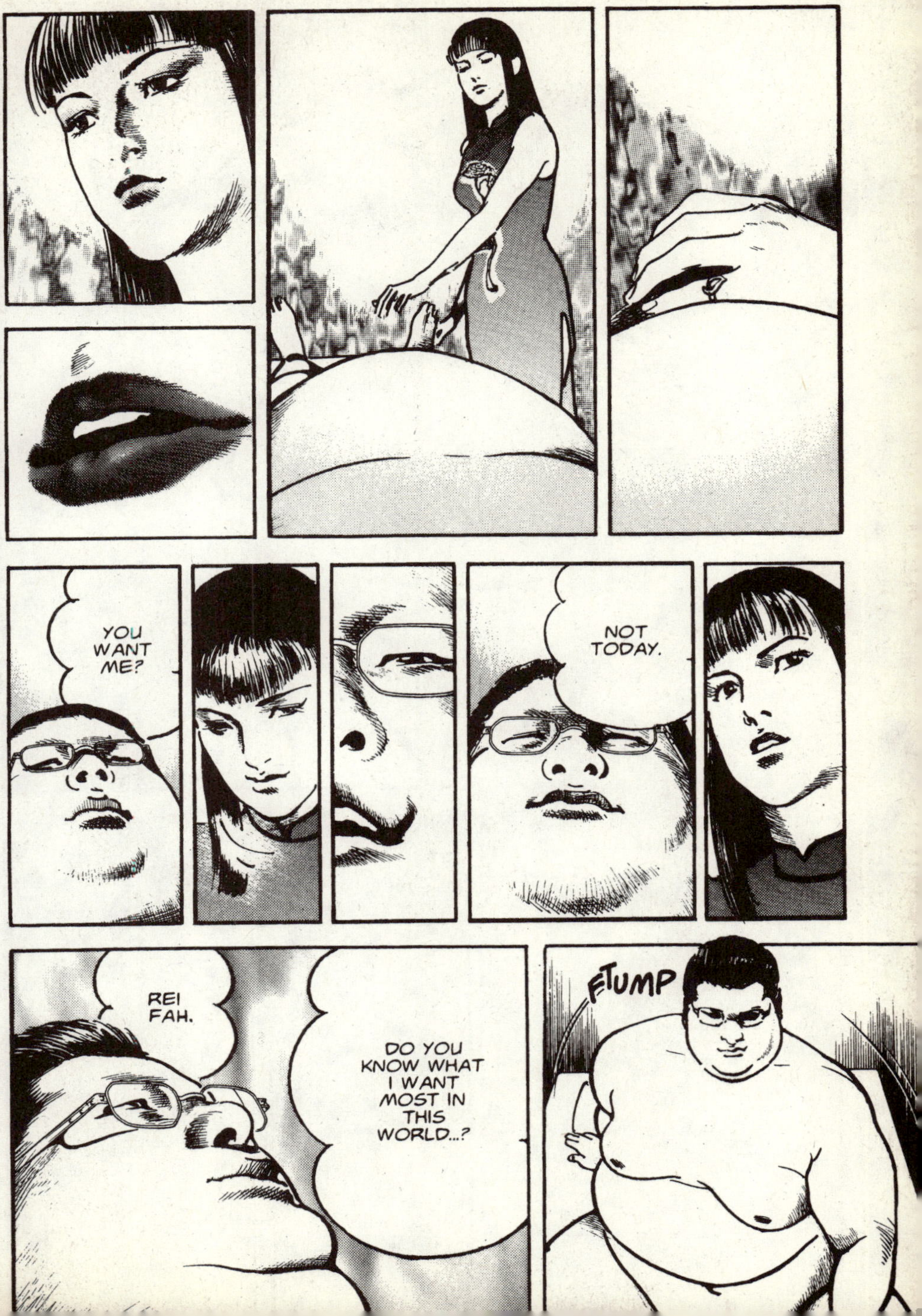
YOU WANT ME?
NOT TODAY.
REI FAH.
DO YOU KNOW WHAT I WANT MOST IN THIS WORLD...?
FTUMP

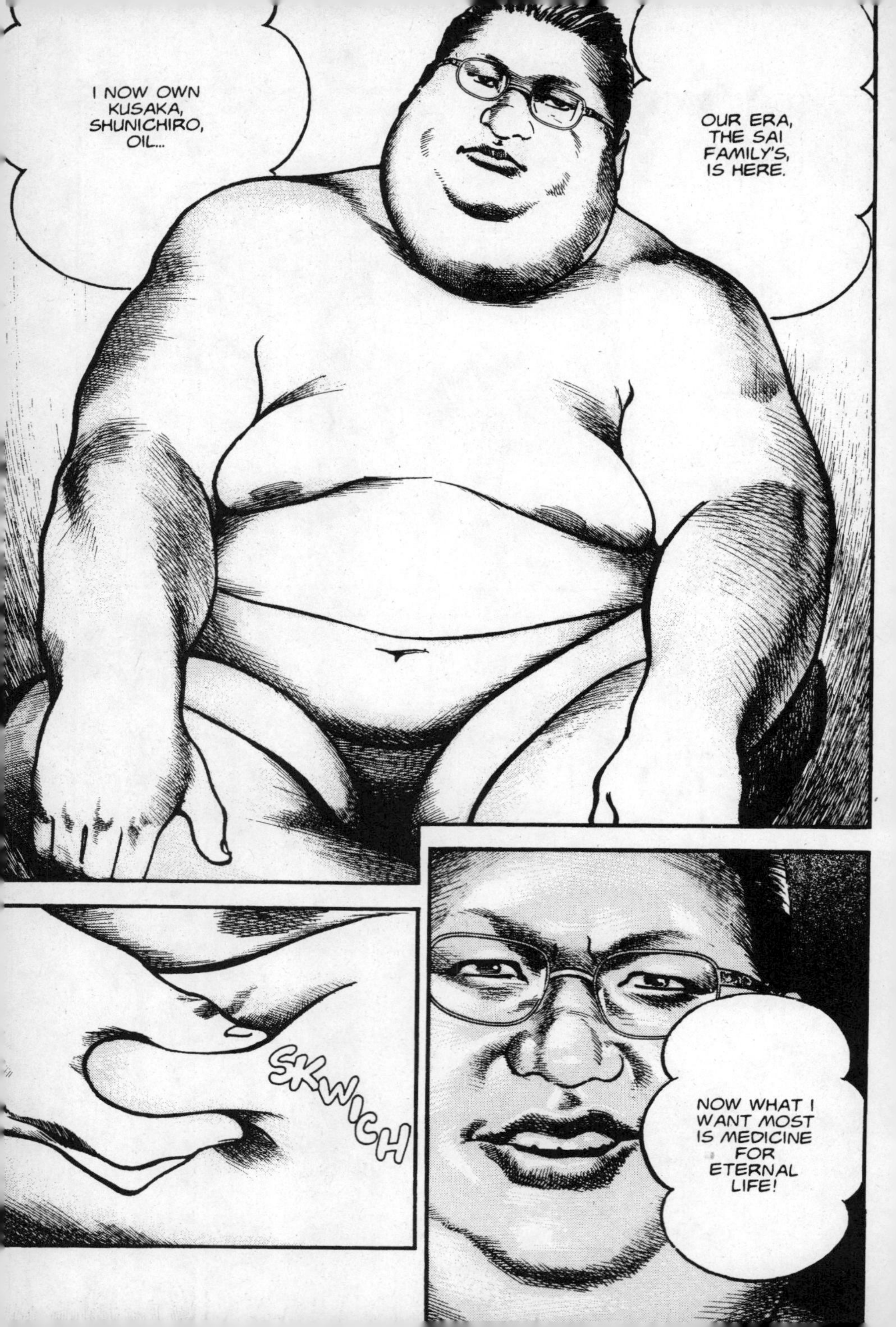
I NOW OWN KUSAKA, SHUNICHIRO, OIL...
OUR ERA, THE SAI FAMILY'S, IS HERE.
SKWICH
NOW WHAT I WANT MOST IS MEDICINE FOR ETERNAL LIFE!

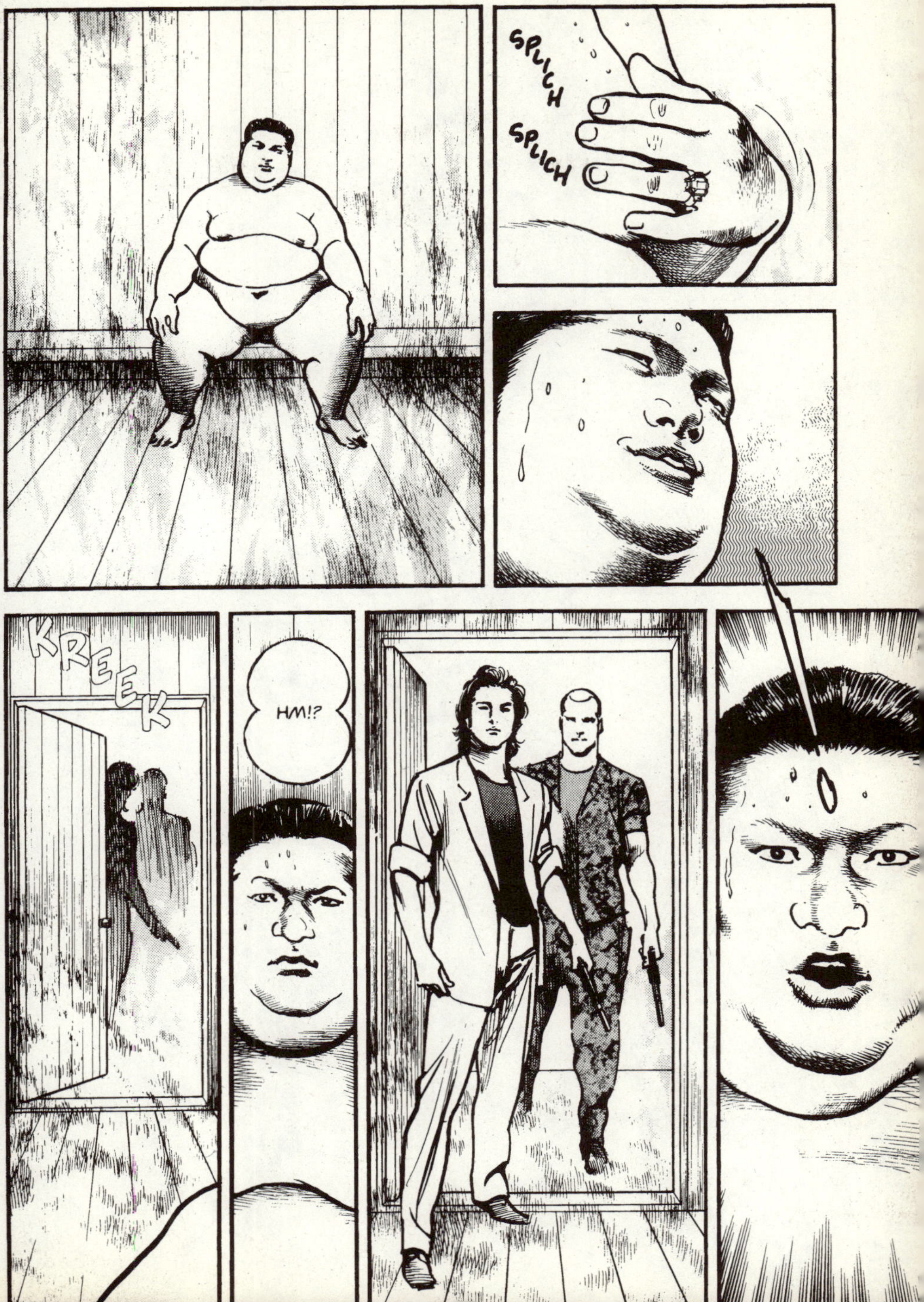
SPLICH
SPLICH
KREEEK
HM!?

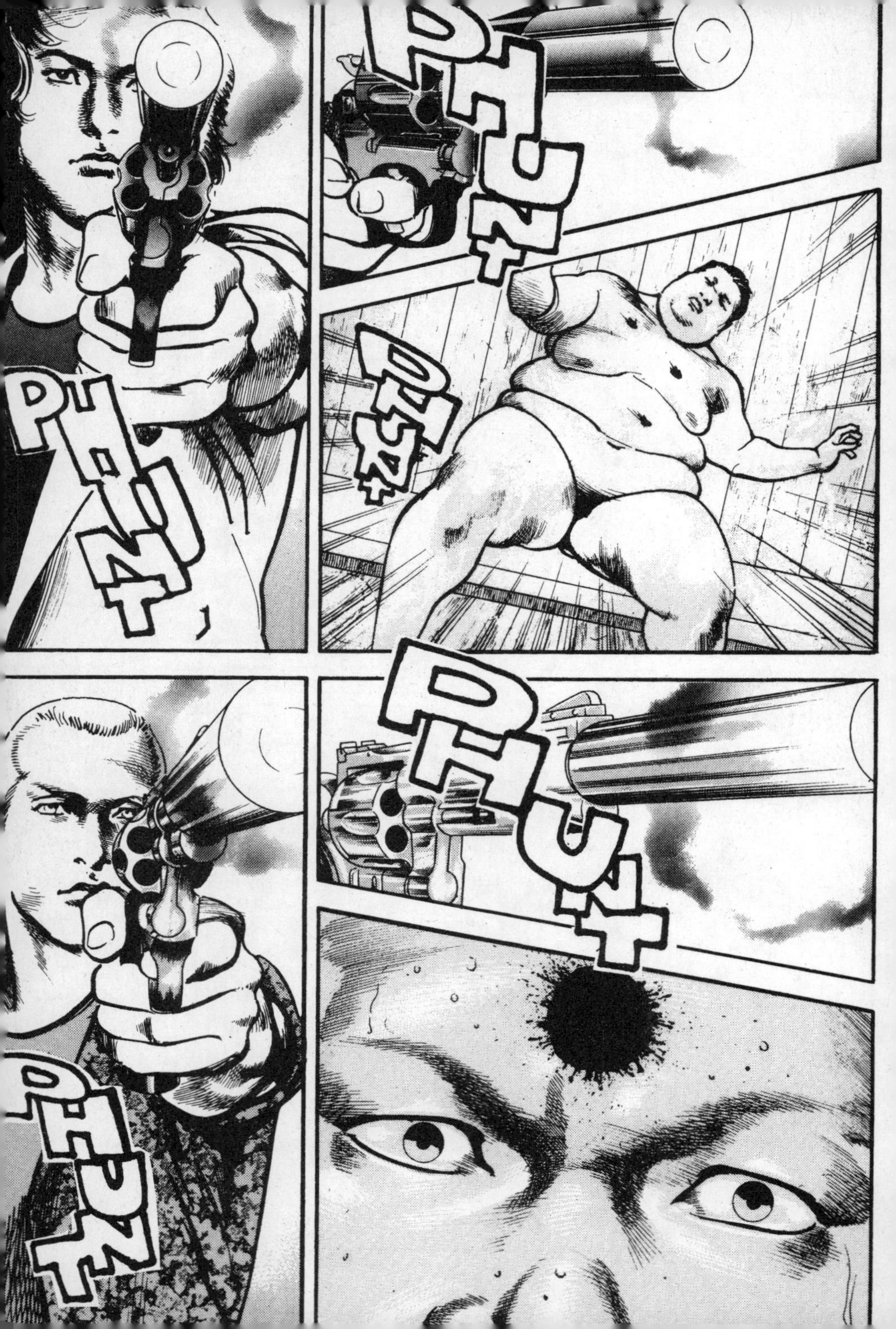
PHUNT
PHUNT
PHUNT
PHUNT
PHUNT

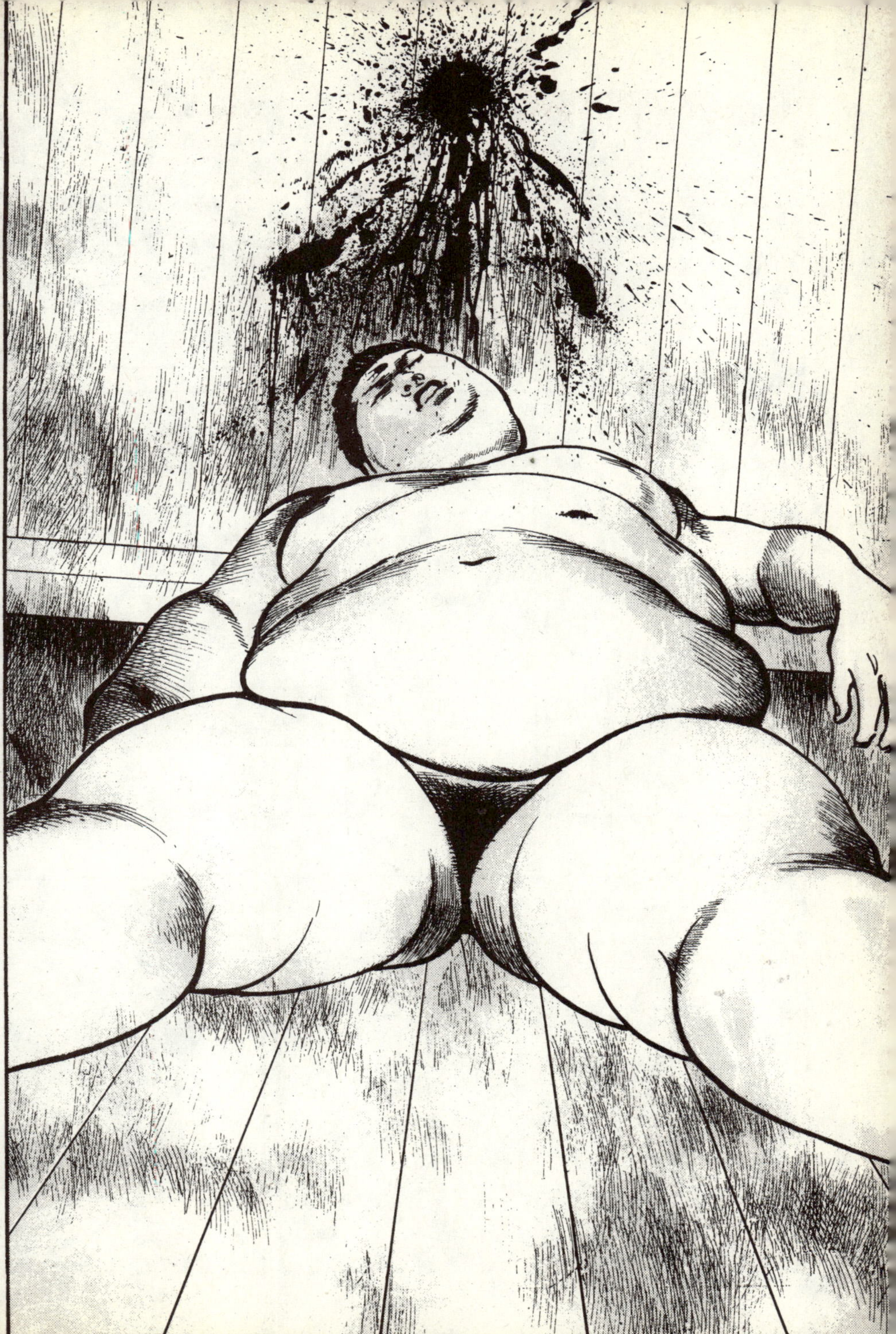

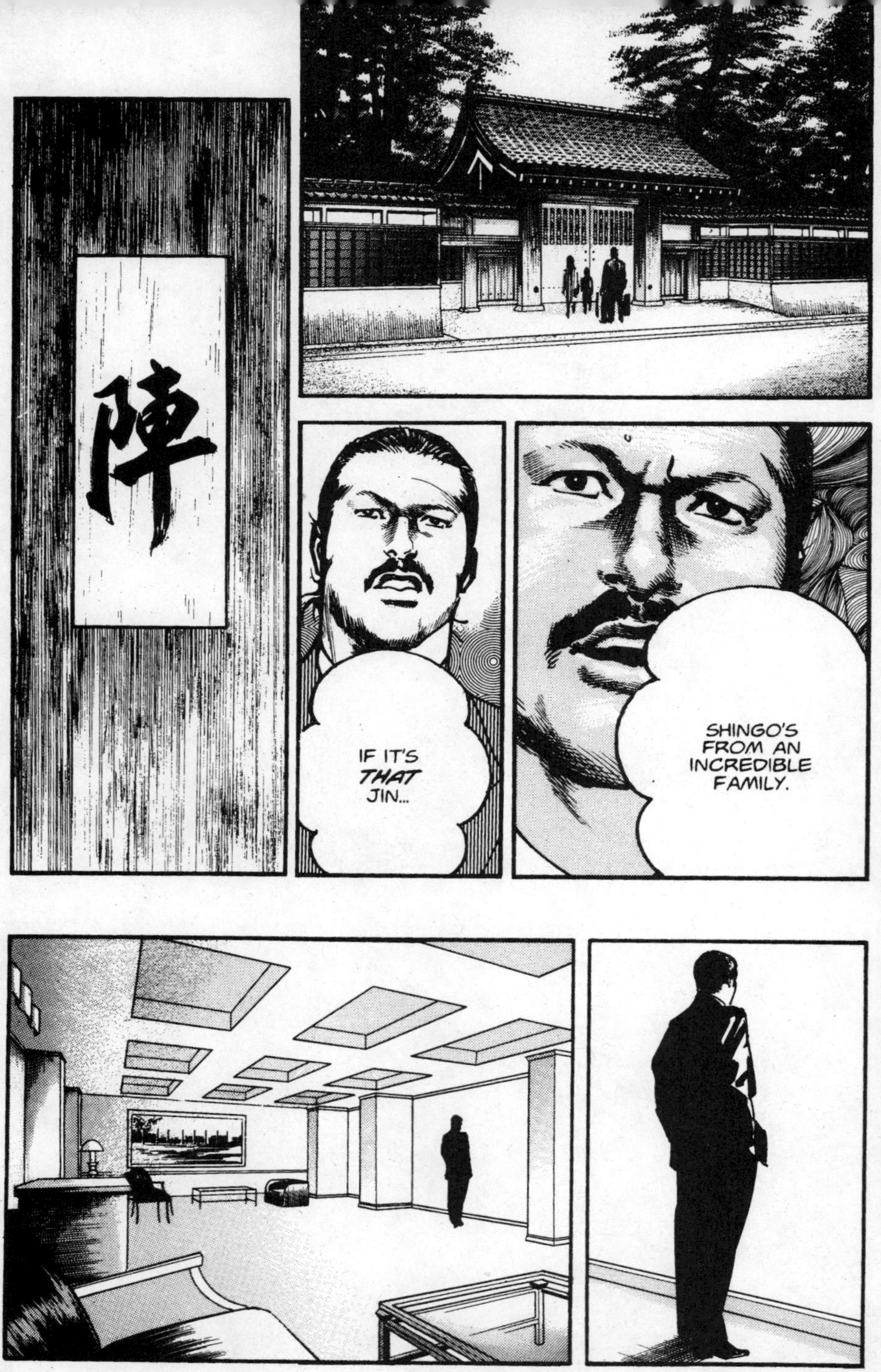
陣
SHINGO'S FROM AN INCREDIBLE FAMILY.
IF IT'S THAT JIN...

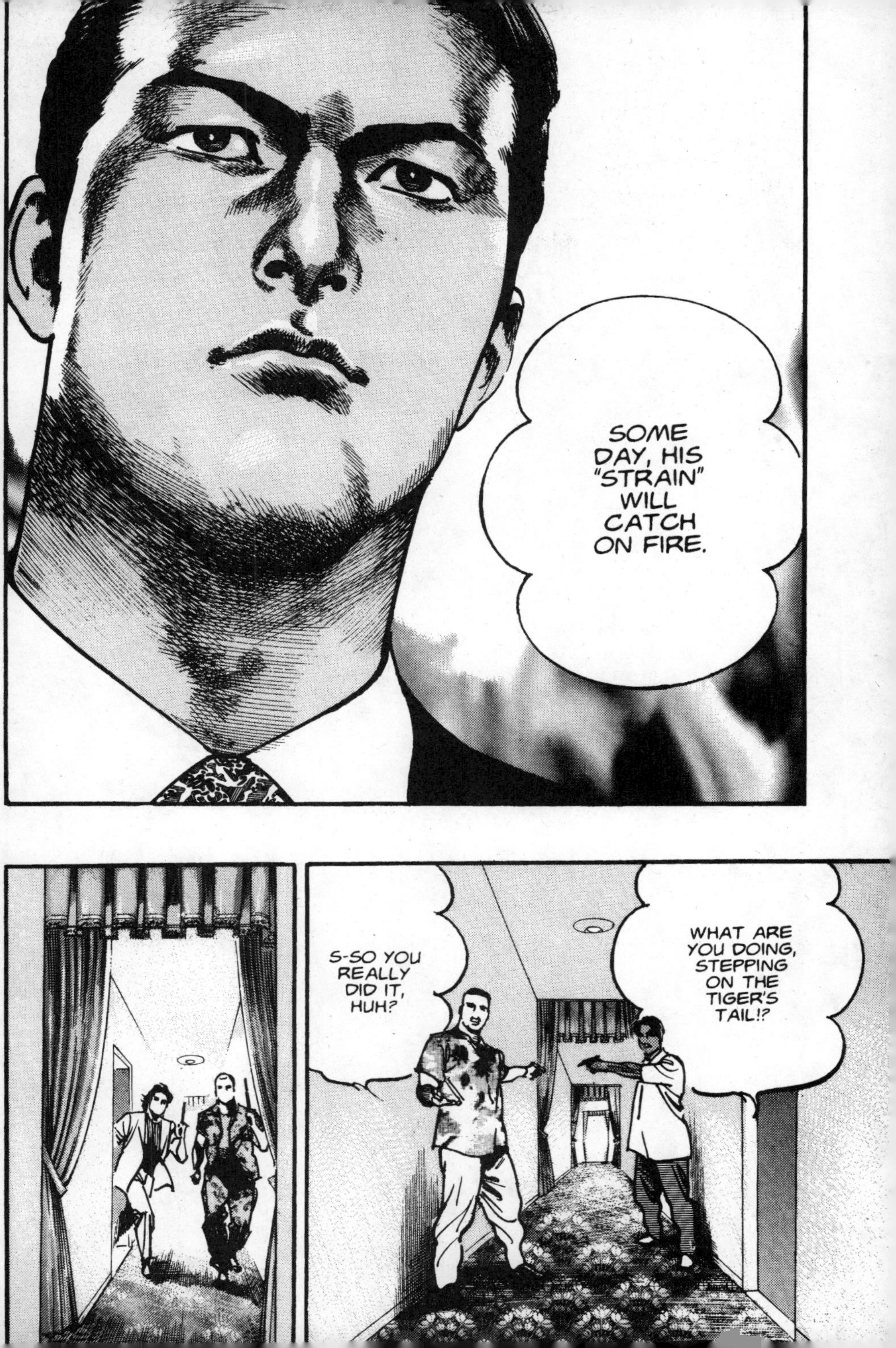
SOME DAY, HIS "STRAIN" WILL CATCH ON FIRE.
S-SO YOU REALLY DID IT, HUH?
WHAT ARE YOU DOING, STEPPING ON THE TIGER'S TAIL!?

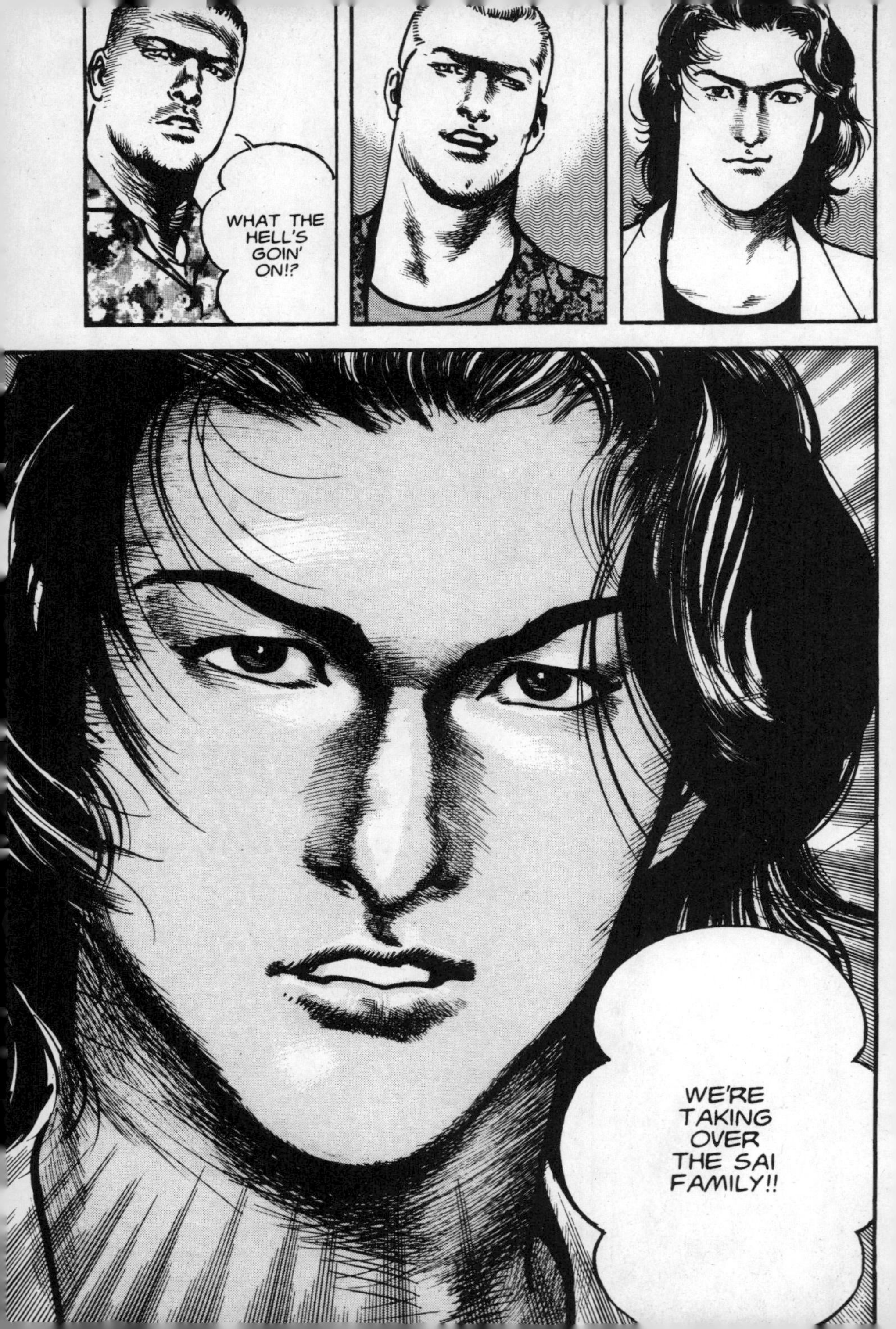
WHAT THE HELL'S GOIN' ON!?
WE'RE TAKING OVER THE SAI FAMILY!!

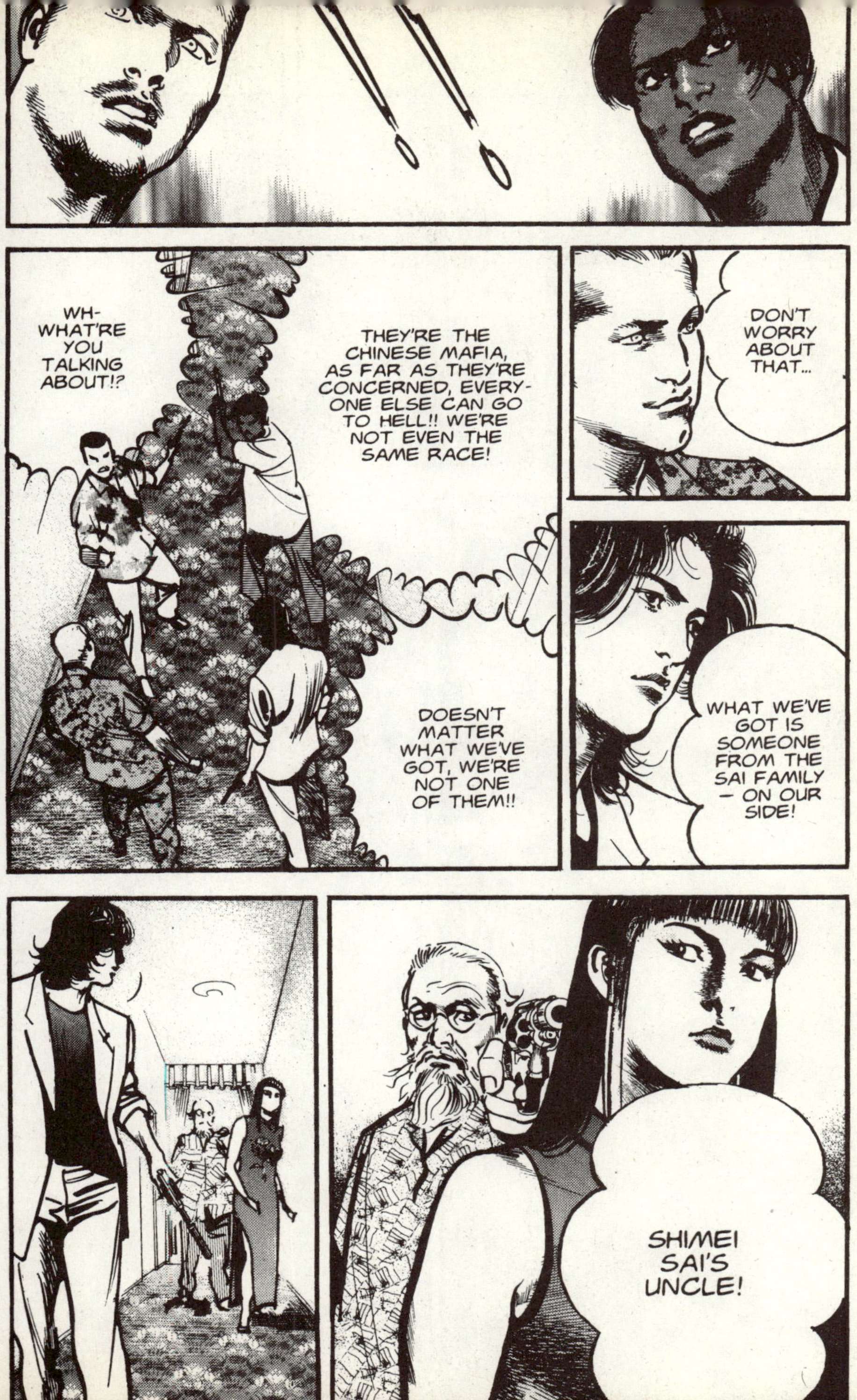

WH- WHAT'RE YOU TALKING ABOUT!?
THEY'RE THE CHINESE MAFIA, AS FAR AS THEY'RE CONCERNED, EVERY-ONE ELSE CAN GO TO HELL!! WE'RE NOT EVEN THE SAME RACE!
DOESN'T MATTER WHAT WE'VE GOT, WE'RE NOT ONE OF THEM!!
DON'T WORRY ABOUT THAT...
WHAT WE'VE GOT IS SOMEONE FROM THE SAI FAMILY – ON OUR SIDE!
SHIMEI SAI'S UNCLE!

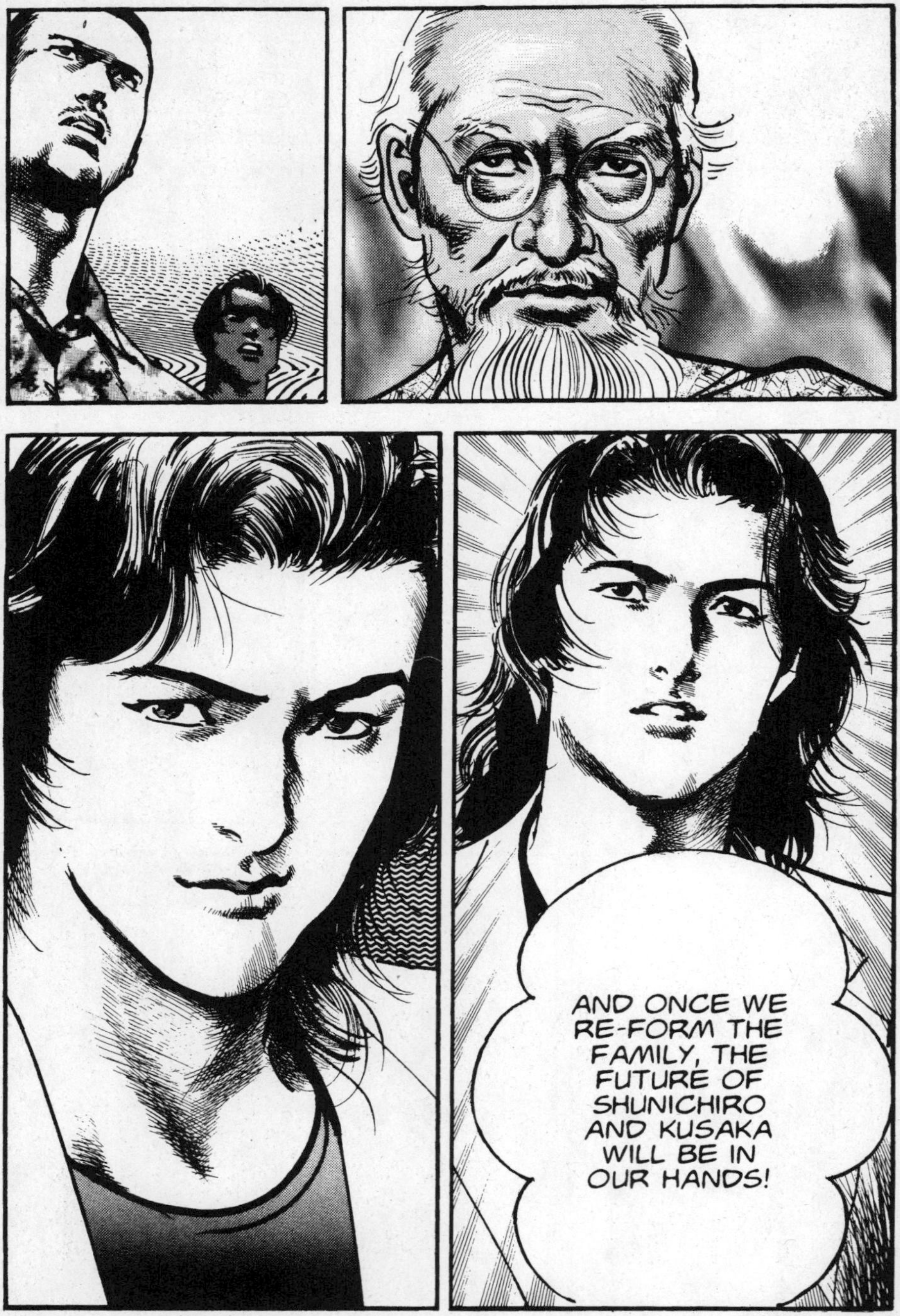
AND ONCE WE RE-FORM THE FAMILY, THE FUTURE OF SHUNICHIRO AND KUSAKA WILL BE IN OUR HANDS!

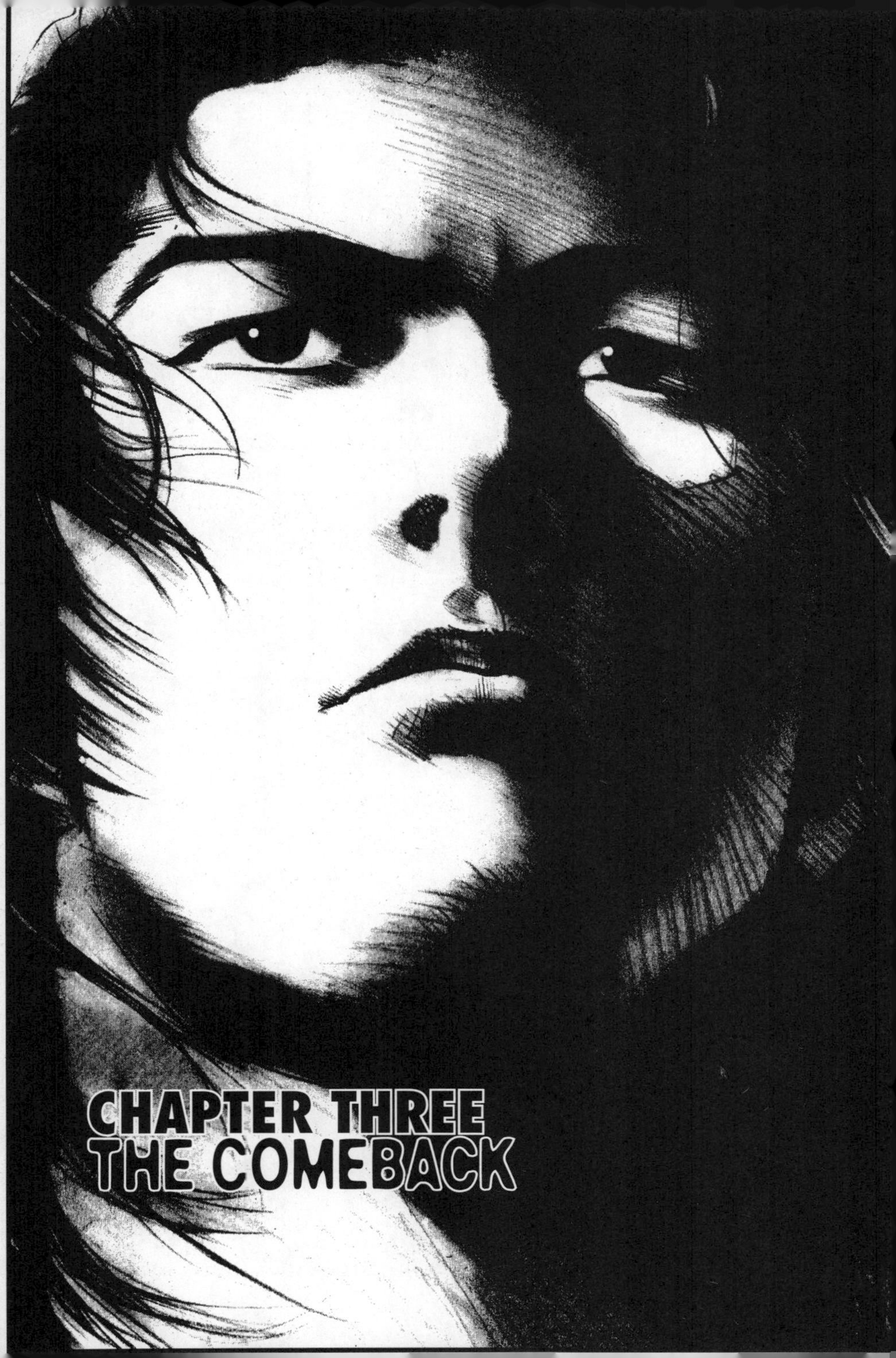
CHAPTER THREE
THE COMEBACK

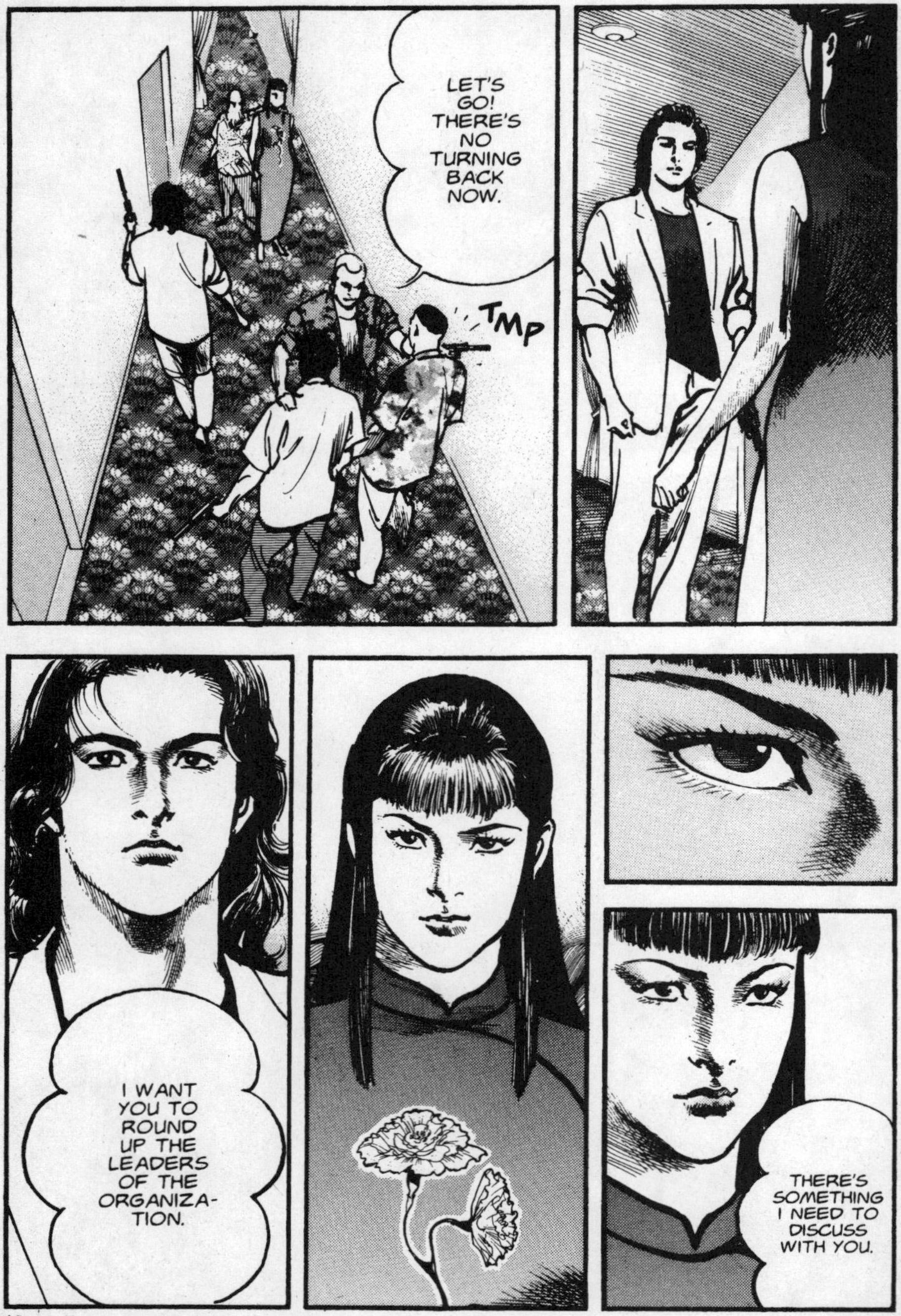
LET'S GO! THERE'S NO TURNING BACK NOW.
TMP
I WANT YOU TO ROUND UP THE LEADERS OF THE ORGANIZA-TION.
THERE'S SOMETHING I NEED TO DISCUSS WITH YOU.

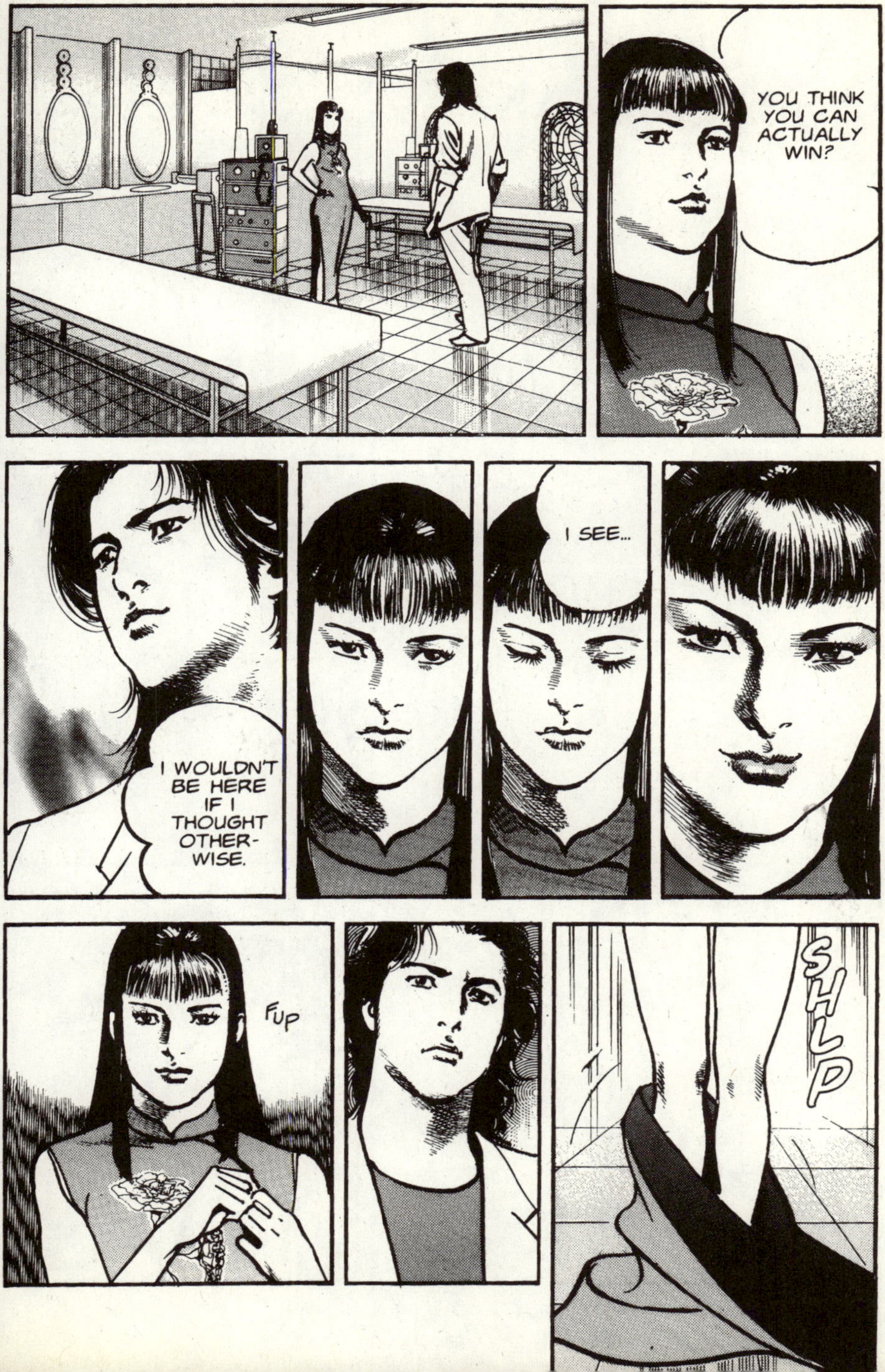
YOU THINK YOU CAN ACTUALLY WIN?
I WOULDN'T BE HERE IF I THOUGHT OTHER-WISE.
I SEE...
FUP
SHLP

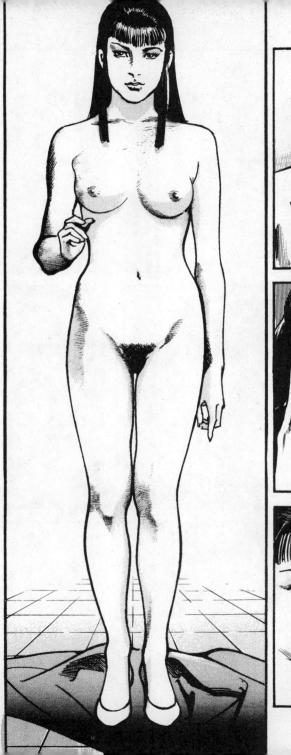

WHO
ARE
YOU...?

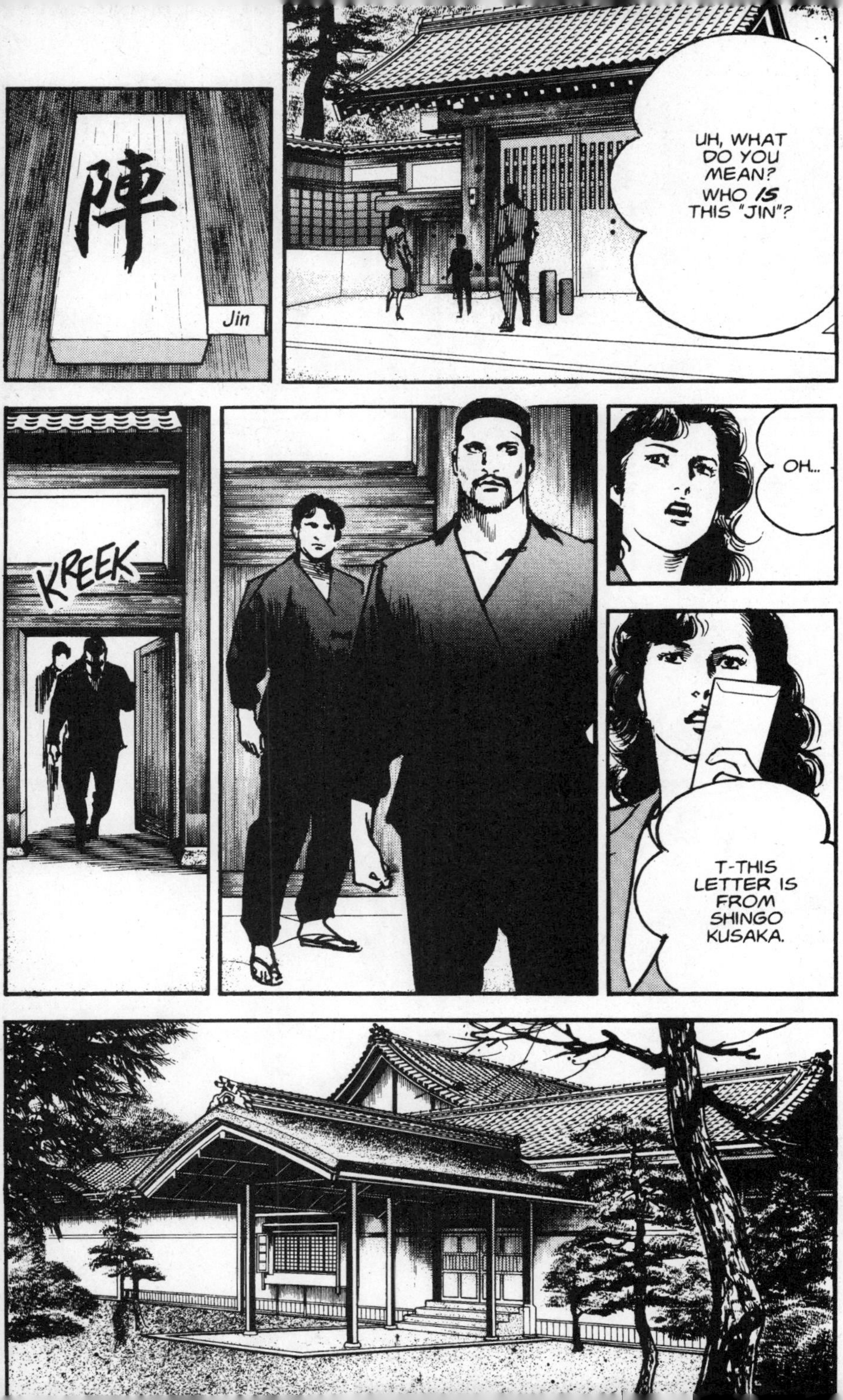
陣
Jin
UH, WHAT DO YOU MEAN? WHO IS THIS "JIN"?
KREEK
OH...
T-THIS LETTER IS FROM SHINGO KUSAKA.

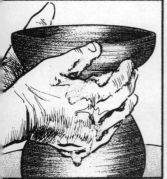

SIR, YOU HAVE VISITORS.

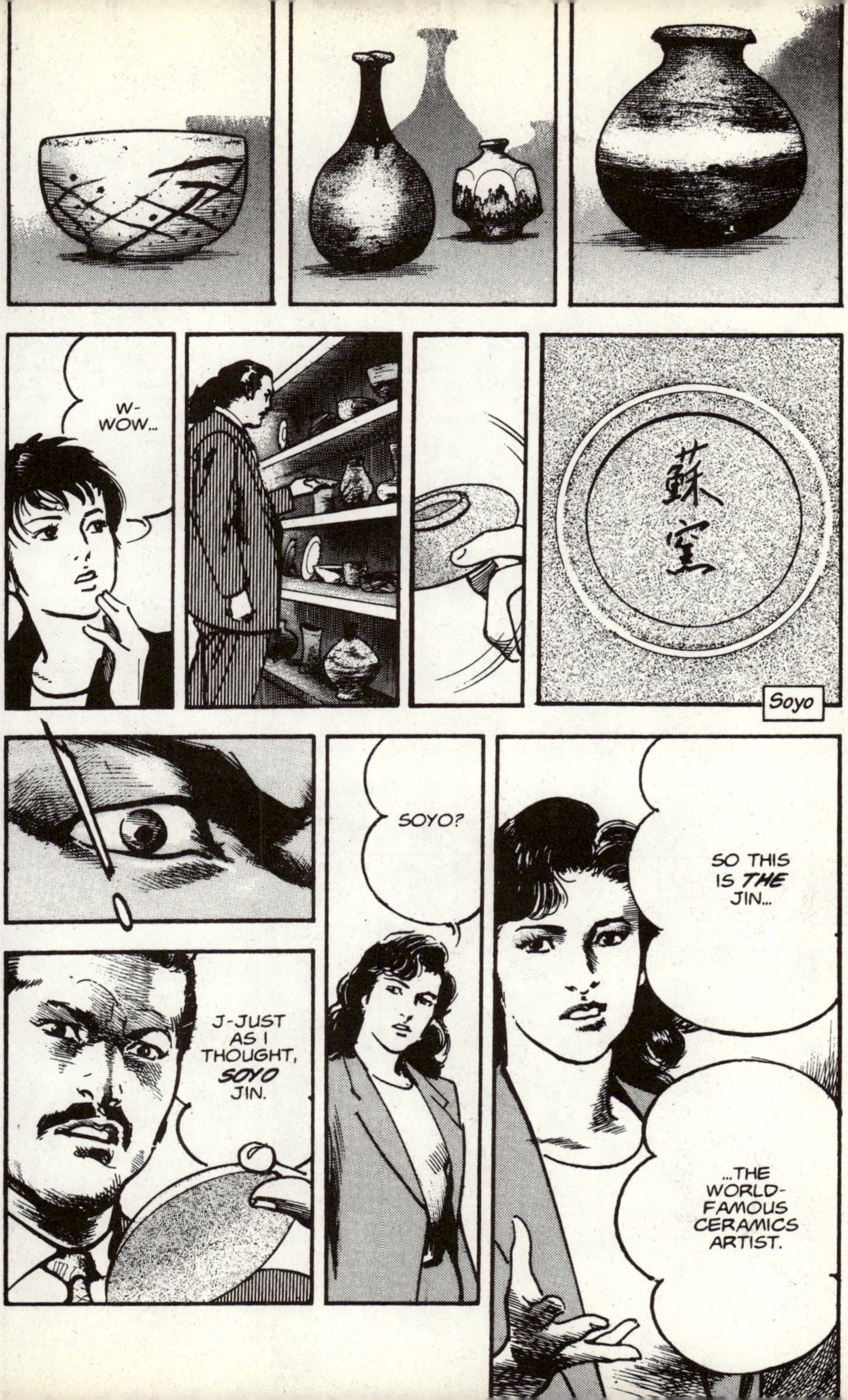
W-WOW...
蘇窯
Soyo
SOYO?
SO THIS IS THE JIN...
...THE WORLD-FAMOUS CERAMICS ARTIST.
J-JUST AS I THOUGHT, SOYO JIN.

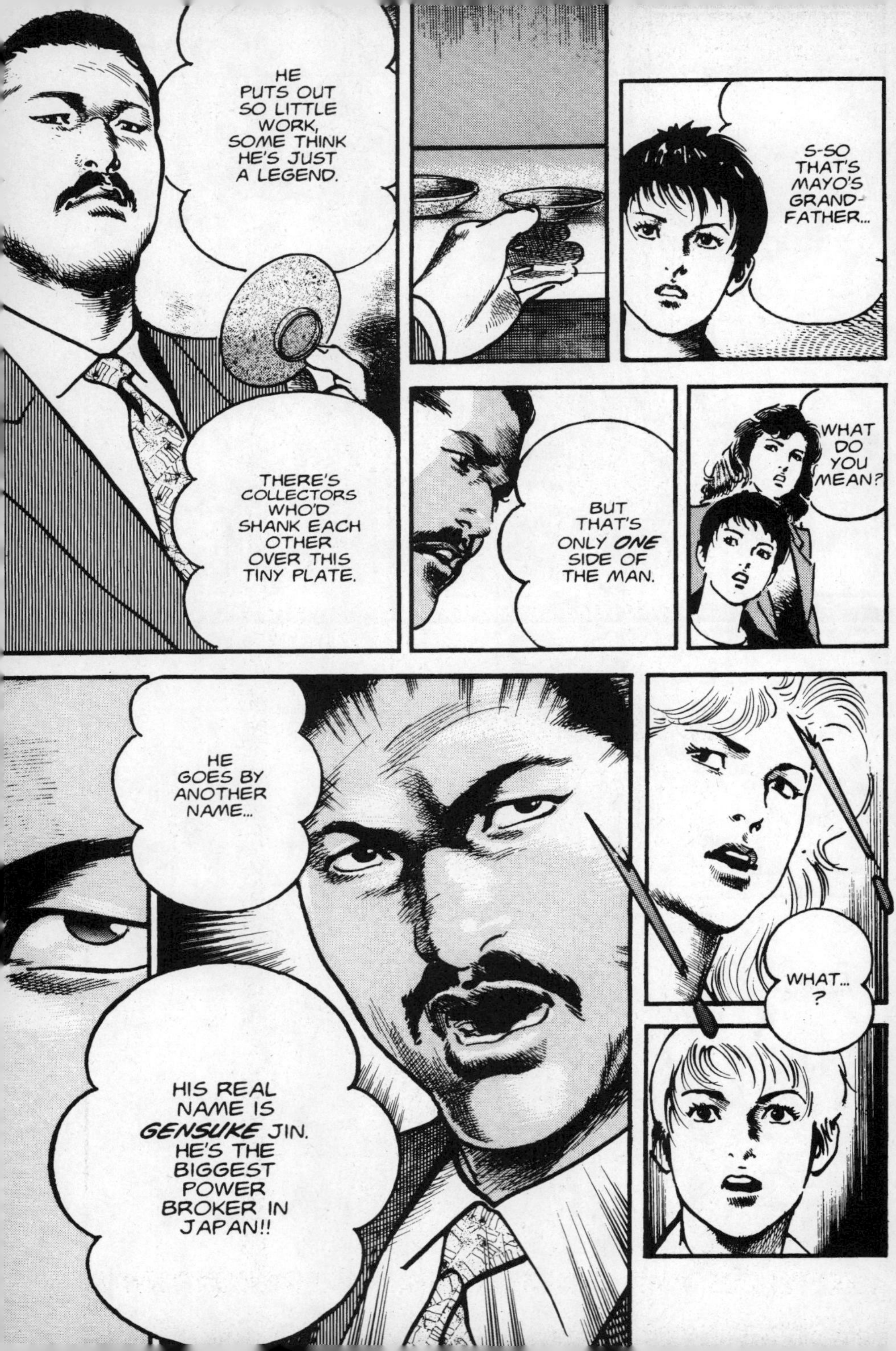
HE PUTS OUT SO LITTLE WORK, SOME THINK HE'S JUST A LEGEND.
THERE'S COLLECTORS WHO'D SHANK EACH OTHER OVER THIS TINY PLATE.
S-SO THAT'S MAYO'S GRAND-FATHER...
BUT THAT'S ONLY ONE SIDE OF THE MAN.
WHAT DO YOU MEAN?
HE GOES BY ANOTHER NAME...
HIS REAL NAME IS GENSUKE JIN. HE'S THE BIGGEST POWER BROKER IN JAPAN!!
WHAT... ?

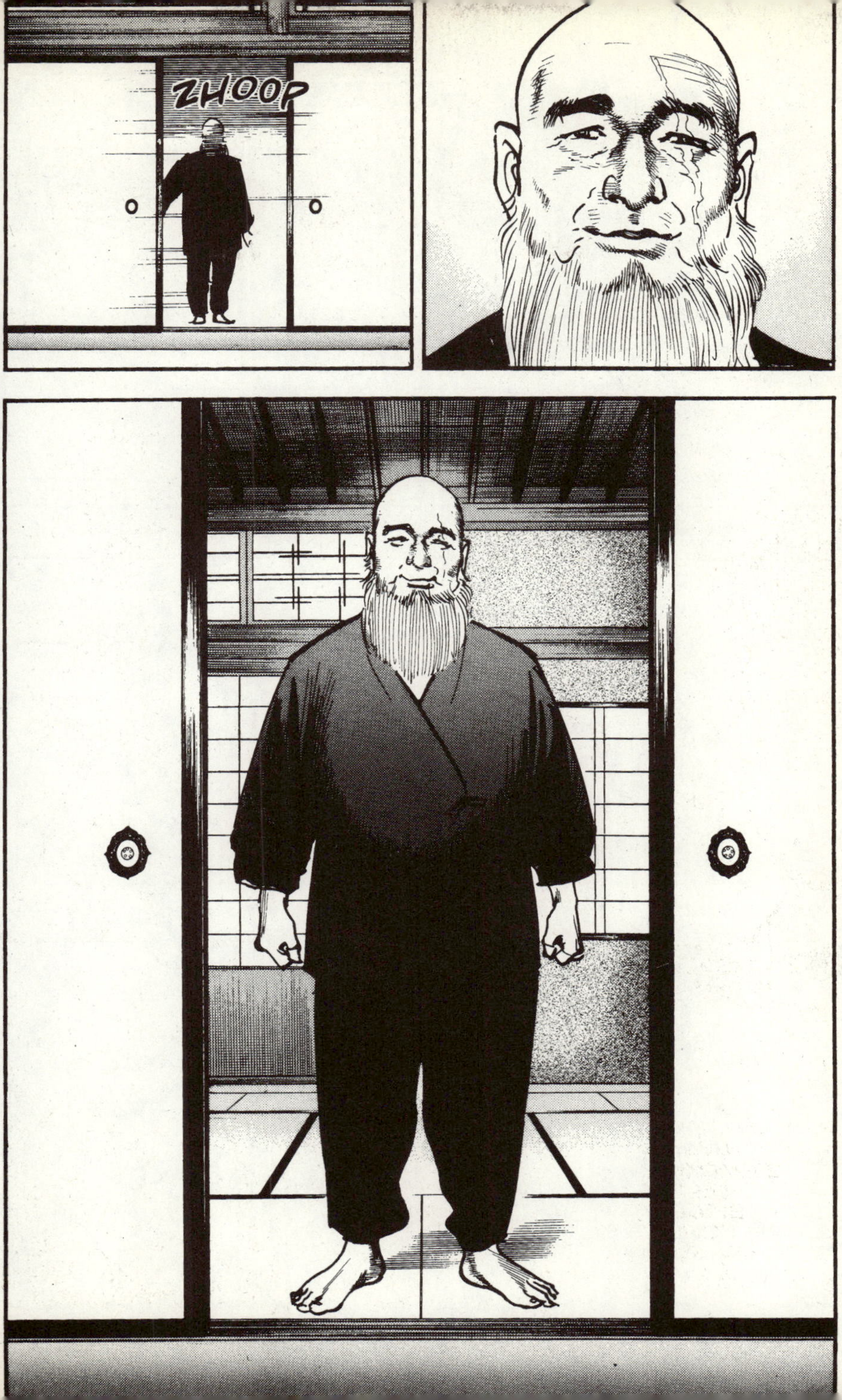
ZHOOP

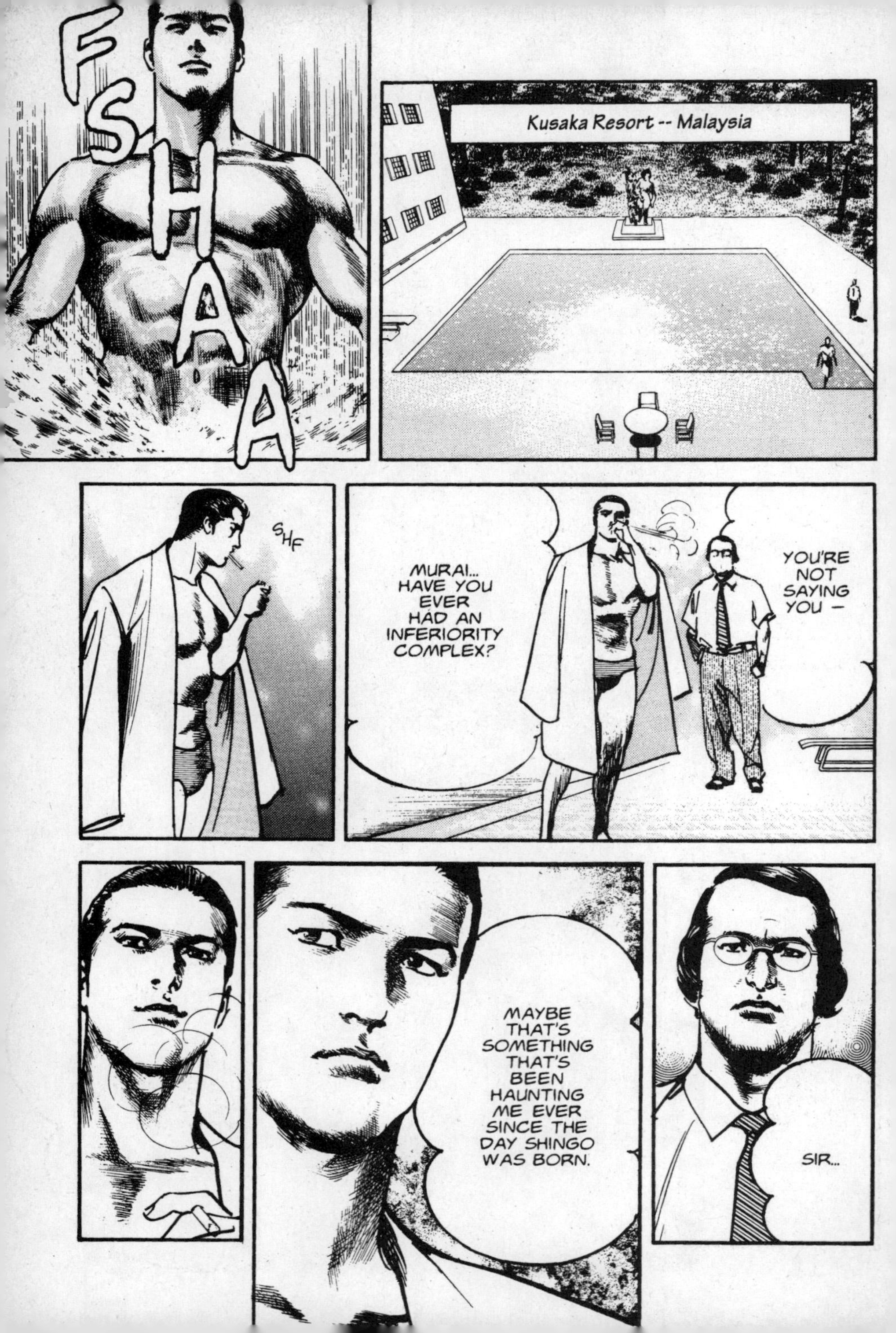
FSHAA
Kusaka Resort -- Malaysia
SHF
MURAI... HAVE YOU EVER HAD AN INFERIORITY COMPLEX?
YOU'RE NOT SAYING YOU —
MAYBE THAT'S SOMETHING THAT'S BEEN HAUNTING ME EVER SINCE THE DAY SHINGO WAS BORN.
SIR...

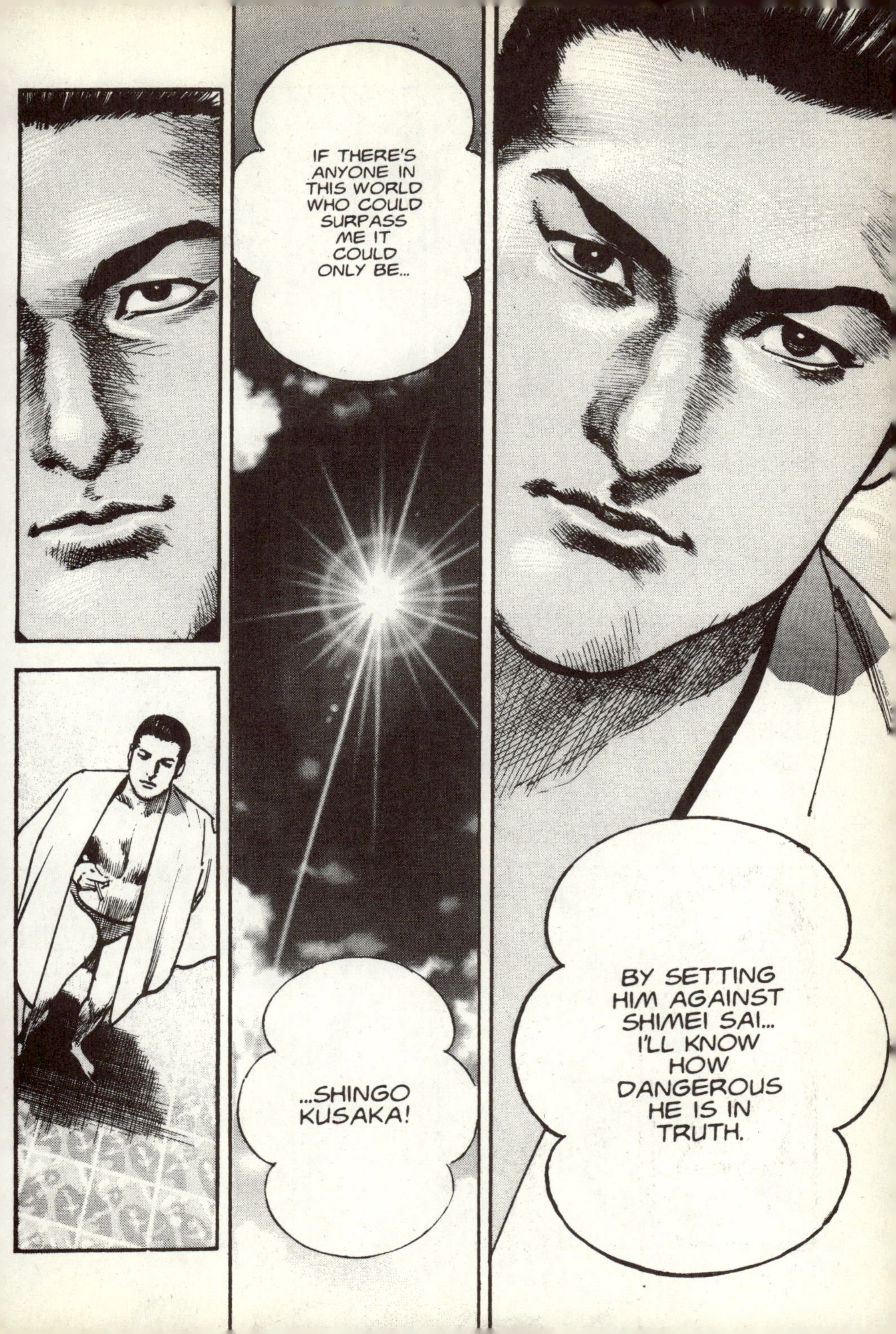
IF THERE'S ANYONE IN THIS WORLD WHO COULD SURPASS ME IT COULD ONLY BE...
BY SETTING HIM AGAINST SHIMEI SAI... I'LL KNOW HOW DANGEROUS HE IS IN TRUTH.
...SHINGO KUSAKA!

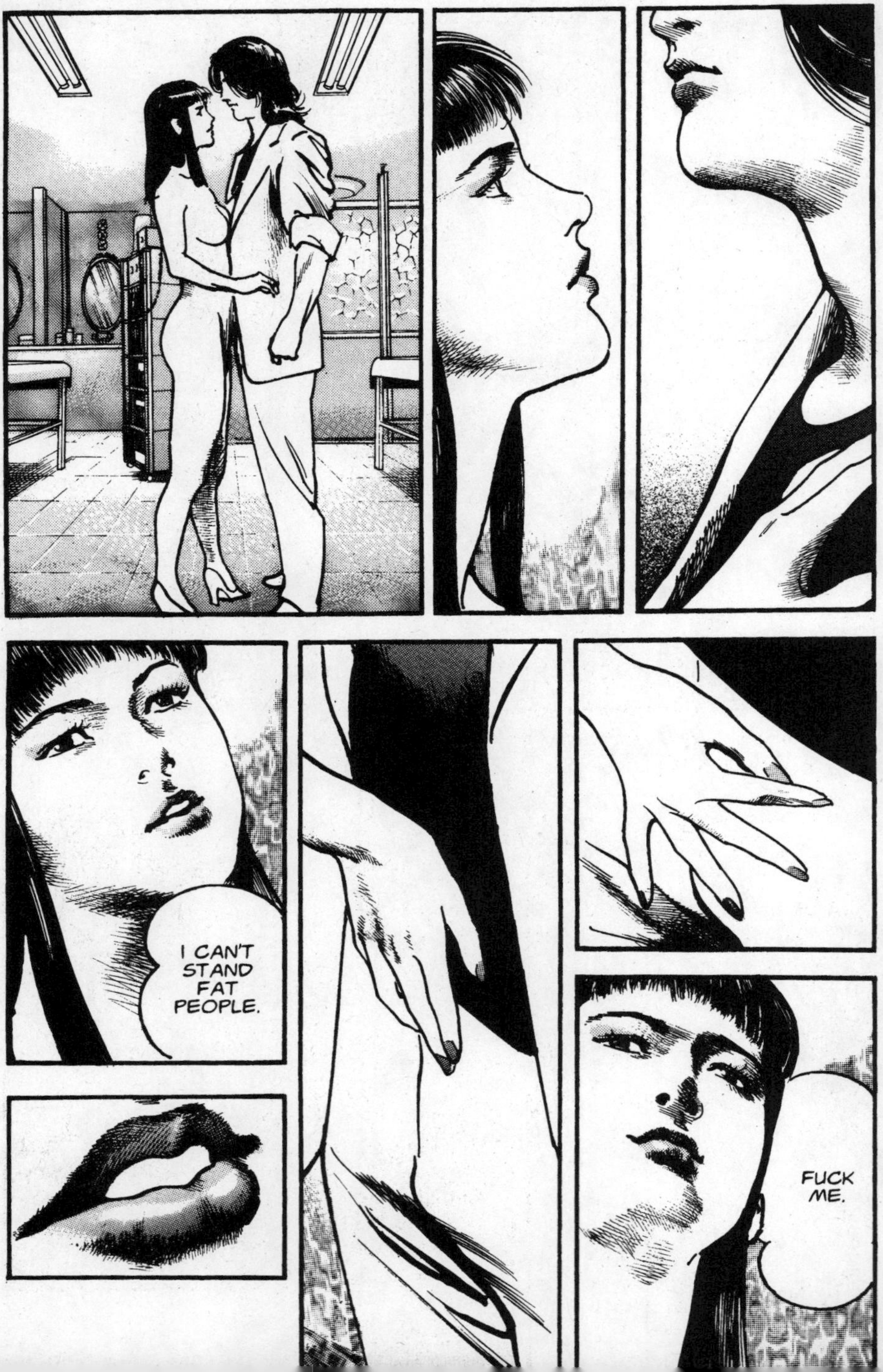
I CAN'T STAND FAT PEOPLE.
FUCK ME.

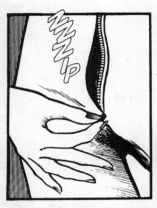

ONCE YOU HAVE MY BODY AT YOUR SIDE... EVERYTHING ELSE IN THE ORGANIZATION WILL BE YOURS.

TUGG

YOUR BODY? IT'S MEANING-LESS.

GET DRESSED!

IF IT'S A NEW BOSS YOU WANT, CHANGE THE WAY YOU LIVE.

THUMP

73

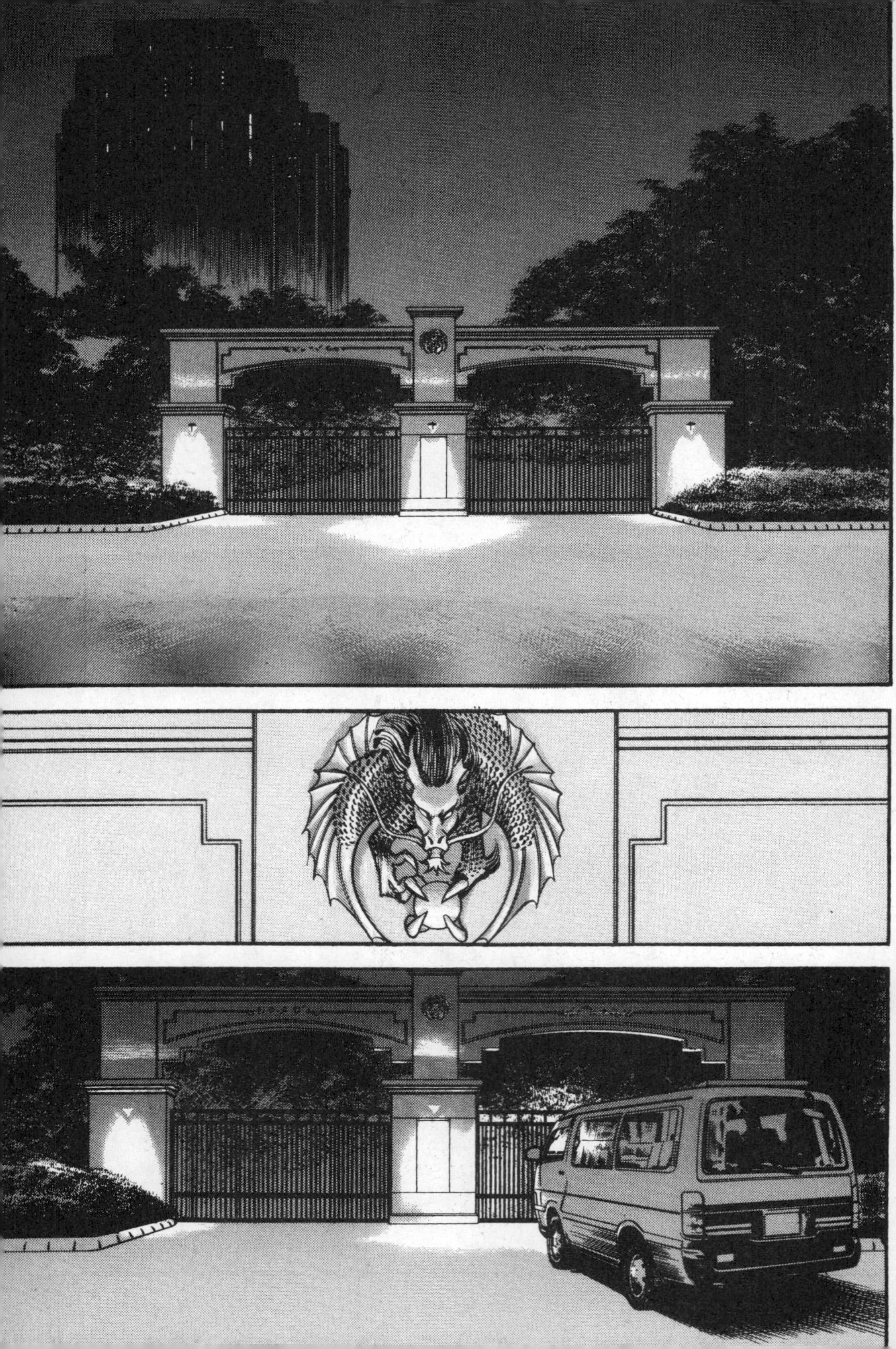

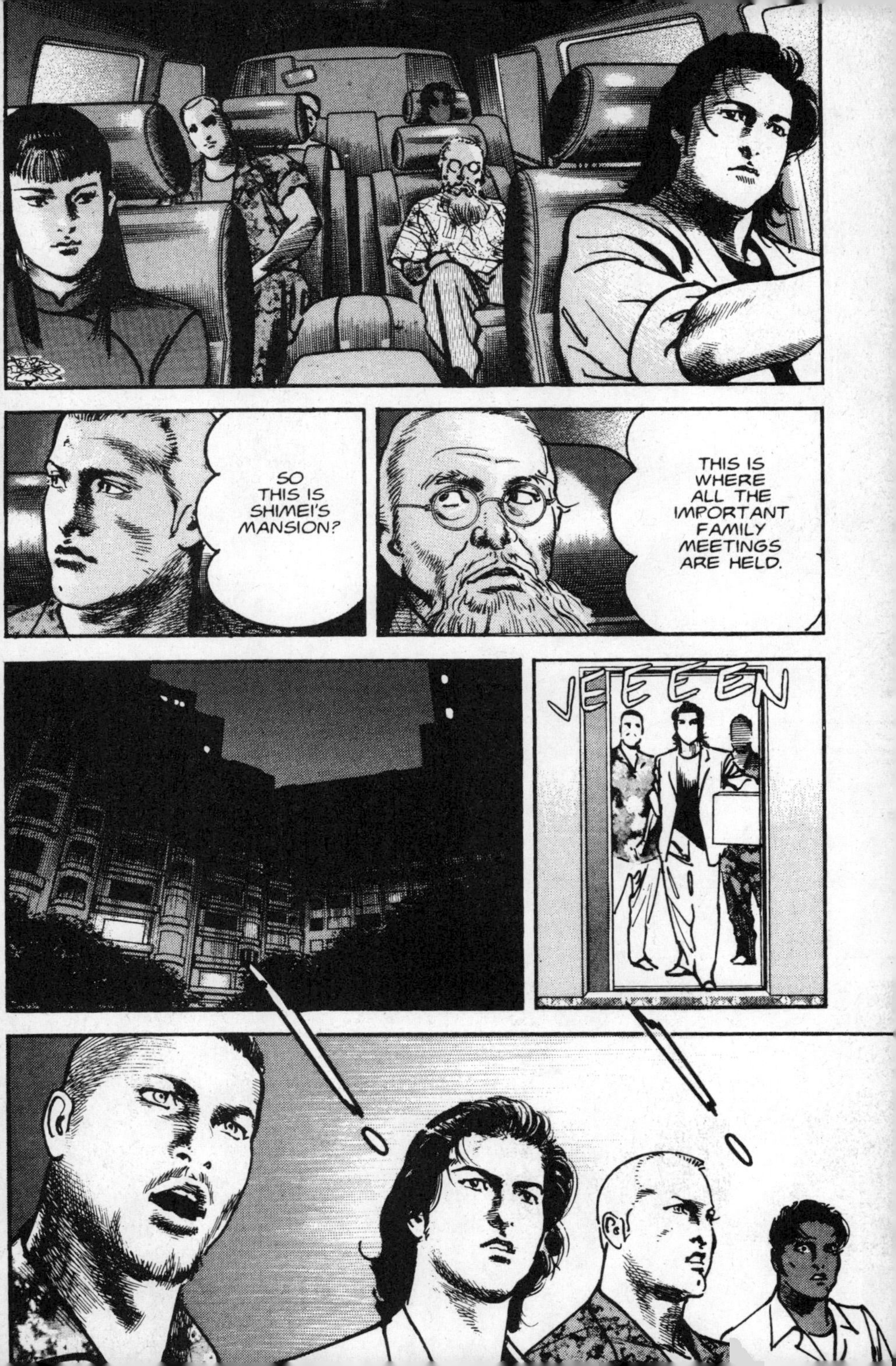
SO THIS IS SHIMEI'S MANSION?
THIS IS WHERE ALL THE IMPORTANT FAMILY MEETINGS ARE HELD.
VEEEEN

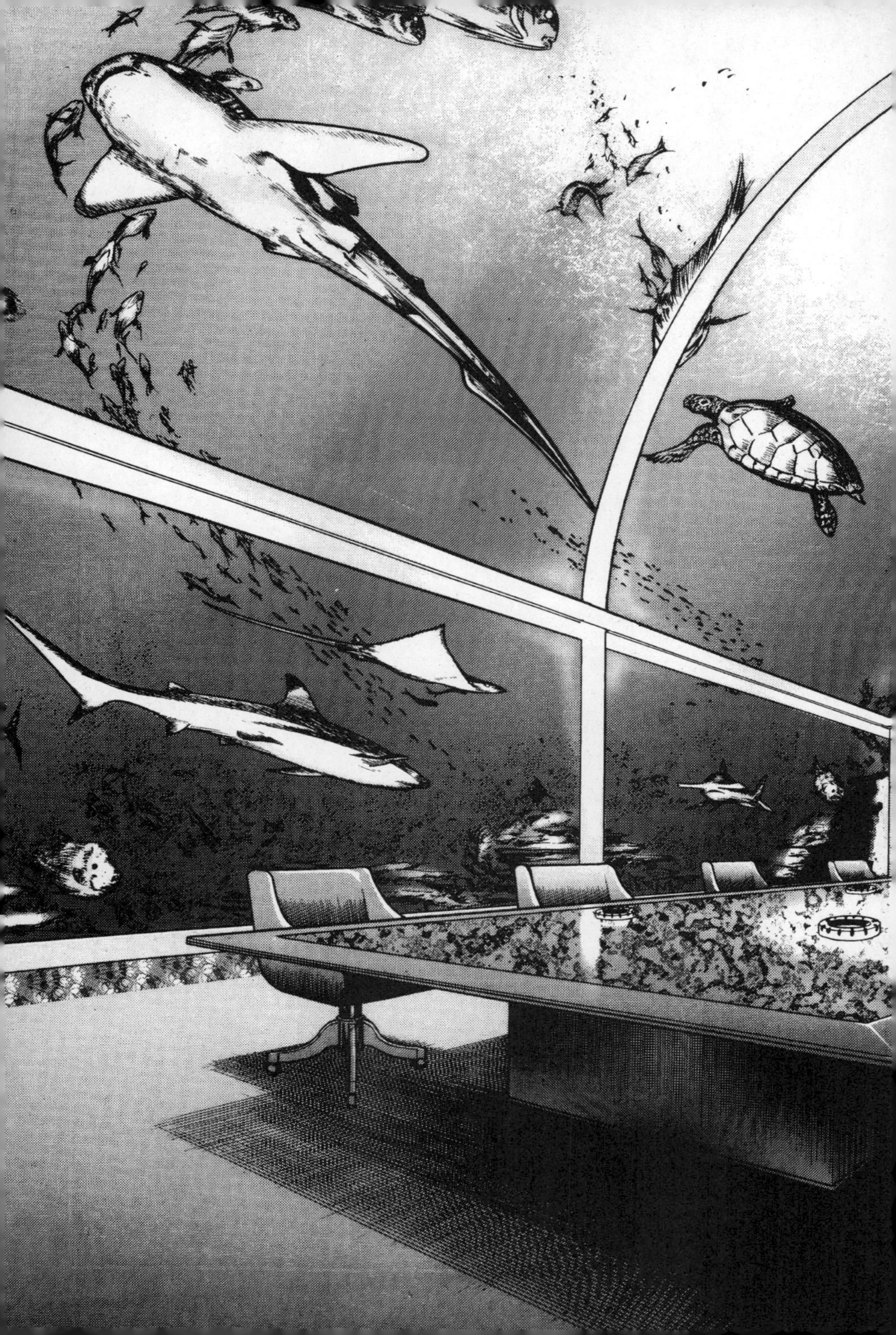

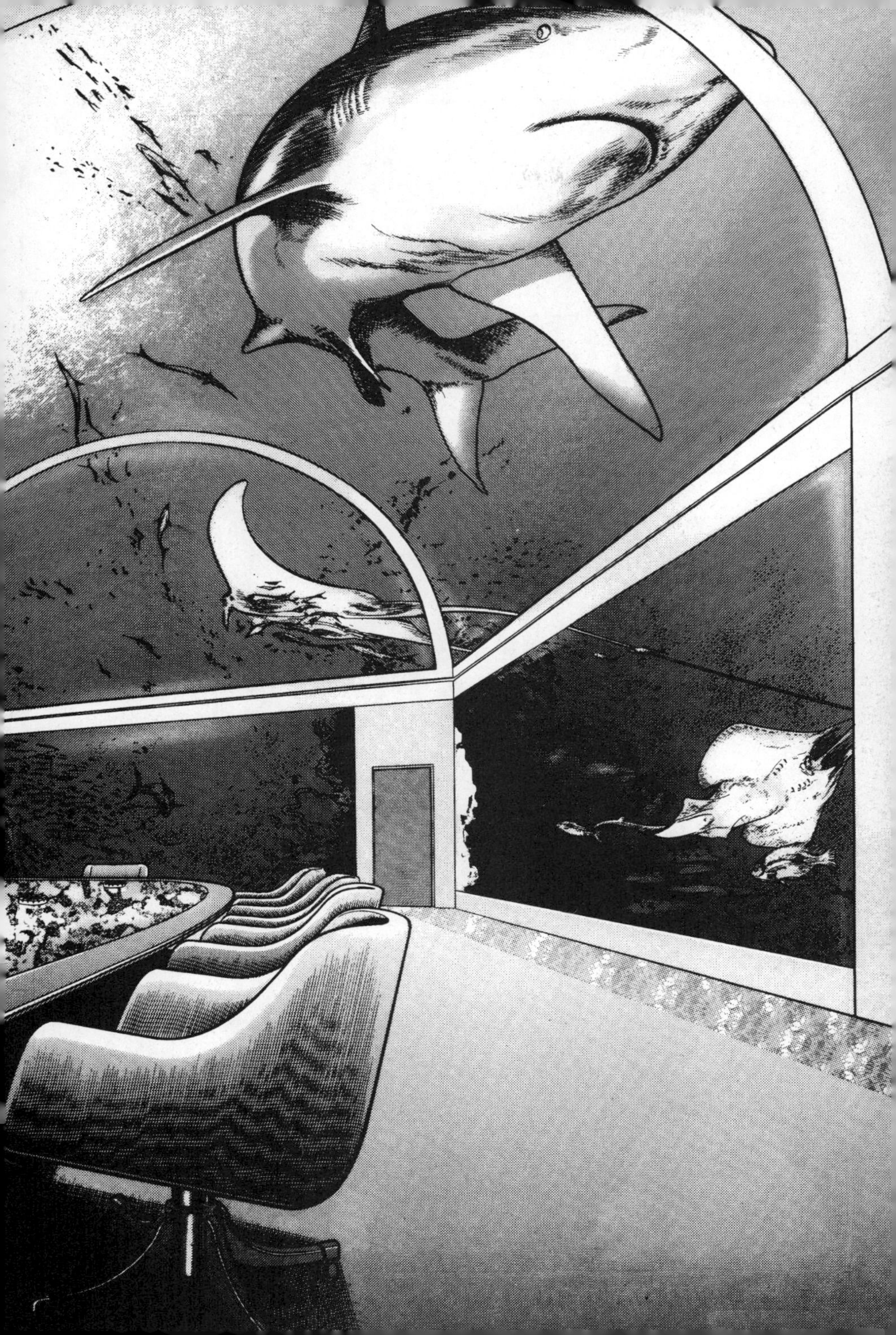

WH-WHAT THE—

AQUARIA ARE A HOBBY OF HIS.

THIS IS WHERE THE "EIGHT DRAGONS"... IN OTHER WORDS, THE EIGHT LEADERS OF THE ORGANIZATION, MEET WITH SHIMEI.

ALL THE KEY DECISIONS ARE MADE HERE.

THE EIGHT DRAGONS WILL BE HERE SOON.

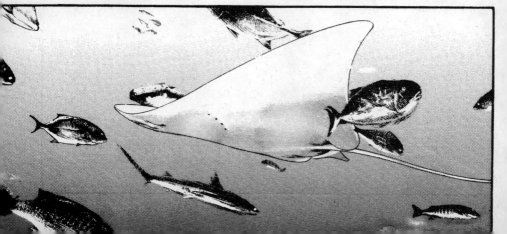

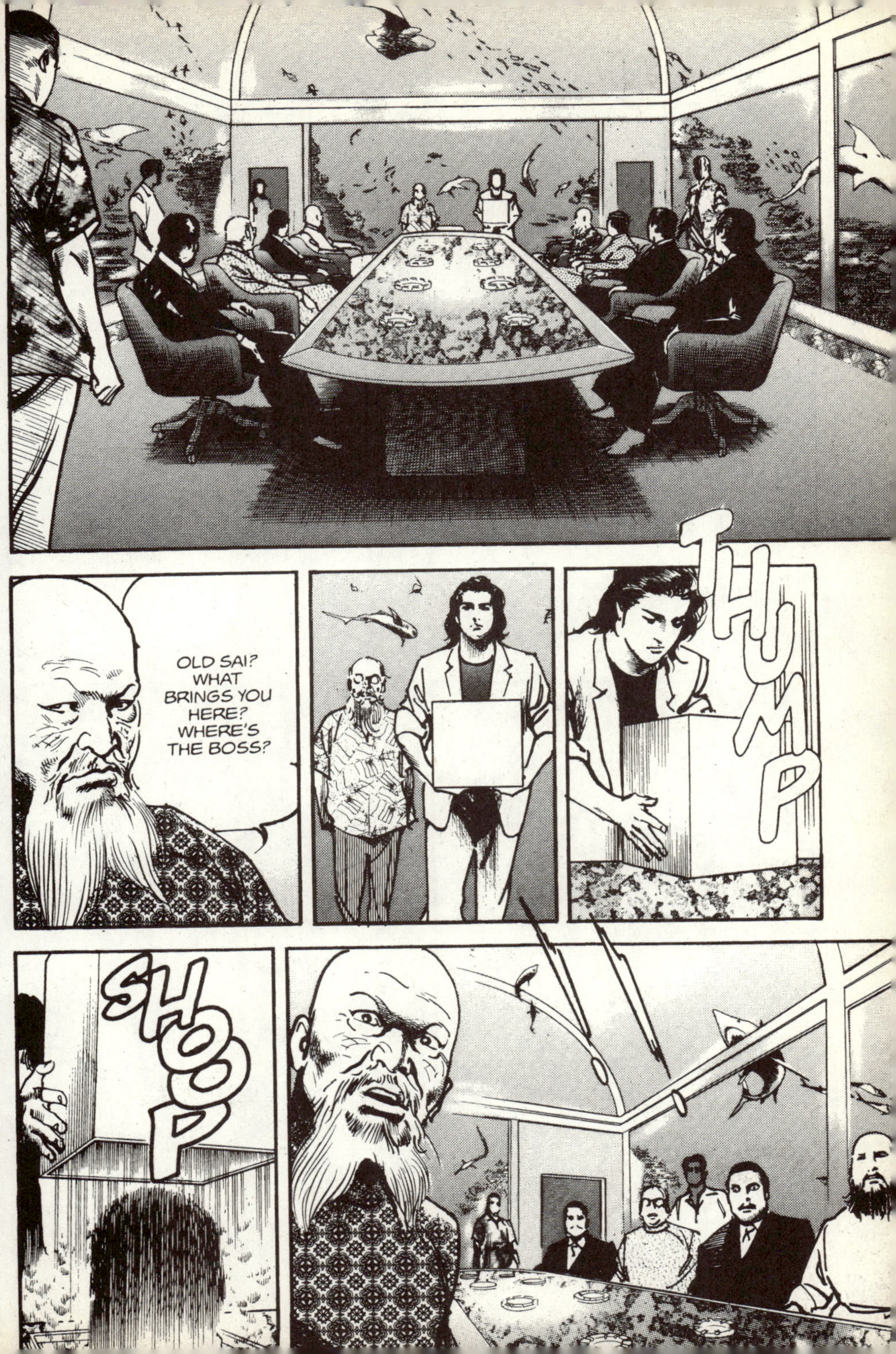
OLD SAI? WHAT BRINGS YOU HERE? WHERE'S THE BOSS?
THUMP
SHOOP

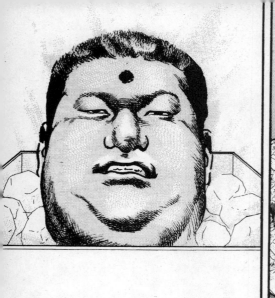

AS YOU CAN SEE, THE HEAD OF OUR FAMILY, SHIMEI SAI, HAS DIED.

I'M HERE TO ANNOUNCE THAT I AM THE NEW FAMILY HEAD.

HUH !?

hee hee

hee

YOU SENILE, OLD MAN? MAKING BAD JOKES LIKE—

PHUNT

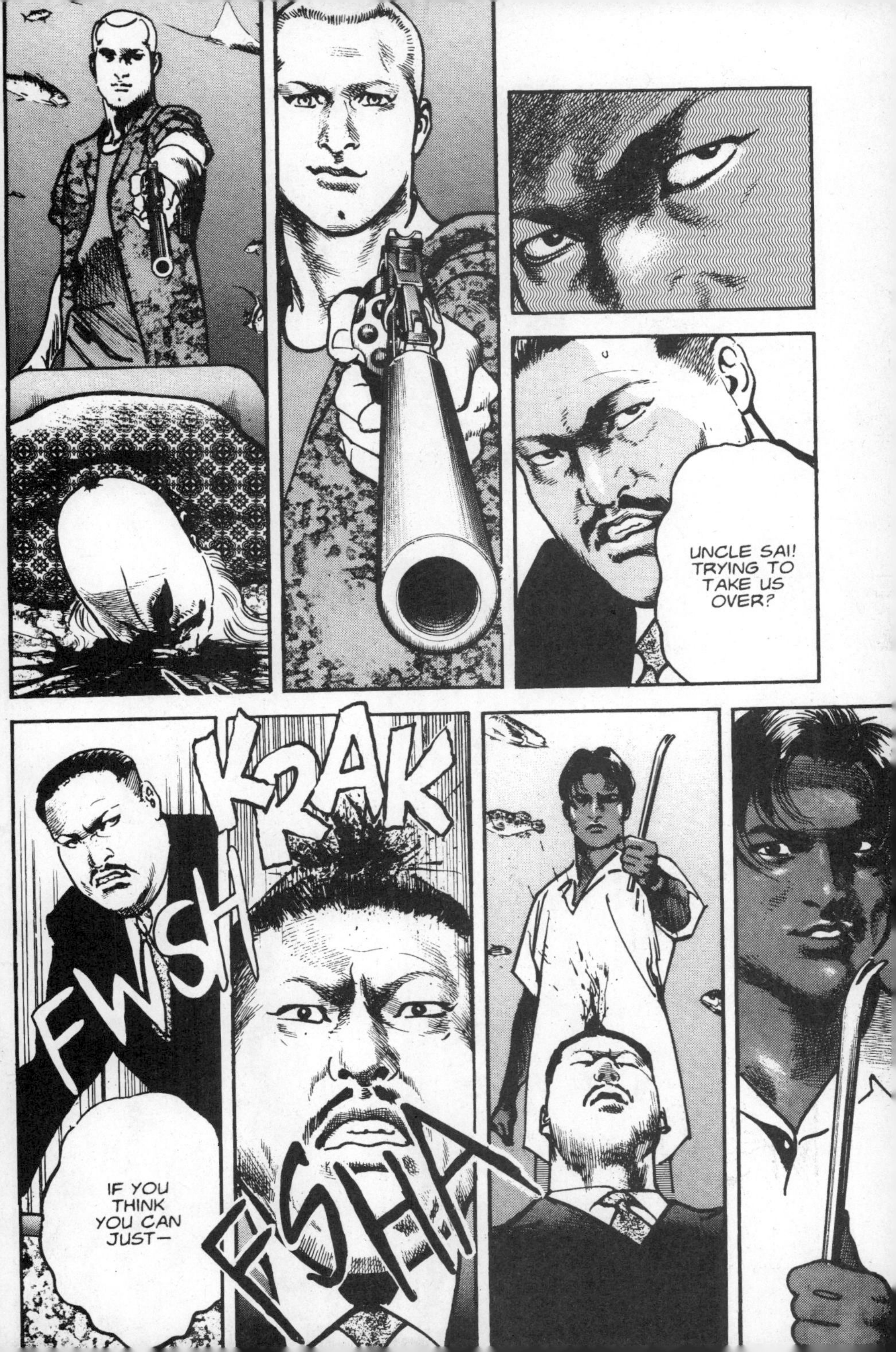
UNCLE SAI! TRYING TO TAKE US OVER?
IF YOU THINK YOU CAN JUST—
FWSH
K2AK
FSHA

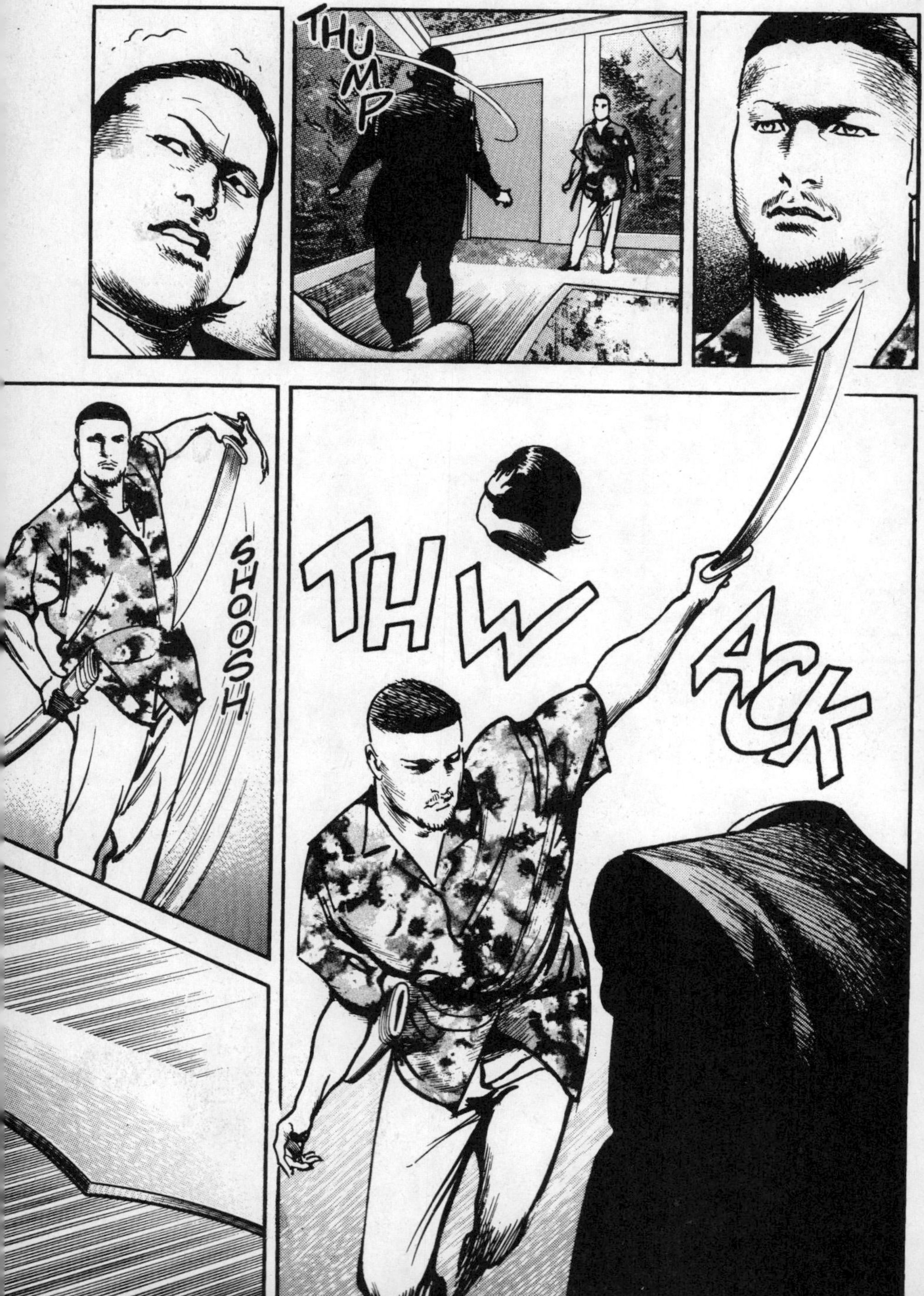
THUMP
SHOOOSH
THWACK

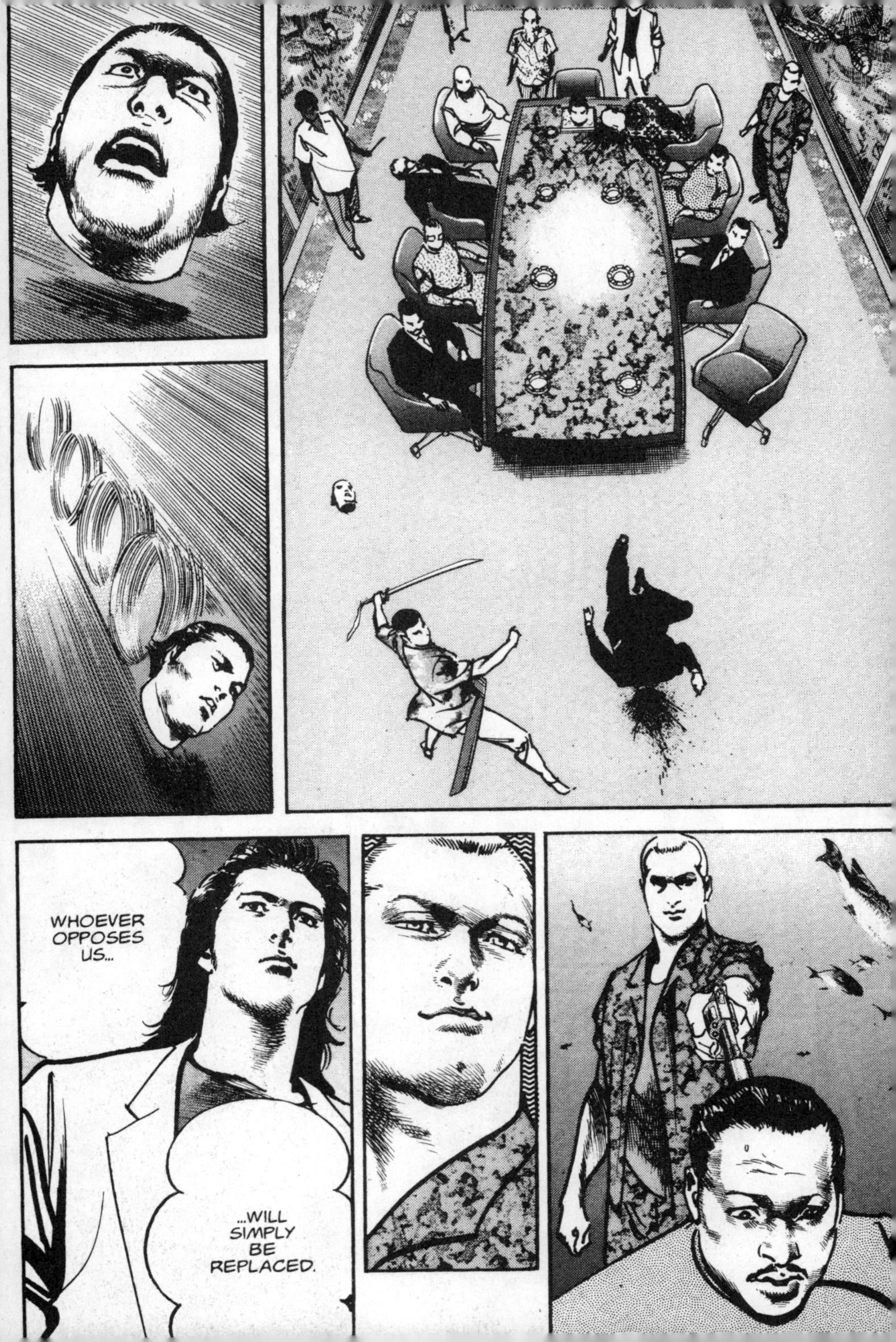
WHOEVER OPPOSES US...
...WILL SIMPLY BE REPLACED.

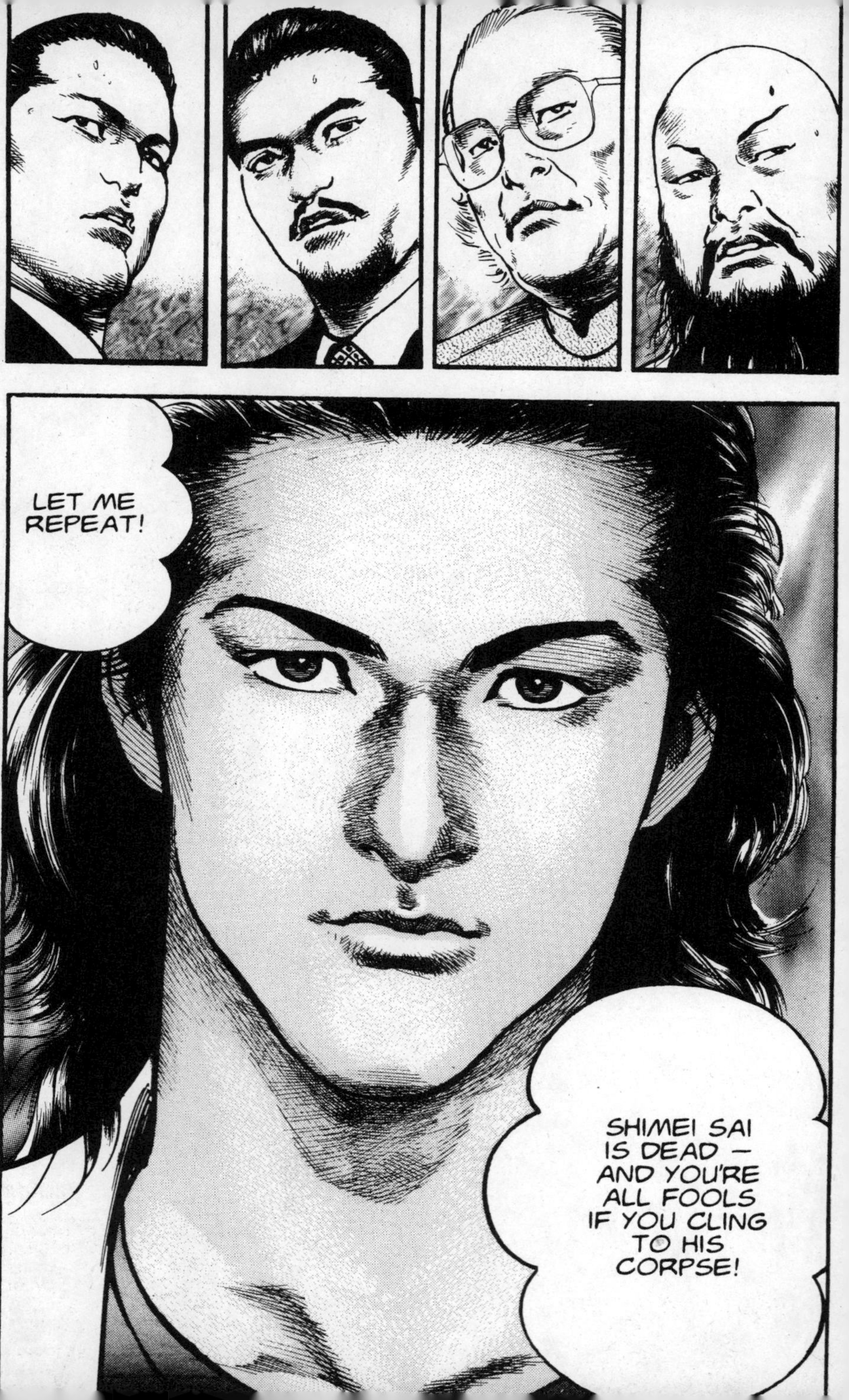
LET ME REPEAT!
SHIMEI SAI IS DEAD — AND YOU'RE ALL FOOLS IF YOU CLING TO HIS CORPSE!

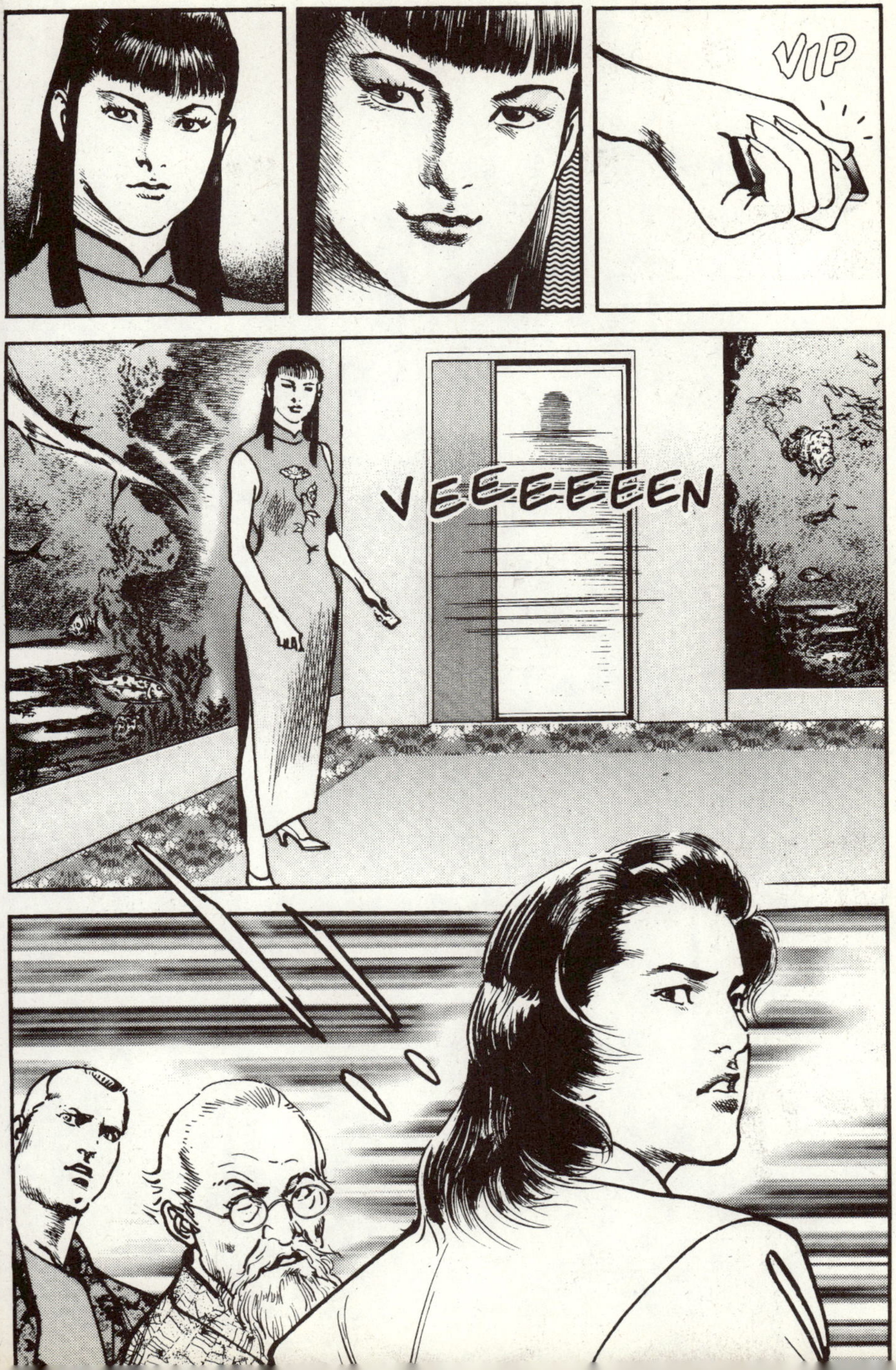
VIP
VEEEEEEN

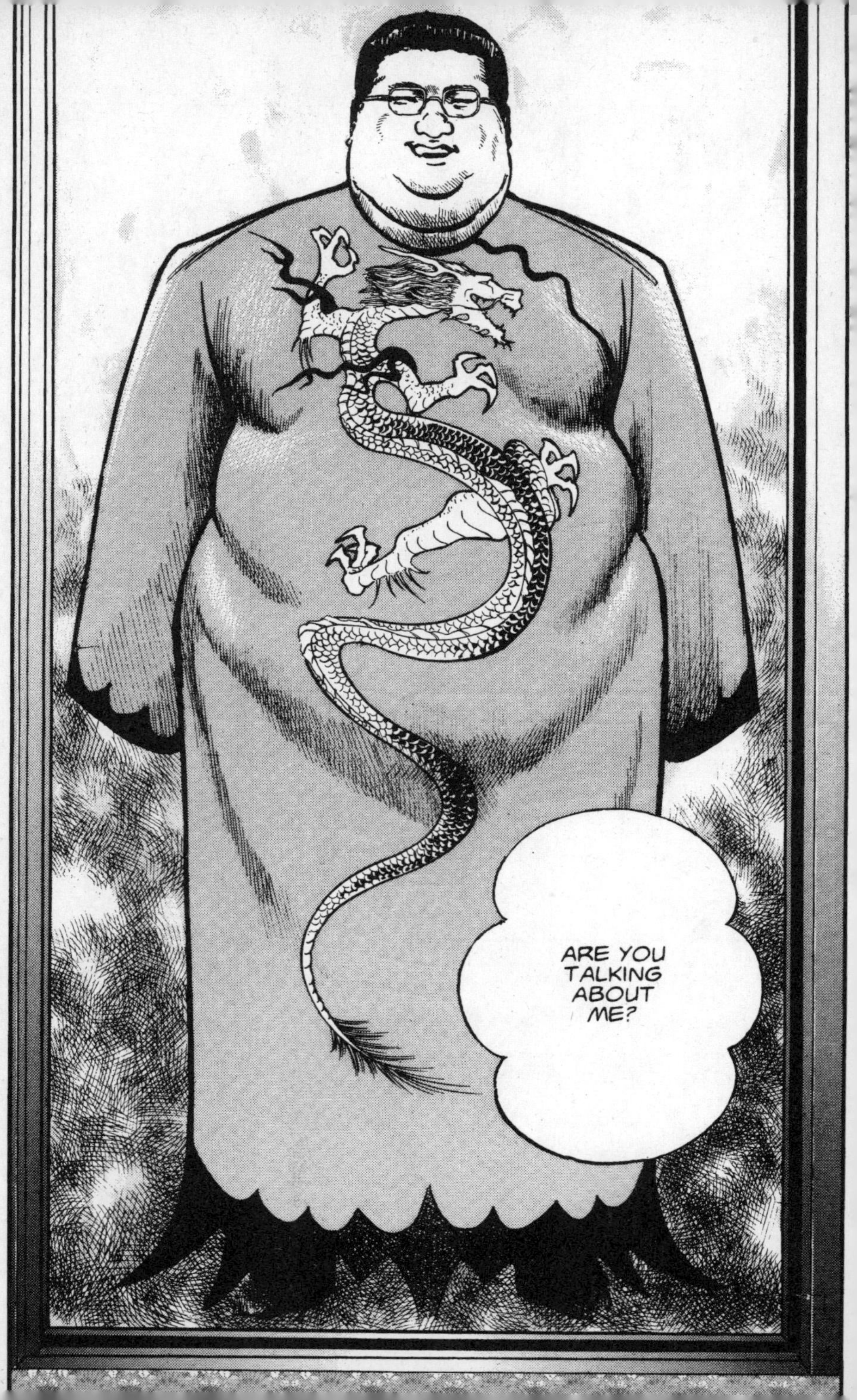
ARE YOU TALKING ABOUT ME?

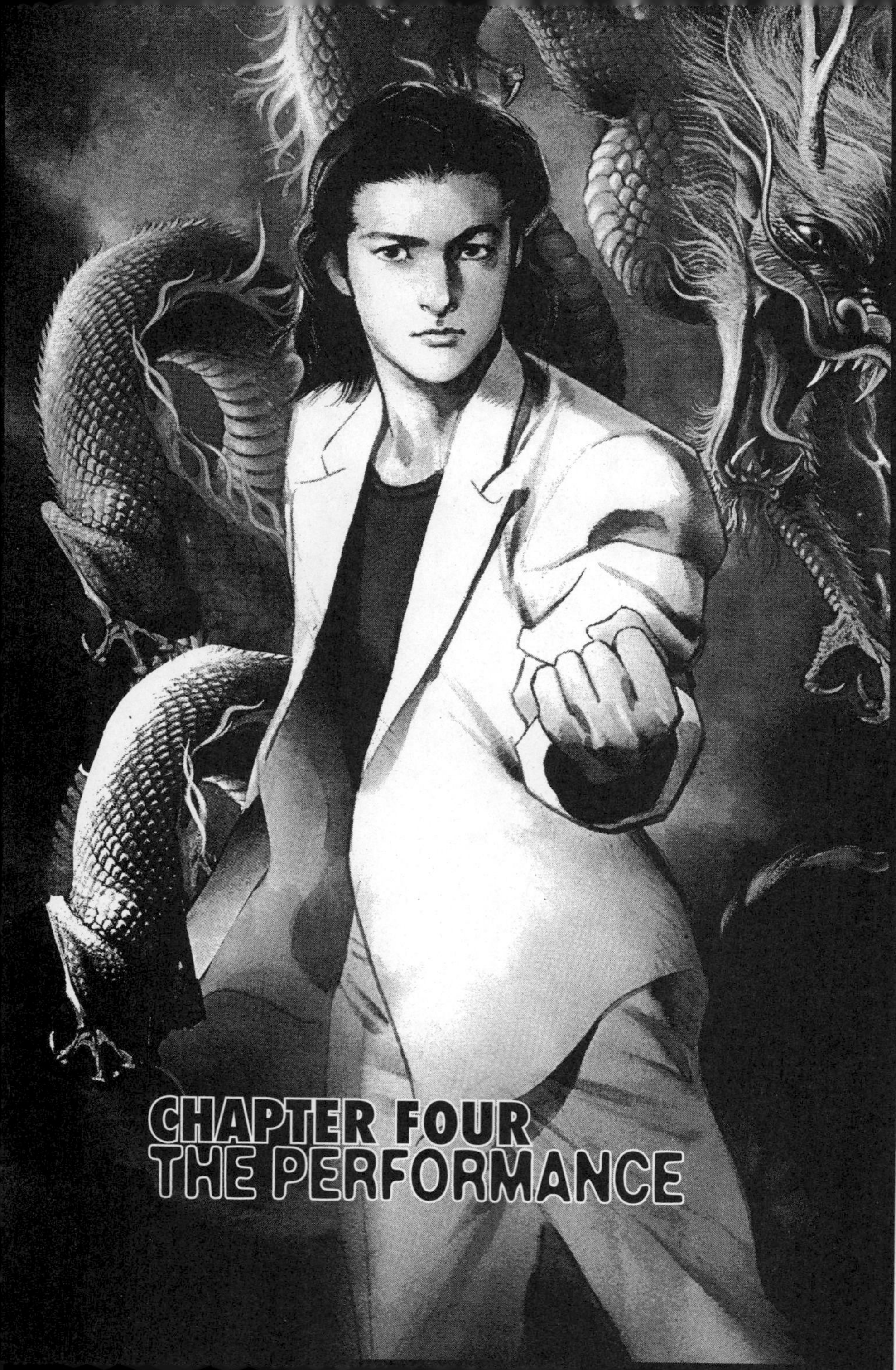
CHAPTER FOUR
THE PERFORMANCE

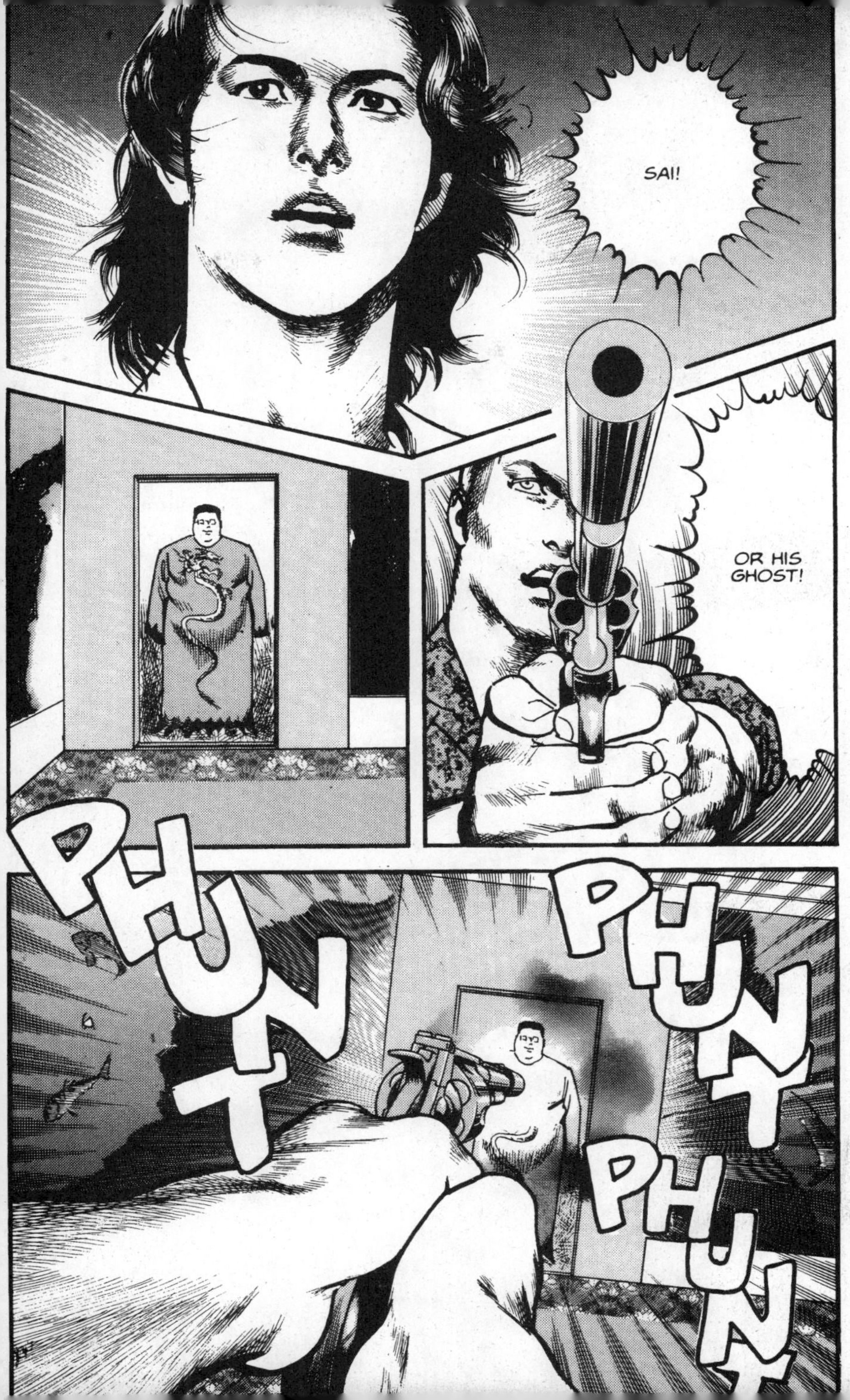
SAI!
OR HIS GHOST!
PHUNT
PHUNT
PHUNT

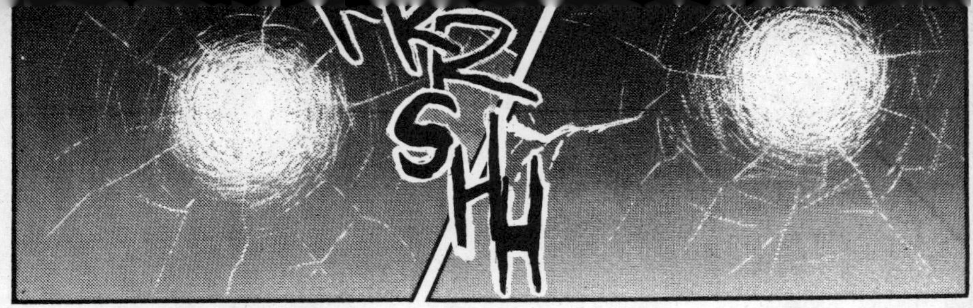
KRSHH

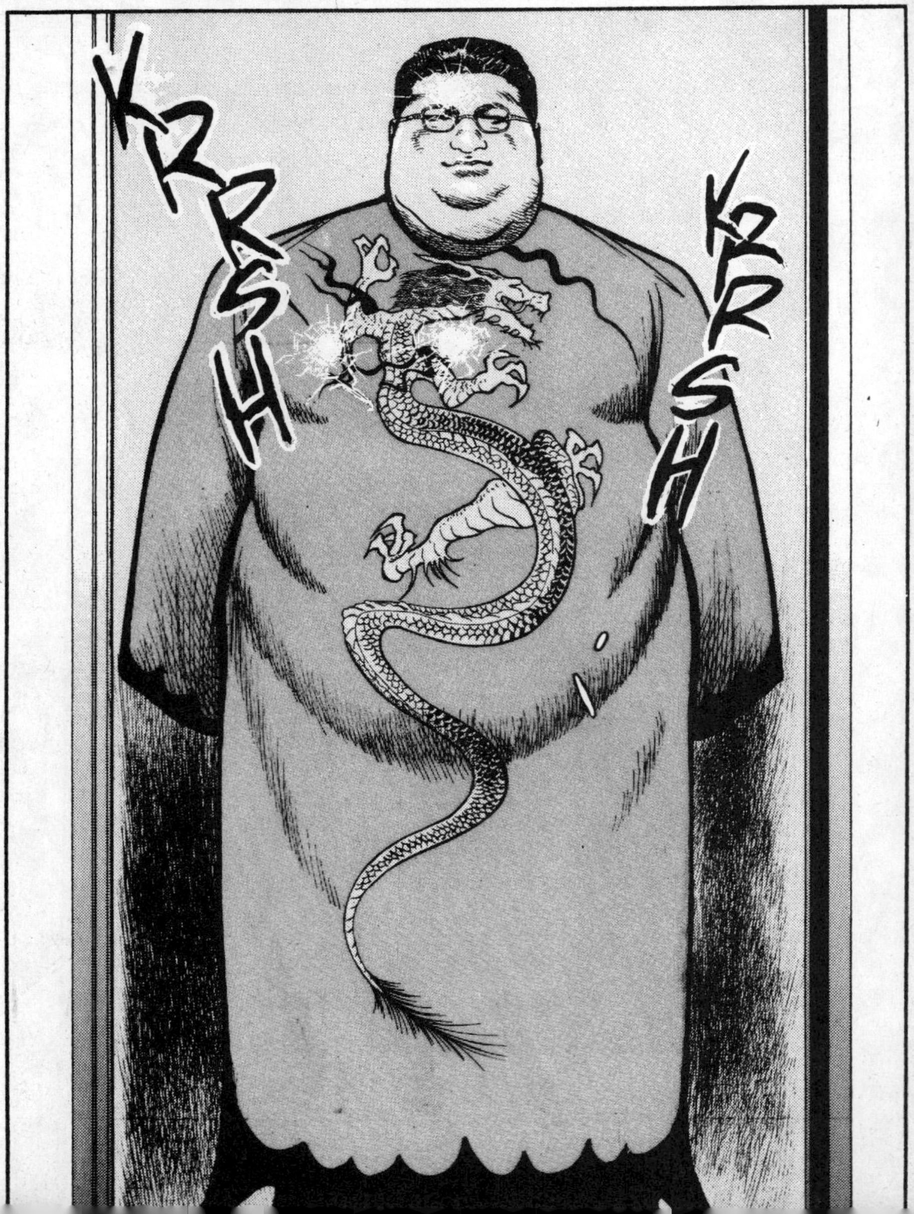
KRRSH
KRRSH

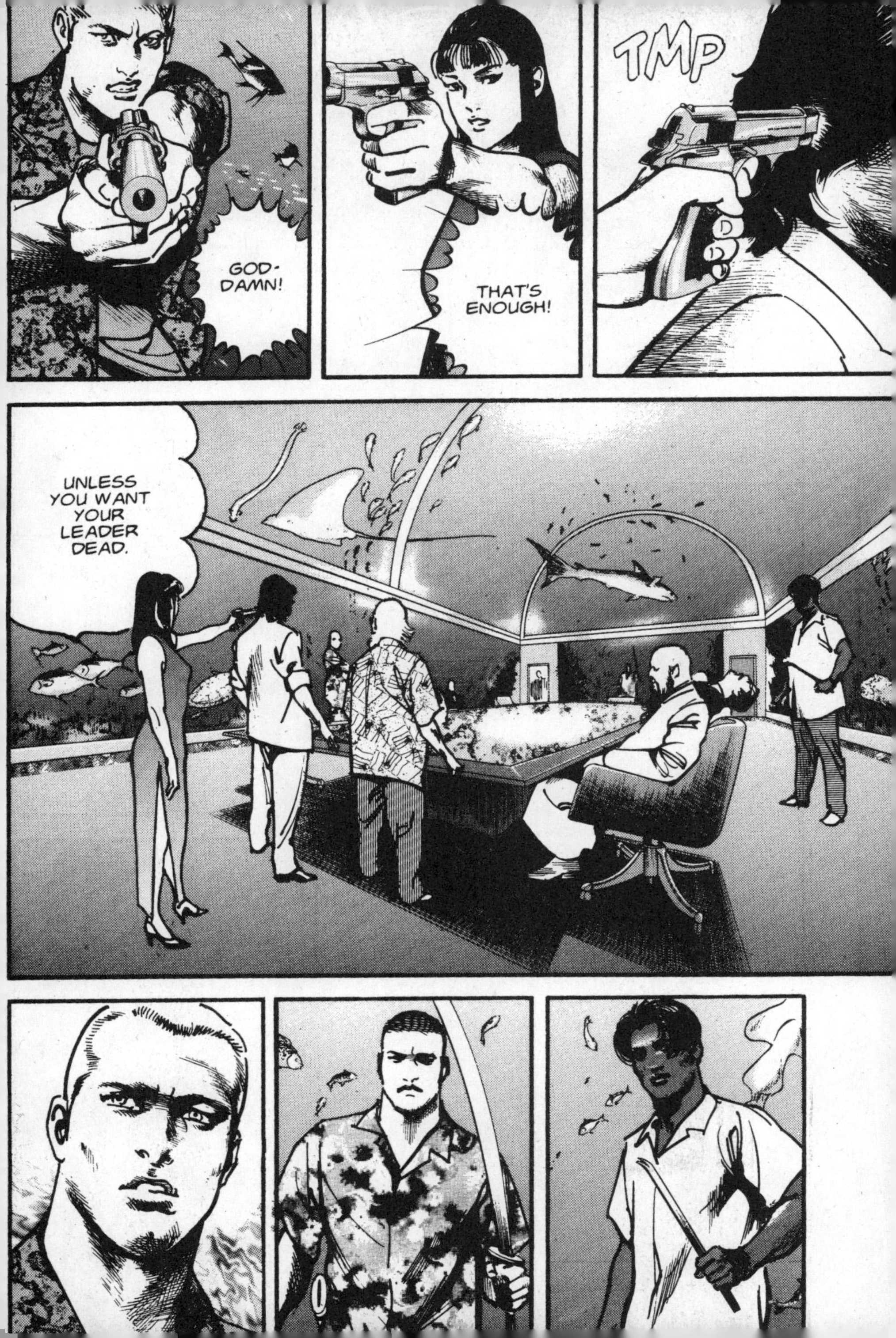
GOD-DAMN!
THAT'S ENOUGH!
TMP
UNLESS YOU WANT YOUR LEADER DEAD.

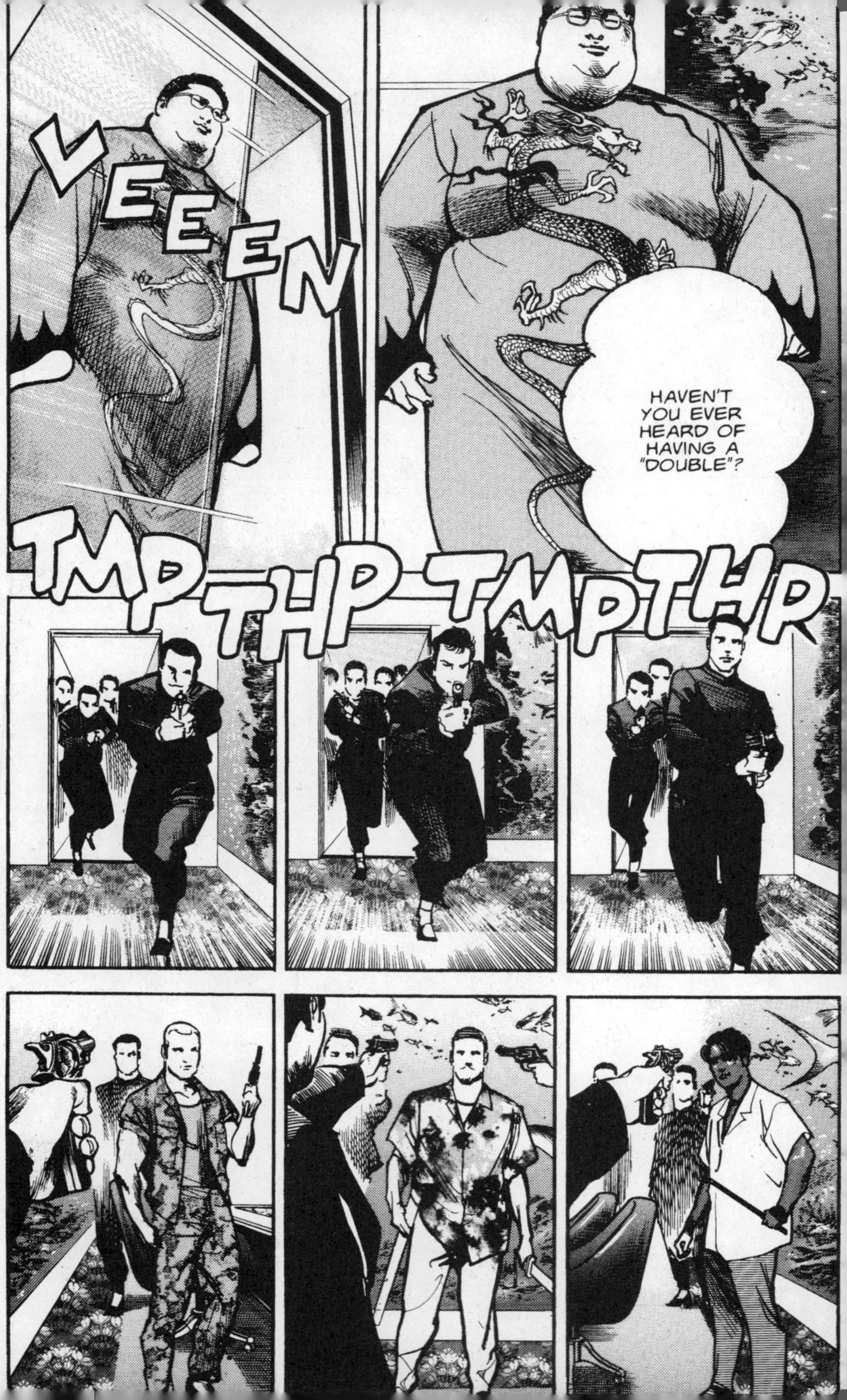
VEEEEN
HAVEN'T YOU EVER HEARD OF HAVING A "DOUBLE"?
TMP THP TMPTHP

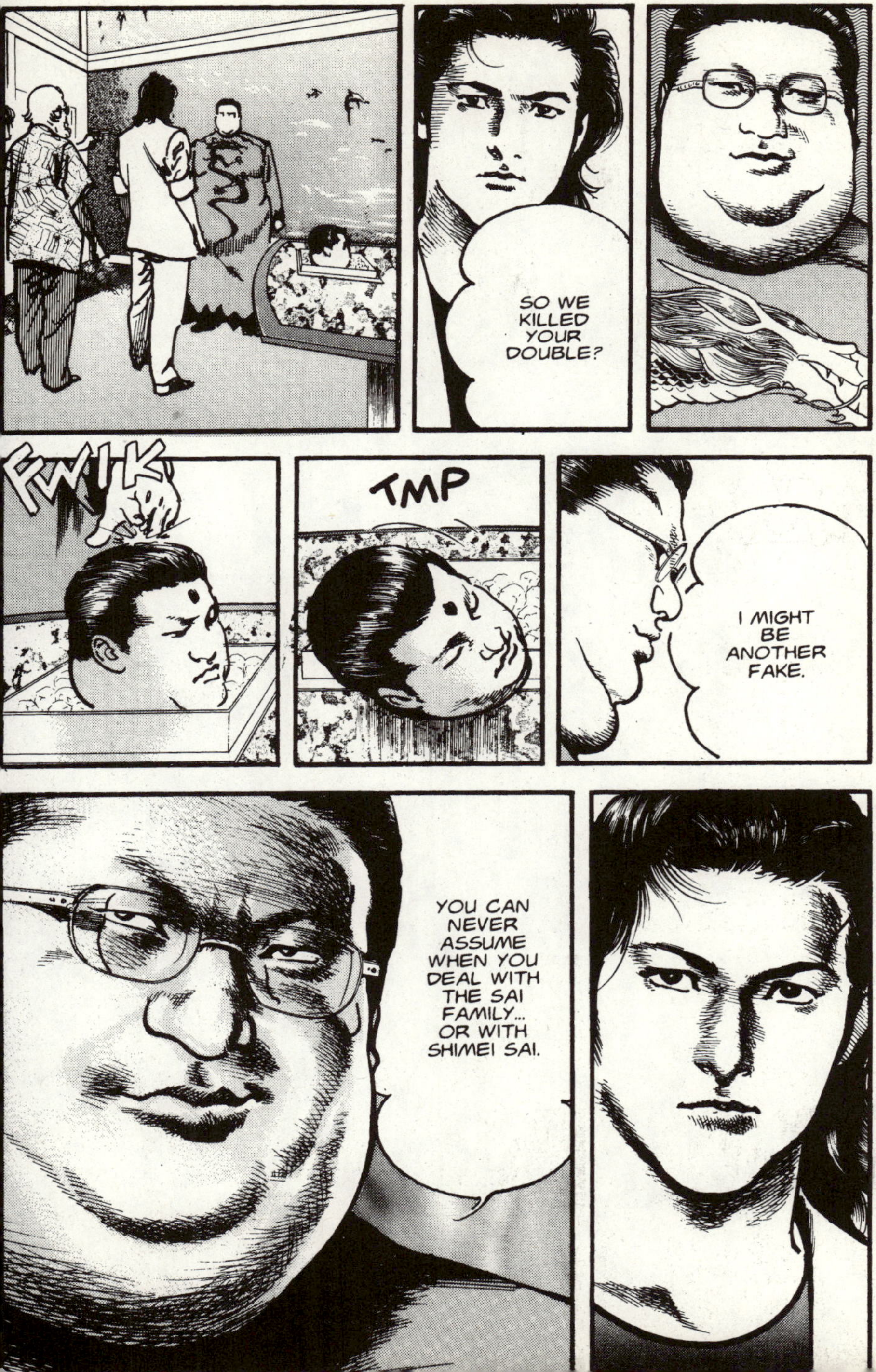
SO WE KILLED YOUR DOUBLE?
FWIK
TMP
I MIGHT BE ANOTHER FAKE.
YOU CAN NEVER ASSUME WHEN YOU DEAL WITH THE SAI FAMILY... OR WITH SHIMEI SAI.

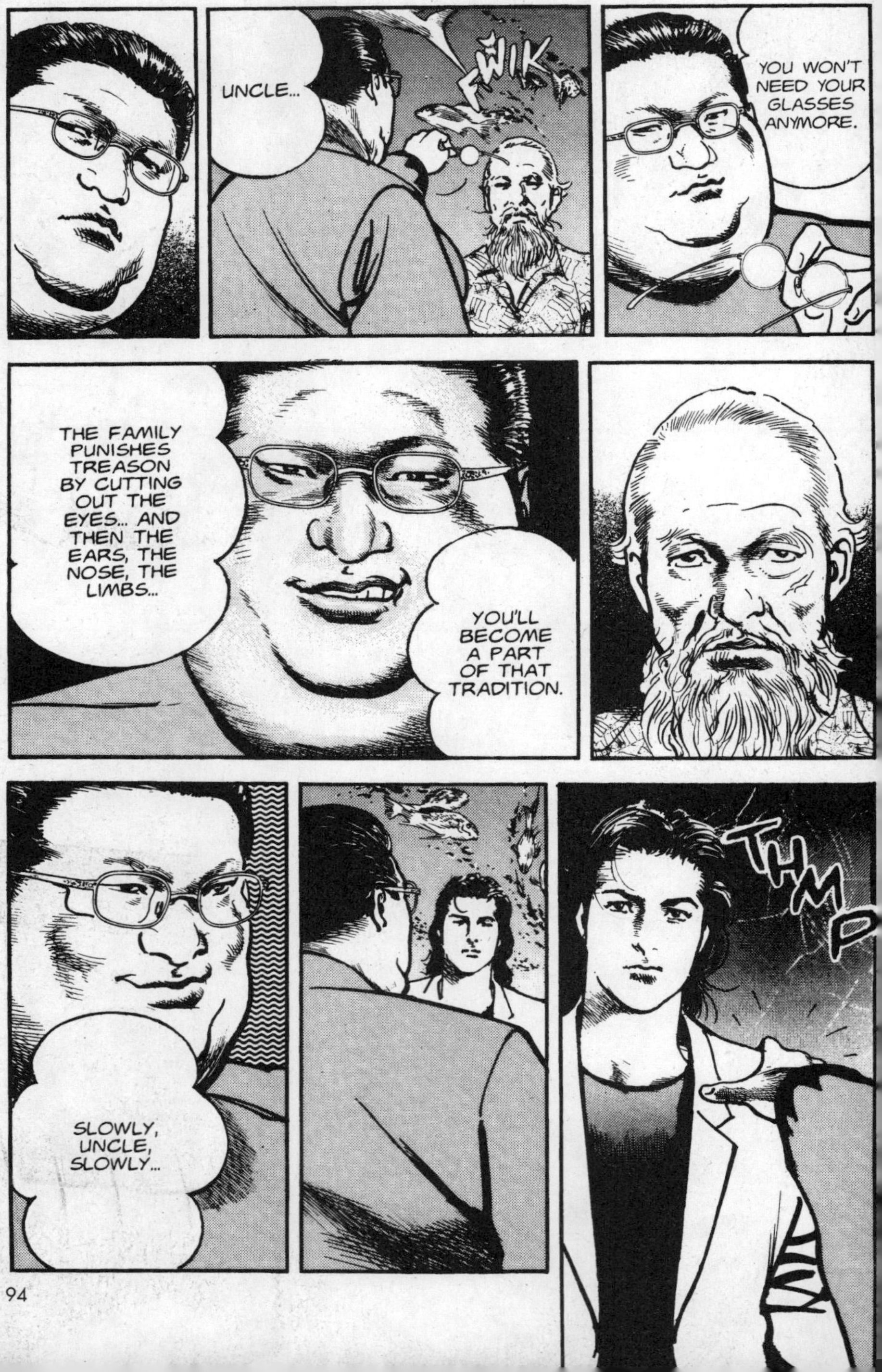
UNCLE...
FWIK
YOU WON'T NEED YOUR GLASSES ANYMORE.
THE FAMILY PUNISHES TREASON BY CUTTING OUT THE EYES... AND THEN THE EARS, THE NOSE, THE LIMBS...
YOU'LL BECOME A PART OF THAT TRADITION.
SLOWLY, UNCLE, SLOWLY...
THMP

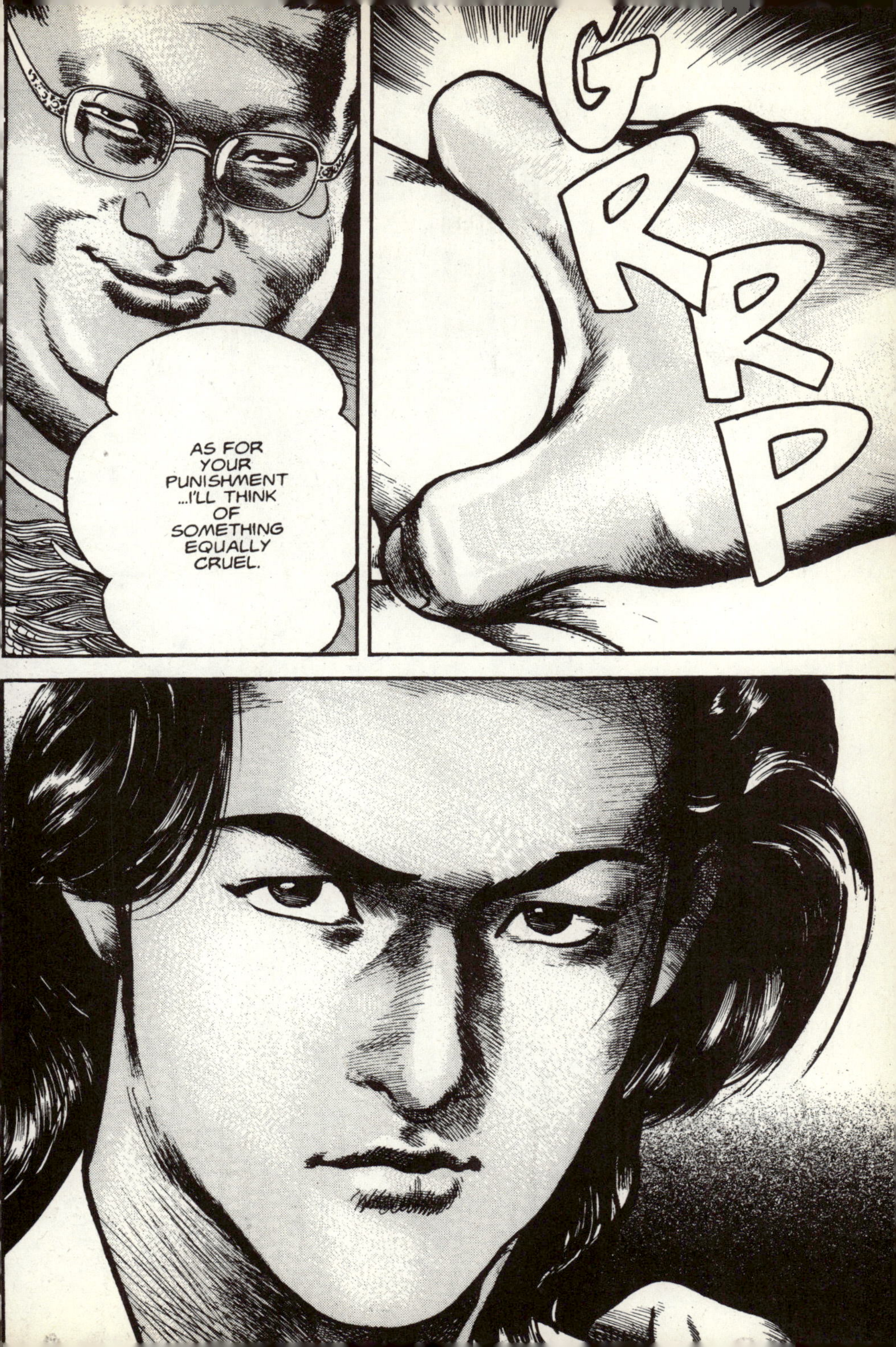
AS FOR YOUR PUNISHMENT ...I'LL THINK OF SOMETHING EQUALLY CRUEL.
GRRP

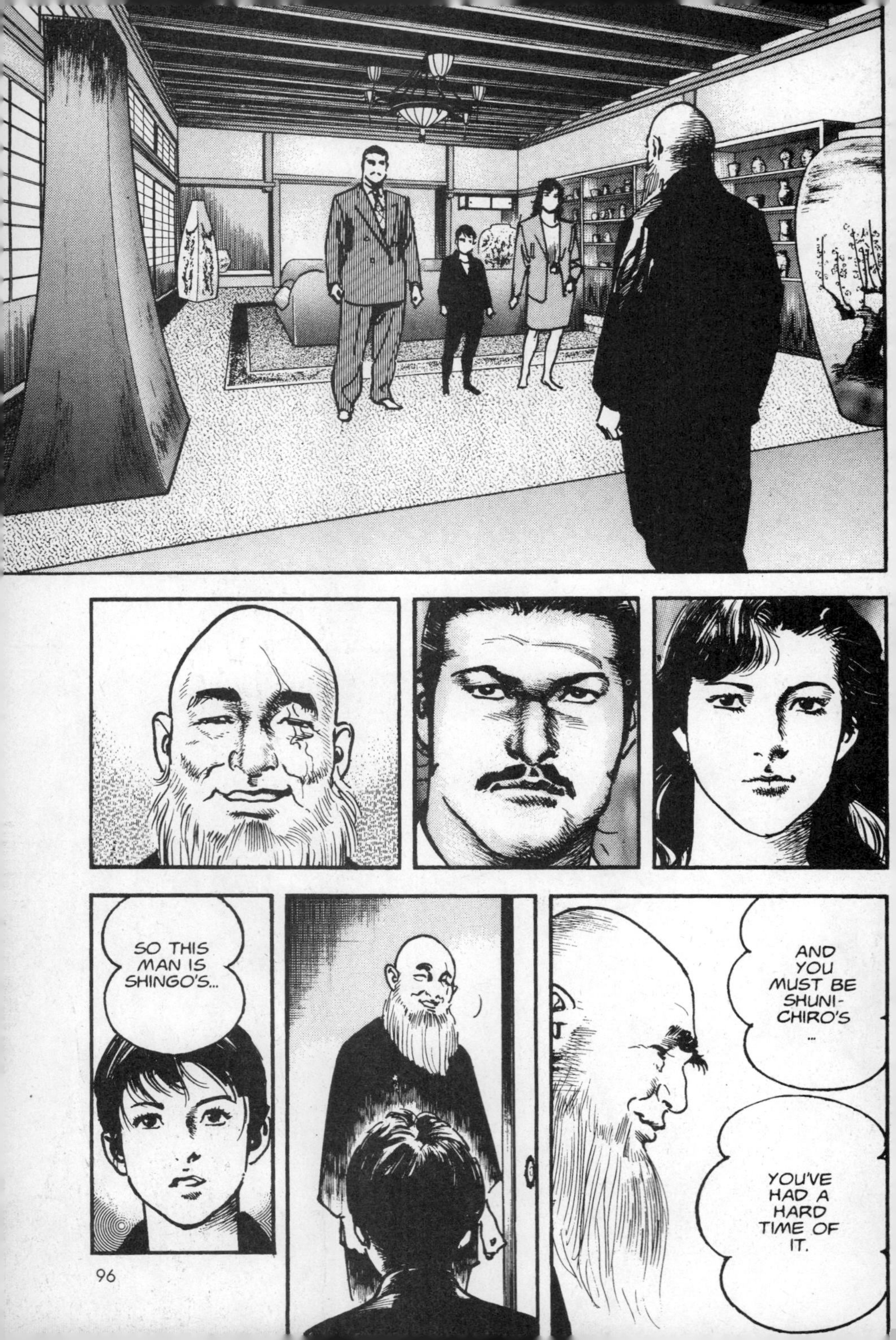
SO THIS MAN IS SHINGO'S...
AND YOU MUST BE SHUNI-CHIRO'S ...
YOU'VE HAD A HARD TIME OF IT.

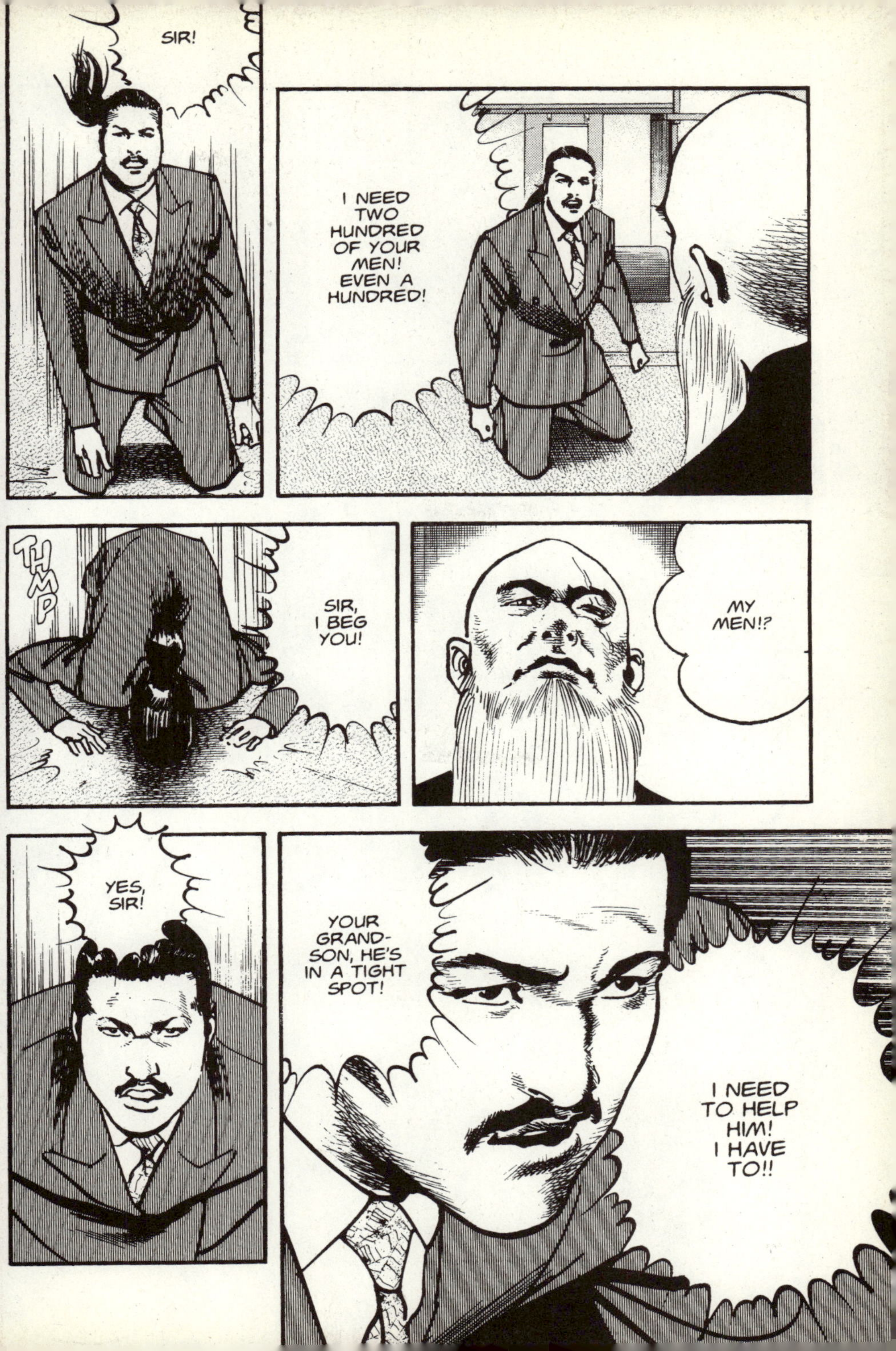
SIR!
I NEED TWO HUNDRED OF YOUR MEN! EVEN A HUNDRED!
THMP
SIR, I BEG YOU!
MY MEN!?
YES, SIR!
YOUR GRAND-SON, HE'S IN A TIGHT SPOT!
I NEED TO HELP HIM! I HAVE TO!!

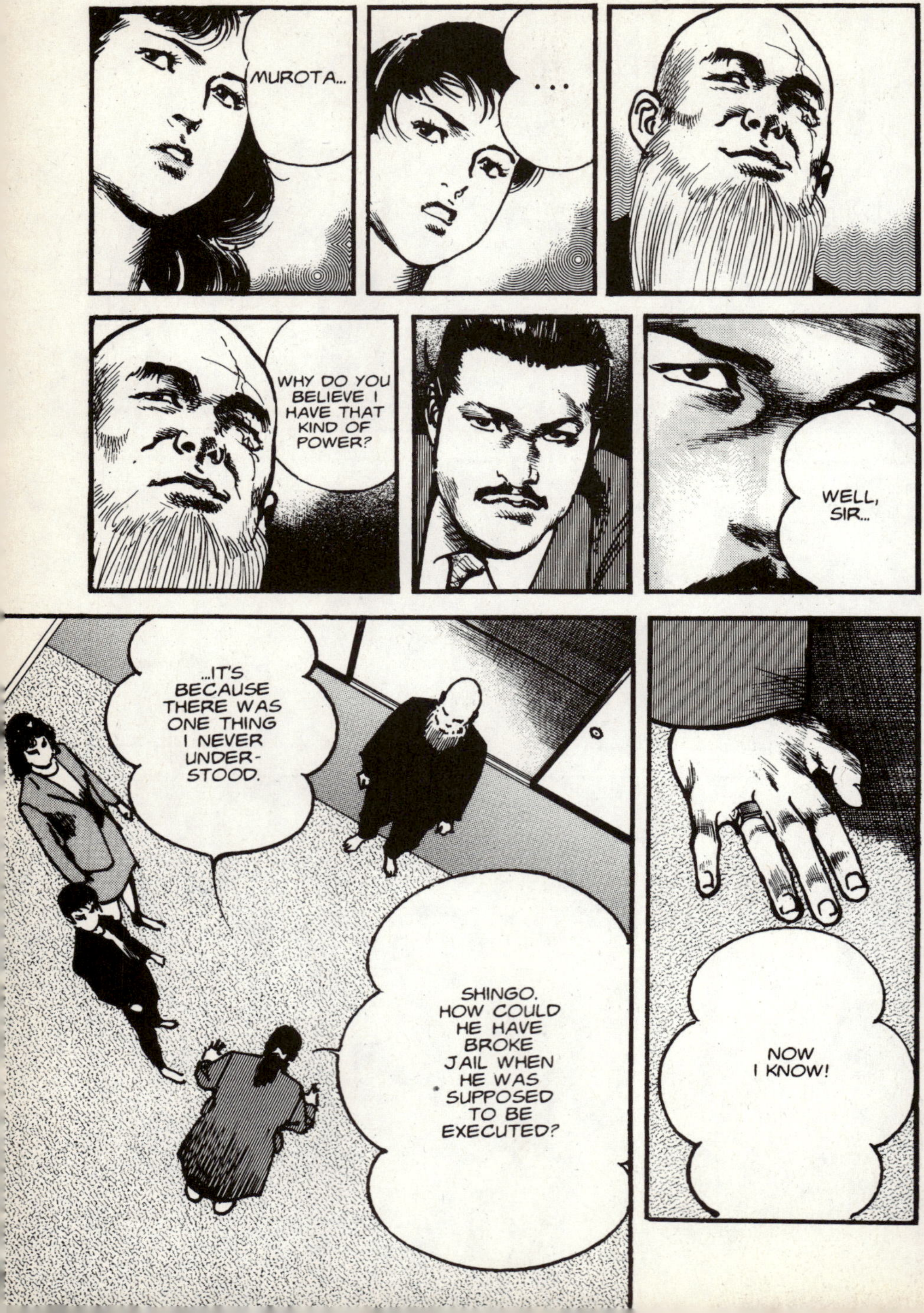

MUROTA...
...
WHY DO YOU BELIEVE I HAVE THAT KIND OF POWER?
WELL, SIR...
...IT'S BECAUSE THERE WAS ONE THING I NEVER UNDER-STOOD.
SHINGO. HOW COULD HE HAVE BROKE JAIL WHEN HE WAS SUPPOSED TO BE EXECUTED?
NOW I KNOW!

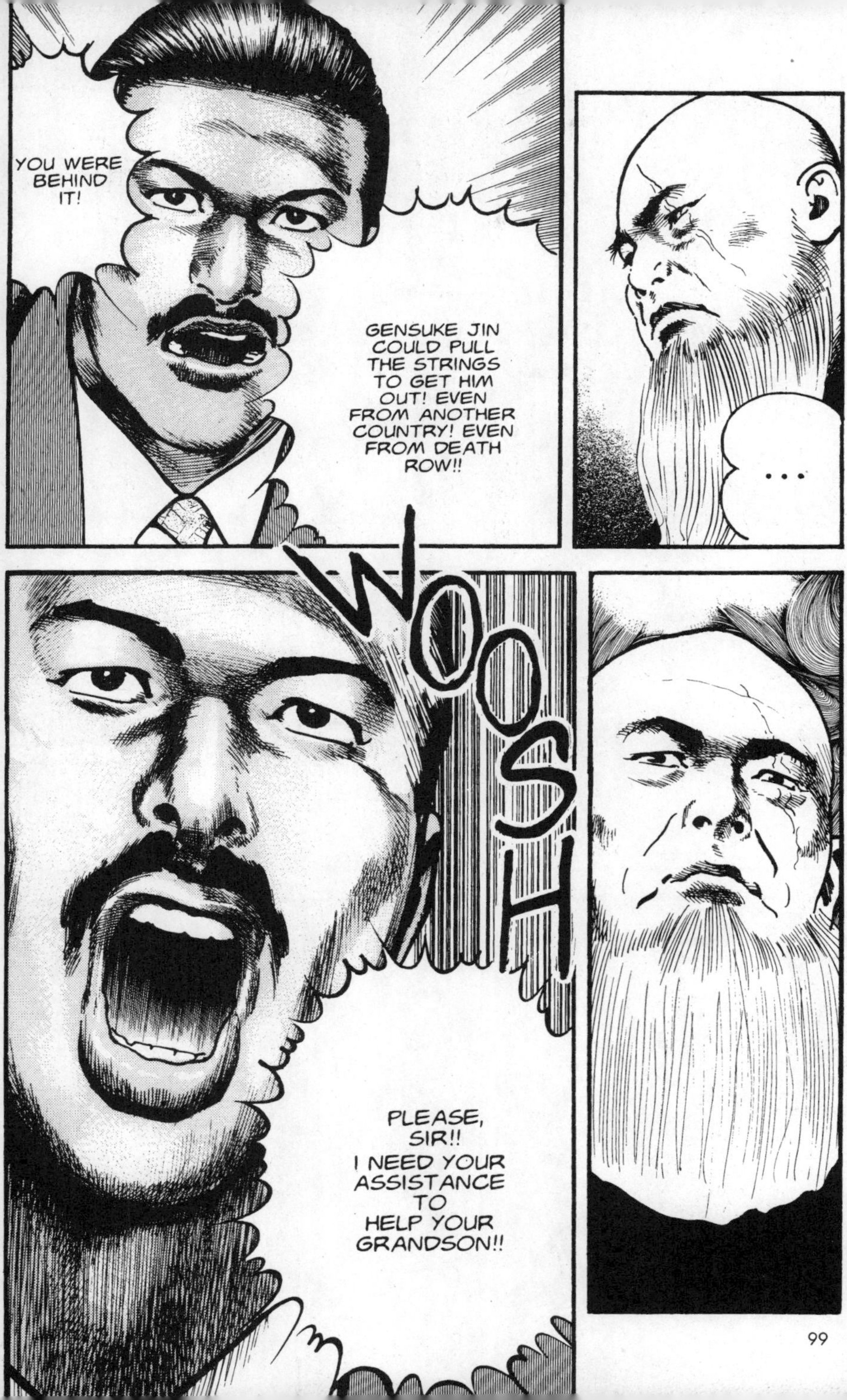

YOU WERE BEHIND IT!
GENSUKE JIN COULD PULL THE STRINGS TO GET HIM OUT! EVEN FROM ANOTHER COUNTRY! EVEN FROM DEATH ROW!!
...
WOOSH
PLEASE, SIR!! I NEED YOUR ASSISTANCE TO HELP YOUR GRANDSON!!

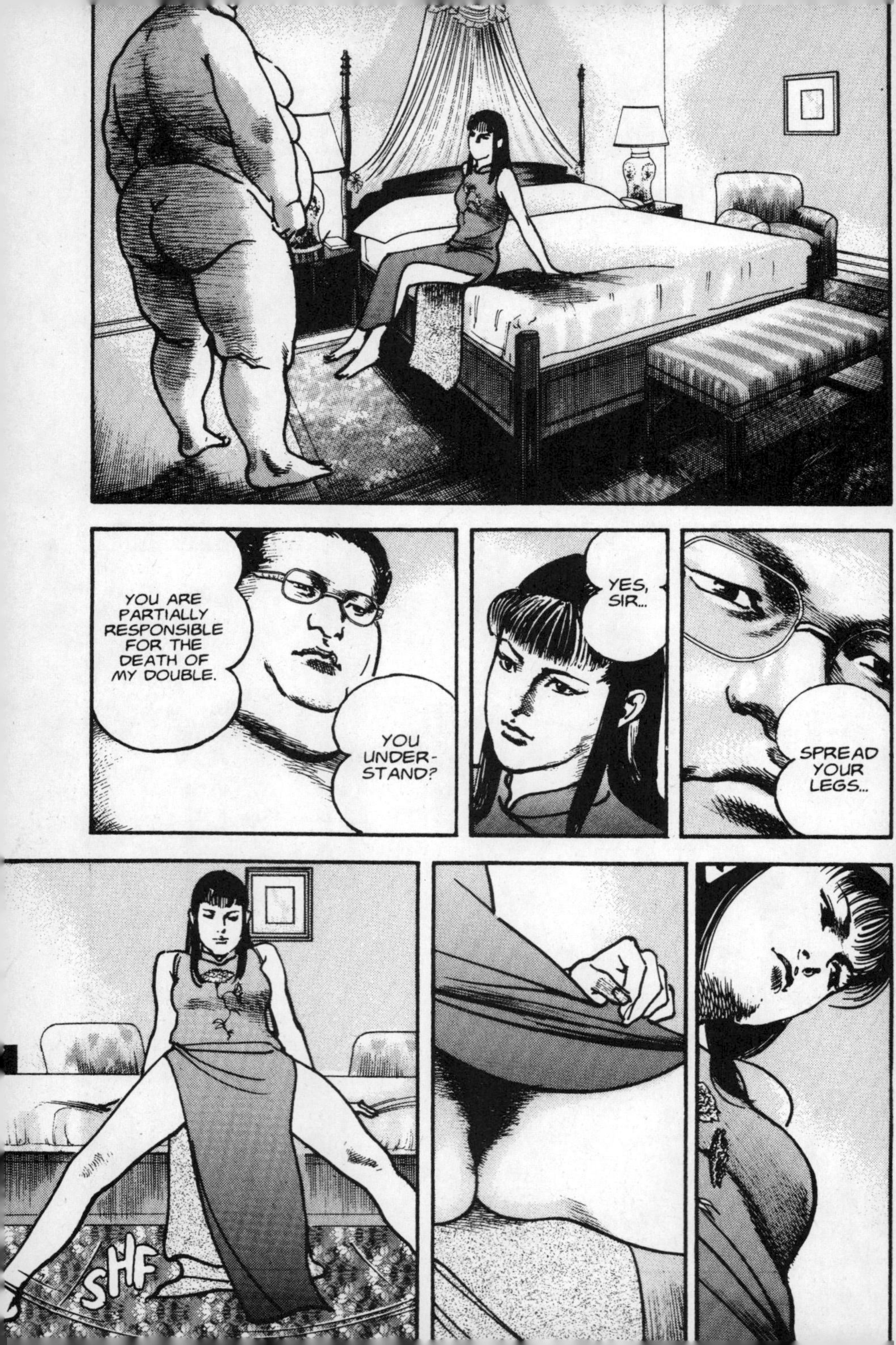
YOU ARE PARTIALLY RESPONSIBLE FOR THE DEATH OF MY DOUBLE.
YOU UNDER-STAND?
YES, SIR...
SPREAD YOUR LEGS...
SHF

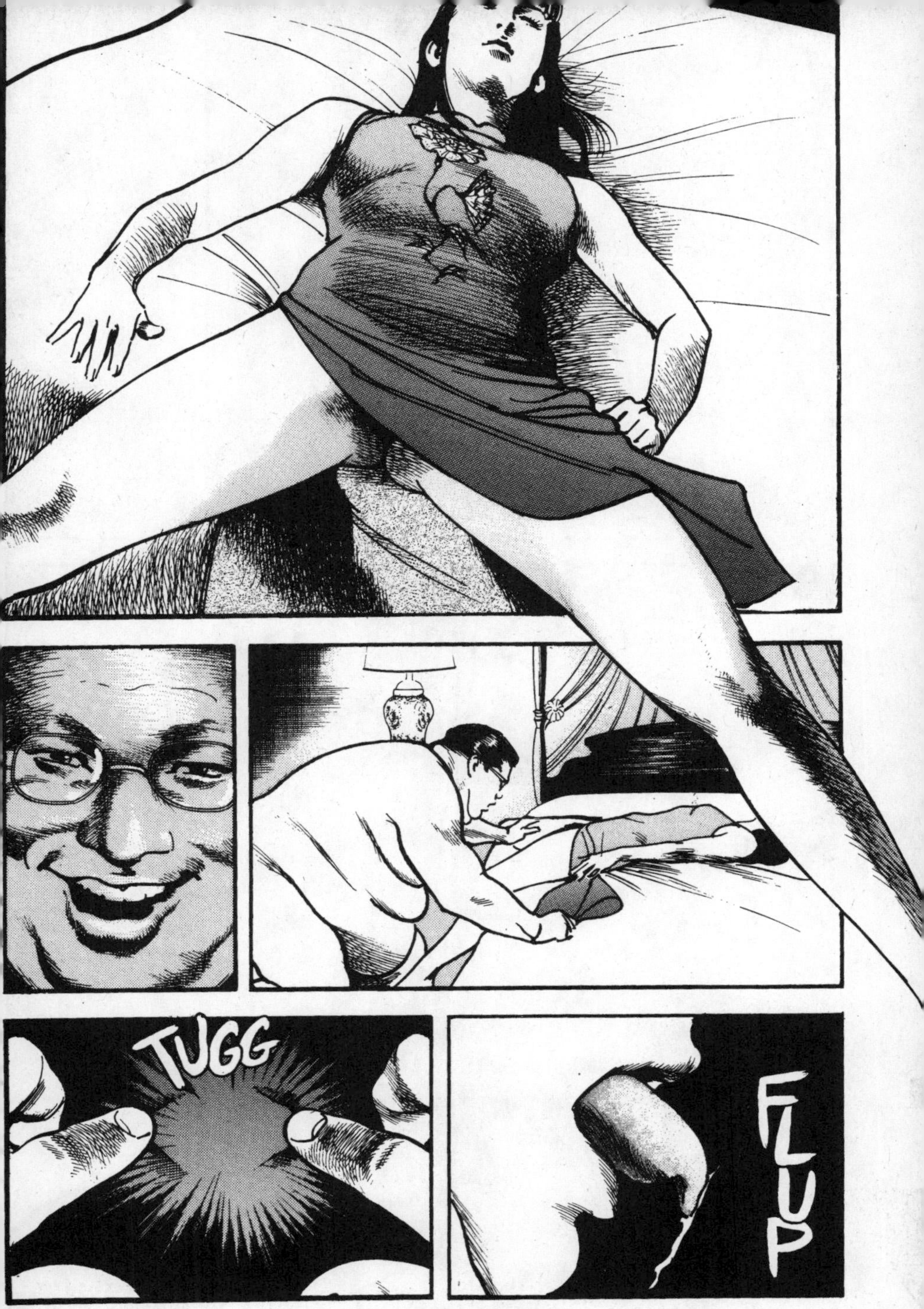
TUGG
FLUP

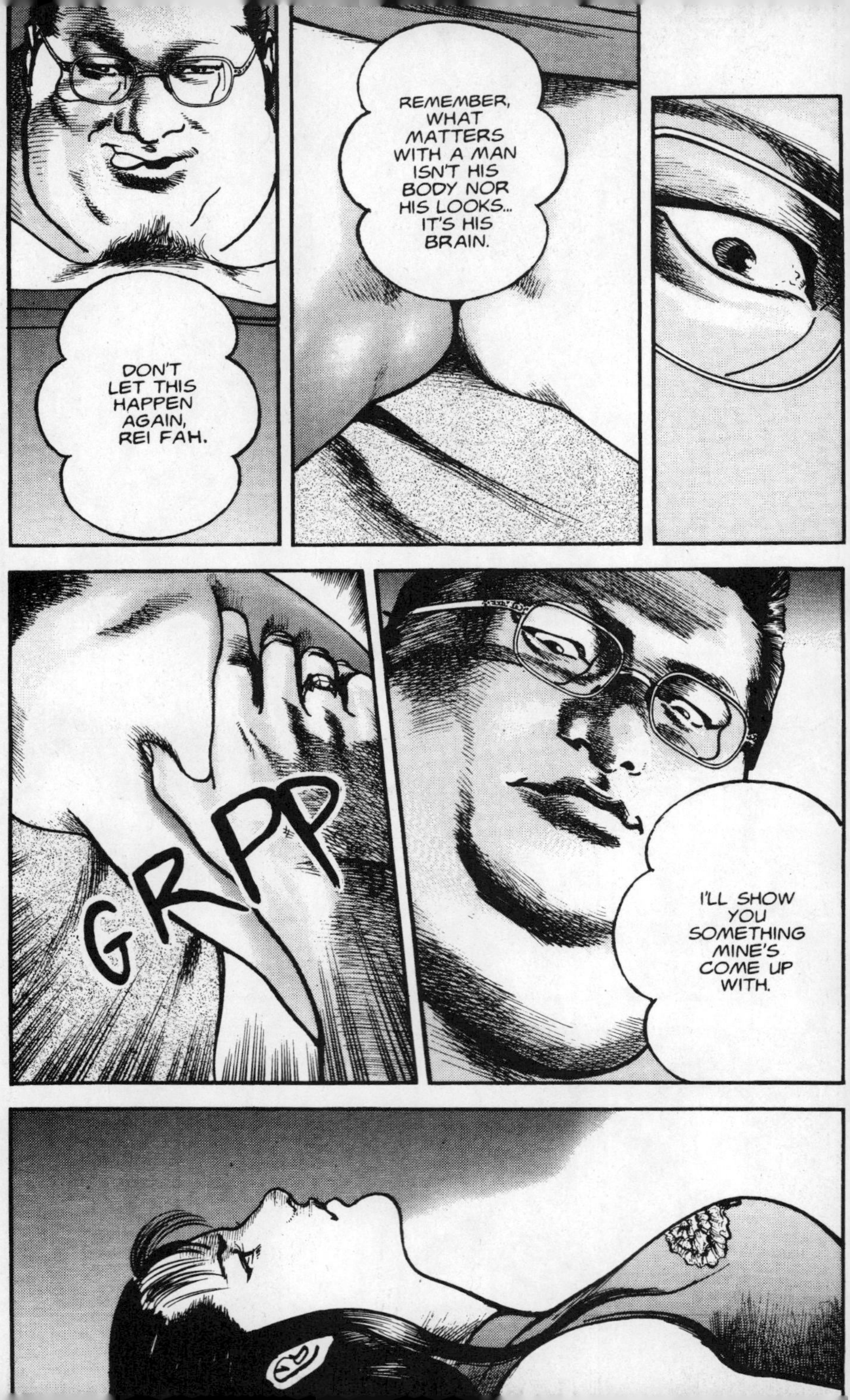
REMEMBER, WHAT MATTERS WITH A MAN ISN'T HIS BODY NOR HIS LOOKS... IT'S HIS BRAIN.
DON'T LET THIS HAPPEN AGAIN, REI FAH.
I'LL SHOW YOU SOMETHING MINE'S COME UP WITH.
GRPP

WHY AM I HERE?

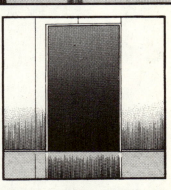

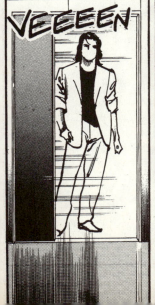

VEEEEN

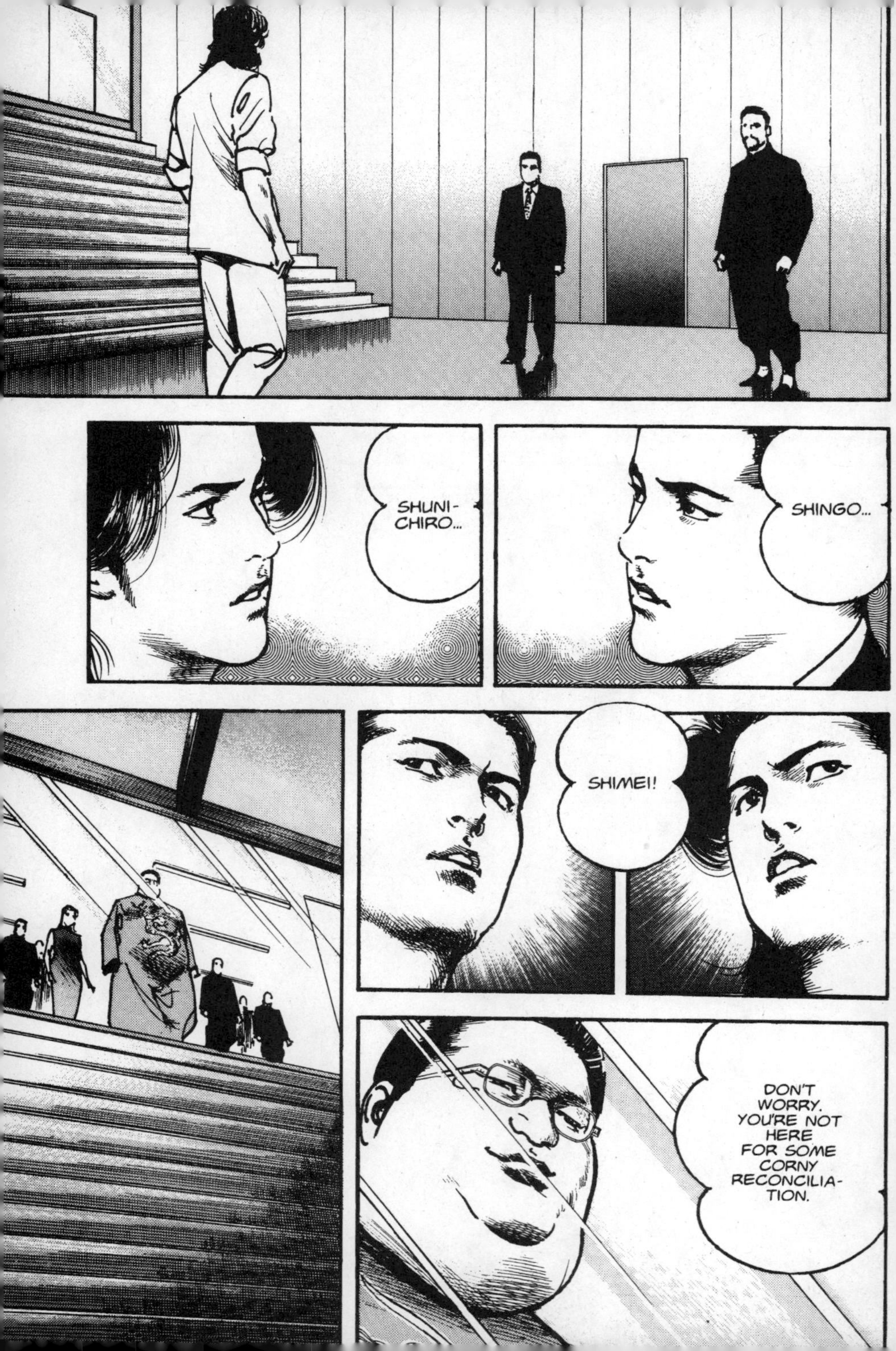
SHUNI-
CHIRO...
SHINGO...
SHIMEI!
DON'T WORRY. YOU'RE NOT HERE FOR SOME CORNY RECONCILIA- TION.

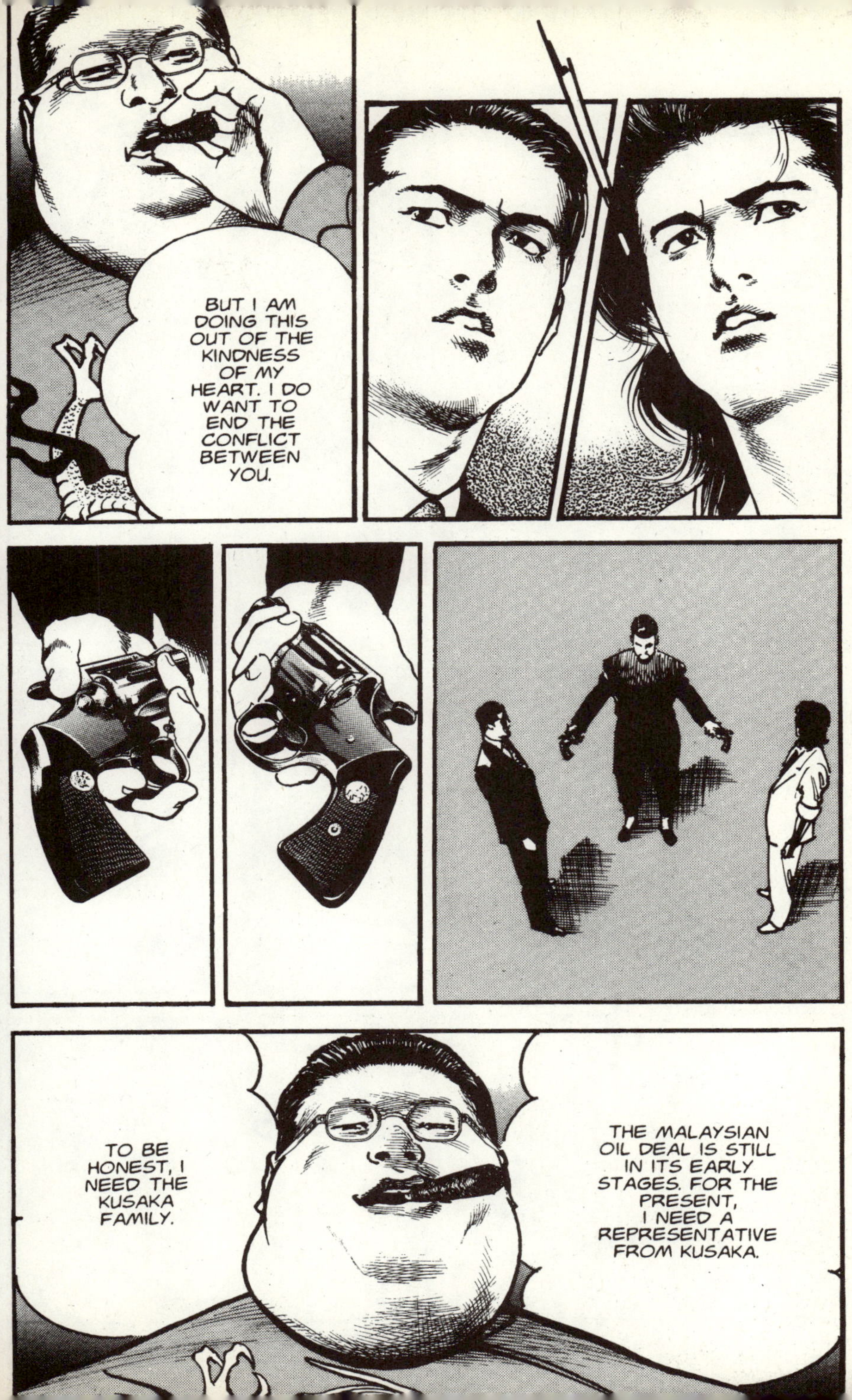

BUT I AM DOING THIS OUT OF THE KINDNESS OF MY HEART. I DO WANT TO END THE CONFLICT BETWEEN YOU.
TO BE HONEST, I NEED THE KUSAKA FAMILY.
THE MALAYSIAN OIL DEAL IS STILL IN ITS EARLY STAGES. FOR THE PRESENT, I NEED A REPRESENTATIVE FROM KUSAKA.

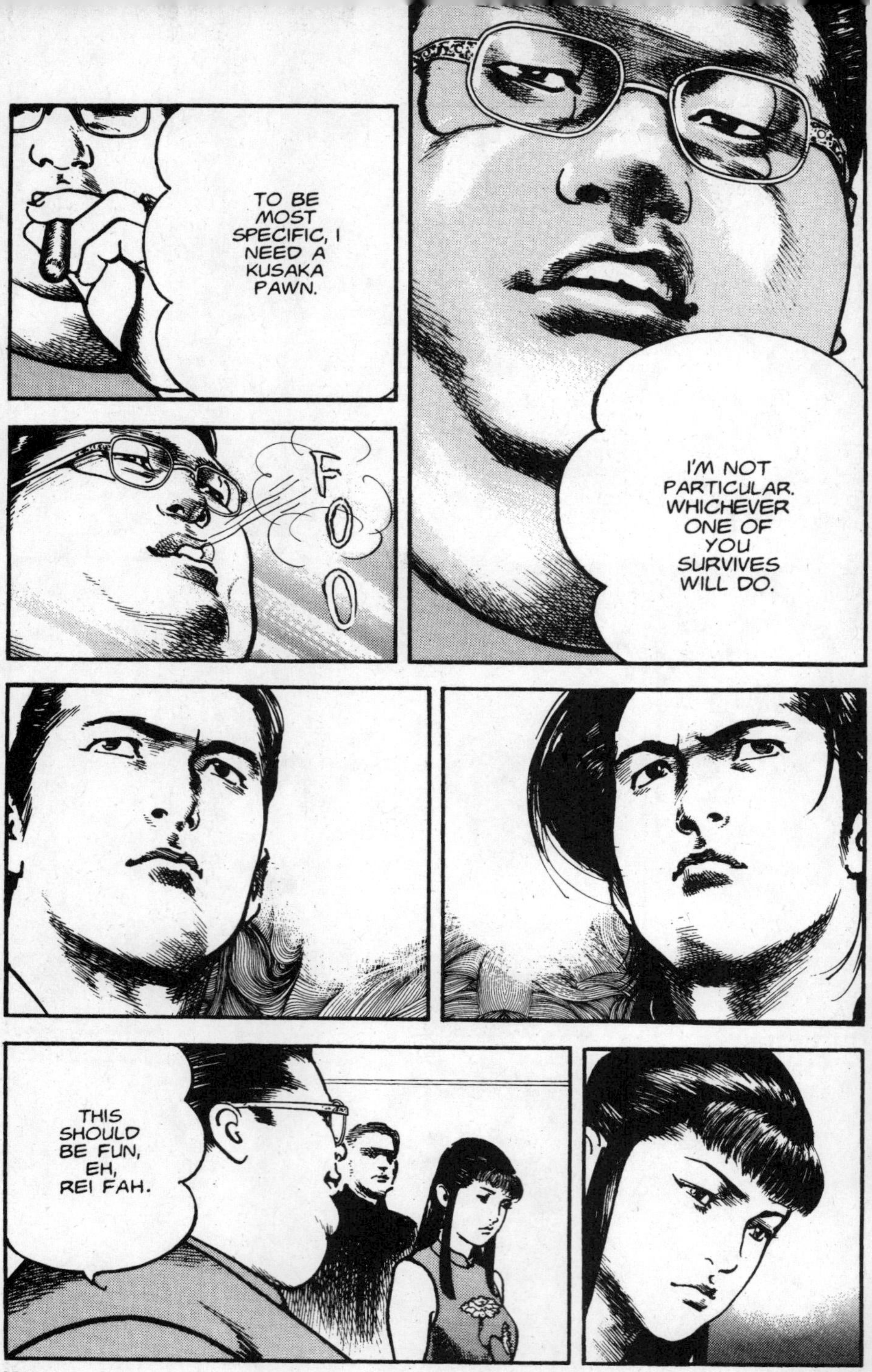
TO BE MOST SPECIFIC, I NEED A KUSAKA PAWN.
FOO
I'M NOT PARTICULAR. WHICHEVER ONE OF YOU SURVIVES WILL DO.
THIS SHOULD BE FUN, EH, REI FAH.

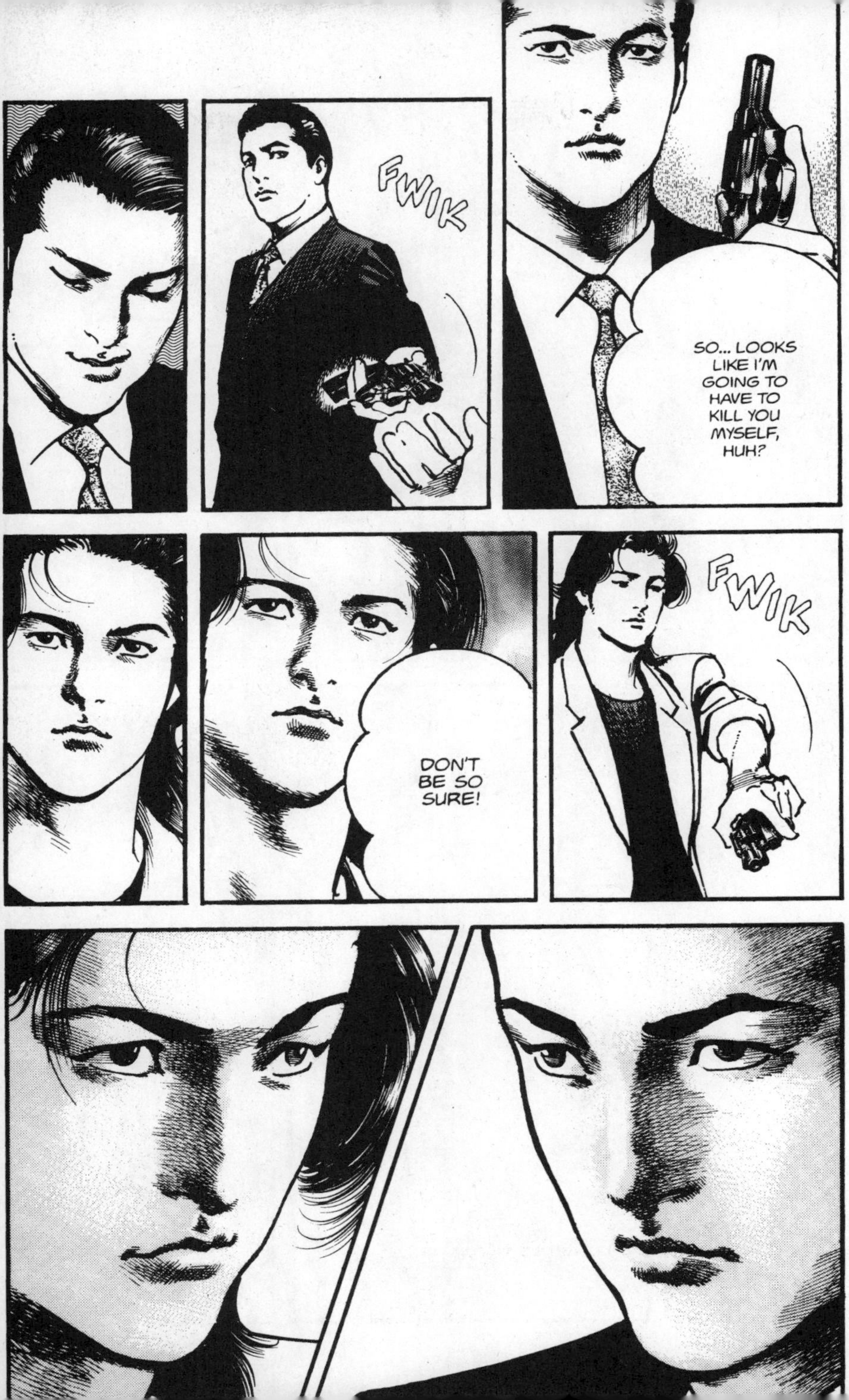
FWIK
SO... LOOKS LIKE I'M GOING TO HAVE TO KILL YOU MYSELF, HUH?
DON'T BE SO SURE!
FWIK

PLEASE, SIR!

BUT YOU'RE WRONG. I'M SORRY. IT WASN'T I WHO SAVED SHINGO.

B-BUT WHO?

WHO ELSE WOULD HAVE THAT KIND OF POWER?

SOMEONE WITH THE POWER TO PUT HIM IN JAIL WOULD ALSO HAVE THE POWER TO HAVE HIM RELEASED...

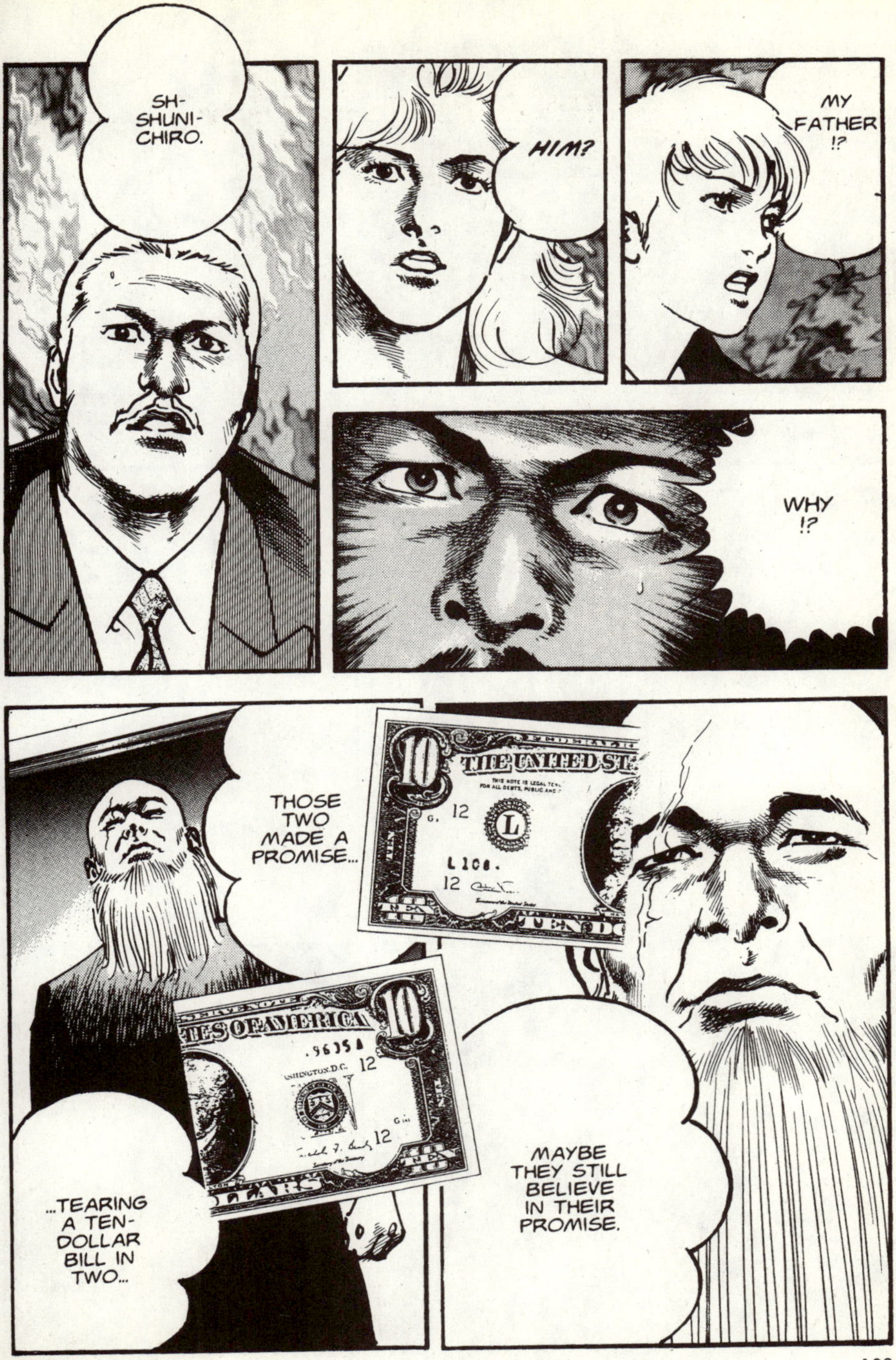
SH-SHUNICHIRO.
HIM?
MY FATHER!?
WHY!?
THOSE TWO MADE A PROMISE...
...TEARING A TEN-DOLLAR BILL IN TWO...
MAYBE THEY STILL BELIEVE IN THEIR PROMISE.

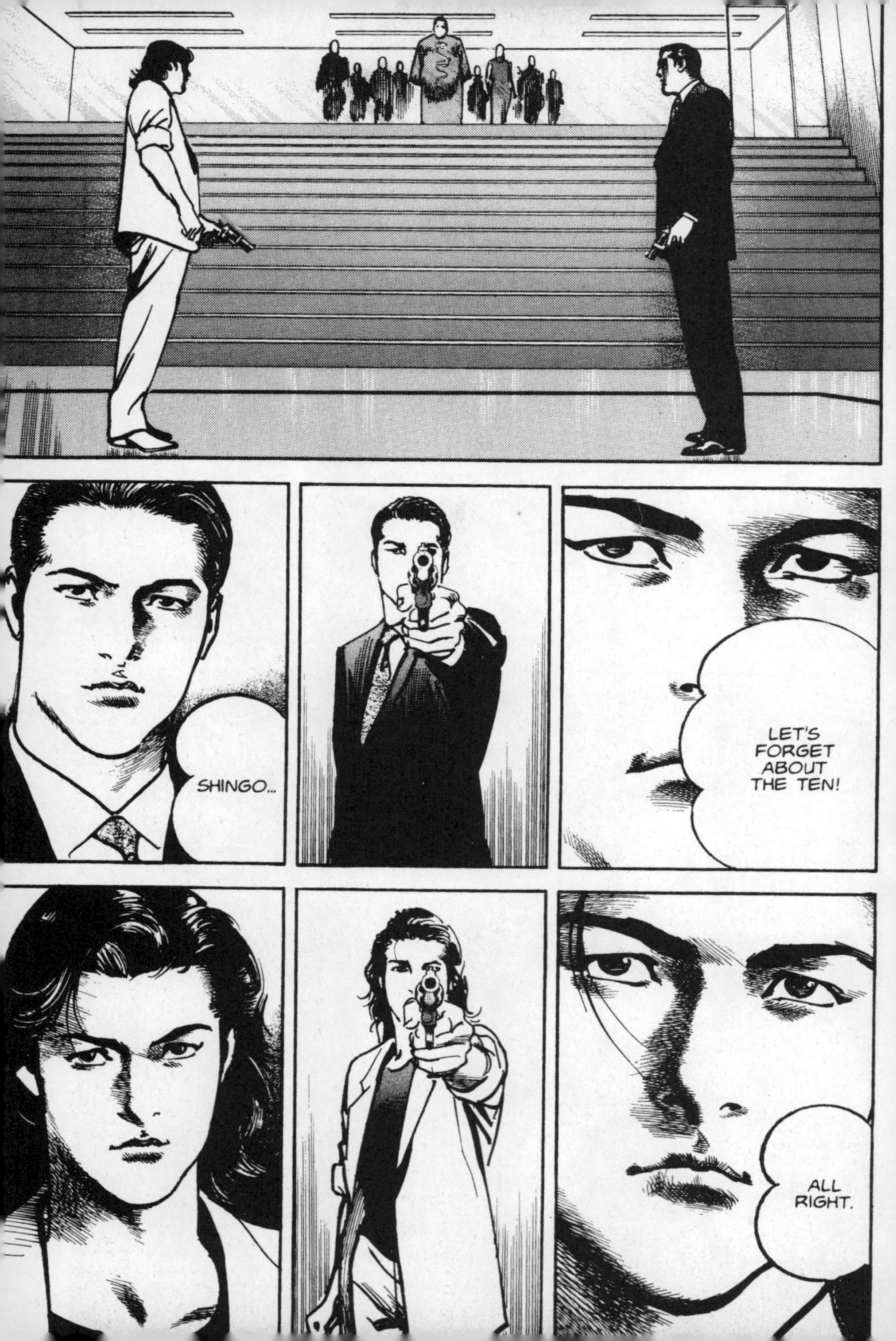
SHINGO...
LET'S FORGET ABOUT THE TEN!
ALL RIGHT.

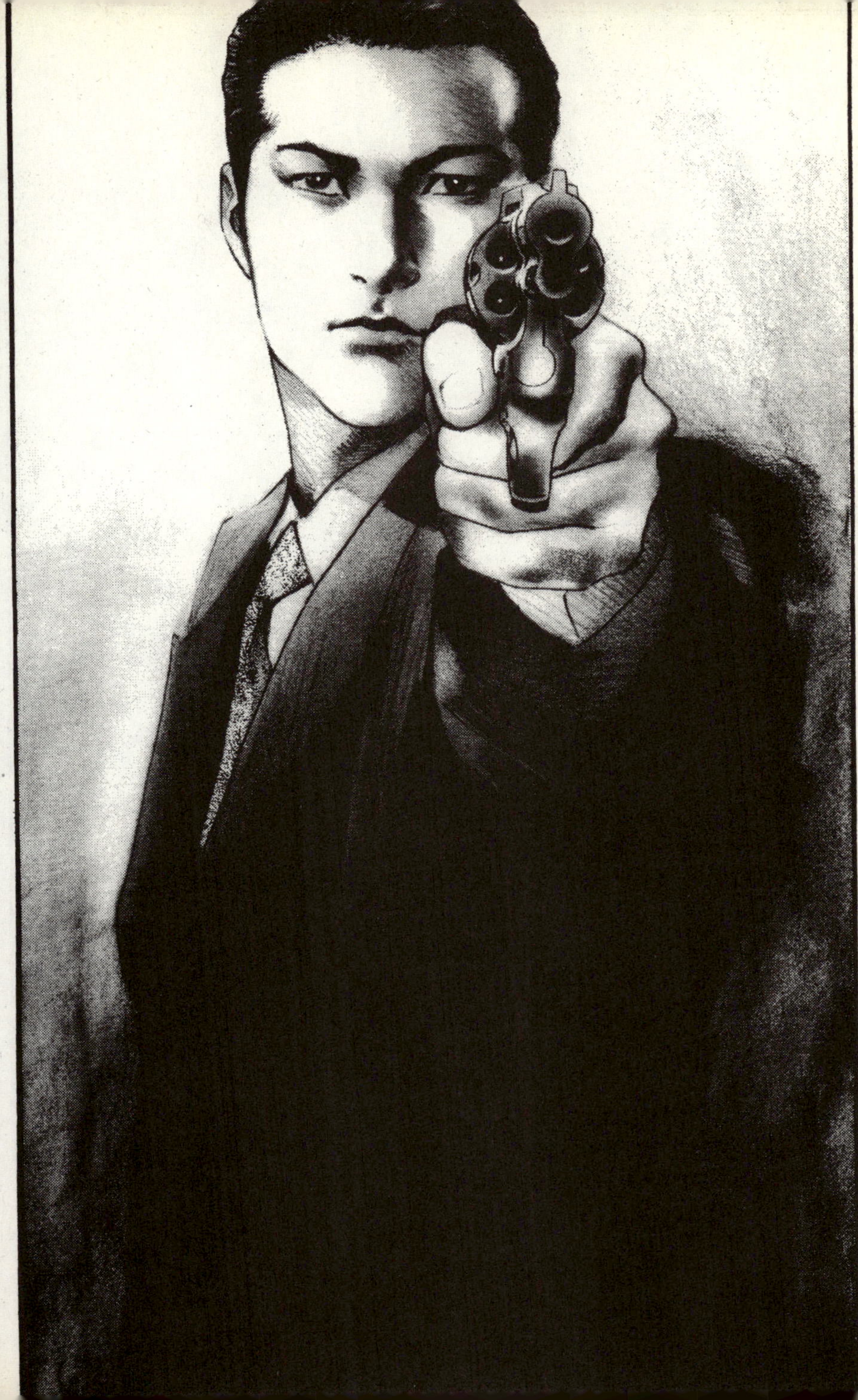

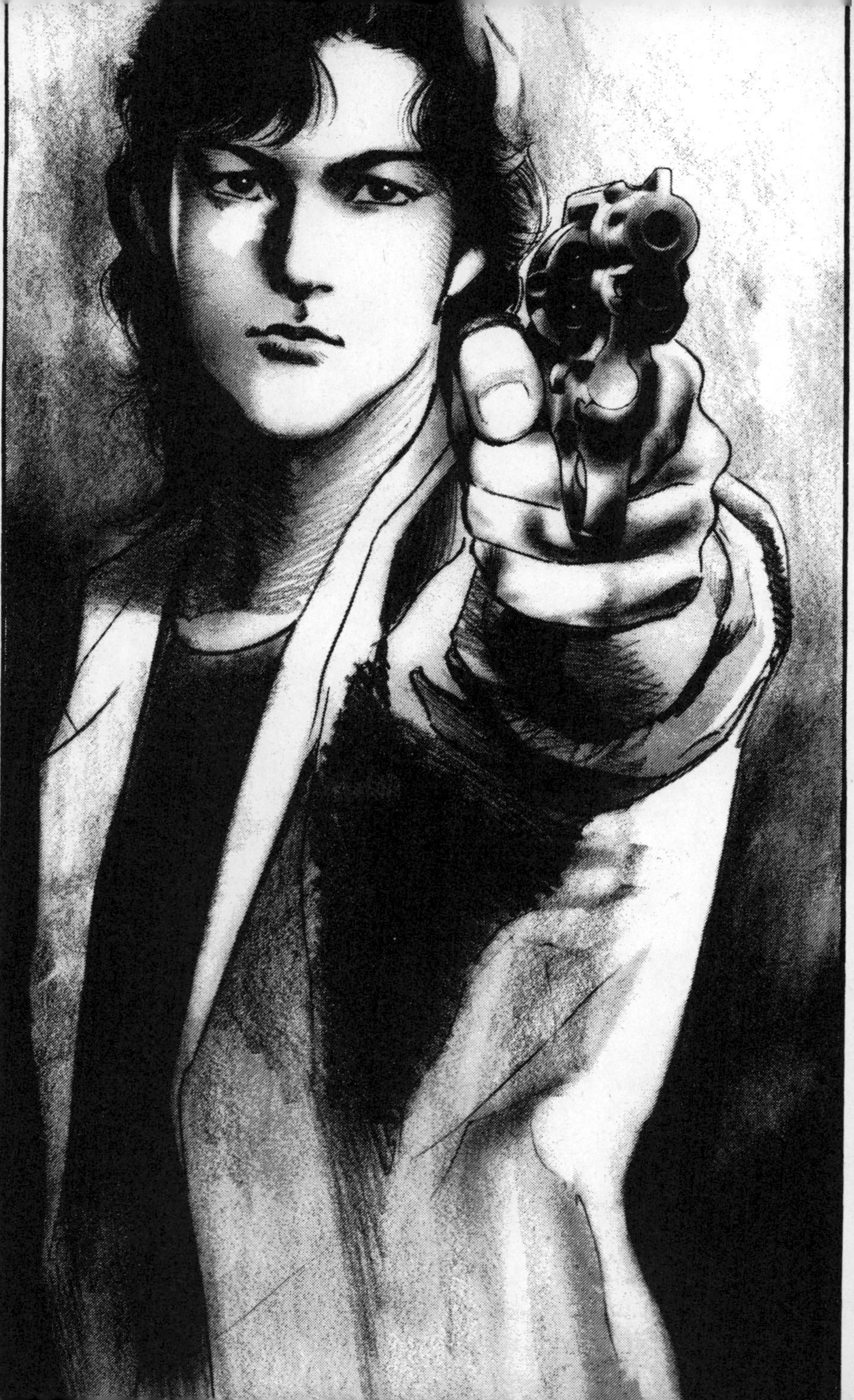

CHAPTER FIVE
THE CHOICE

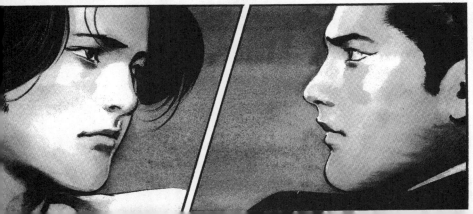

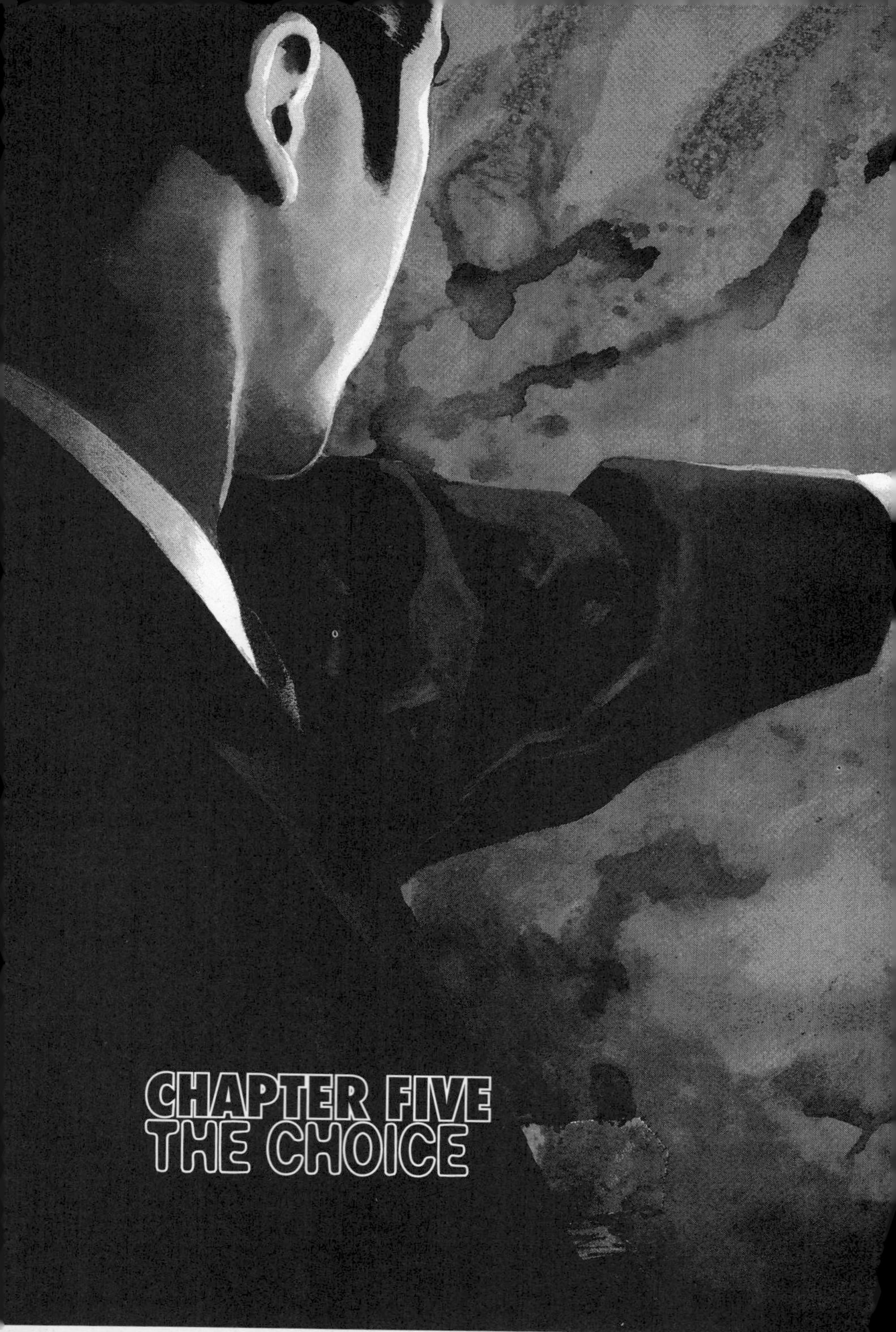
CHAPTER FIVE
THE CHOICE

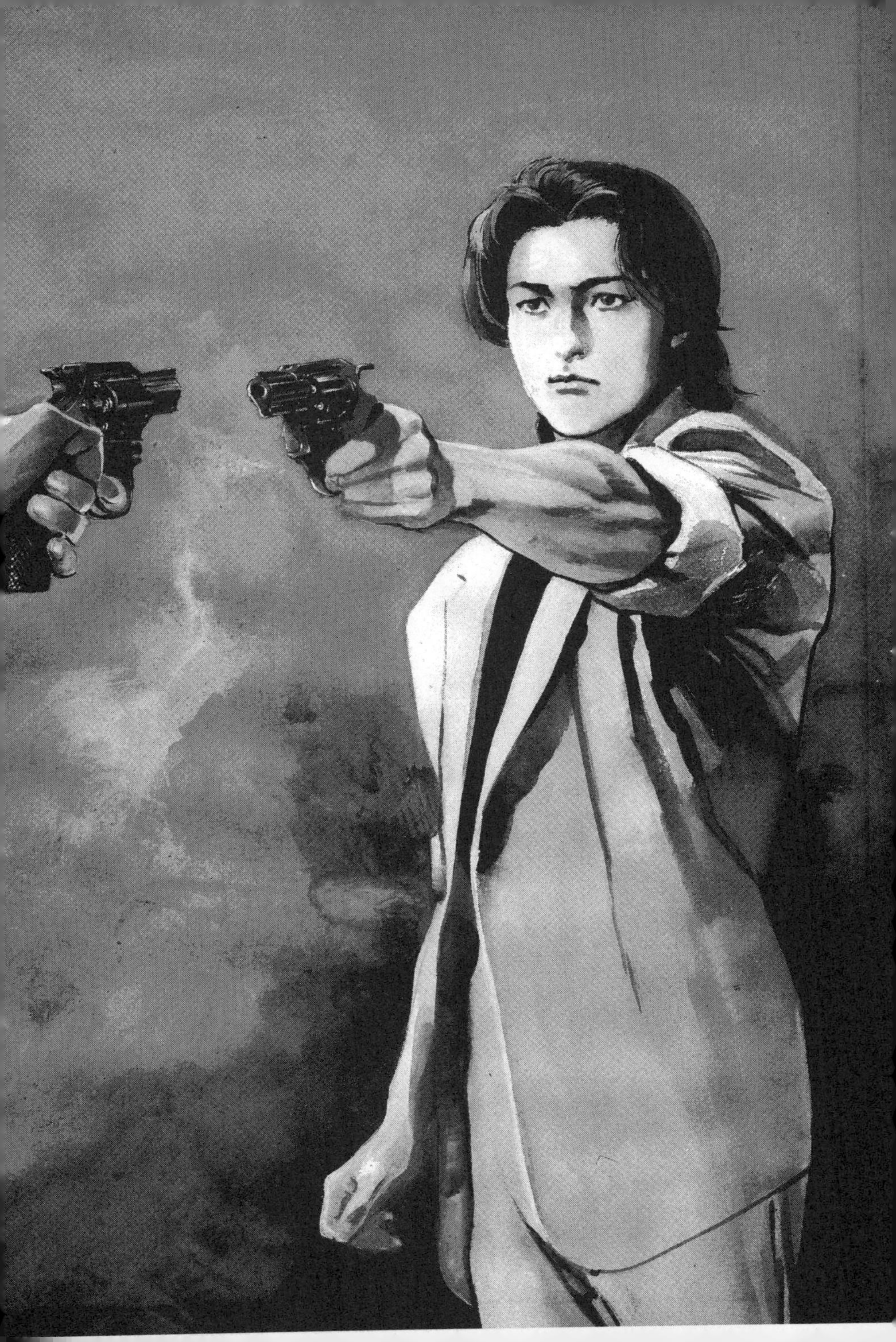

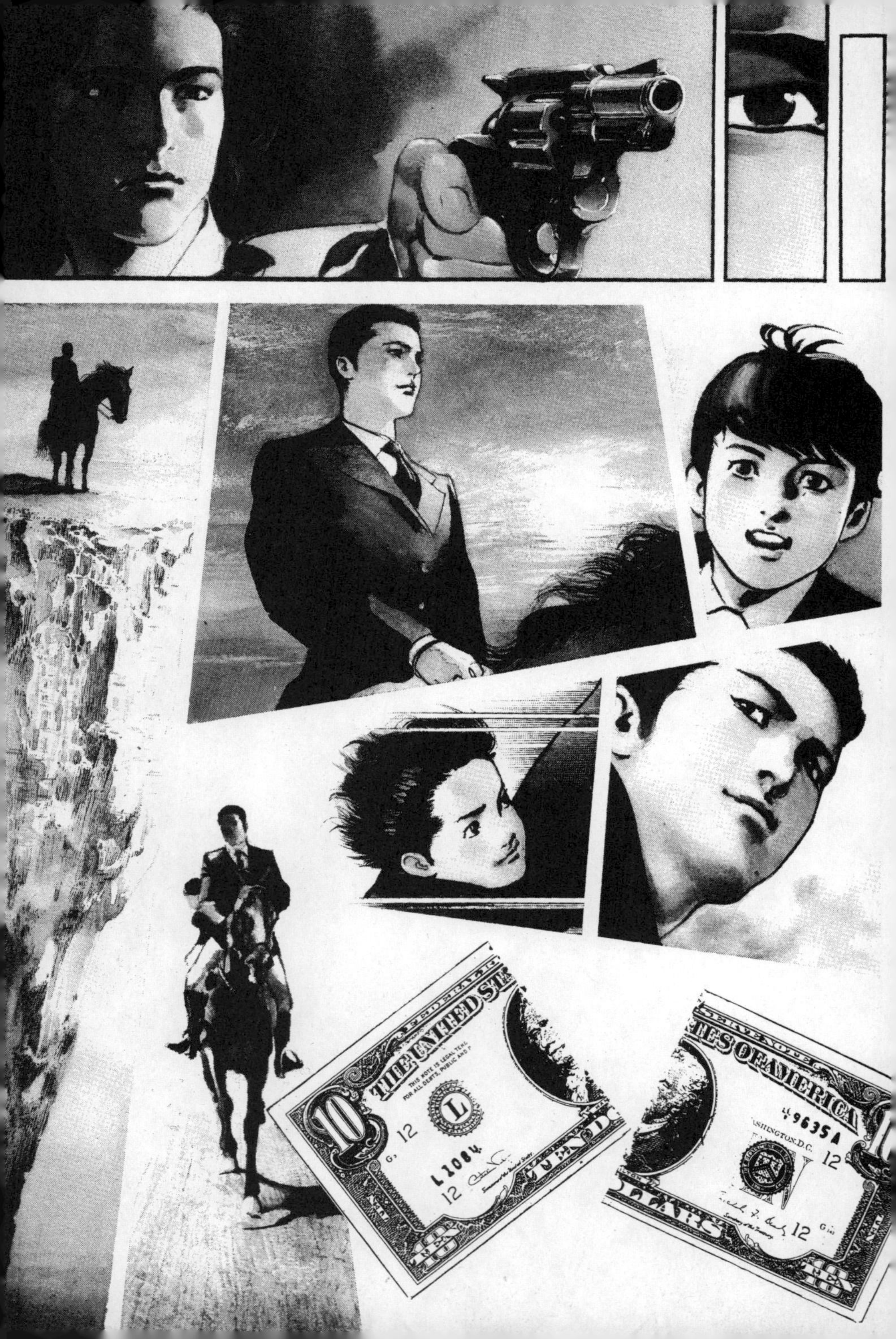
THE UNITED ST
THIS NOTE IS LEGAL TENDER FOR ALL DEBTS, PUBLIC AND P
10
L
12
TES OF AMERICA
SHINGTON, D.C.
12

WHICH ONE WILL GOD CHOOSE...

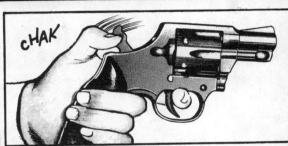

CHAK

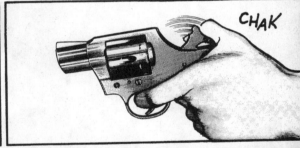

CHAK

BROTHER...

A KILLER COULD NEVER HANDLE KUSAKA.

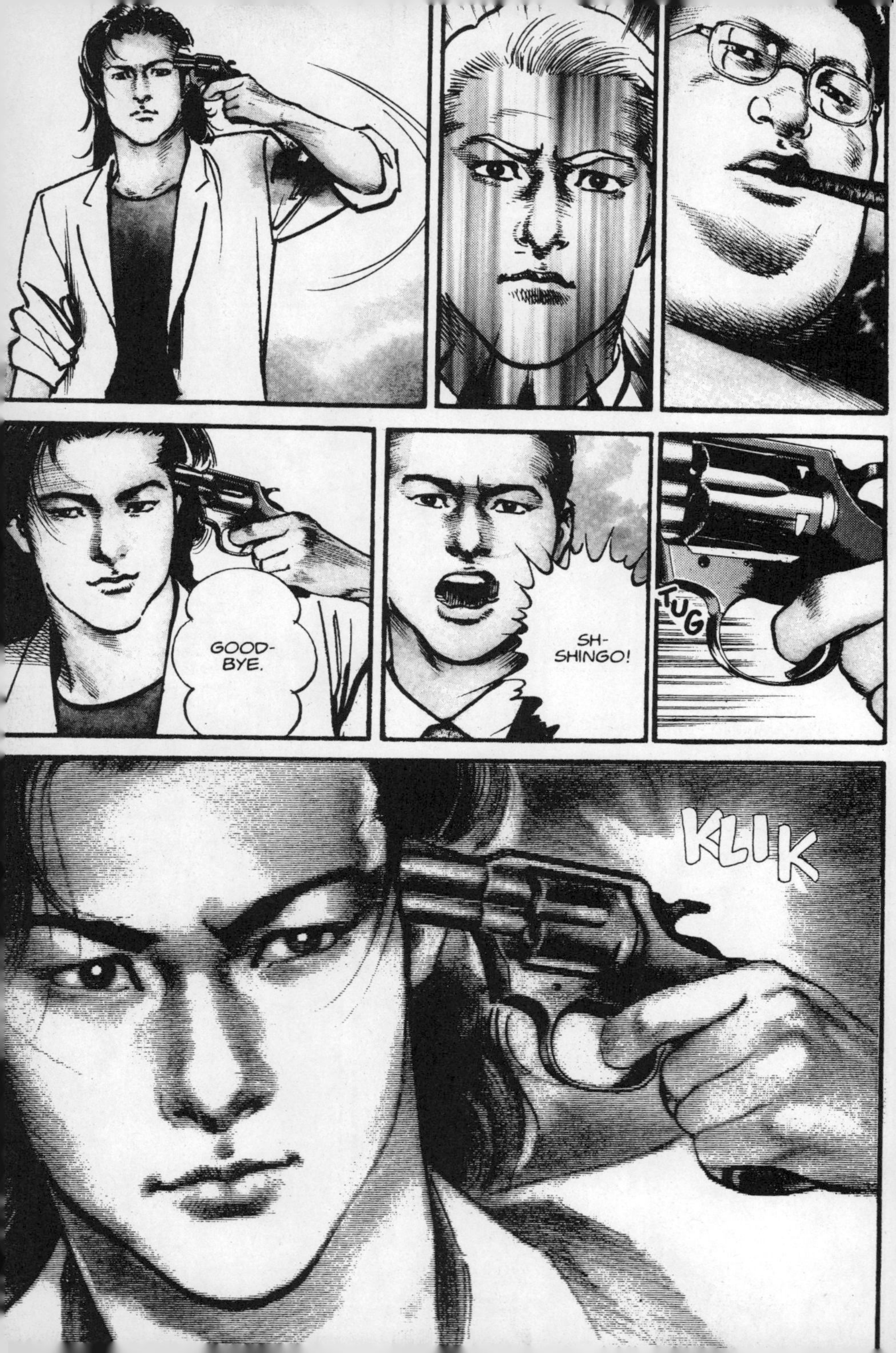
GOOD-BYE.
SH-SHINGO!
TUG
KLIK

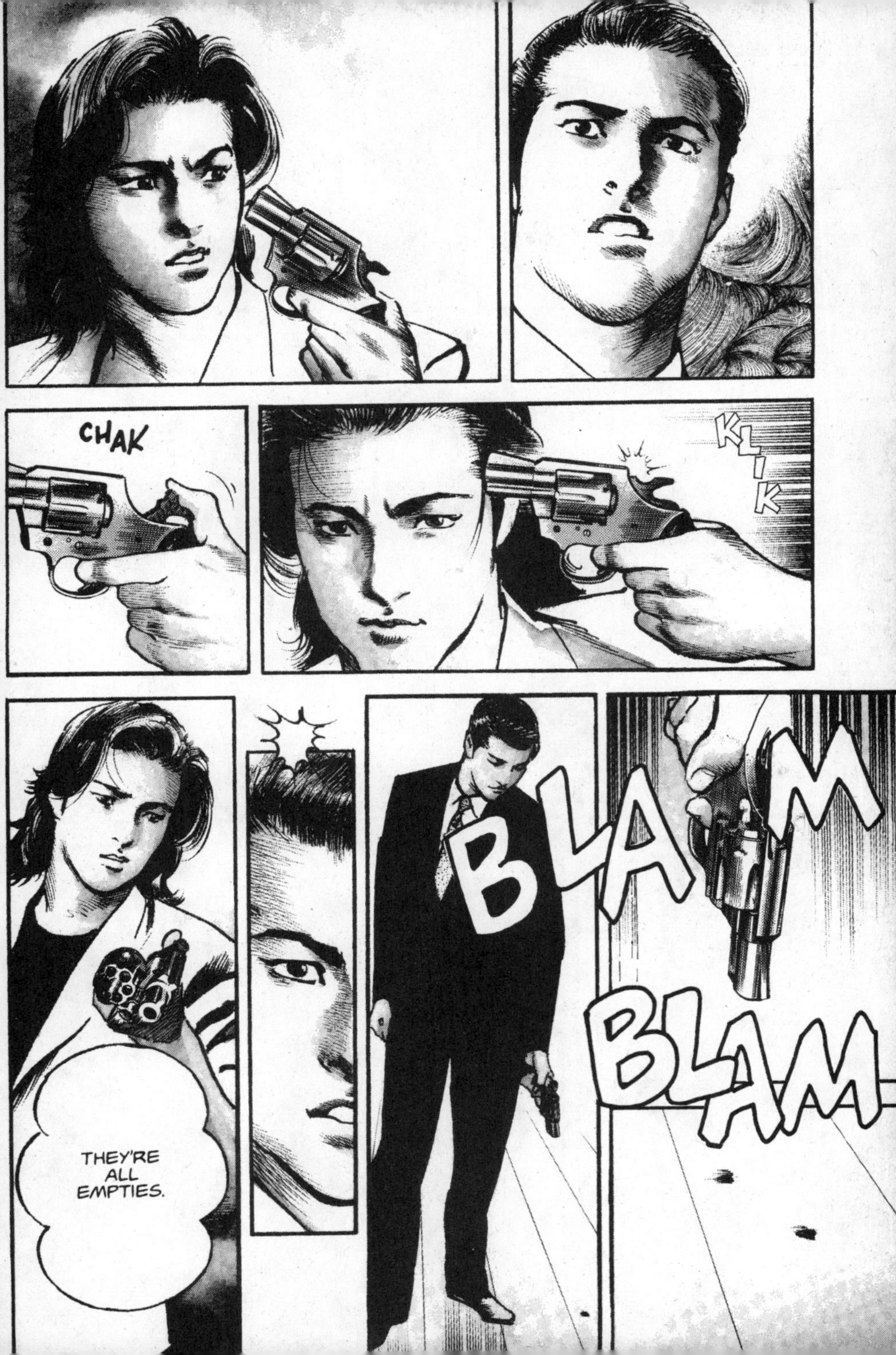
CHAK
KLIK
THEY'RE ALL EMPTIES.
BLAM
BLAM

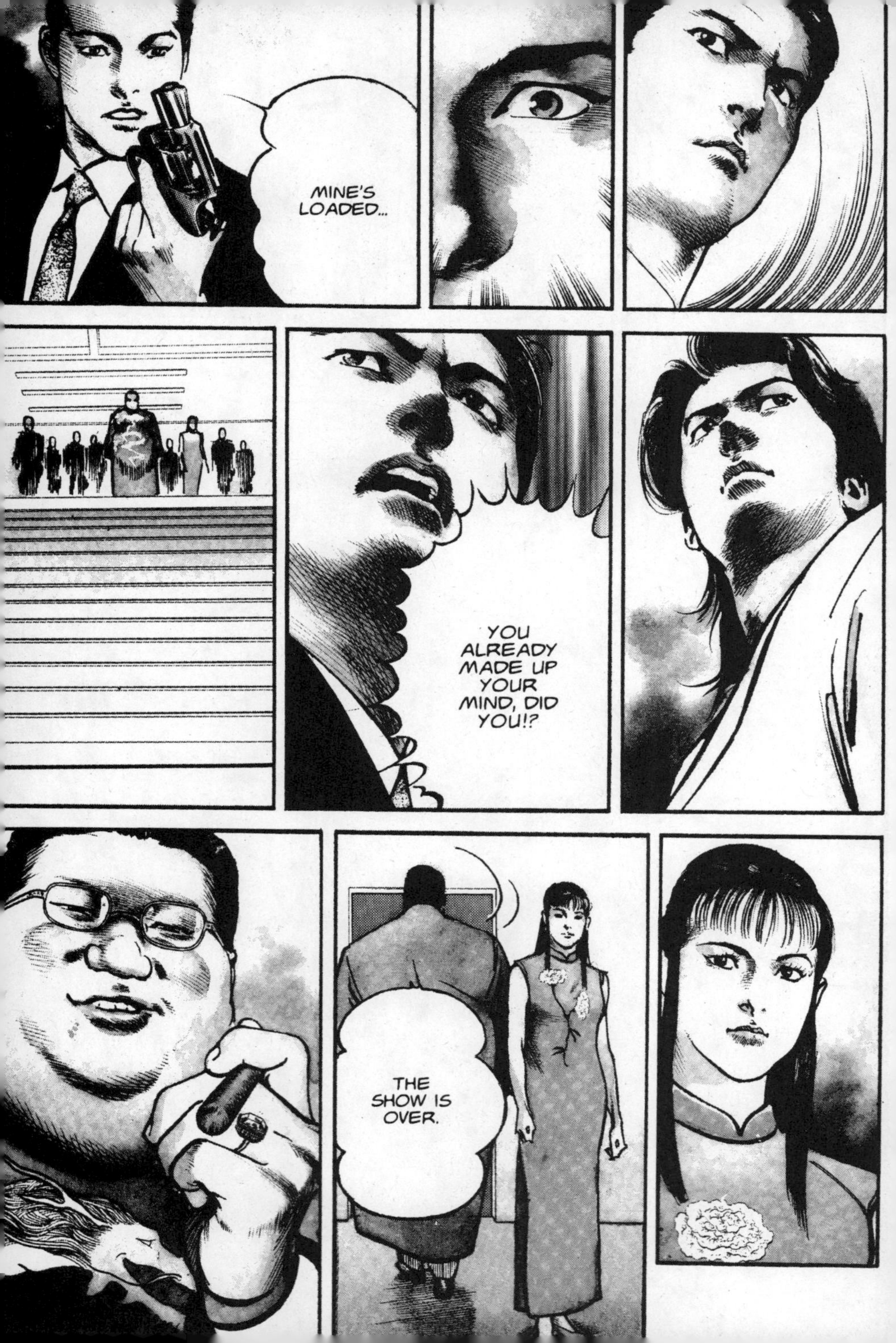
MINE'S LOADED...
YOU ALREADY MADE UP YOUR MIND, DID YOU!?
THE SHOW IS OVER.

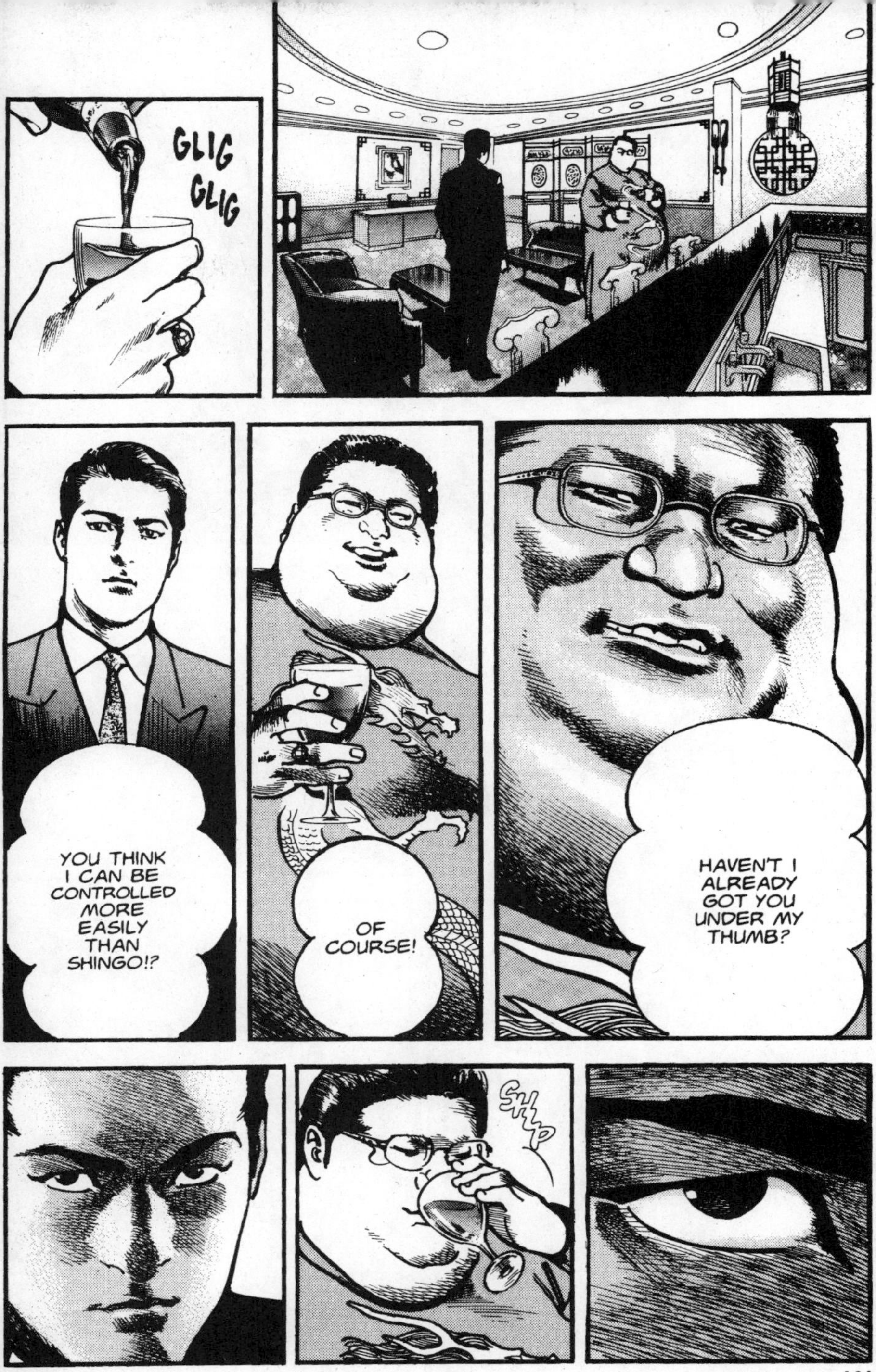

GLIG GLIG
YOU THINK I CAN BE CONTROLLED MORE EASILY THAN SHINGO!?
OF COURSE!
HAVEN'T I ALREADY GOT YOU UNDER MY THUMB?
SHIP

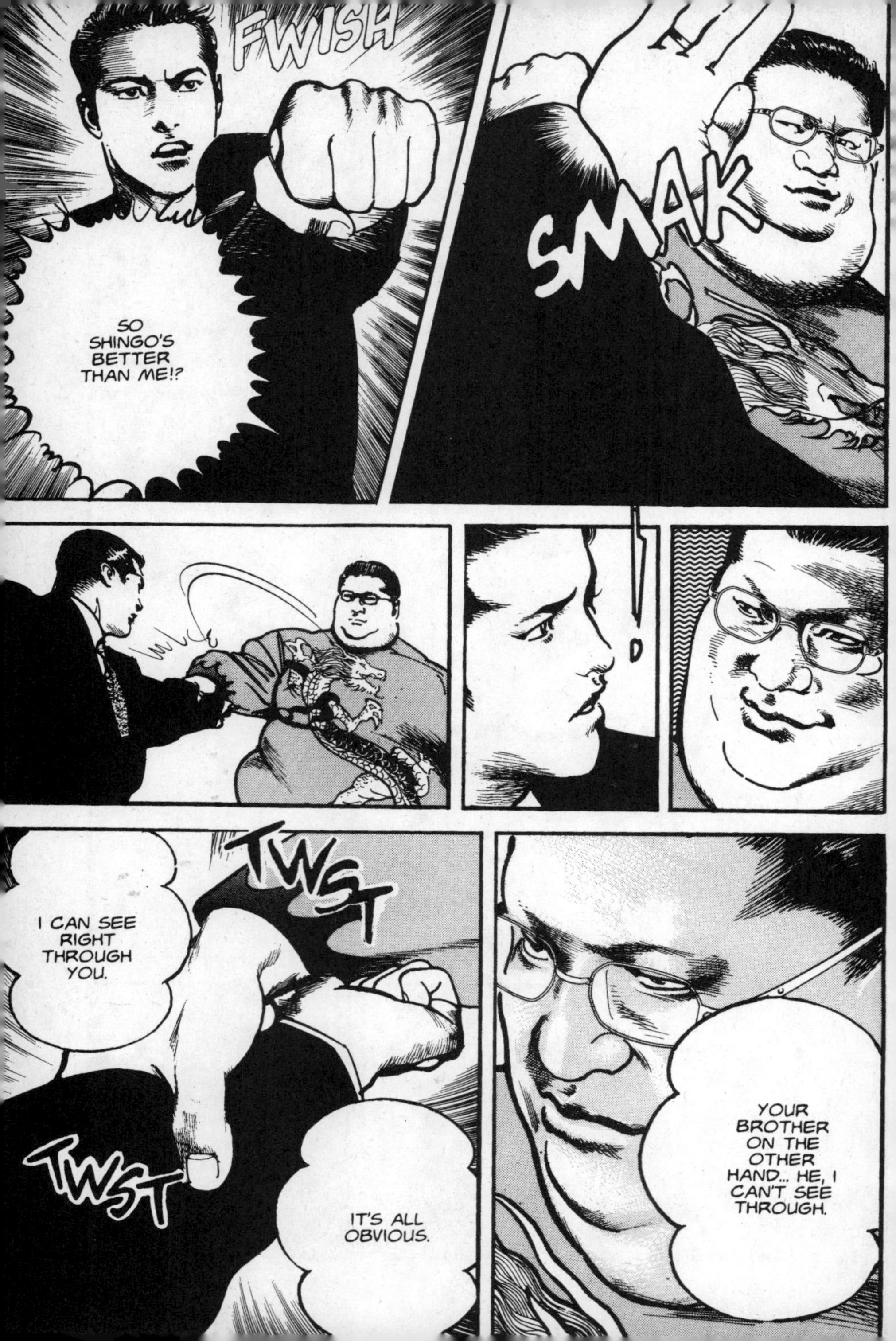
FWISH
SO SHINGO'S BETTER THAN ME!?
SMAK
TWST
I CAN SEE RIGHT THROUGH YOU.
TWST
IT'S ALL OBVIOUS.
YOUR BROTHER ON THE OTHER HAND... HE, I CAN'T SEE THROUGH.

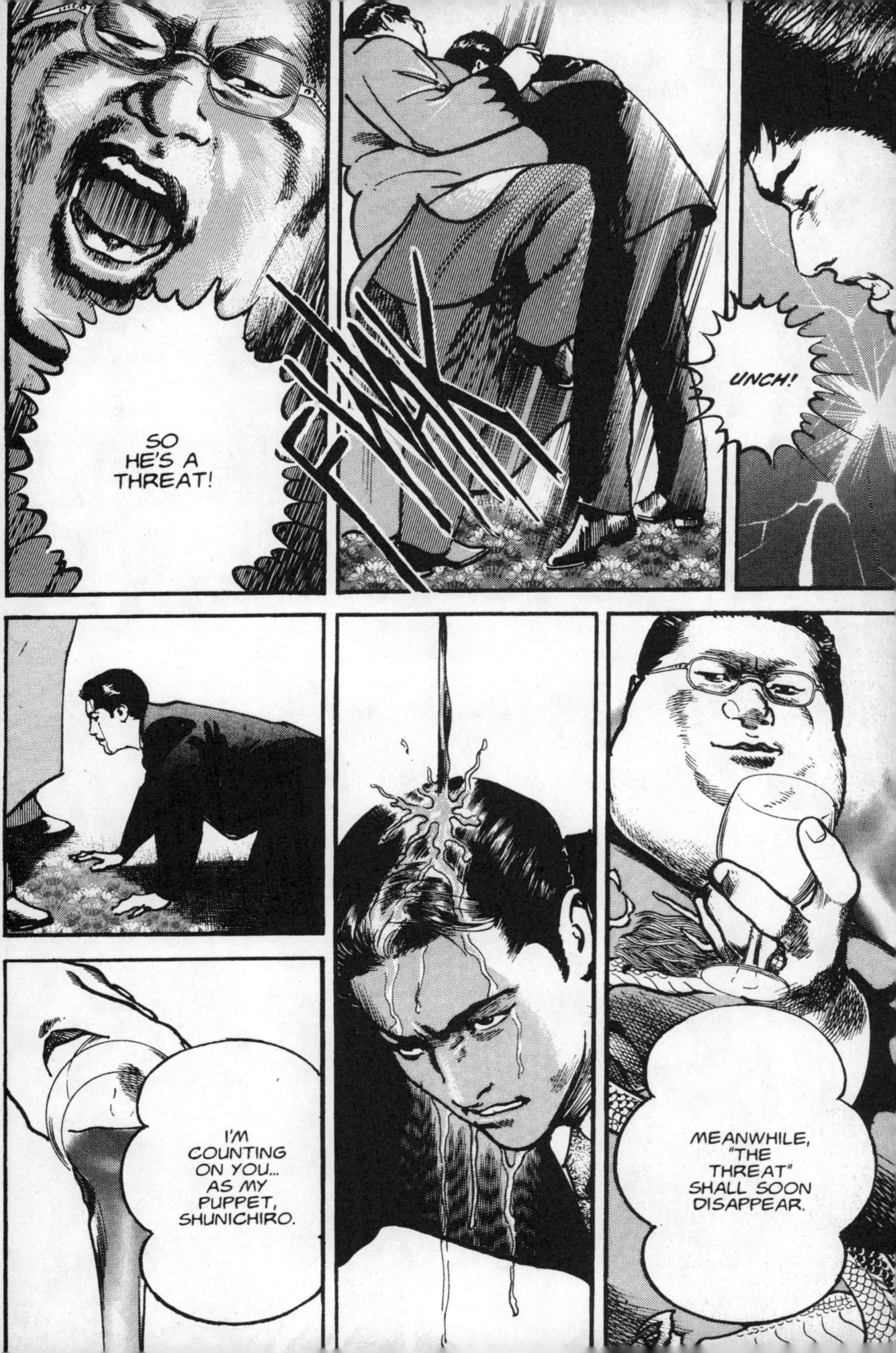
SO HE'S A THREAT!
UNCH!
I'M COUNTING ON YOU... AS MY PUPPET, SHUNICHIRO.
MEANWHILE, "THE THREAT" SHALL SOON DISAPPEAR.

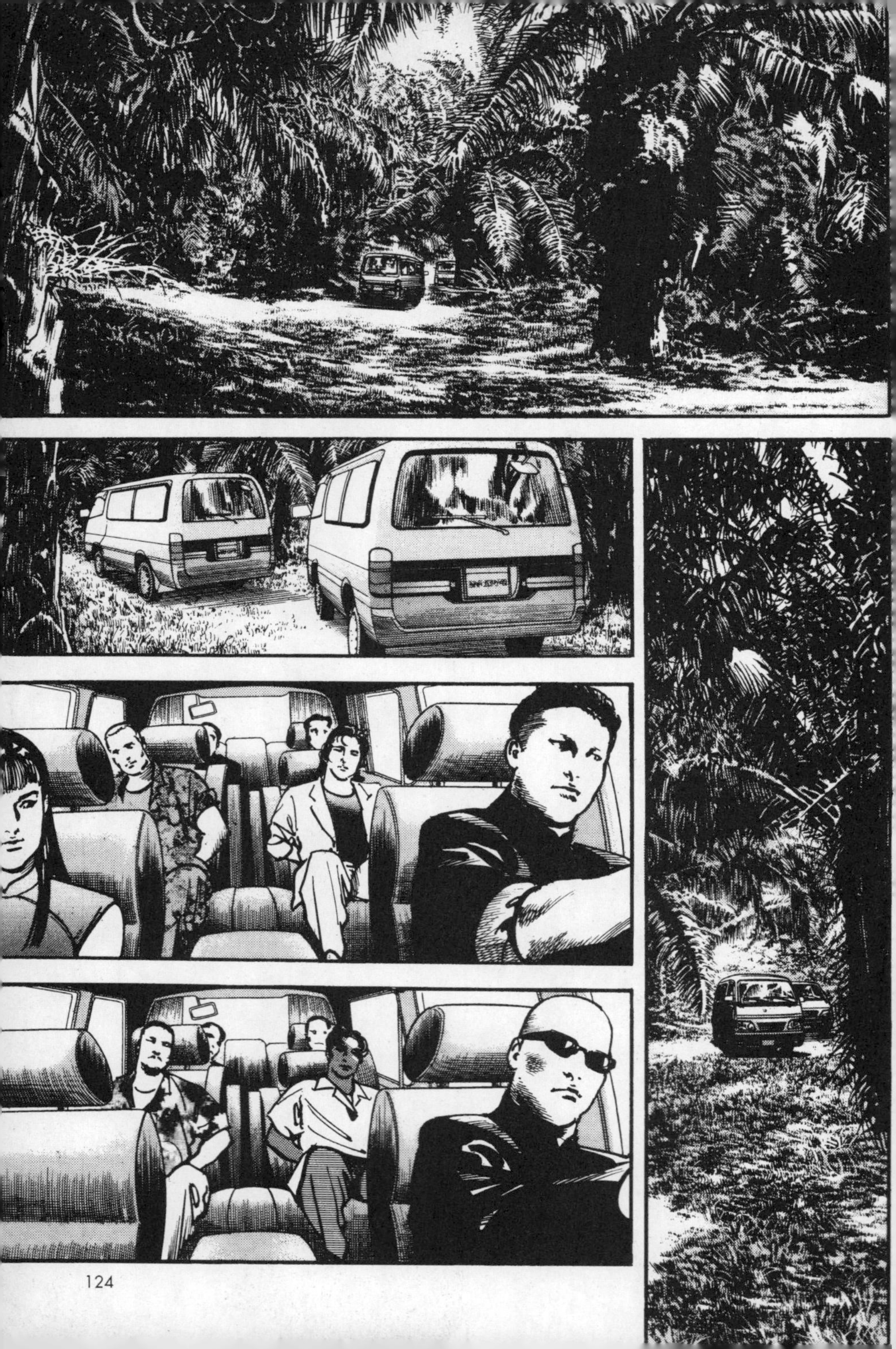

ANGEL.

HA! NO APOLOGIES FROM YOU!

WE SAID WE'D COME ALONG FOR THE RIDE...

SMAK!

LET'S FINISH EM OFF. I DON'T WANNA GET MALARIA OUT HERE.

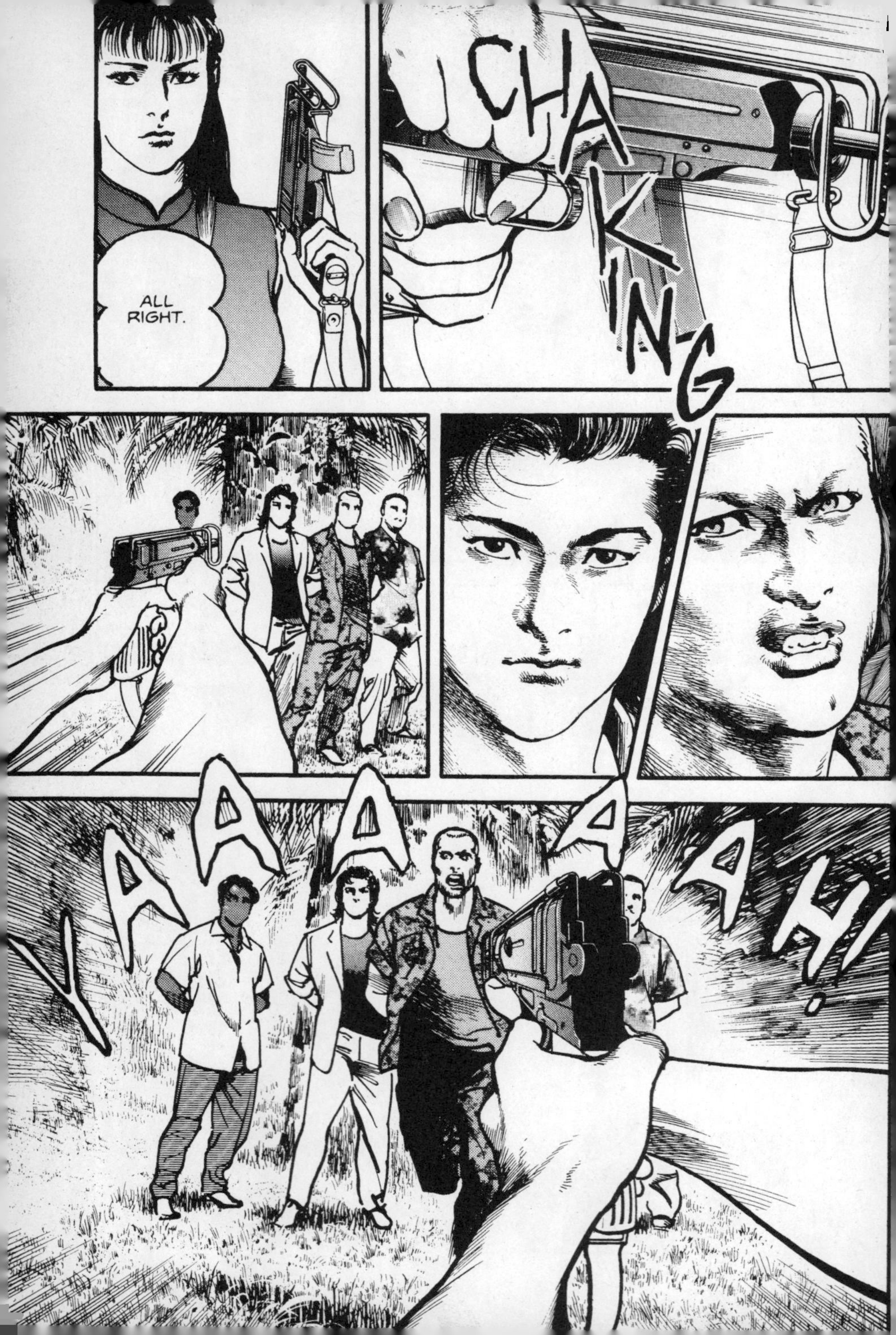
ALL RIGHT.
CHAKING
YAAAAAH!

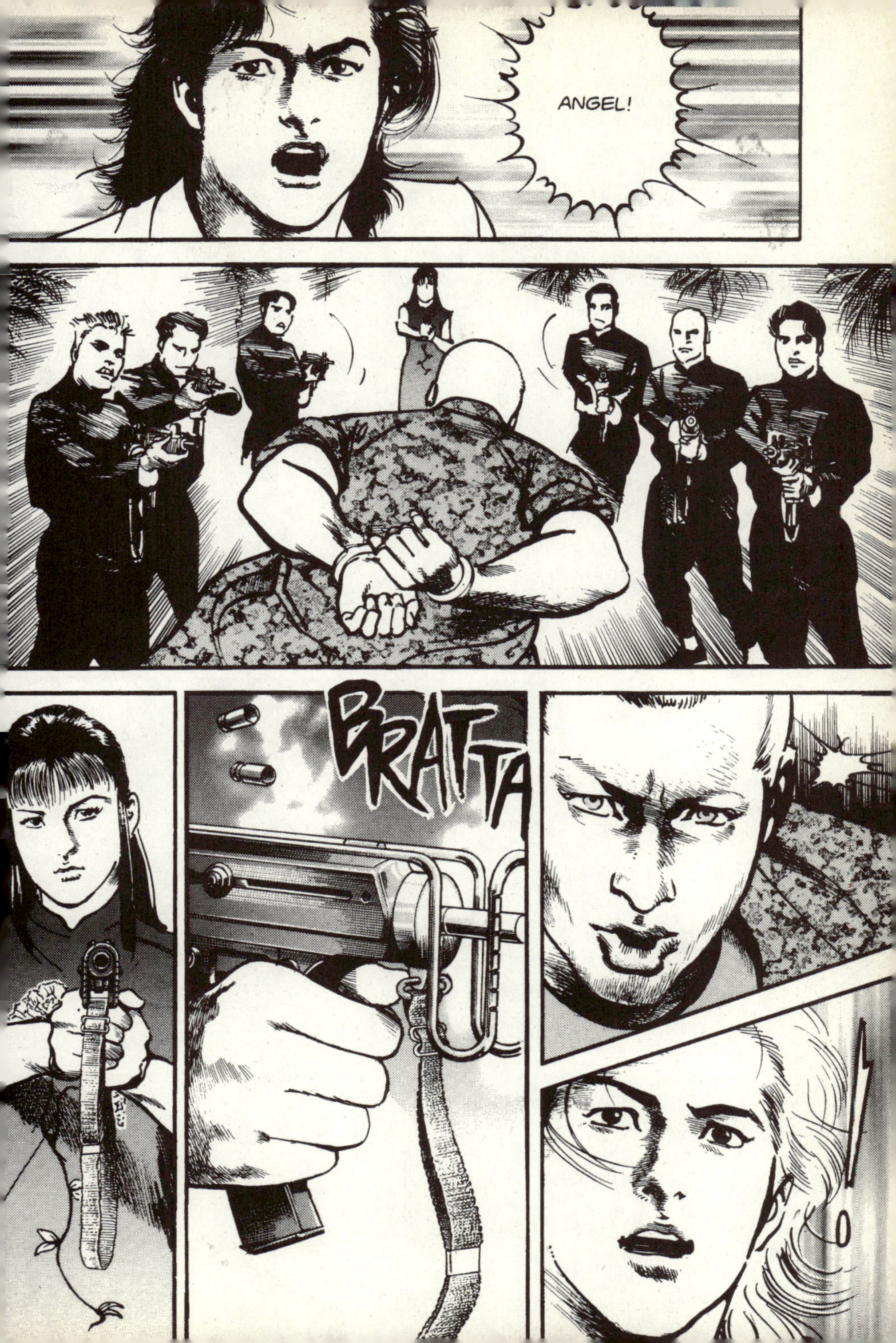

ANGEL!
BRATTA

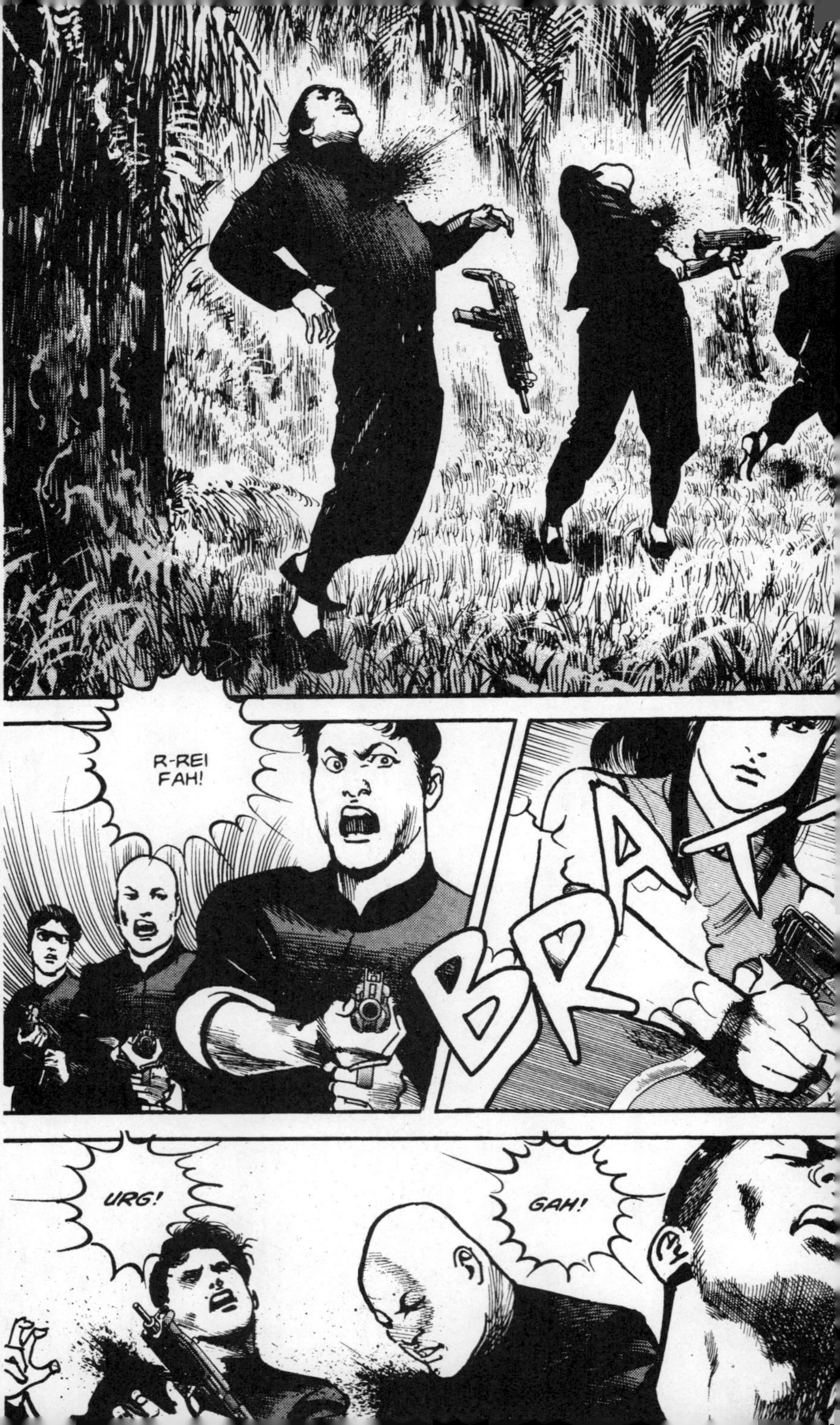
R-REI FAH!
BRAT
URG!
GAH!

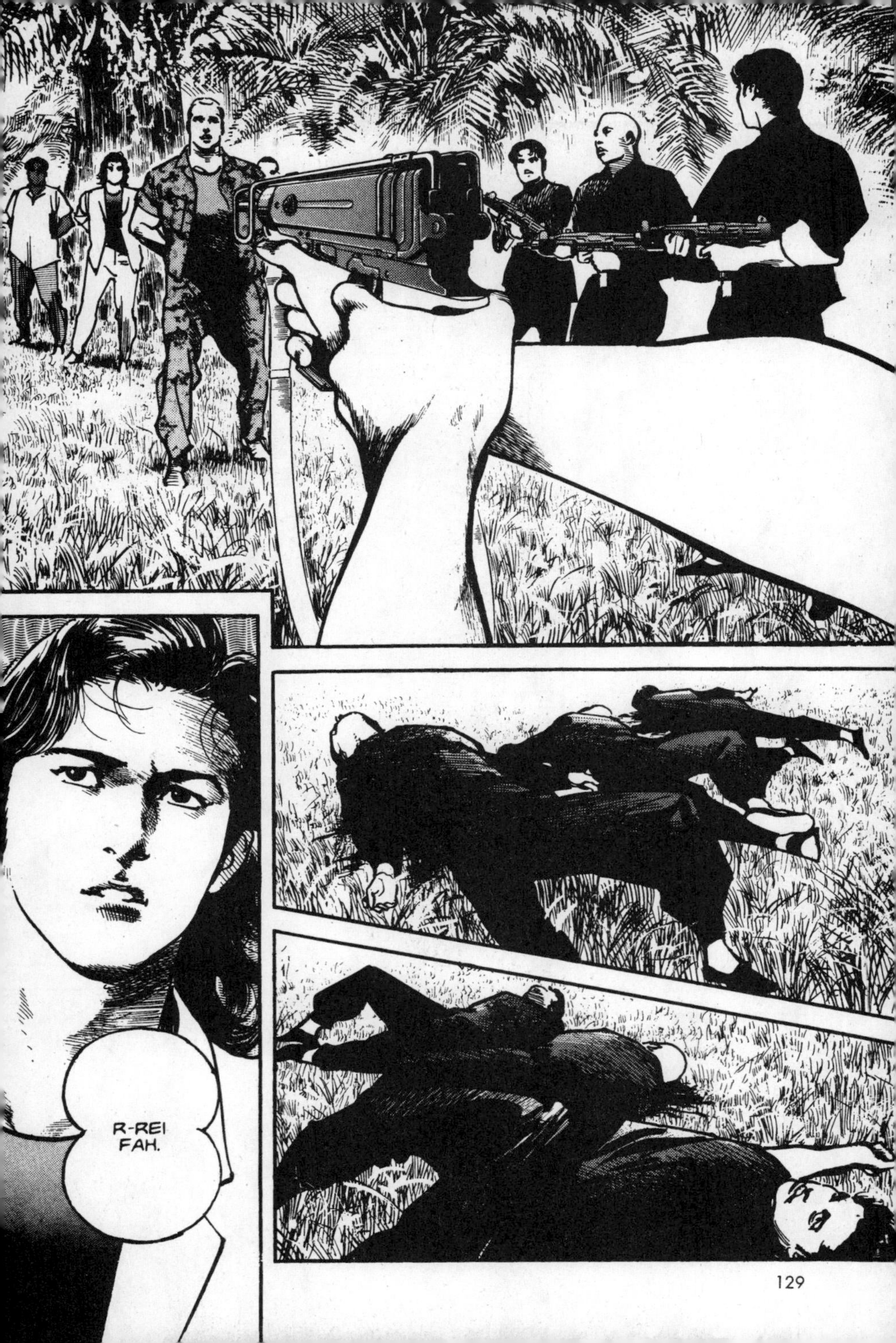
R-REI FAH.

KRICH

WHAT'S THIS ABOUT?

SOMEONE JUMPED US AND YOU ALL GOT AWAY...

FIP

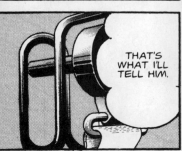

THAT'S WHAT I'LL TELL HIM.

BLAM

UNGH!

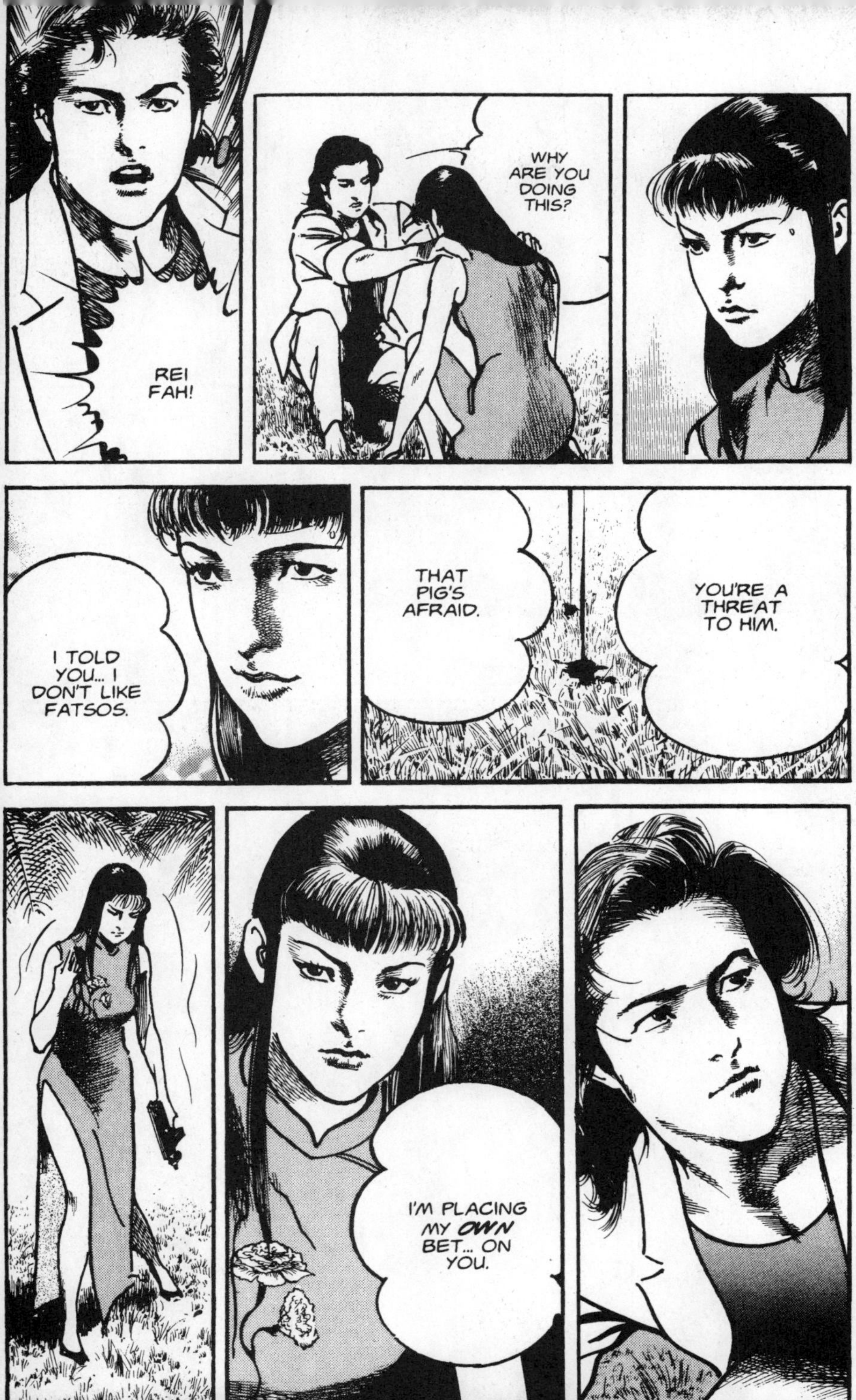
REI FAH!
WHY ARE YOU DOING THIS?
I TOLD YOU... I DON'T LIKE FATSOS.
THAT PIG'S AFRAID.
YOU'RE A THREAT TO HIM.
I'M PLACING MY OWN BET... ON YOU.

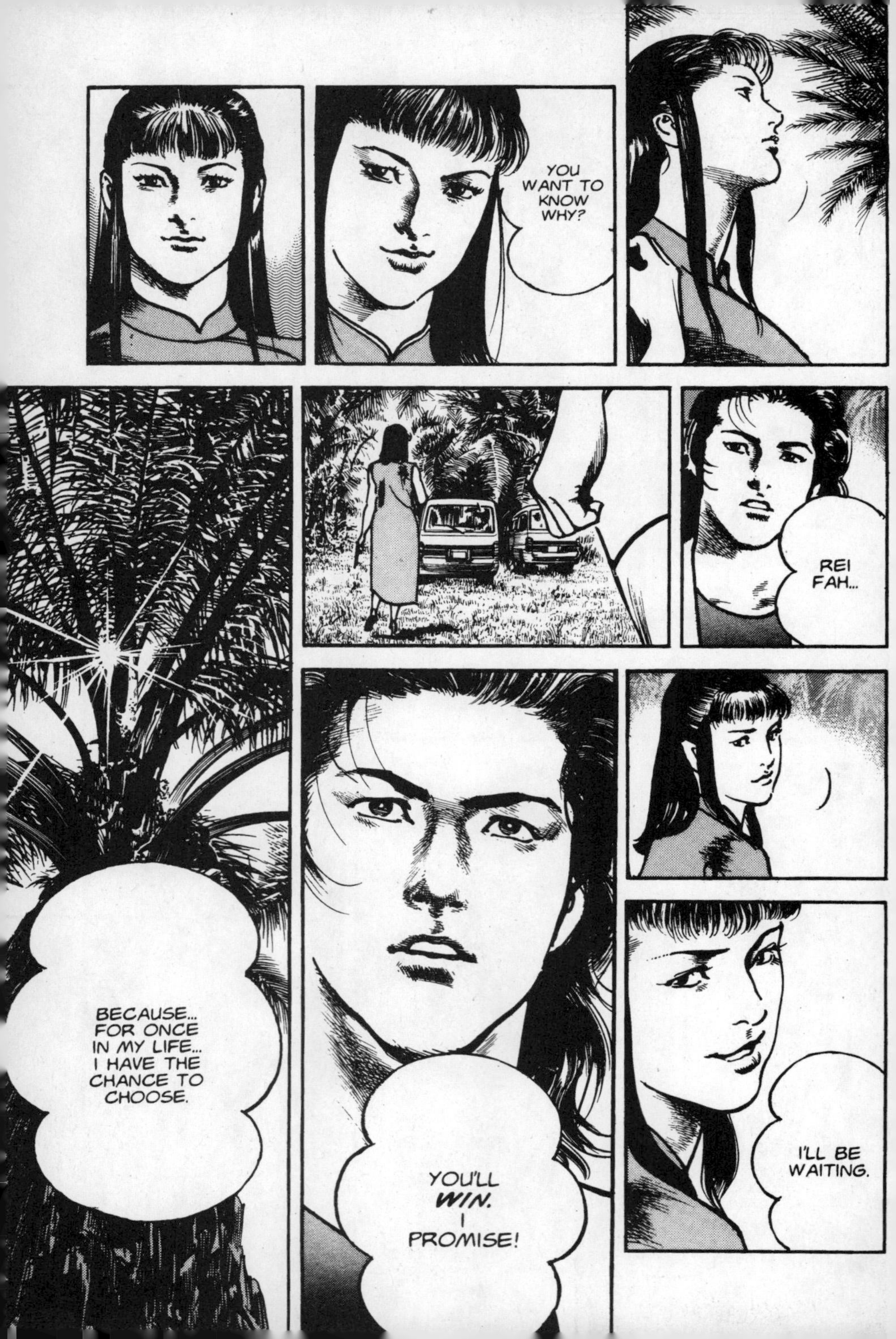
YOU WANT TO KNOW WHY?
REI FAH...
BECAUSE... FOR ONCE IN MY LIFE... I HAVE THE CHANCE TO CHOOSE.
YOU'LL *WIN.* I PROMISE!
I'LL BE WAITING.

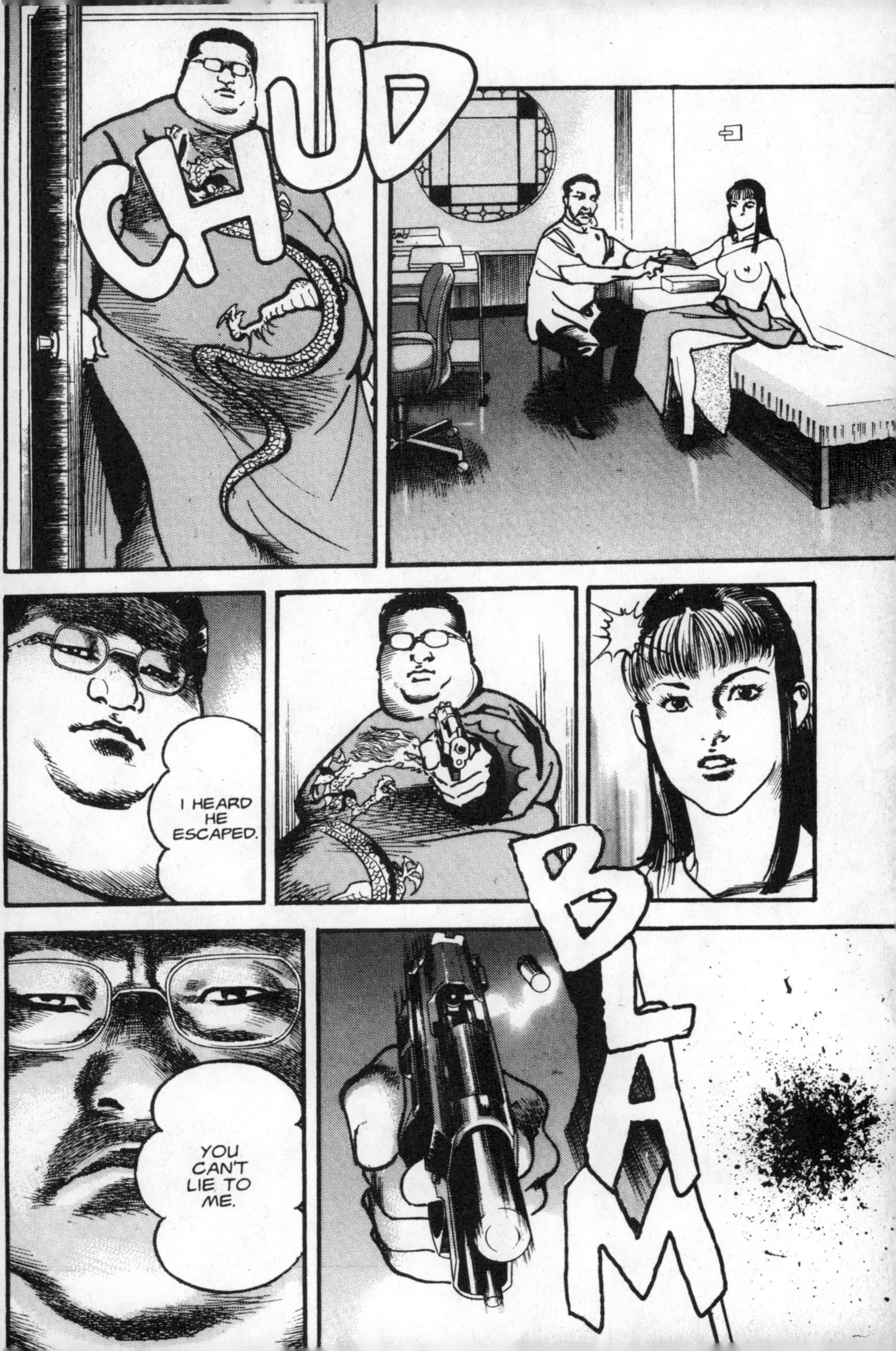
CHUD
I HEARD HE ESCAPED.
YOU CAN'T LIE TO ME.
BLAM

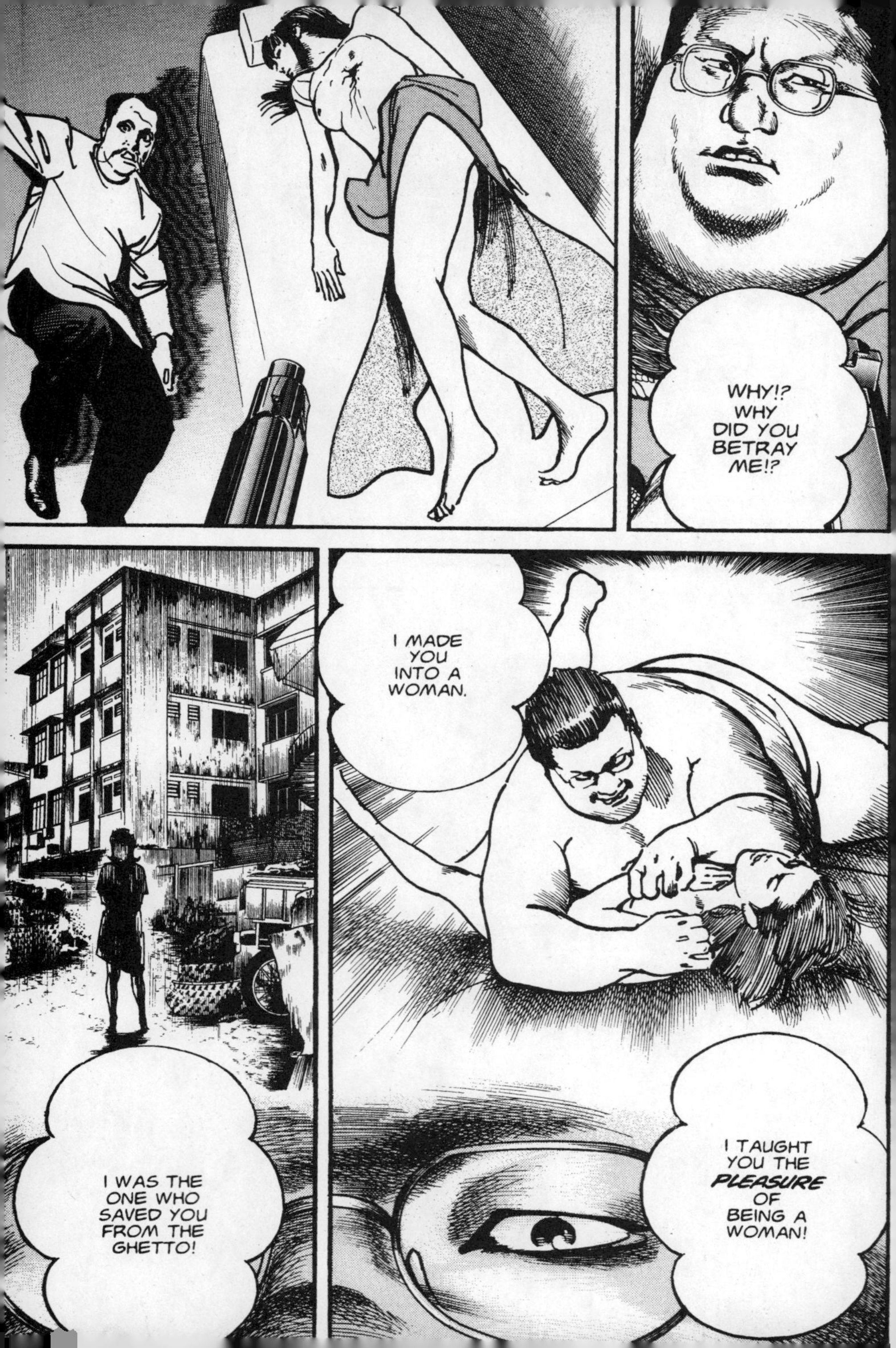
WHY!? WHY DID YOU BETRAY ME!?
I MADE YOU INTO A WOMAN.
I WAS THE ONE WHO SAVED YOU FROM THE GHETTO!
I TAUGHT YOU THE PLEASURE OF BEING A WOMAN!

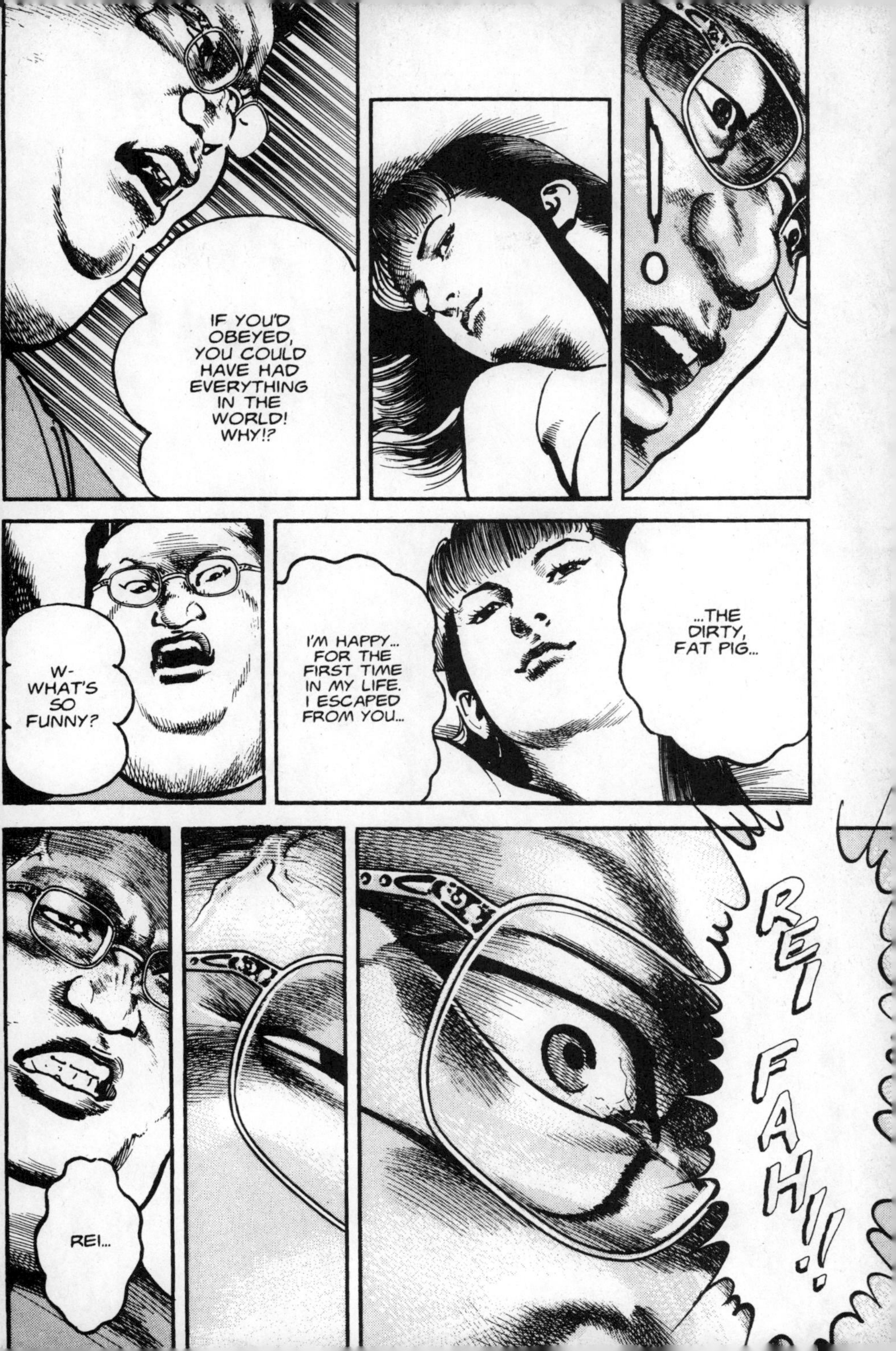
IF YOU'D OBEYED, YOU COULD HAVE HAD EVERYTHING IN THE WORLD! WHY!?
!
...THE DIRTY, FAT PIG...
I'M HAPPY... FOR THE FIRST TIME IN MY LIFE. I ESCAPED FROM YOU...
W-WHAT'S SO FUNNY?
RE!!
FAH!!
REI...

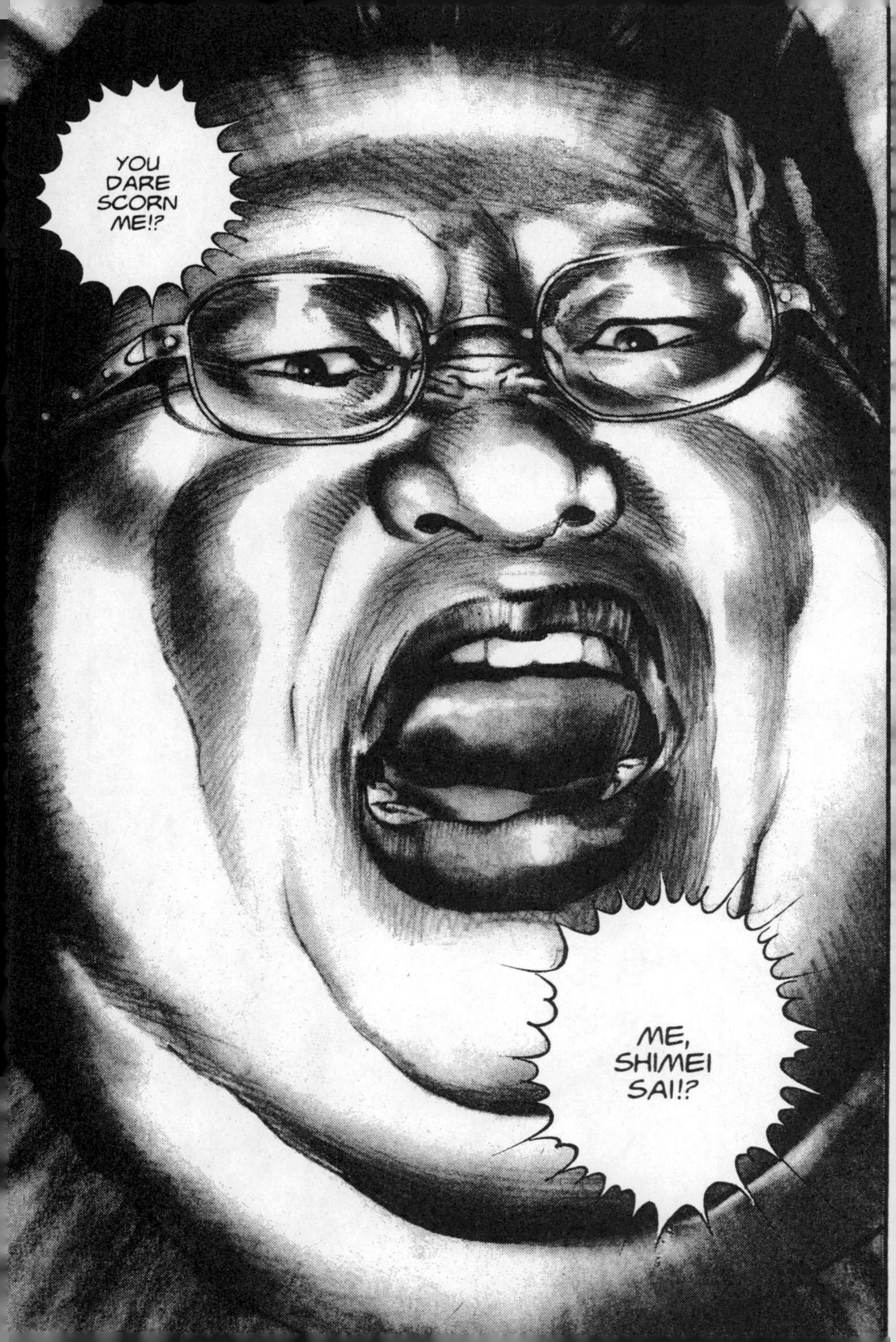
YOU DARE SCORN ME!?
ME, SHIMEI SAI!?

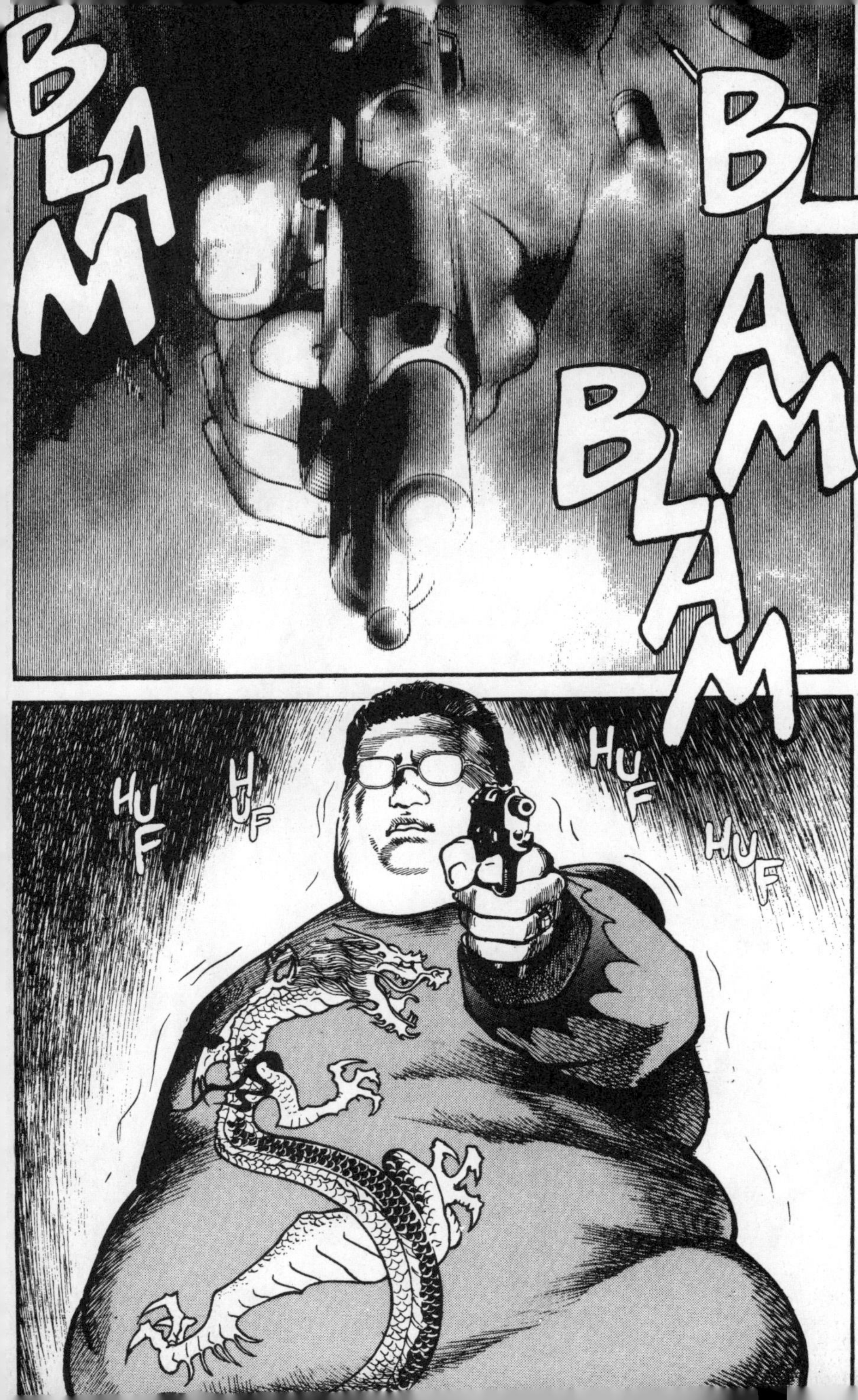
BLAM
BLAM
BLAM
BLAM
HUF HUF
HUF HUF
HUF HUF
HUF HUF

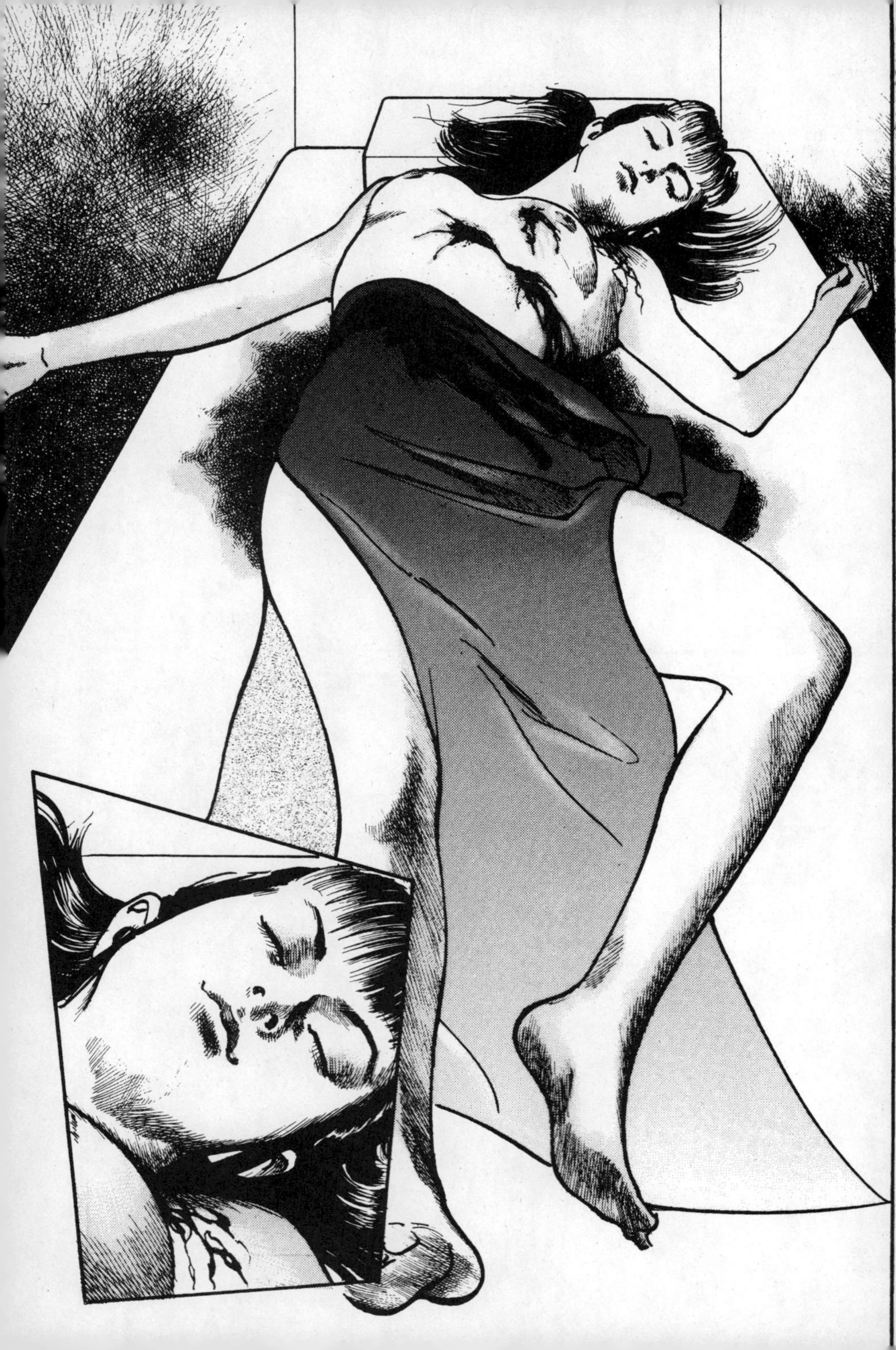

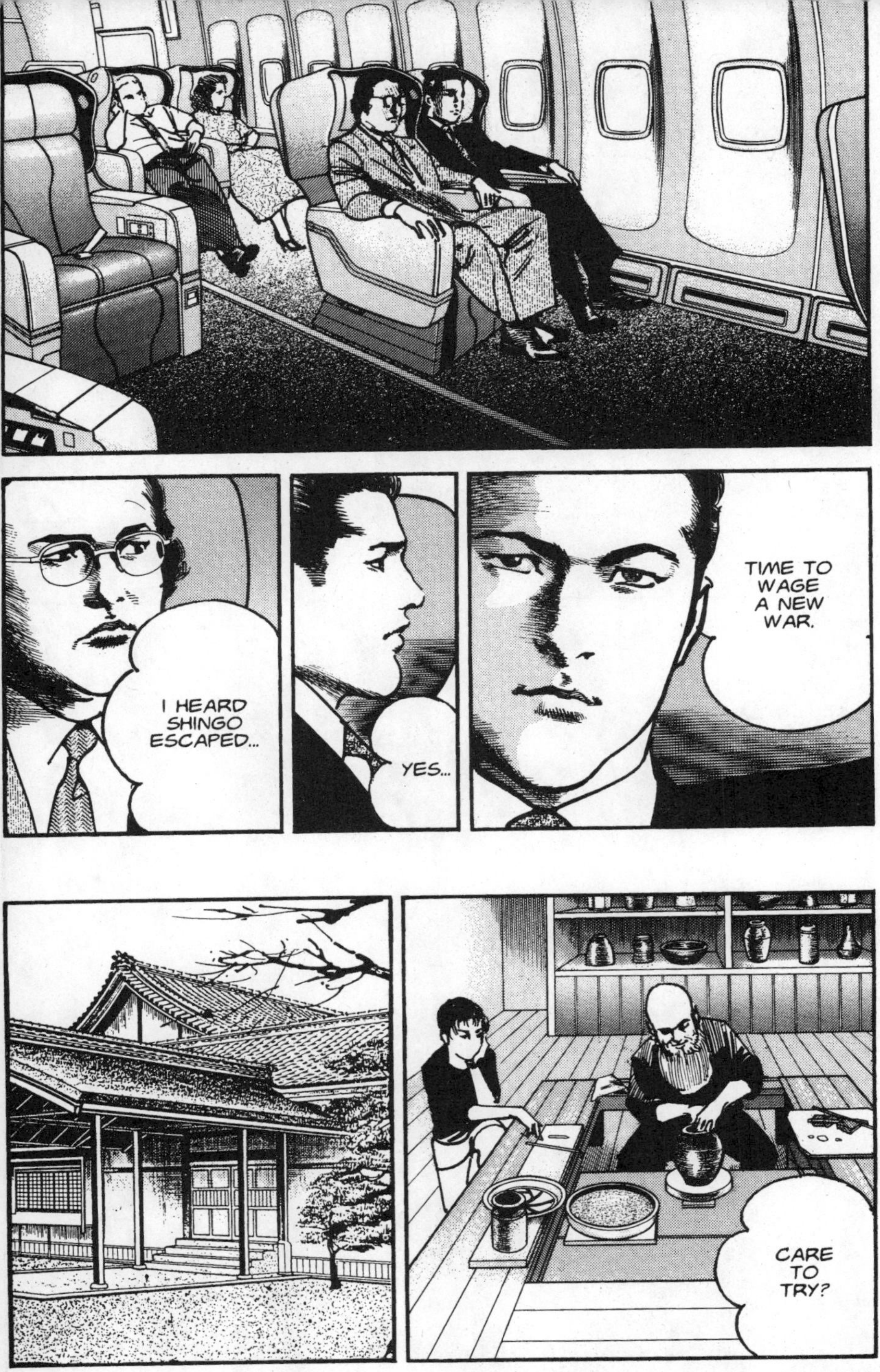
I HEARD SHINGO ESCAPED...
YES...
TIME TO WAGE A NEW WAR.
CARE TO TRY?

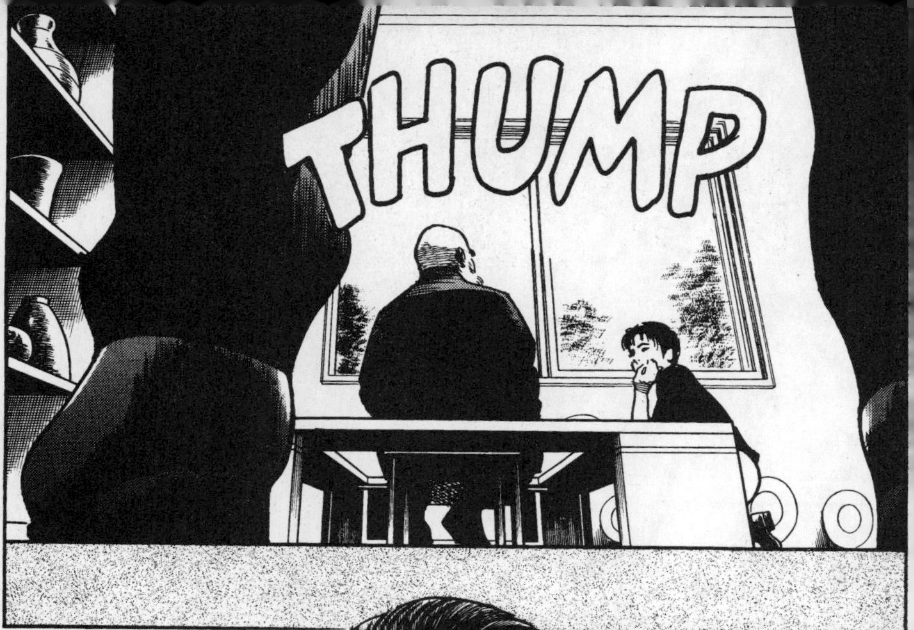
THUMP
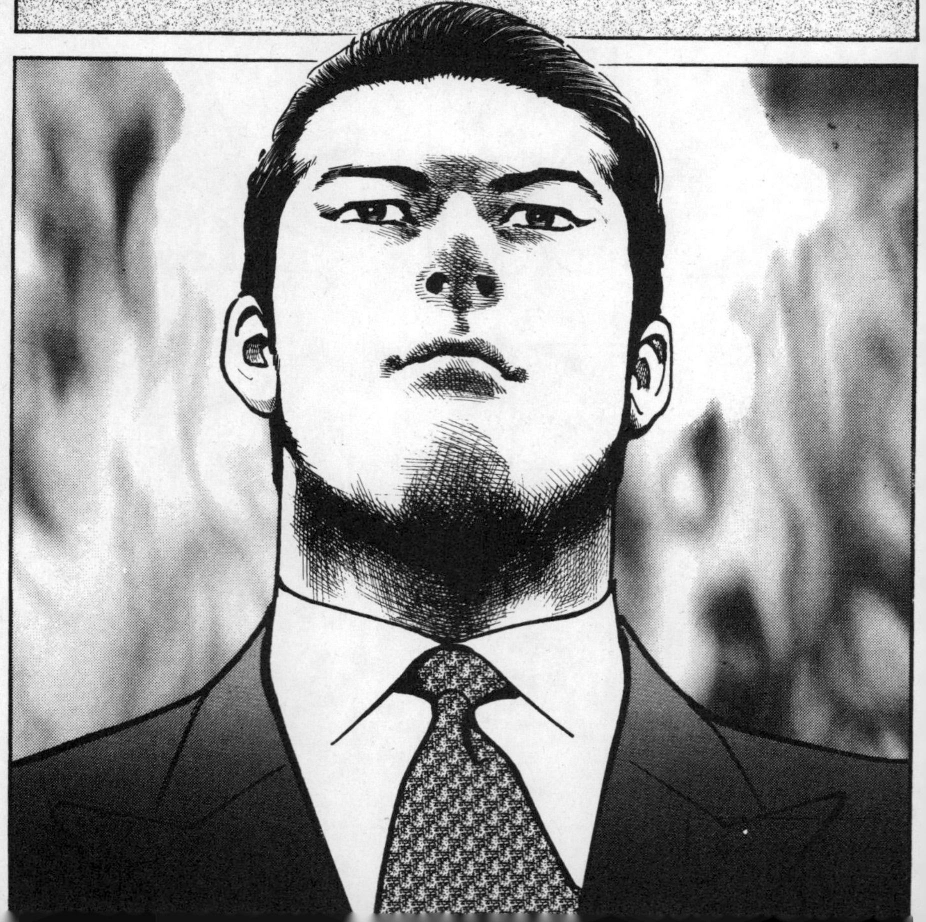

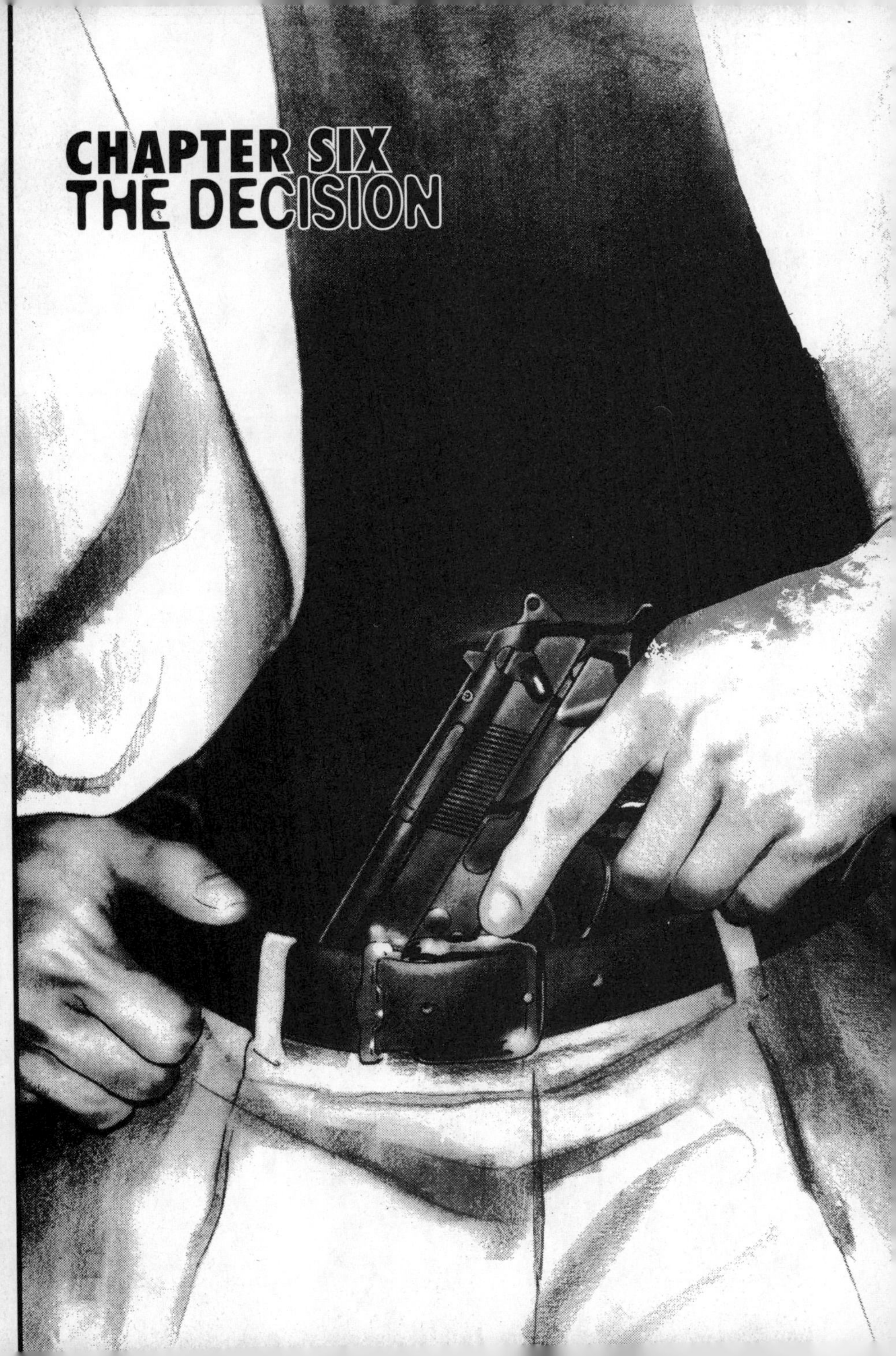
CHAPTER SIX
THE DECISION

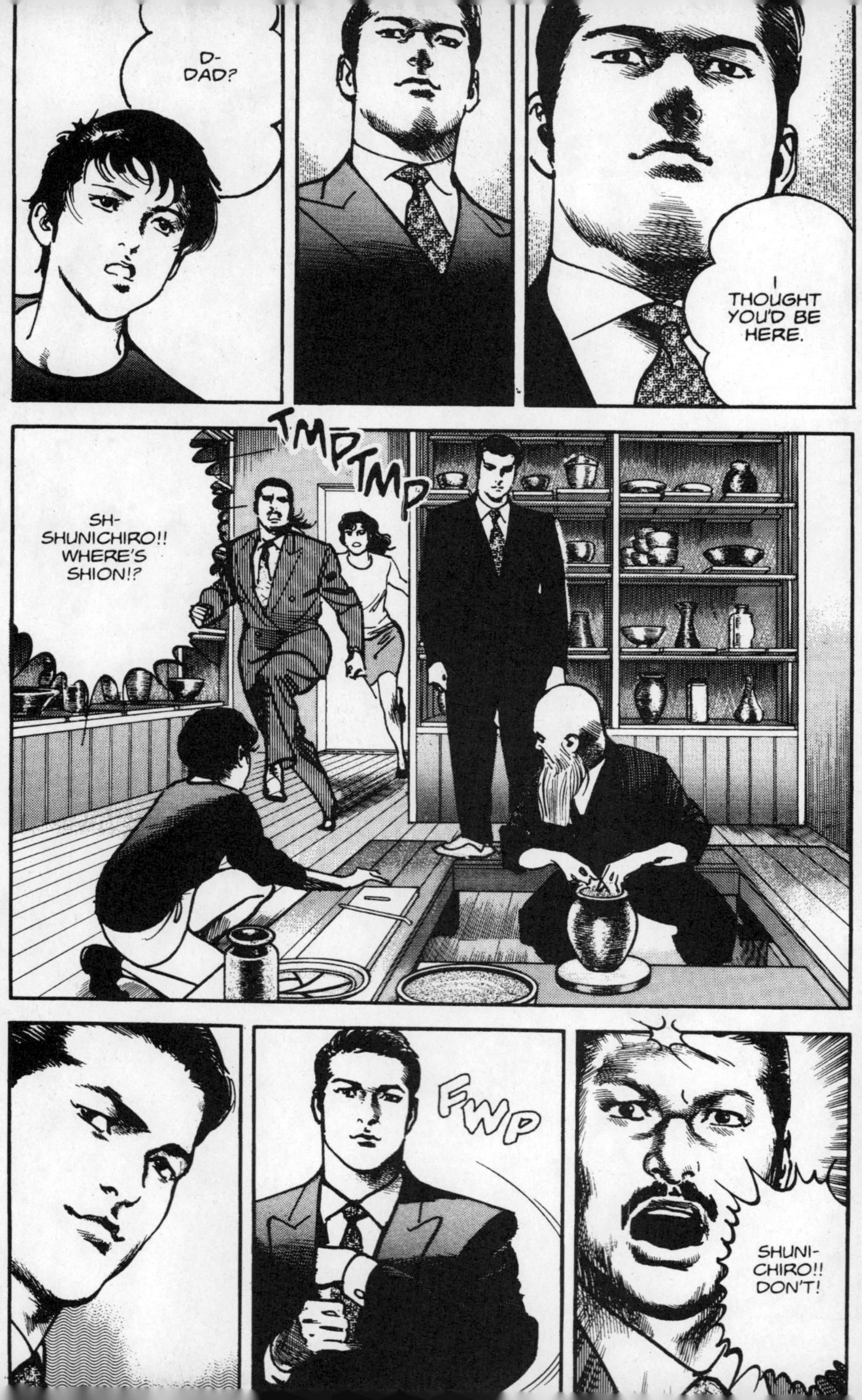
D-
DAD?
I THOUGHT YOU'D BE HERE.
TMP TMP
SH-SHUNICHIRO!! WHERE'S SHION!?
FWP
SHUNI-CHIRO!! DON'T!

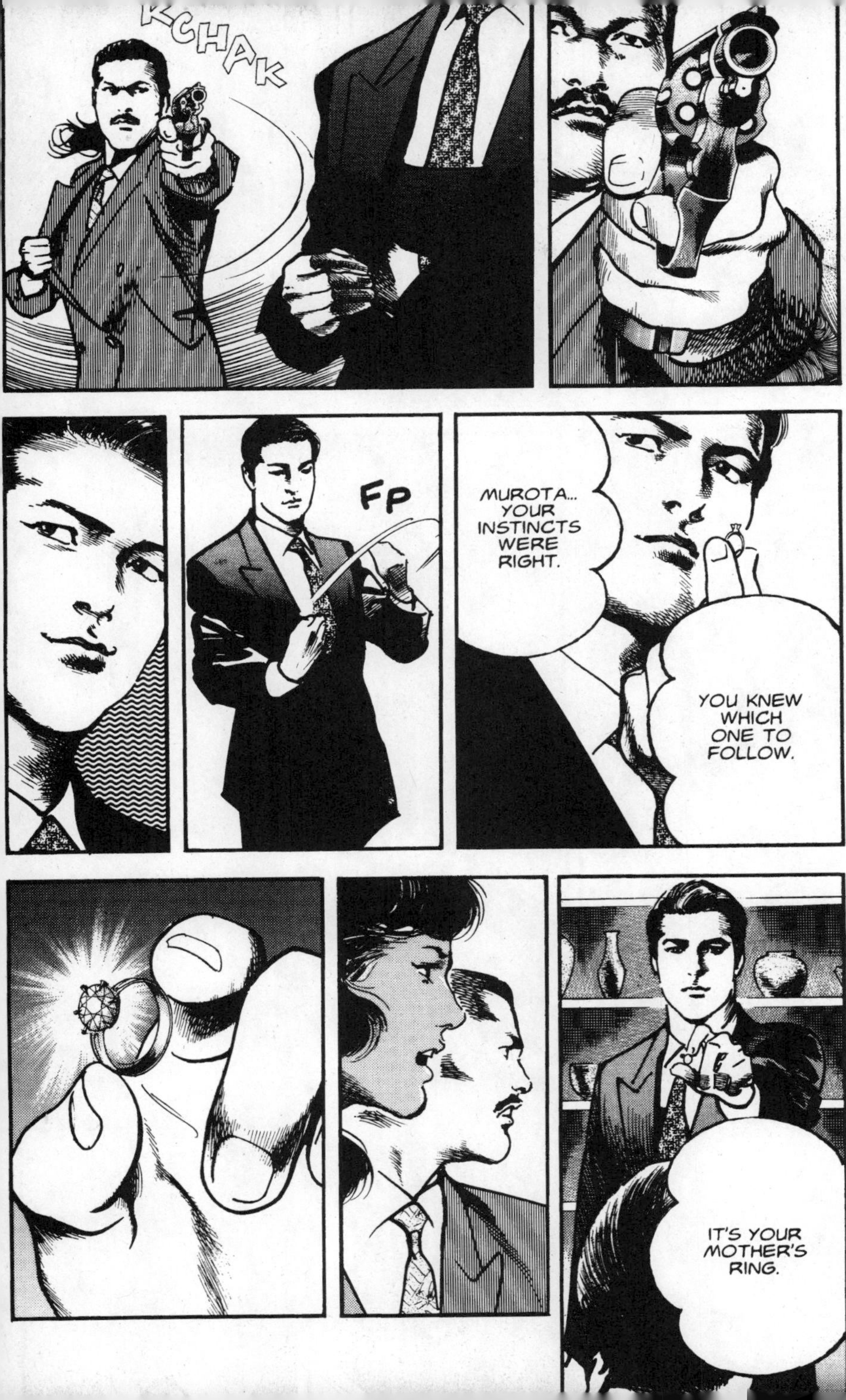
KCHAK
FP
MUROTA... YOUR INSTINCTS WERE RIGHT.
YOU KNEW WHICH ONE TO FOLLOW.
IT'S YOUR MOTHER'S RING.

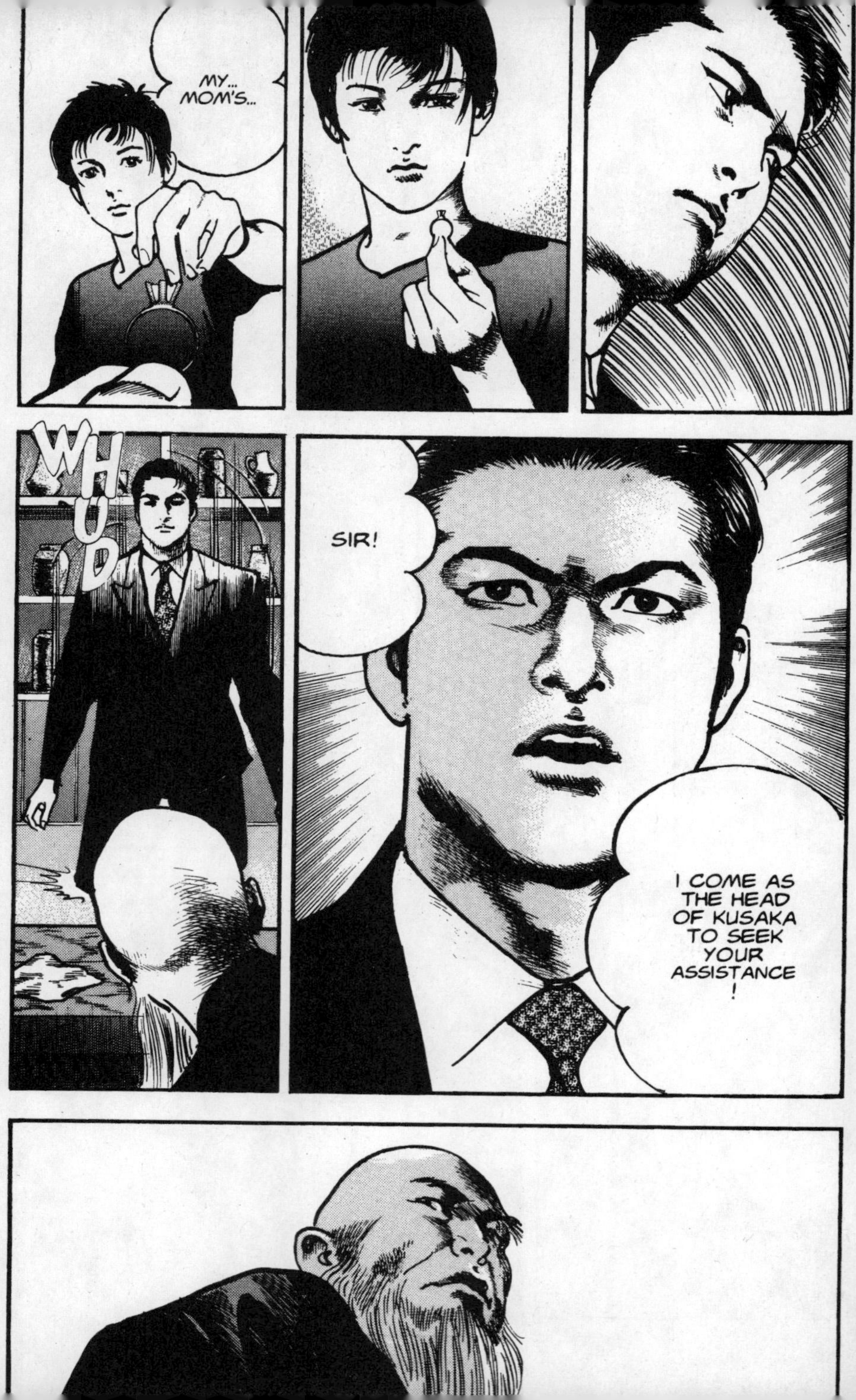
MY... MOM'S...
WHUD
SIR!
I COME AS THE HEAD OF KUSAKA TO SEEK YOUR ASSISTANCE!

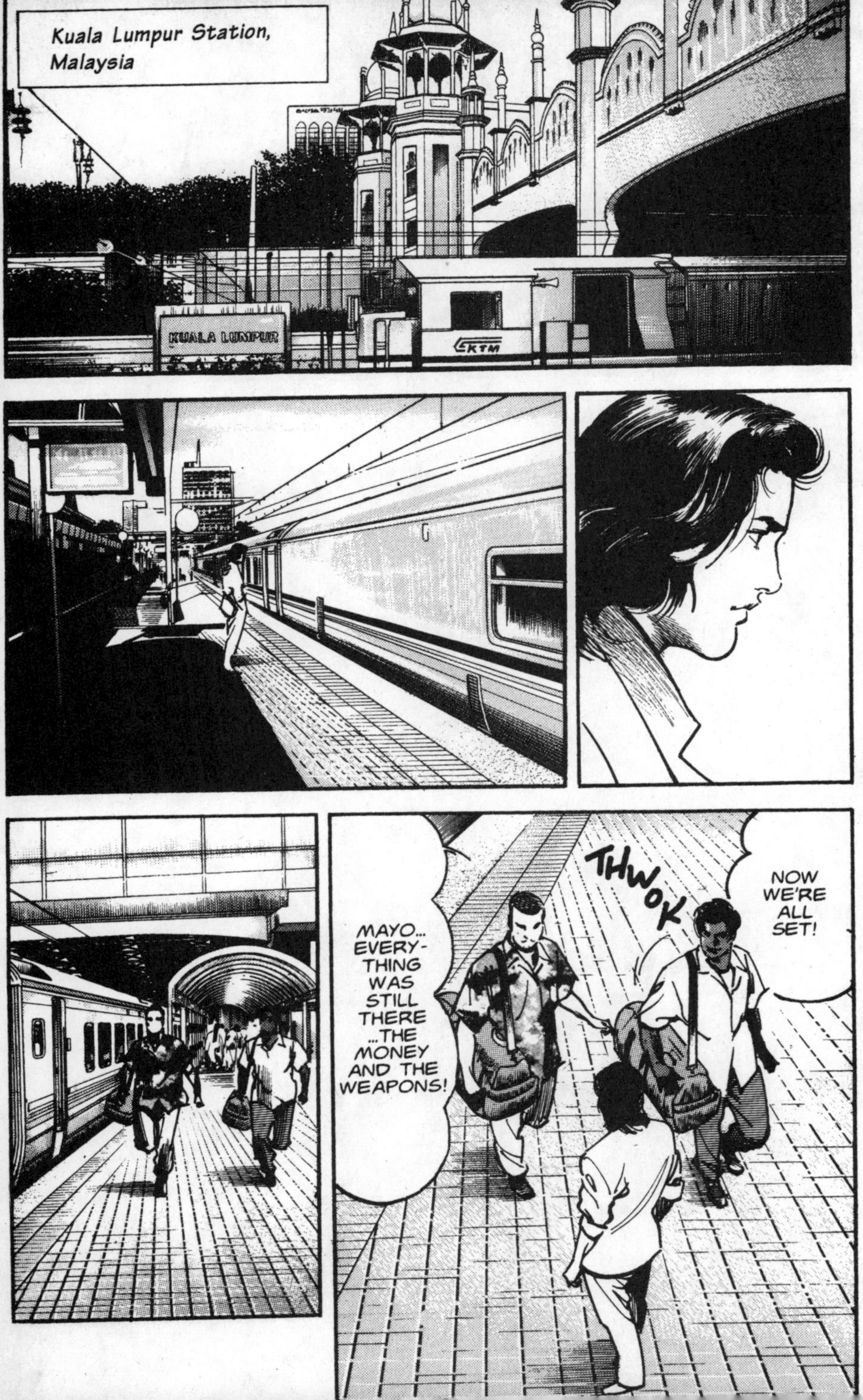
Kuala Lumpur Station, Malaysia
KUALA LUMPUR
KTM
MAYO... EVERY-THING WAS STILL THERE ...THE MONEY AND THE WEAPONS!
THWOK
NOW WE'RE ALL SET!

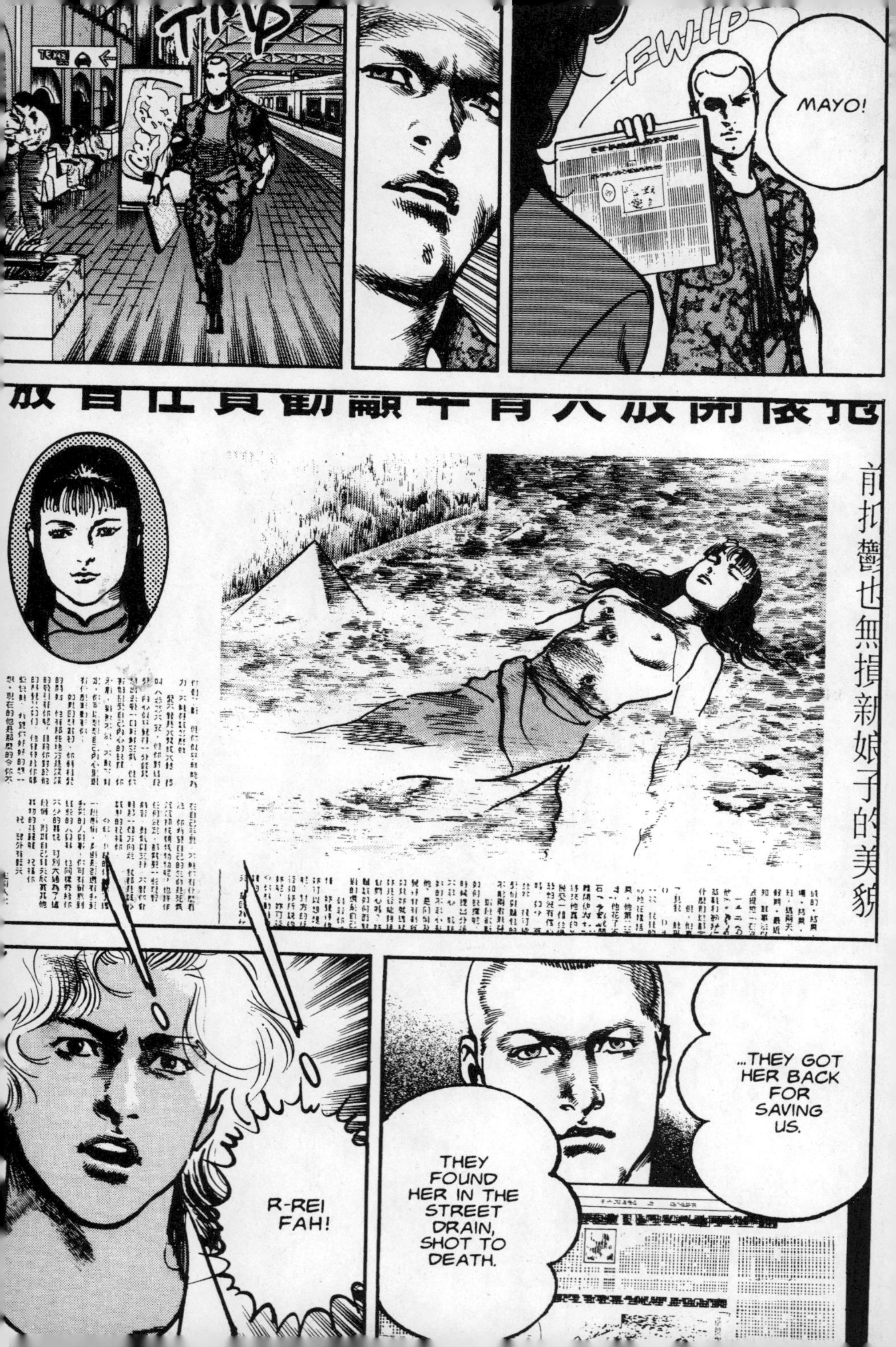
TIP
FWIP
MAYO!
R-REI FAH!
THEY FOUND HER IN THE STREET DRAIN, SHOT TO DEATH.
...THEY GOT HER BACK FOR SAVING US.

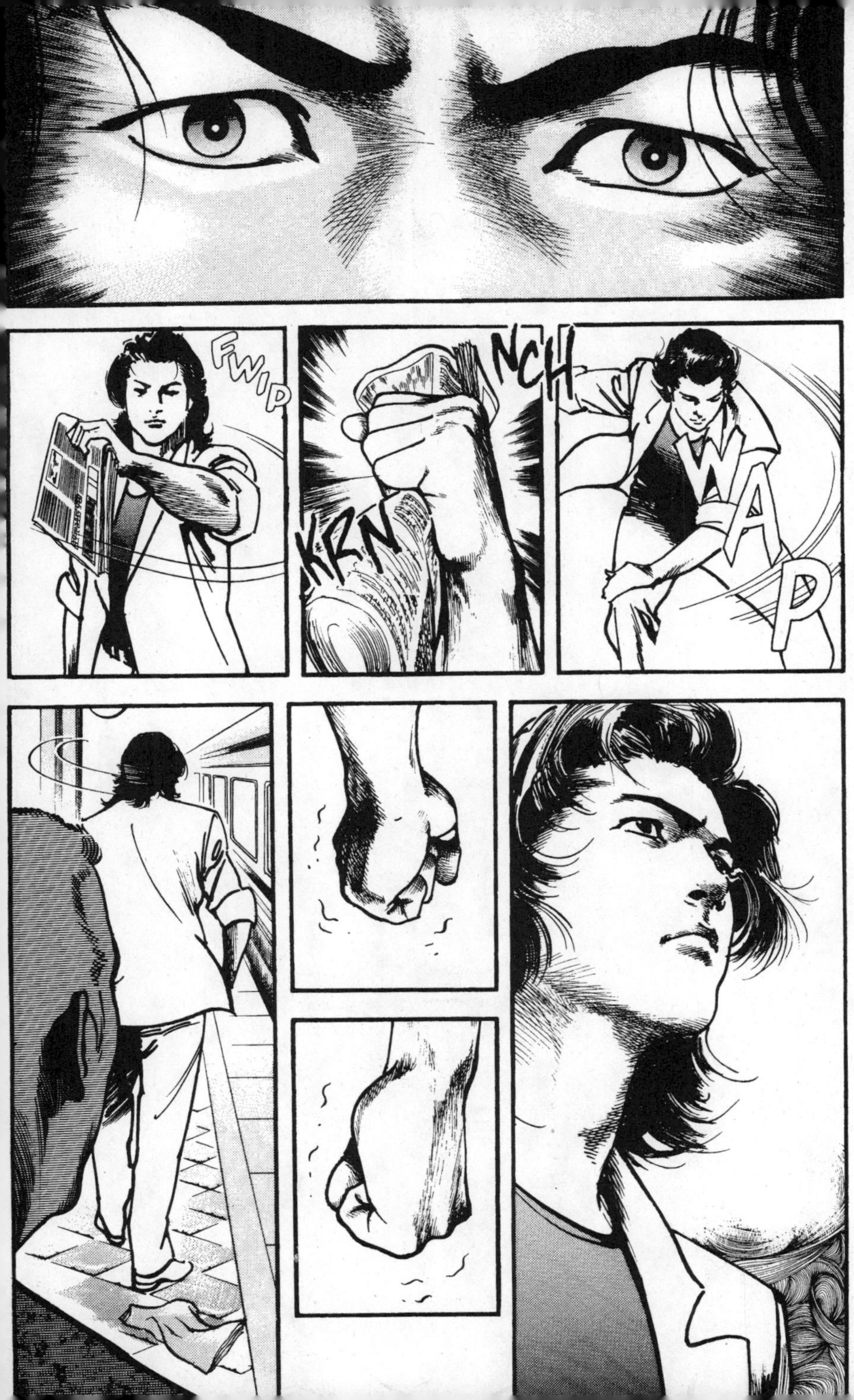
FWIP
KRN
NCH
WAP

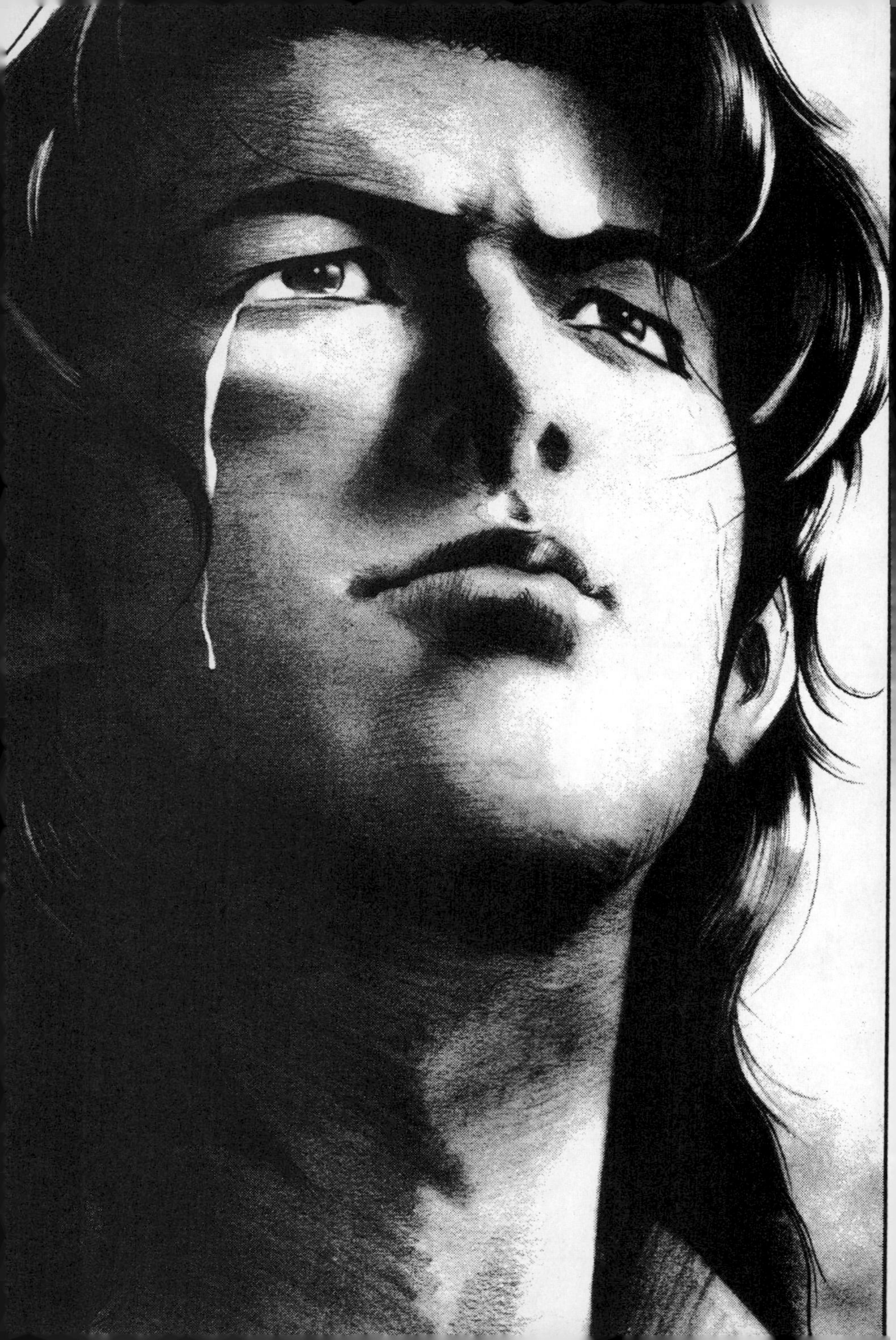

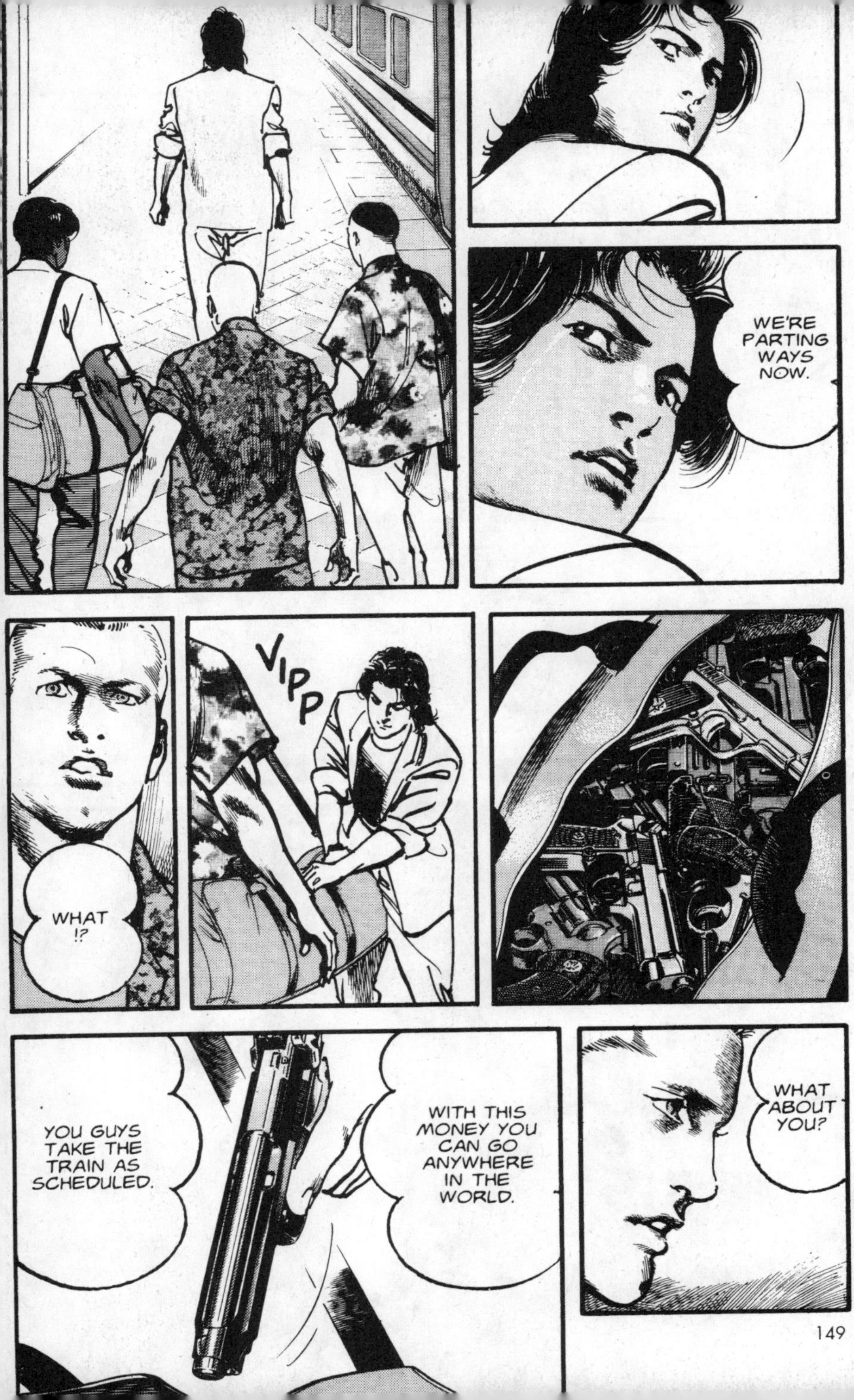
WE'RE PARTING WAYS NOW.
WHAT !?
VIPP
YOU GUYS TAKE THE TRAIN AS SCHEDULED.
WITH THIS MONEY YOU CAN GO ANYWHERE IN THE WORLD.
WHAT ABOUT YOU?

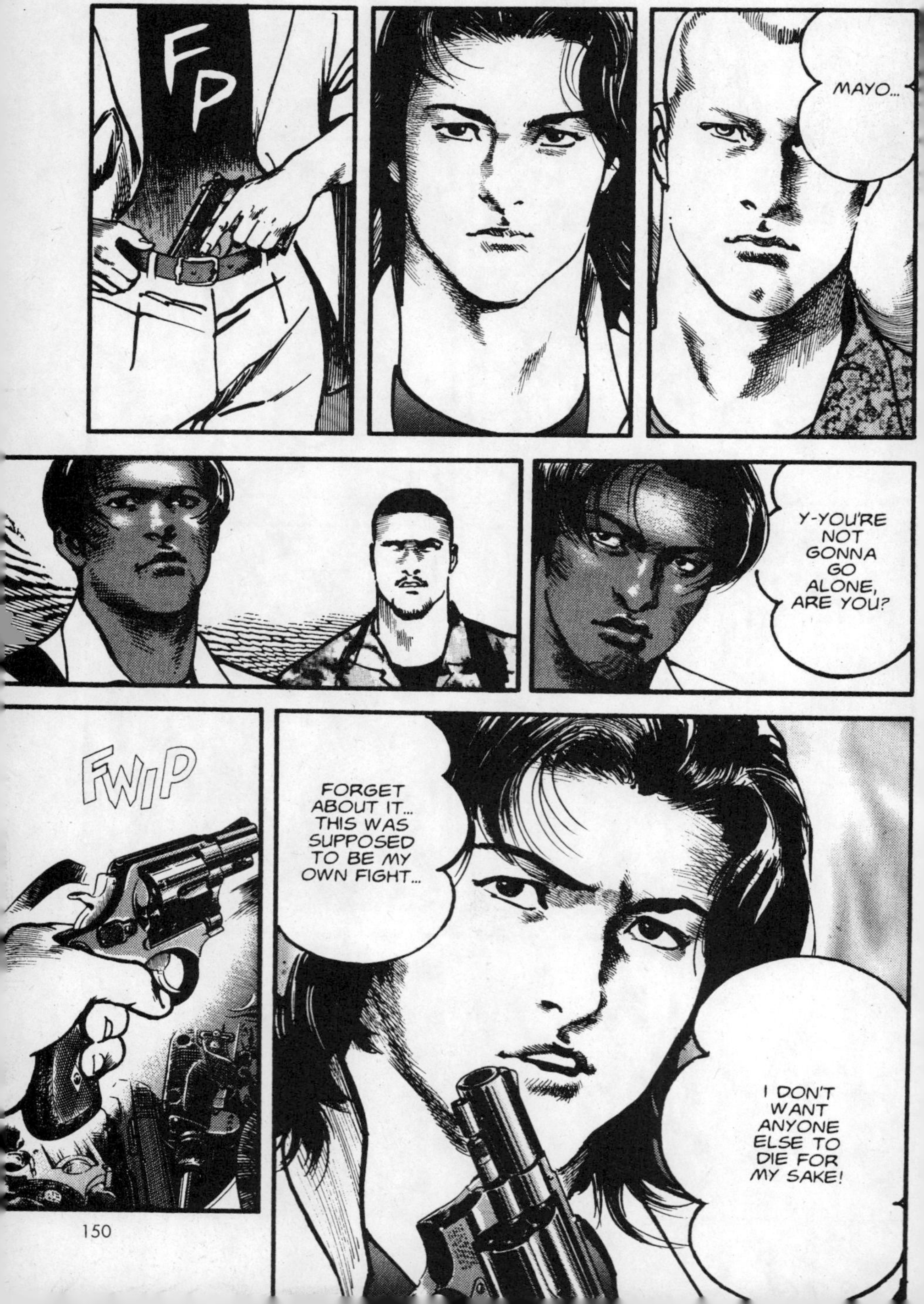
FP
MAYO...
Y-YOU'RE NOT GONNA GO ALONE, ARE YOU?
FWIP
FORGET ABOUT IT... THIS WAS SUPPOSED TO BE MY OWN FIGHT...
I DON'T WANT ANYONE ELSE TO DIE FOR MY SAKE!

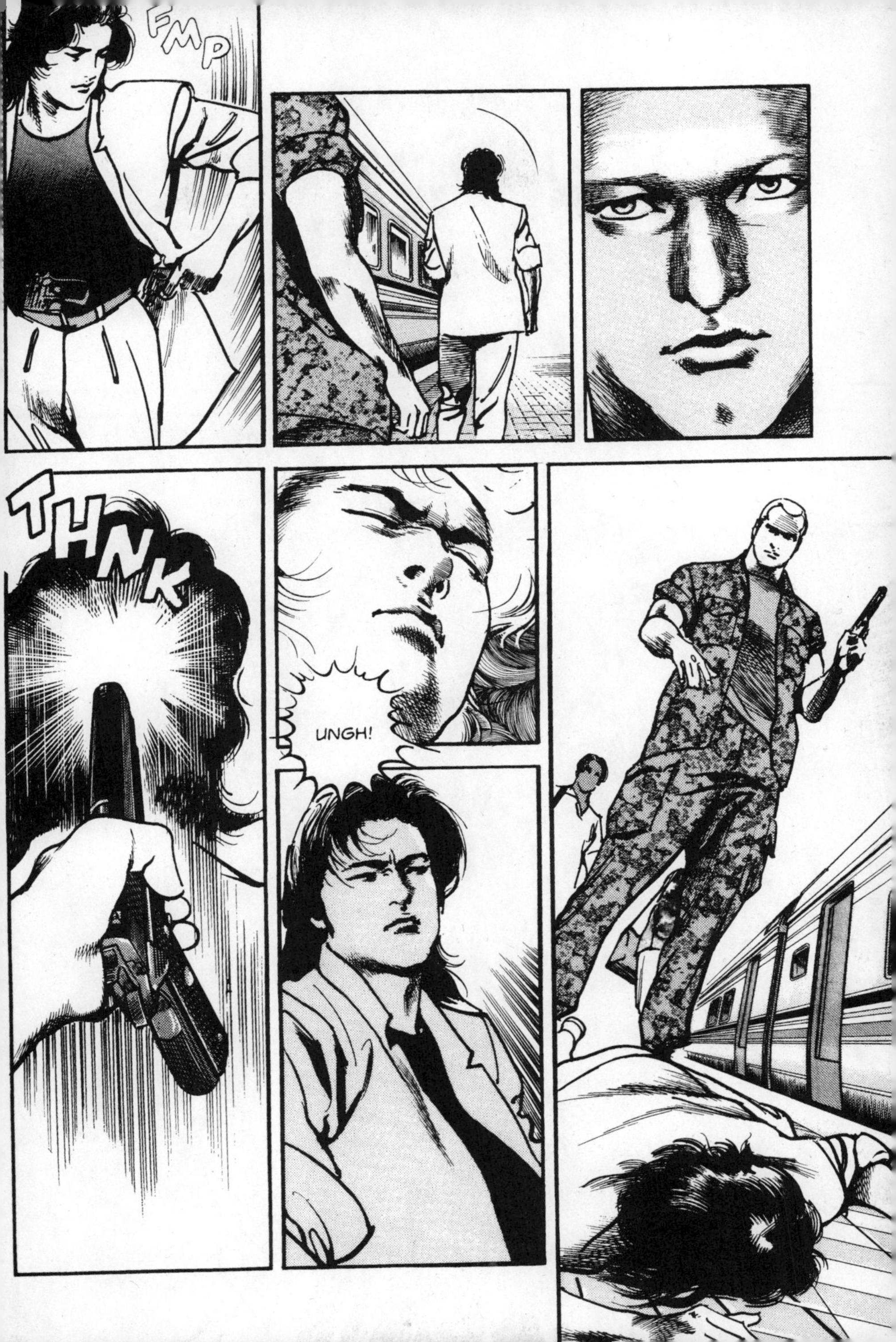
FMP
THNK
UNGH!

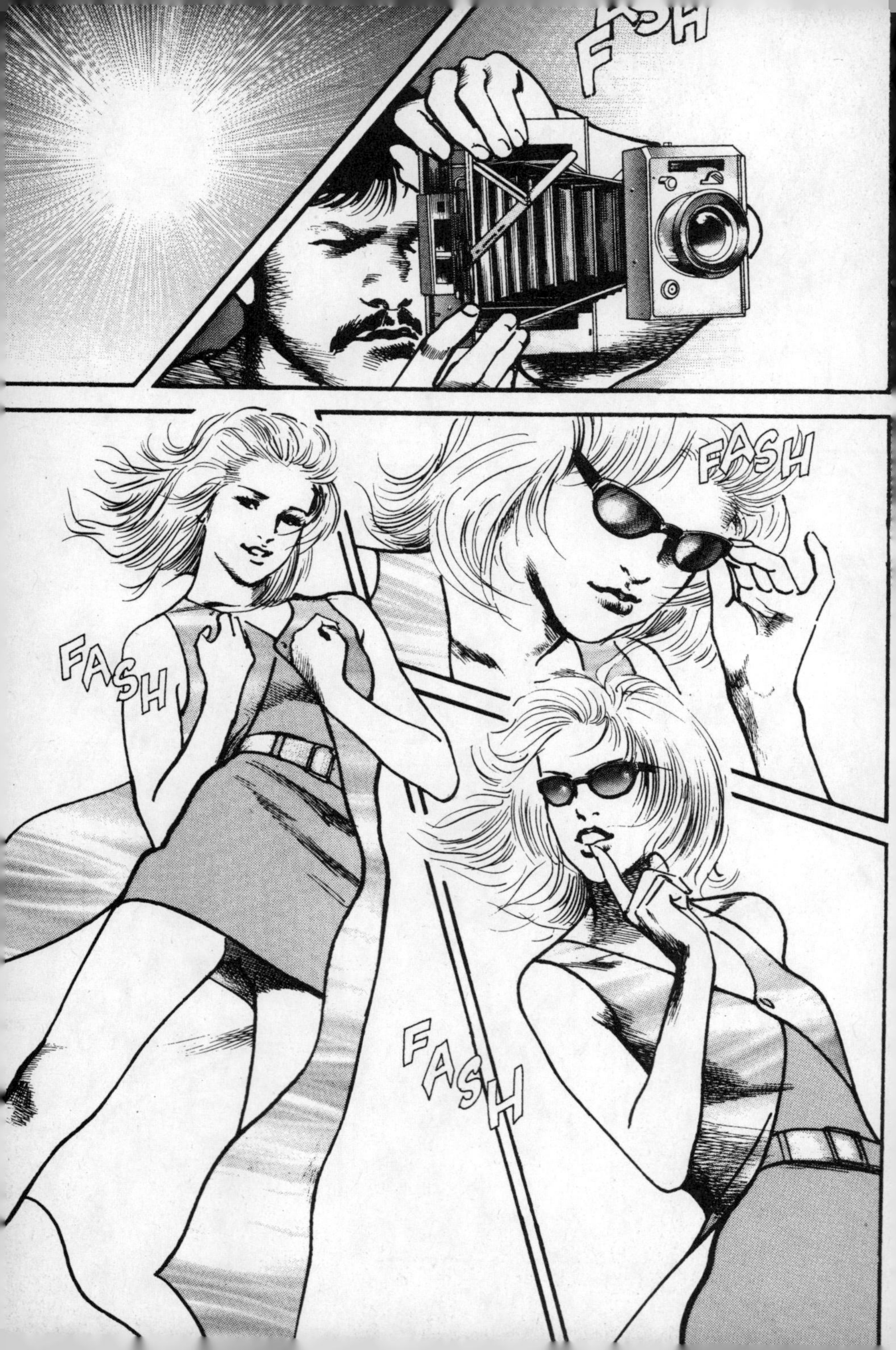
FASH
FASH
FASH
FASH

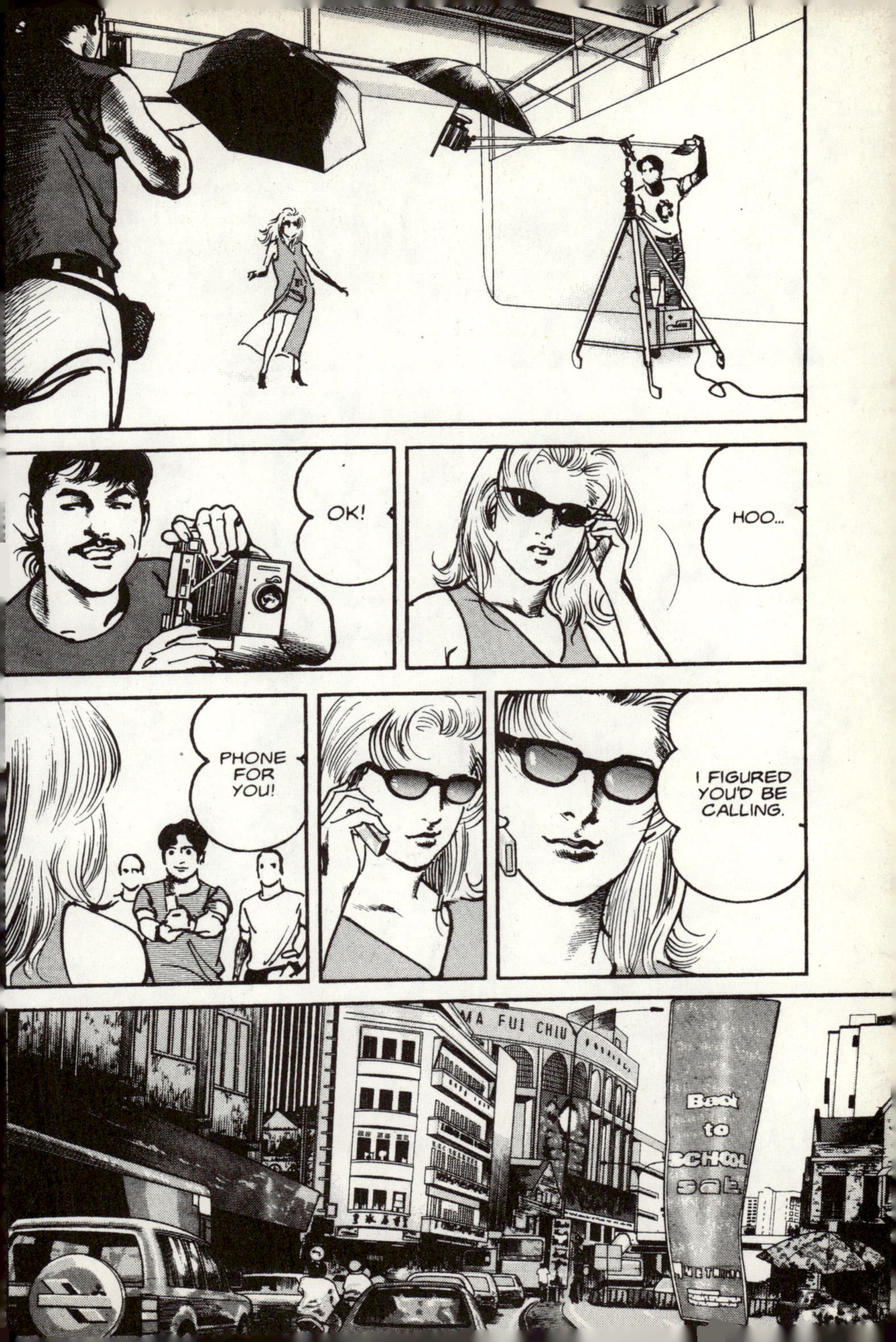
OK!
HOO...
PHONE FOR YOU!
I FIGURED YOU'D BE CALLING.
MA FUI CHIU
Back to SCHOOL sale

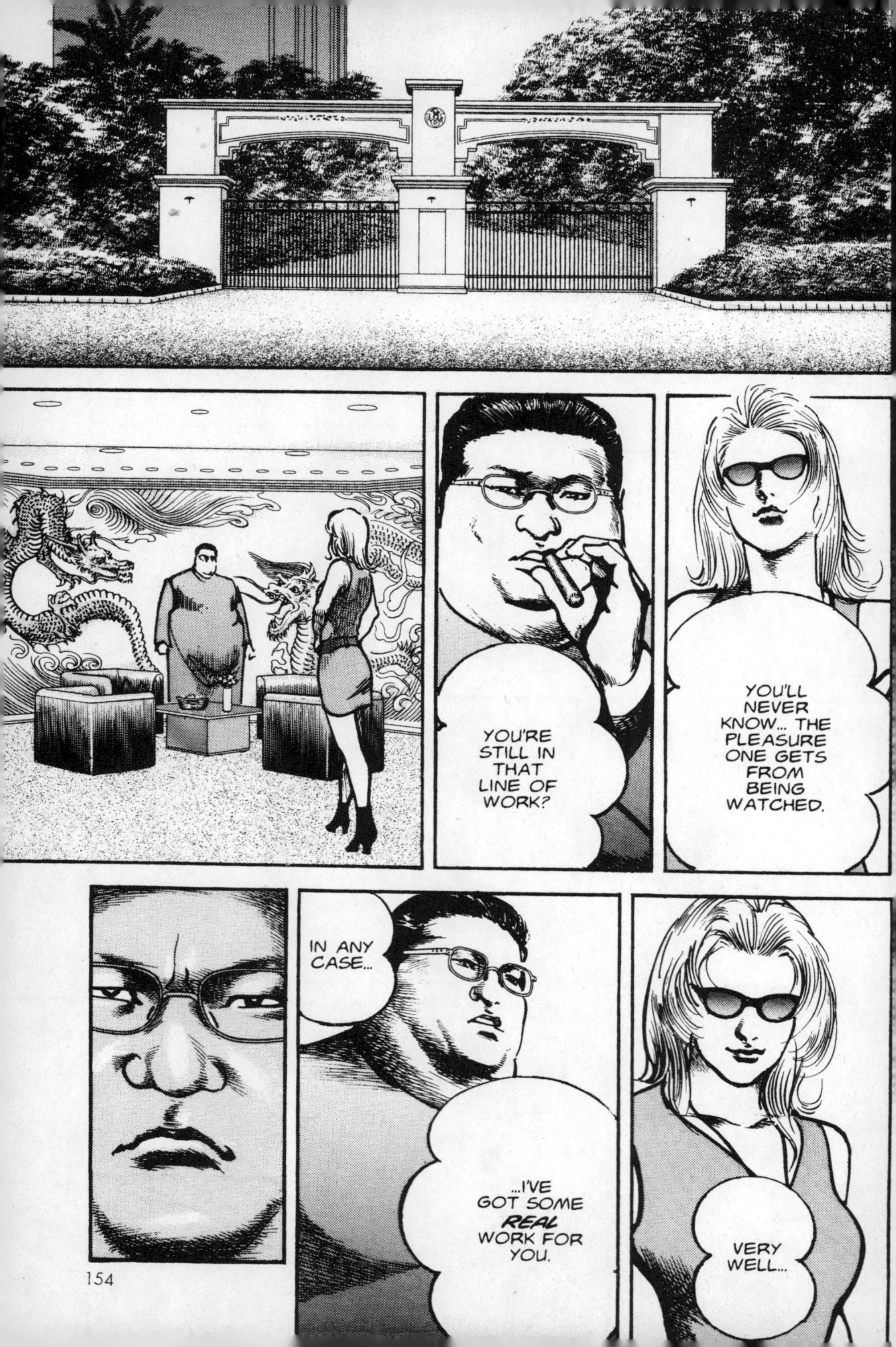

YOU'RE STILL IN THAT LINE OF WORK?
YOU'LL NEVER KNOW... THE PLEASURE ONE GETS FROM BEING WATCHED.
IN ANY CASE...
...I'VE GOT SOME *REAL* WORK FOR YOU.
VERY WELL...

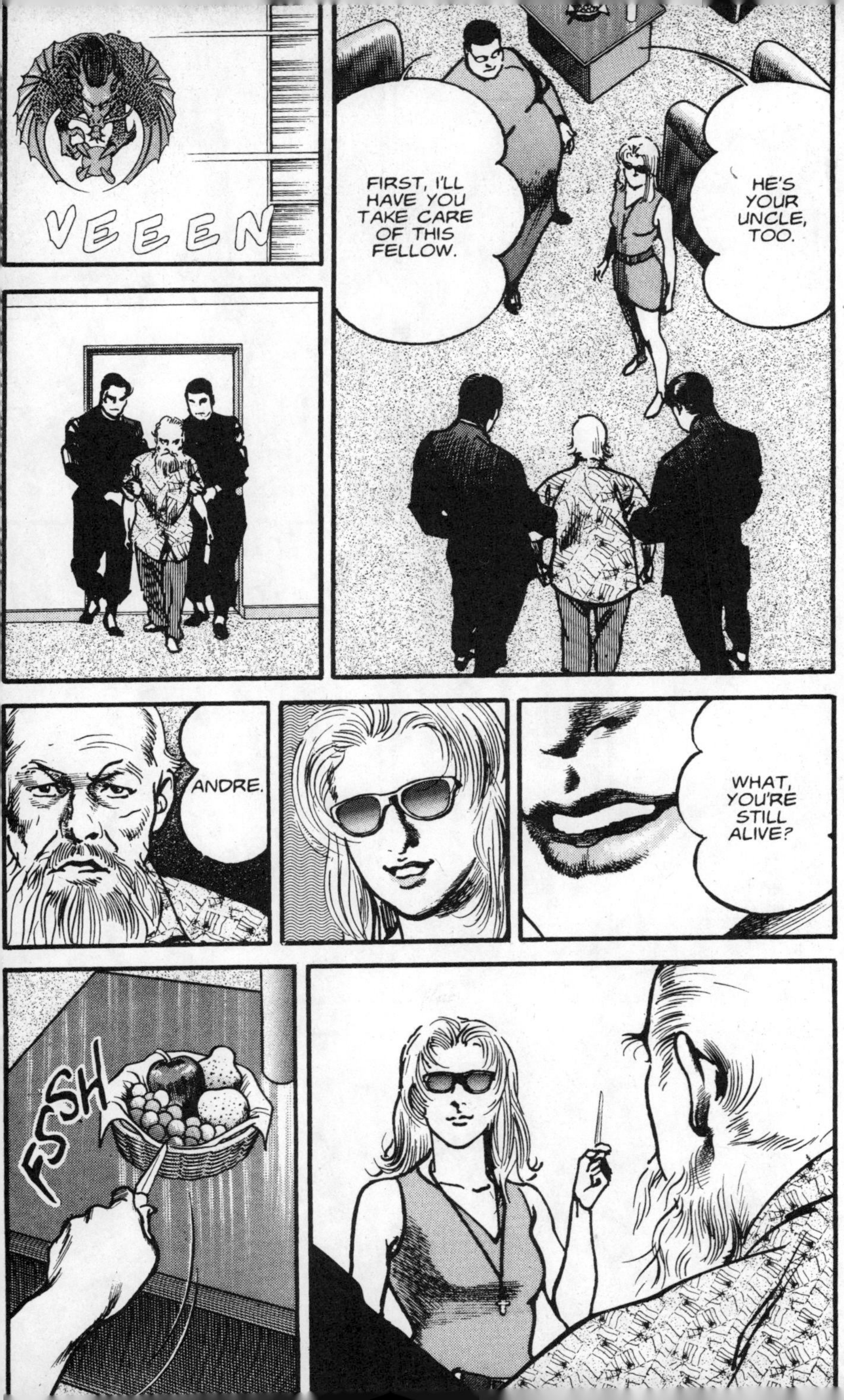
VEEEN
FIRST, I'LL HAVE YOU TAKE CARE OF THIS FELLOW.
HE'S YOUR UNCLE, TOO.
ANDRE.
WHAT, YOU'RE STILL ALIVE?
FSSH

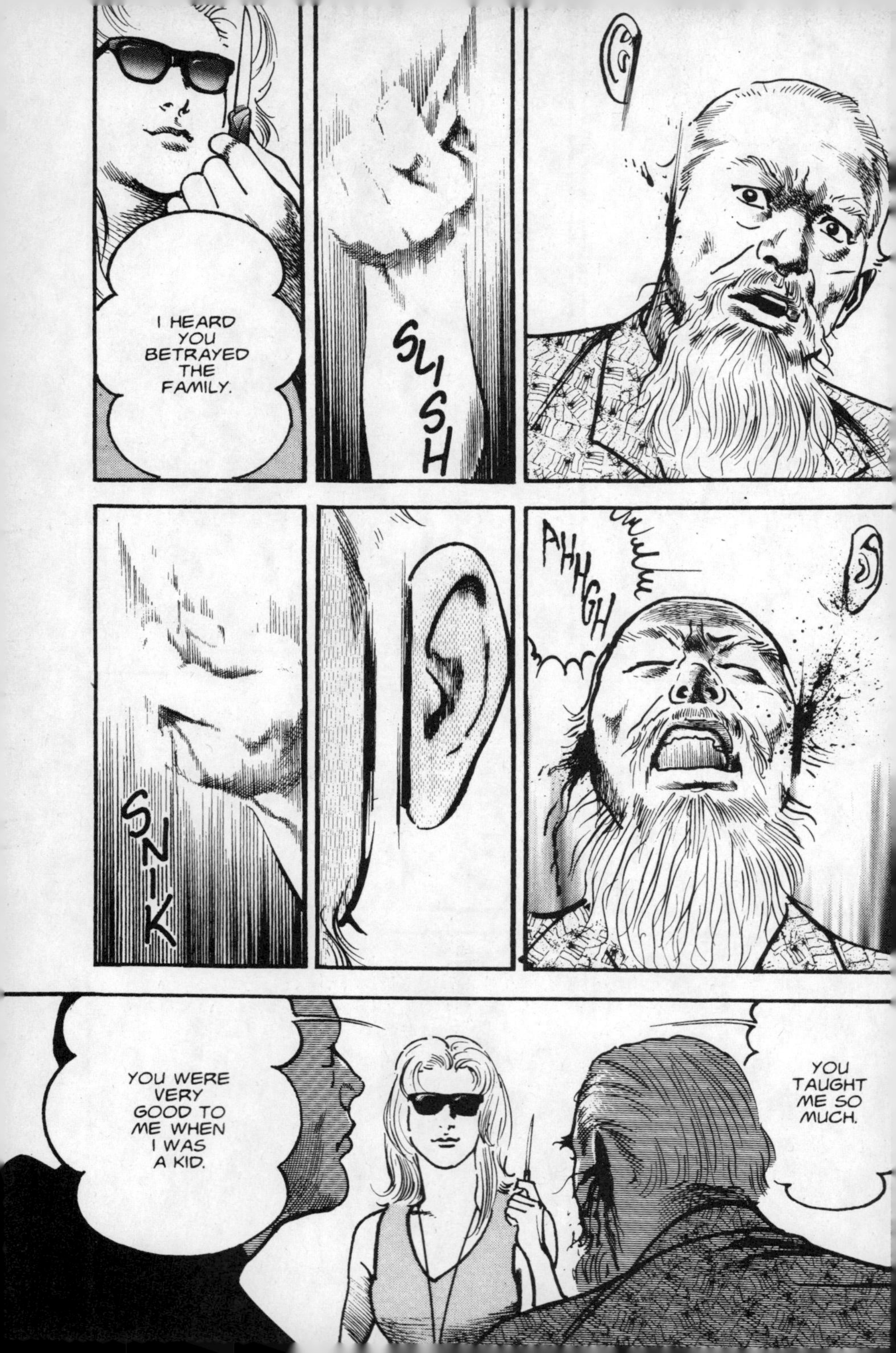
I HEARD YOU BETRAYED THE FAMILY.
SLISH
SNIK
PHHGH
YOU WERE VERY GOOD TO ME WHEN I WAS A KID.
YOU TAUGHT ME SO MUCH.

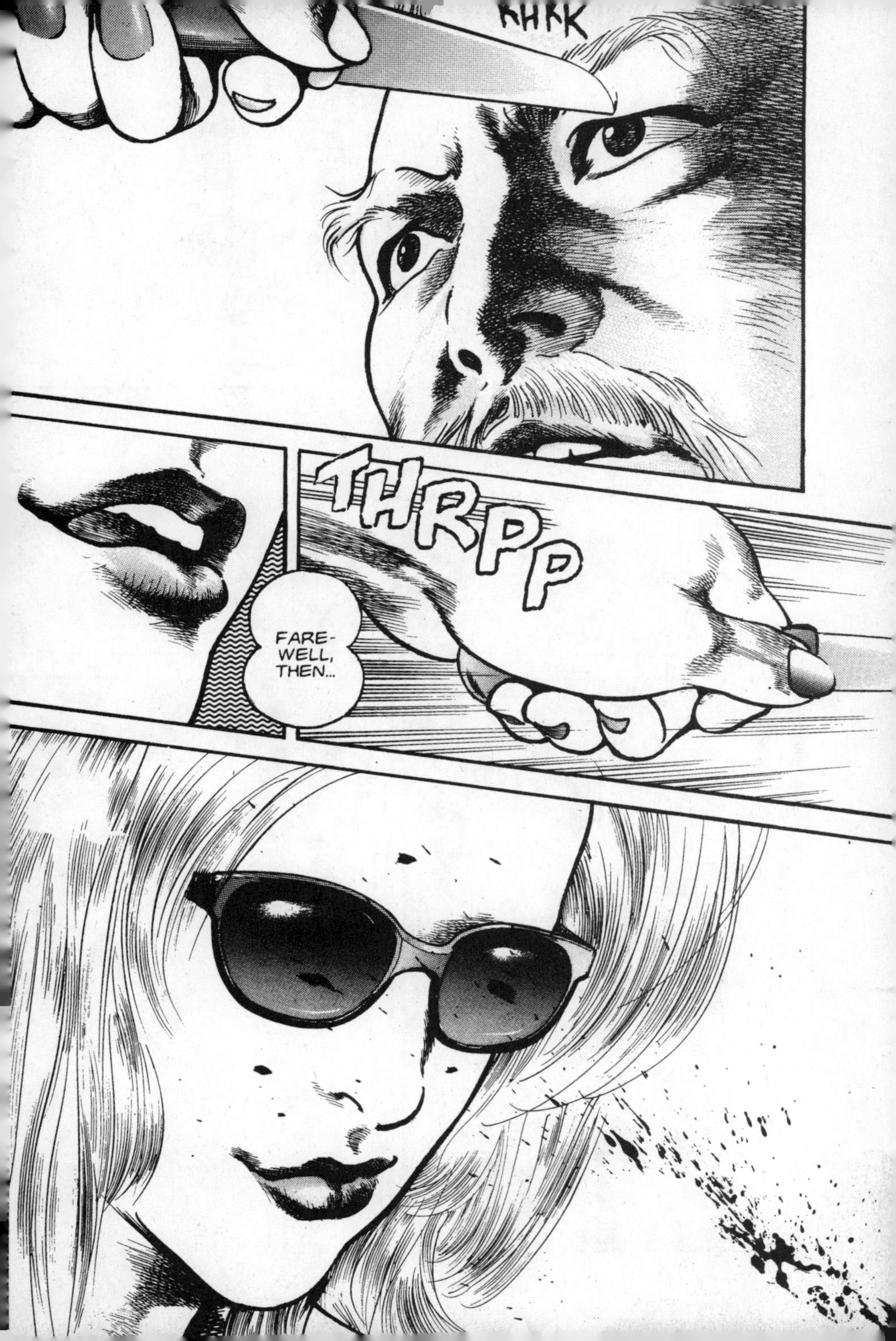
RHRK
THRPP
FARE-WELL, THEN...

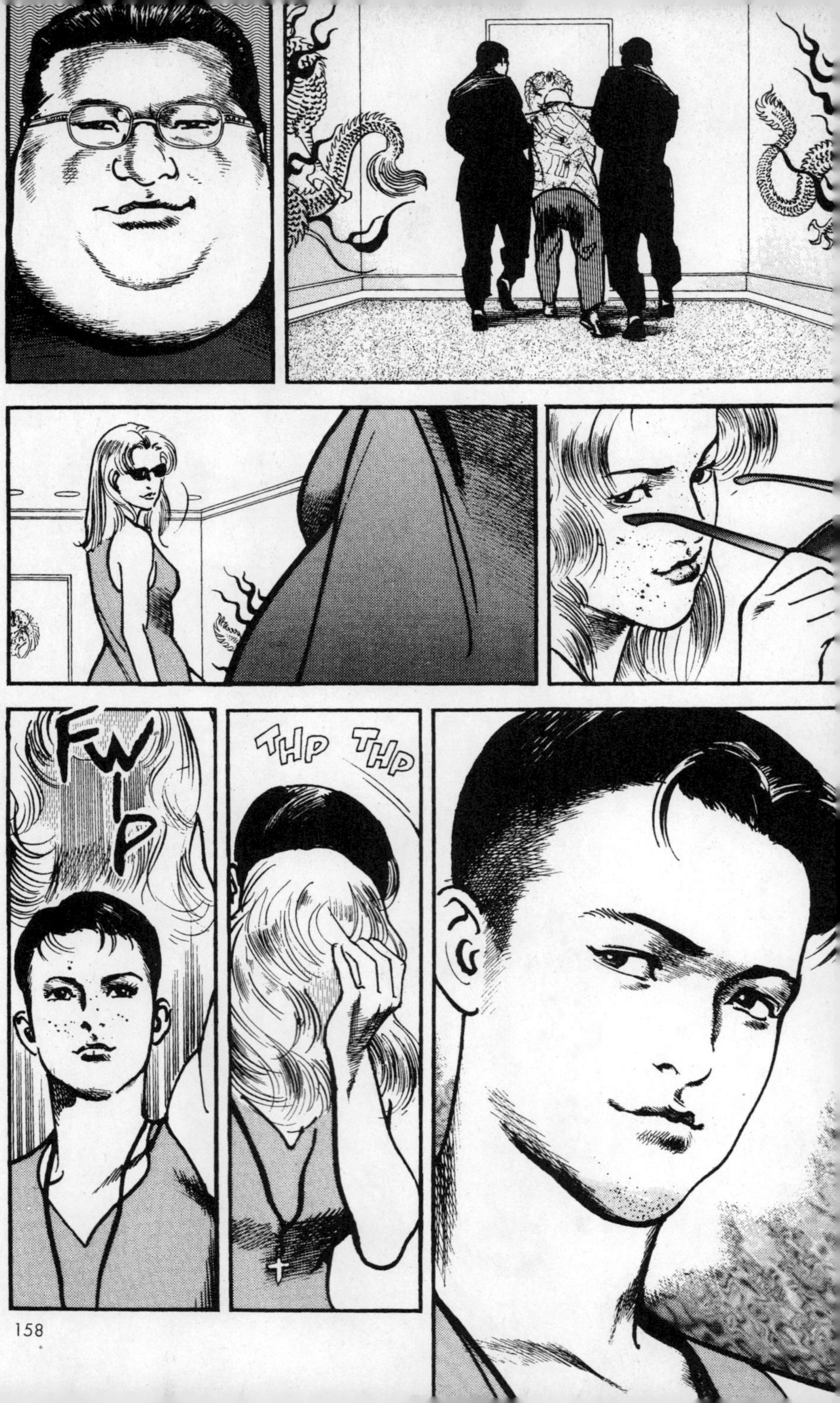
FWIP
THP THP

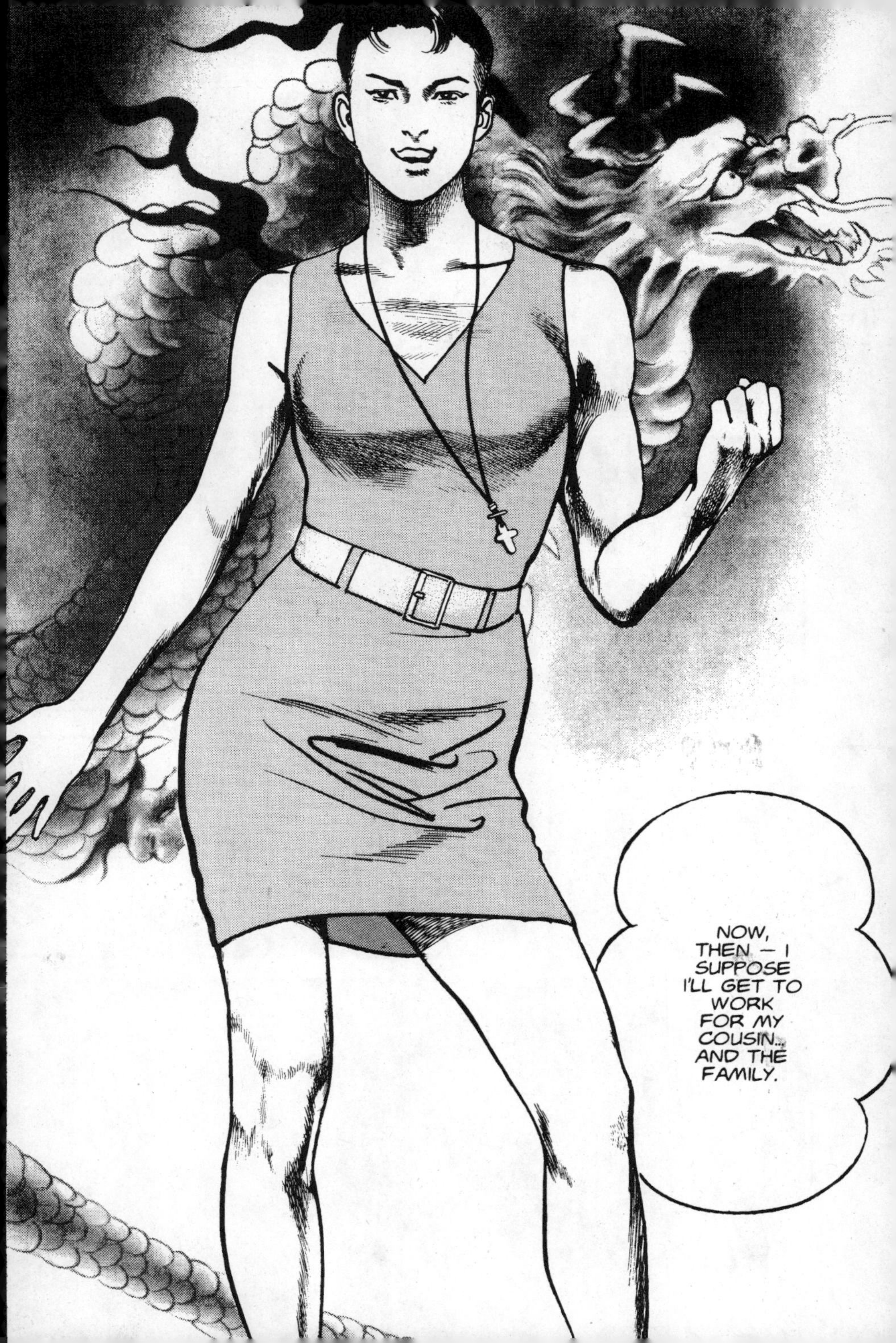
NOW, THEN — I SUPPOSE I'LL GET TO WORK FOR MY COUSIN... AND THE FAMILY.

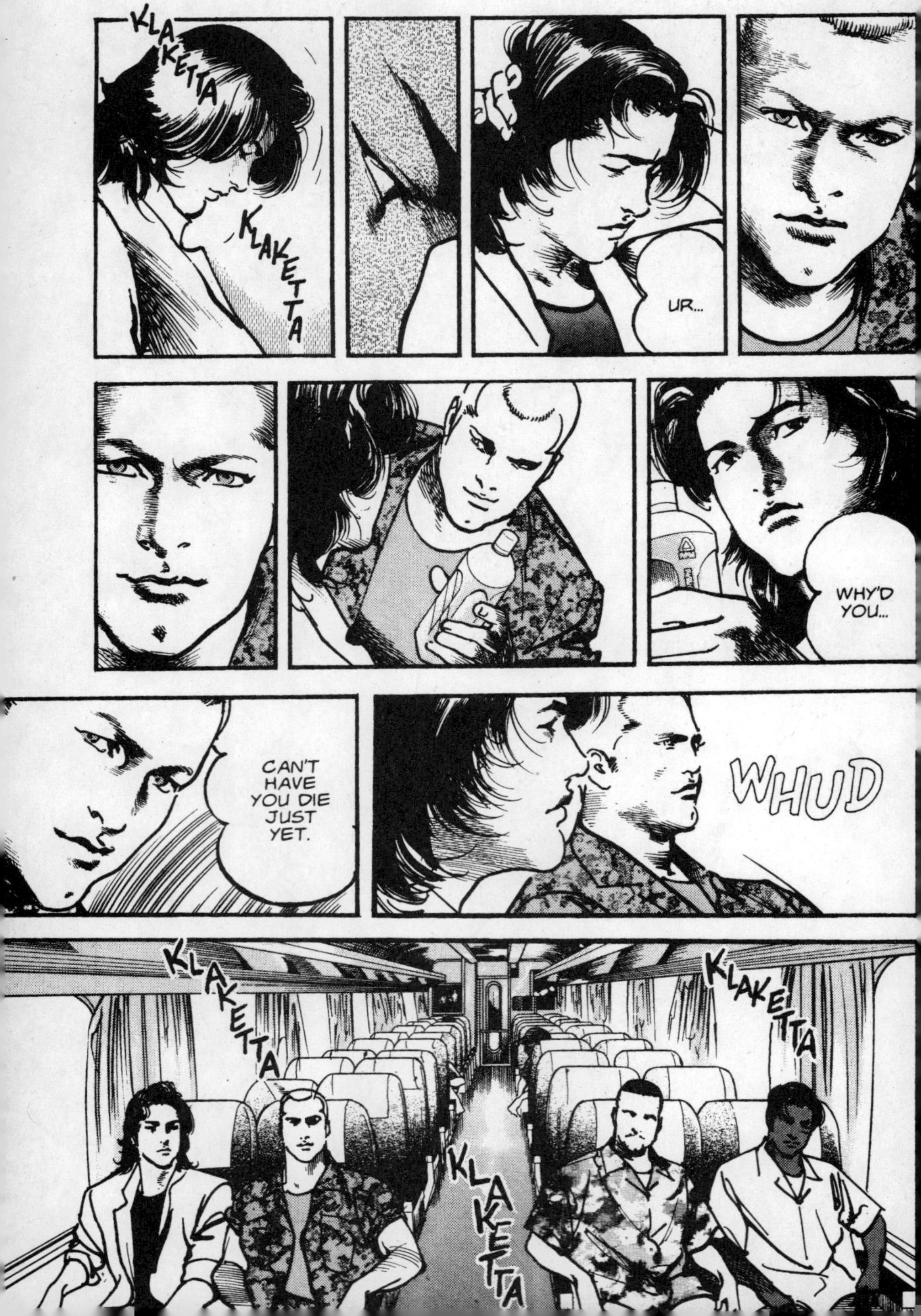
KLAKETTA
KLAKETTA
UR...
WHY'D YOU...
CAN'T HAVE YOU DIE JUST YET.
WHUD
KLAKETTA
KLAKETTA
KLAKETTA

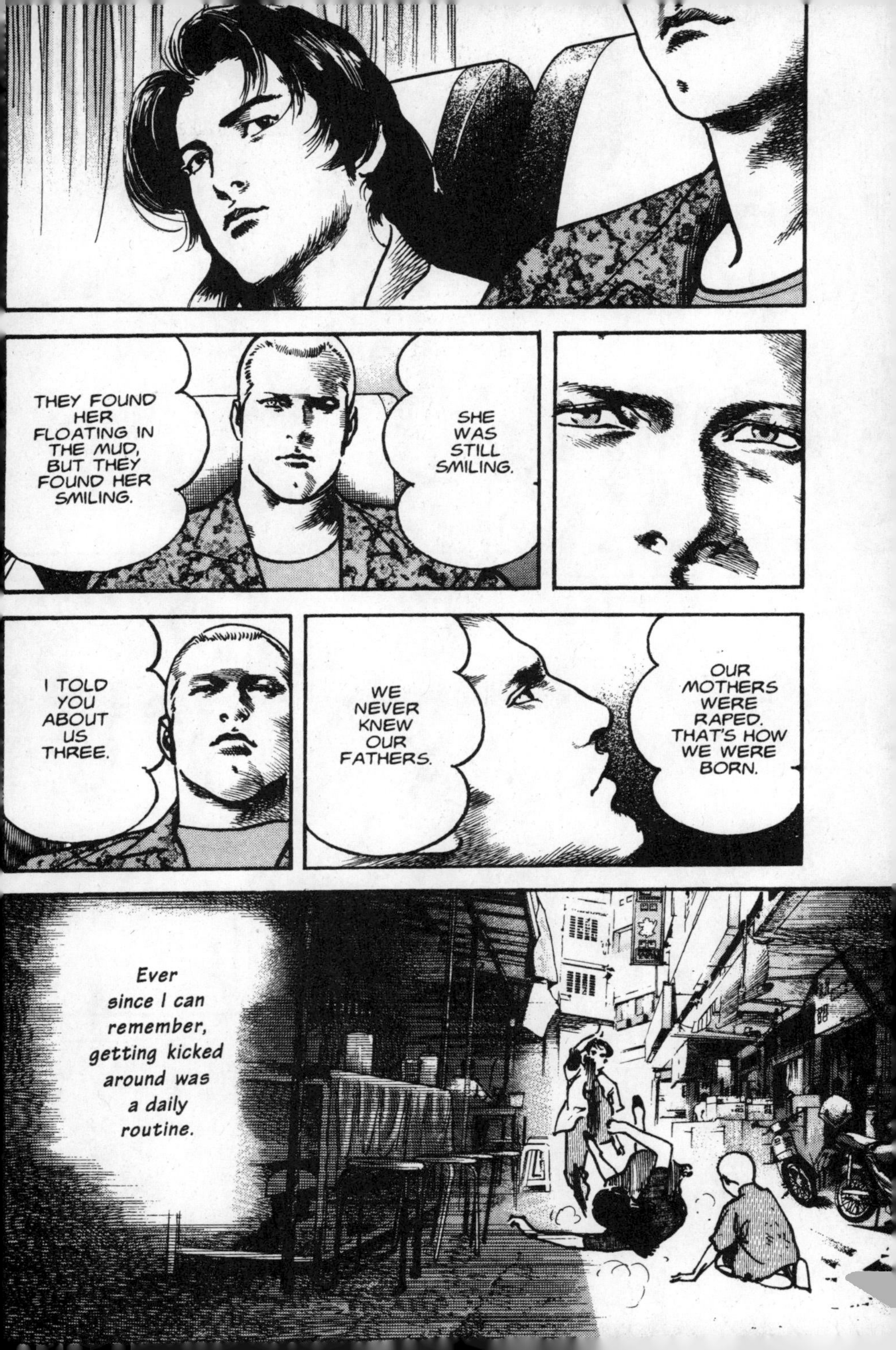
THEY FOUND HER FLOATING IN THE MUD, BUT THEY FOUND HER SMILING.
SHE WAS STILL SMILING.
I TOLD YOU ABOUT US THREE.
WE NEVER KNEW OUR FATHERS.
OUR MOTHERS WERE RAPED. THAT'S HOW WE WERE BORN.
Ever since I can remember, getting kicked around was a daily routine.

THE ONLY THING WE LEARNED WAS HOW TO HATE.

WE DON'T CRY, WE DON'T LAUGH...

WE DON'T UNDERSTAND FEELINGS LIKE THAT...

THAT WOMAN REI FAH, SHE WAS ONE OF US.

...

JUST ONCE... WE'D LIKE TO LAUGH... FOR REAL...

THAT MUCH WE WANT.

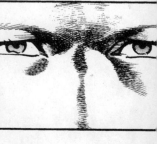

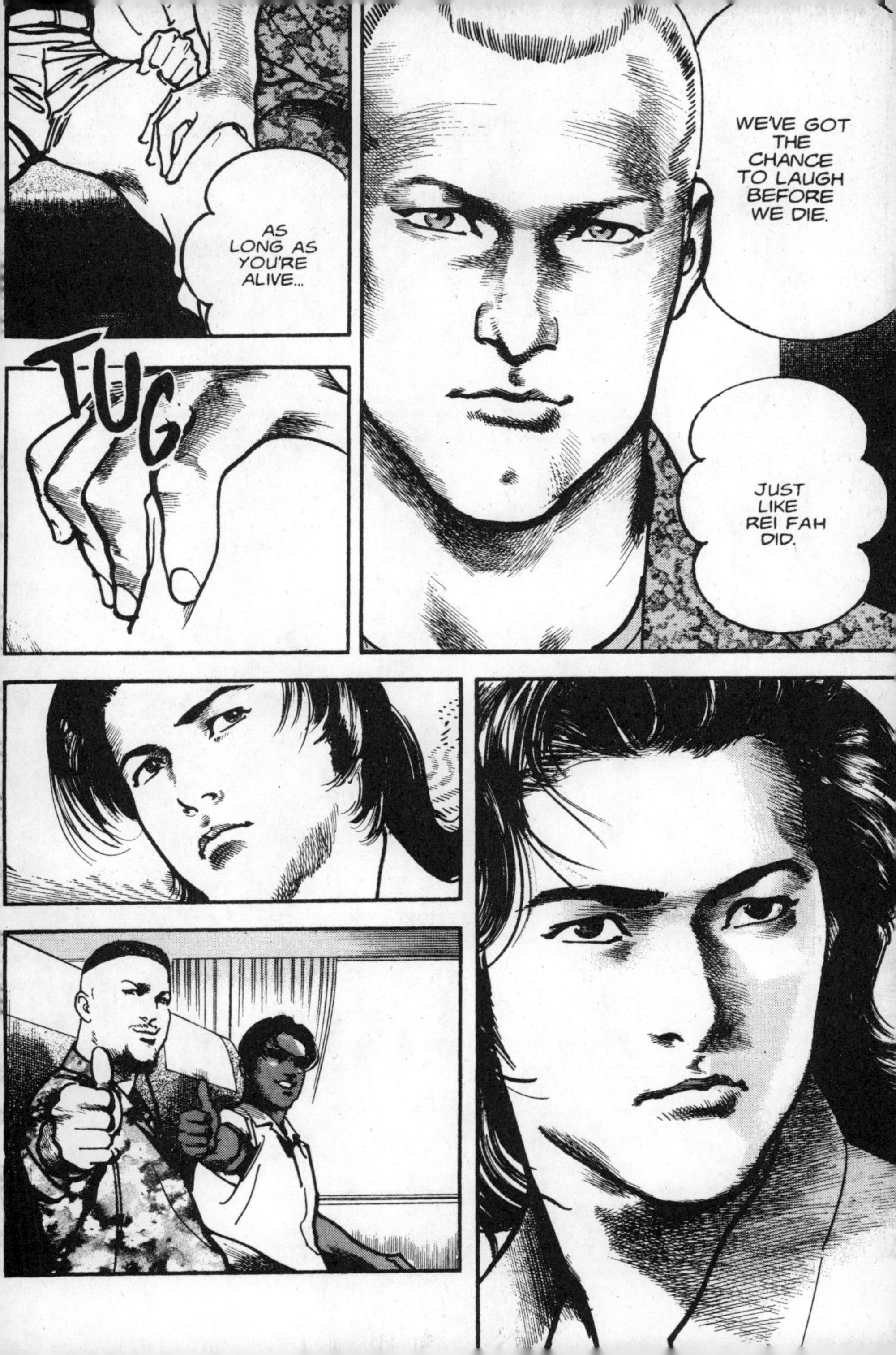
WE'VE GOT THE CHANCE TO LAUGH BEFORE WE DIE.
AS LONG AS YOU'RE ALIVE...
TUG
JUST LIKE REI FAH DID.

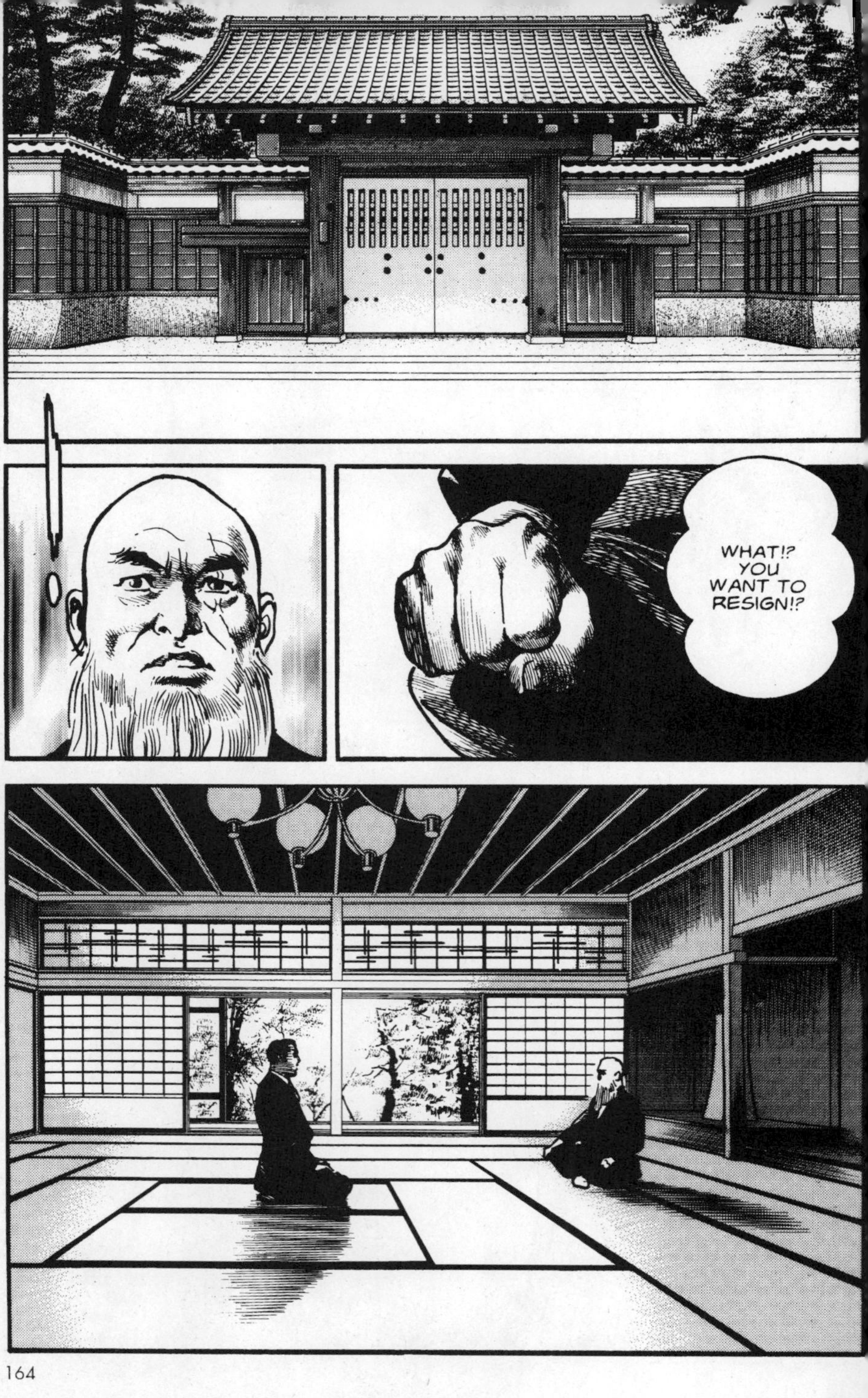
WHAT!? YOU WANT TO RESIGN!?

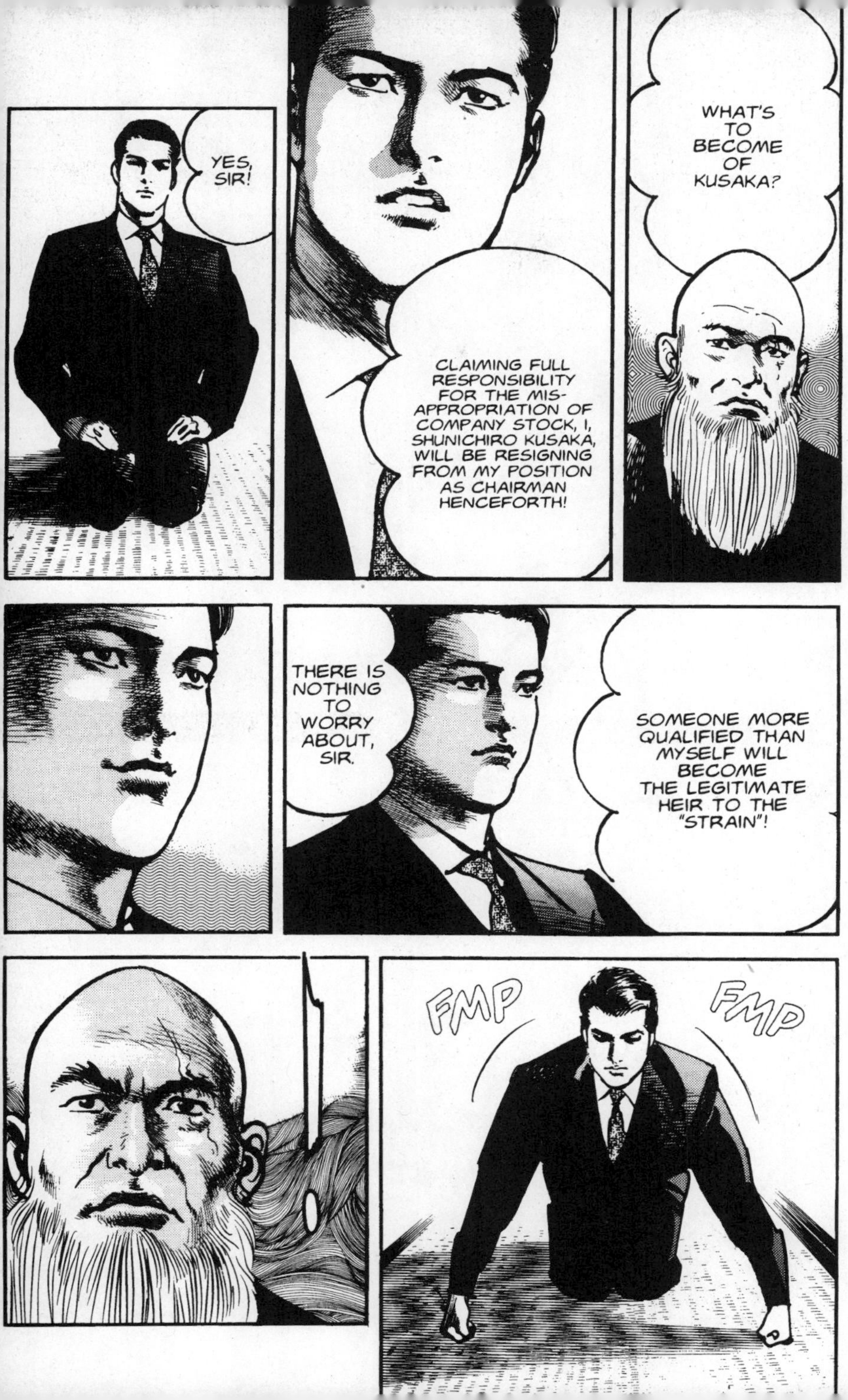
YES, SIR!
CLAIMING FULL RESPONSIBILITY FOR THE MIS-APPROPRIATION OF COMPANY STOCK, I, SHUNICHIRO KUSAKA, WILL BE RESIGNING FROM MY POSITION AS CHAIRMAN HENCEFORTH!
WHAT'S TO BECOME OF KUSAKA?
THERE IS NOTHING TO WORRY ABOUT, SIR.
SOMEONE MORE QUALIFIED THAN MYSELF WILL BECOME THE LEGITIMATE HEIR TO THE "STRAIN"!
FMP
FMP

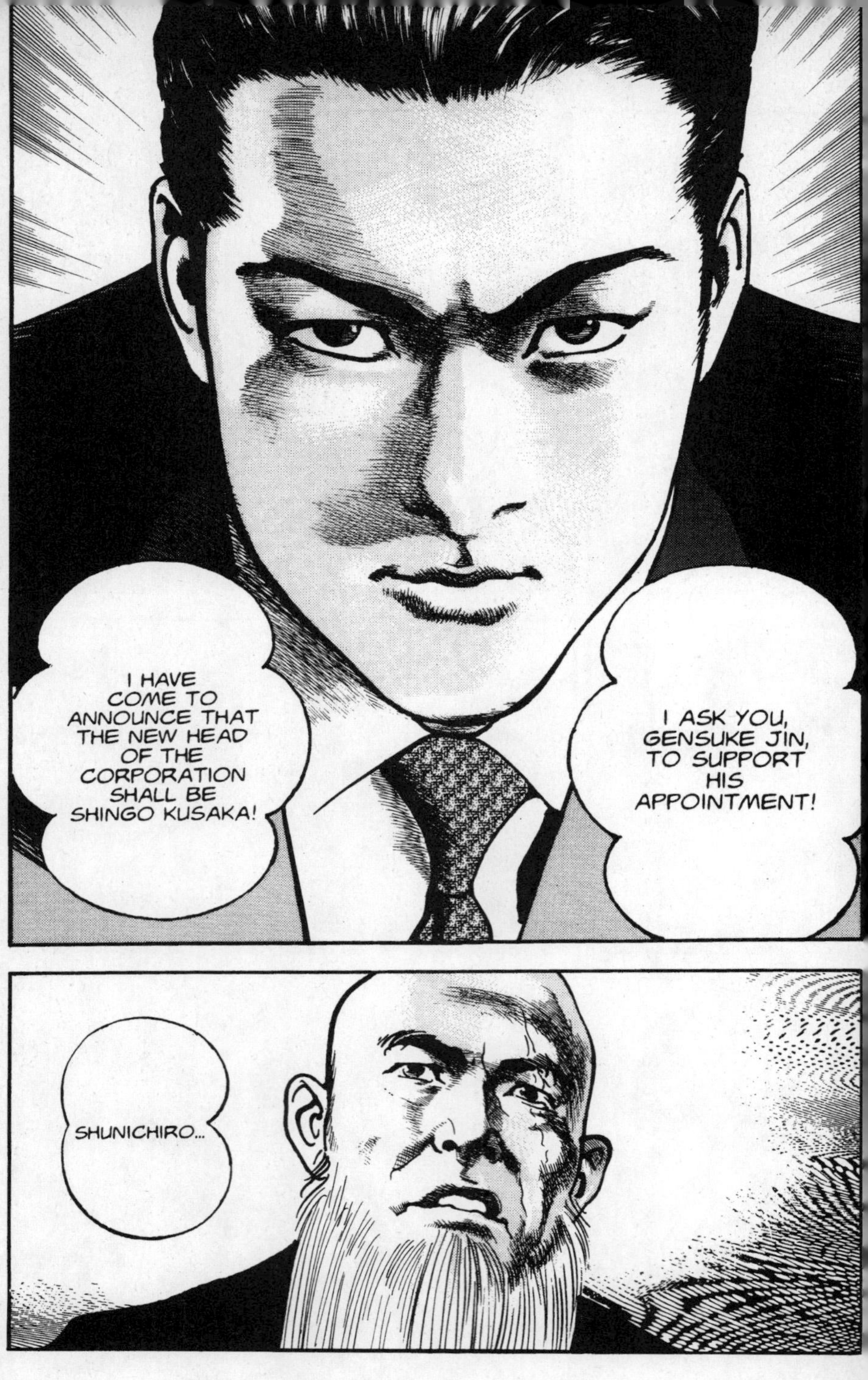
I ASK YOU, GENSUKE JIN, TO SUPPORT HIS APPOINTMENT!
I HAVE COME TO ANNOUNCE THAT THE NEW HEAD OF THE CORPORATION SHALL BE SHINGO KUSAKA!
SHUNICHIRO...

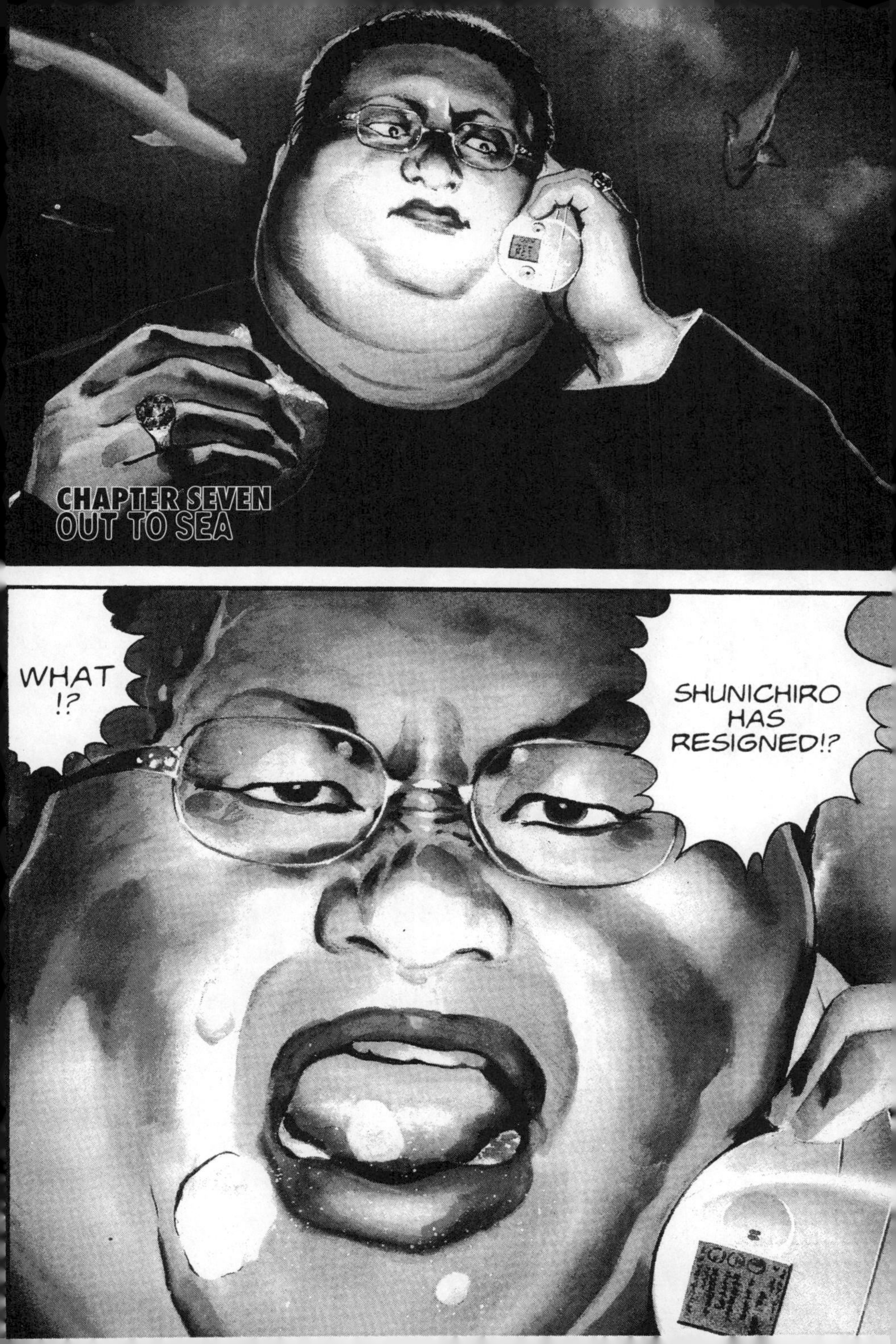
CHAPTER SEVEN
OUT TO SEA
SHUNICHIRO HAS RESIGNED!?
WHAT !?

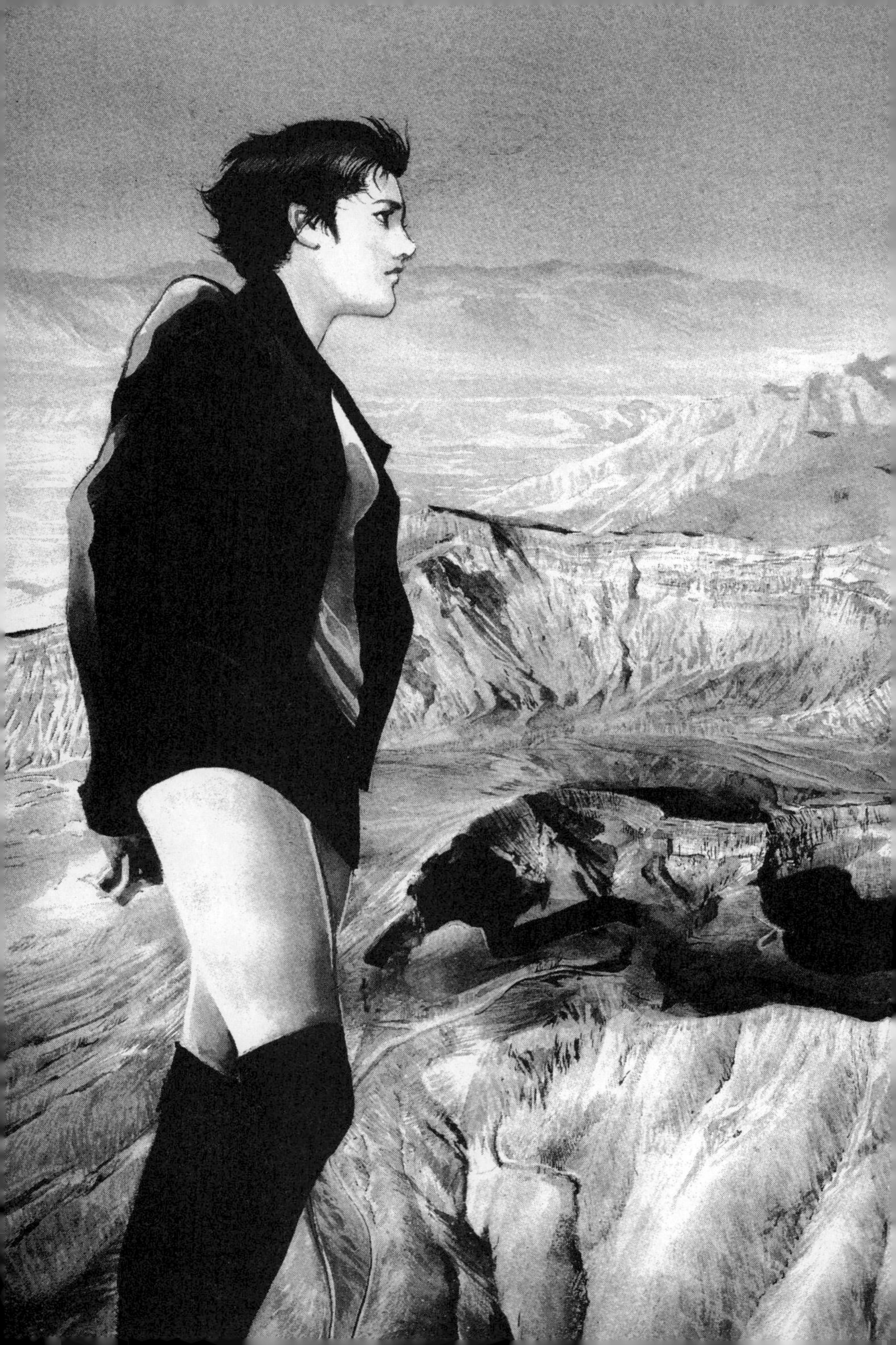

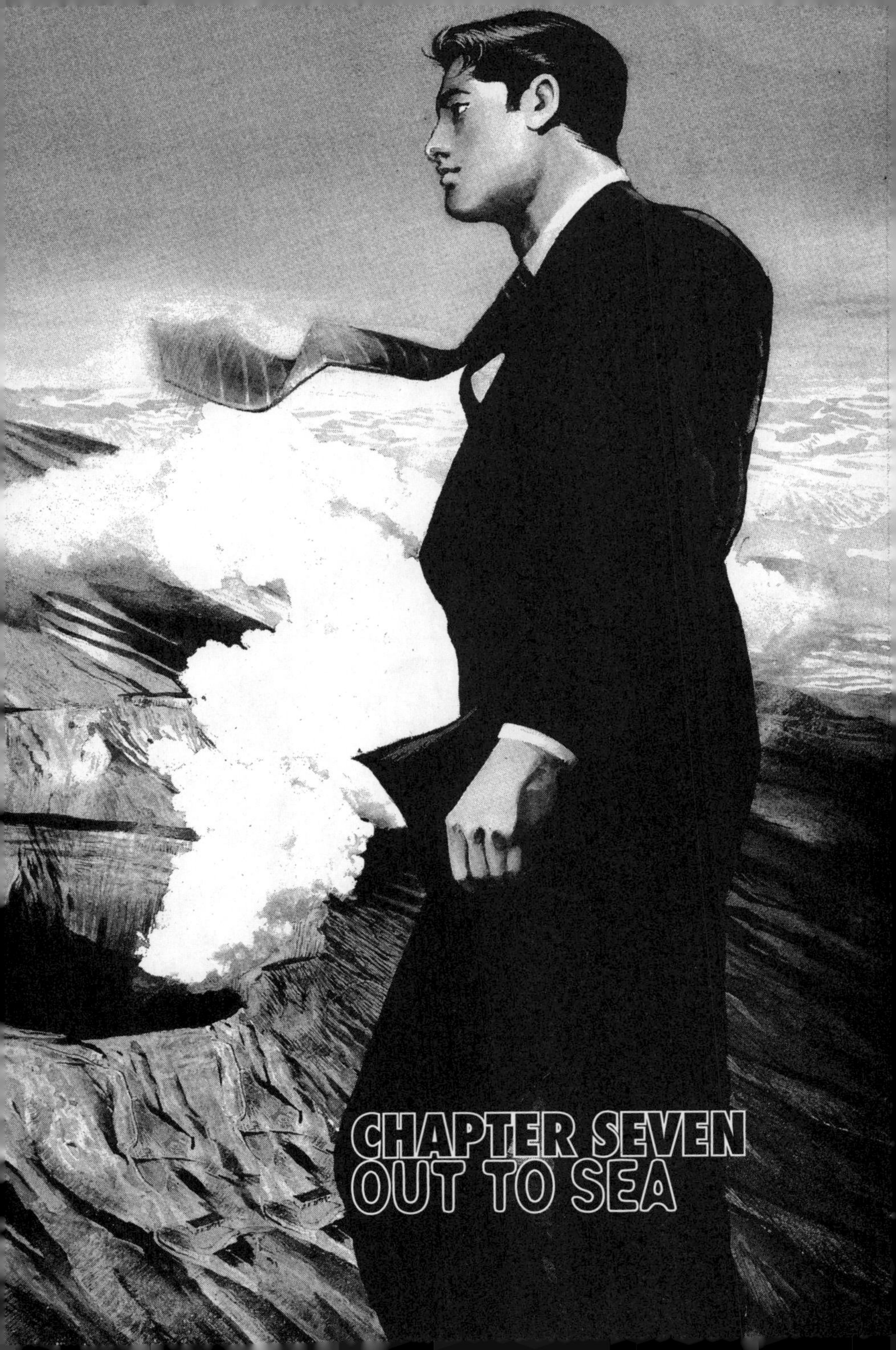
CHAPTER SEVEN
OUT TO SEA

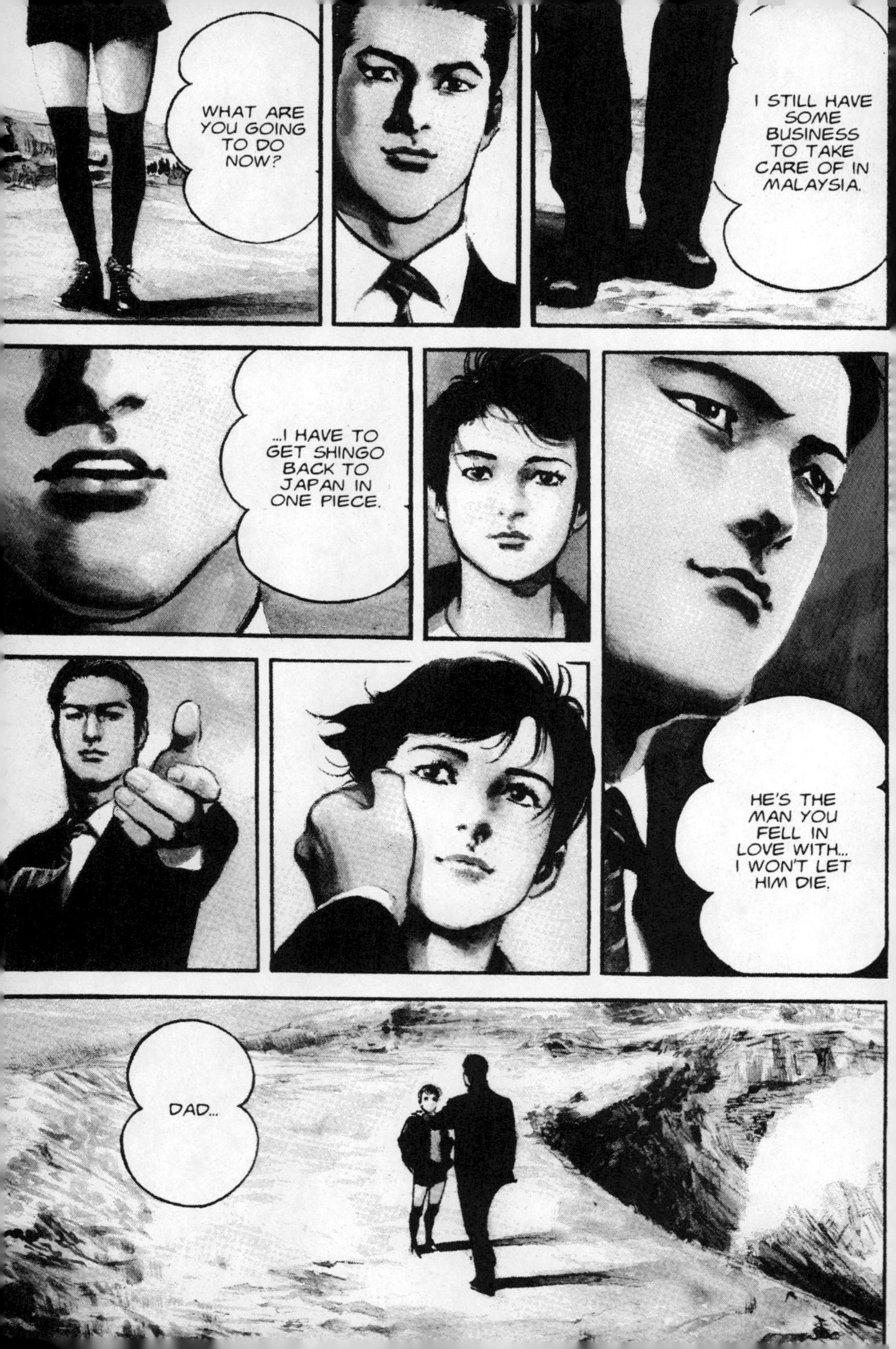
WHAT ARE YOU GOING TO DO NOW?
I STILL HAVE SOME BUSINESS TO TAKE CARE OF IN MALAYSIA.
...I HAVE TO GET SHINGO BACK TO JAPAN IN ONE PIECE.
HE'S THE MAN YOU FELL IN LOVE WITH... I WON'T LET HIM DIE.
DAD...

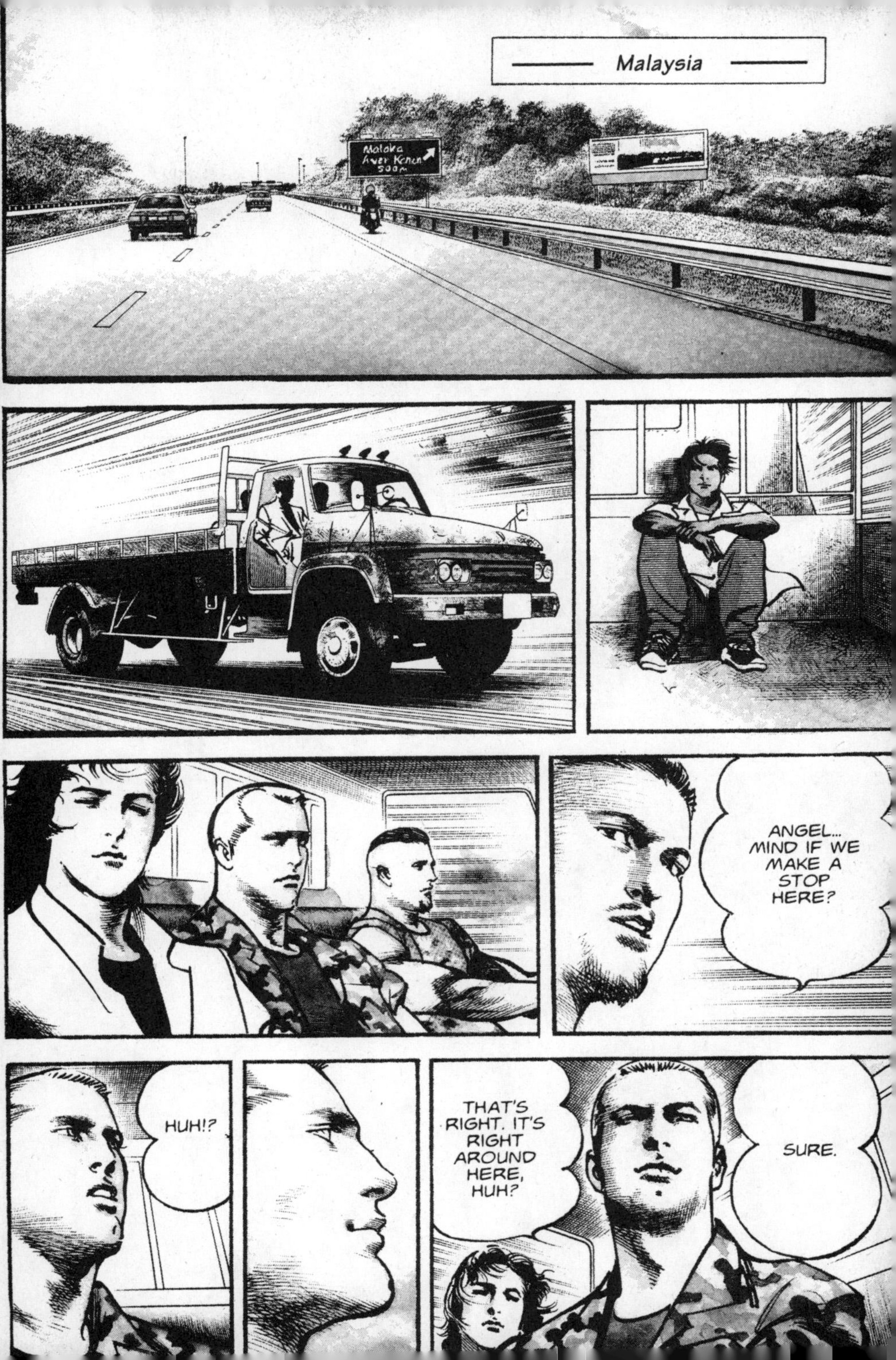
Malaysia
Malaka
Ayer Keroh
500m
ANGEL... MIND IF WE MAKE A STOP HERE?
HUH!?
THAT'S RIGHT. IT'S RIGHT AROUND HERE, HUH?
SURE.

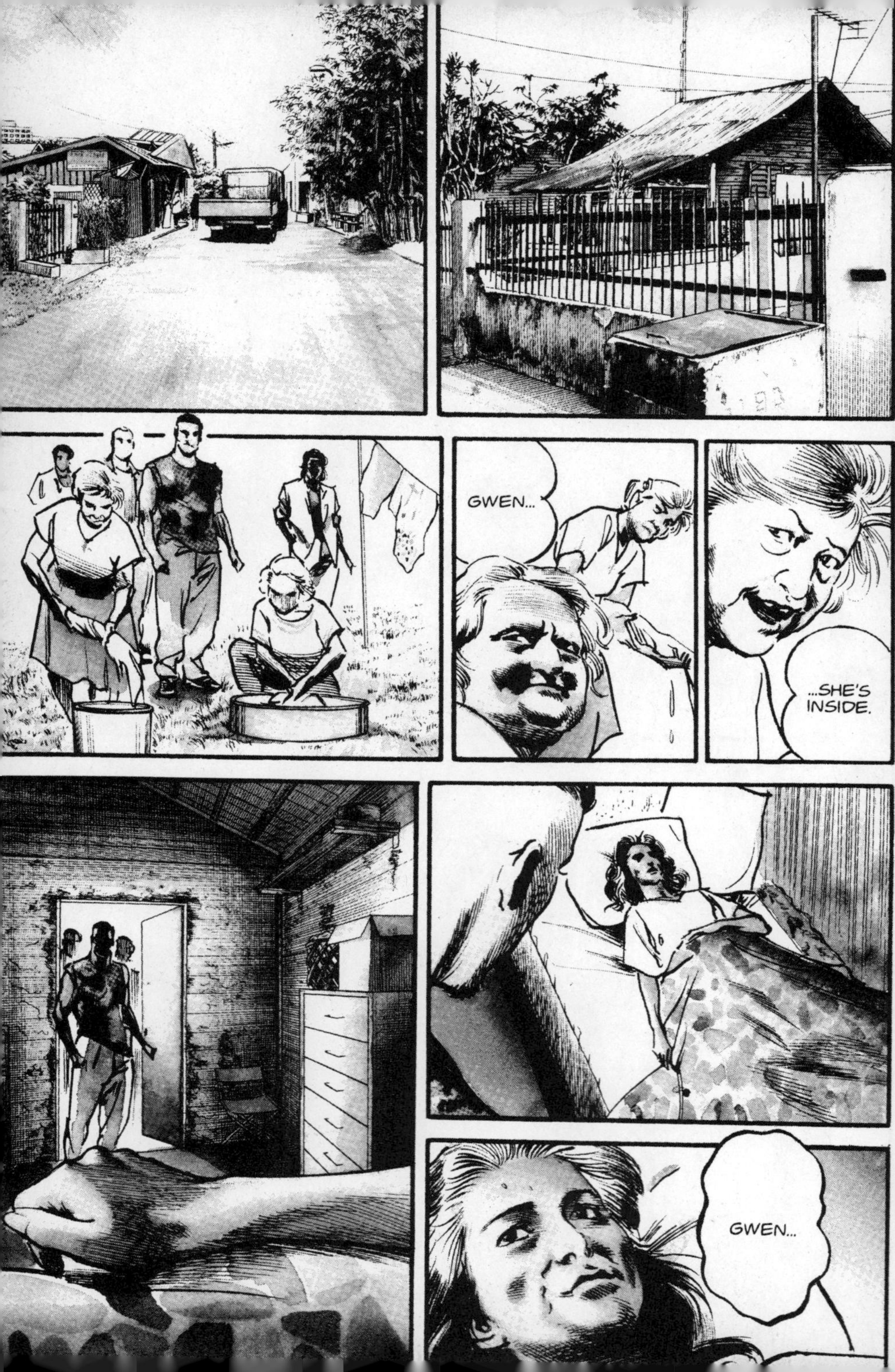
GWEN...
...SHE'S INSIDE.
GWEN...

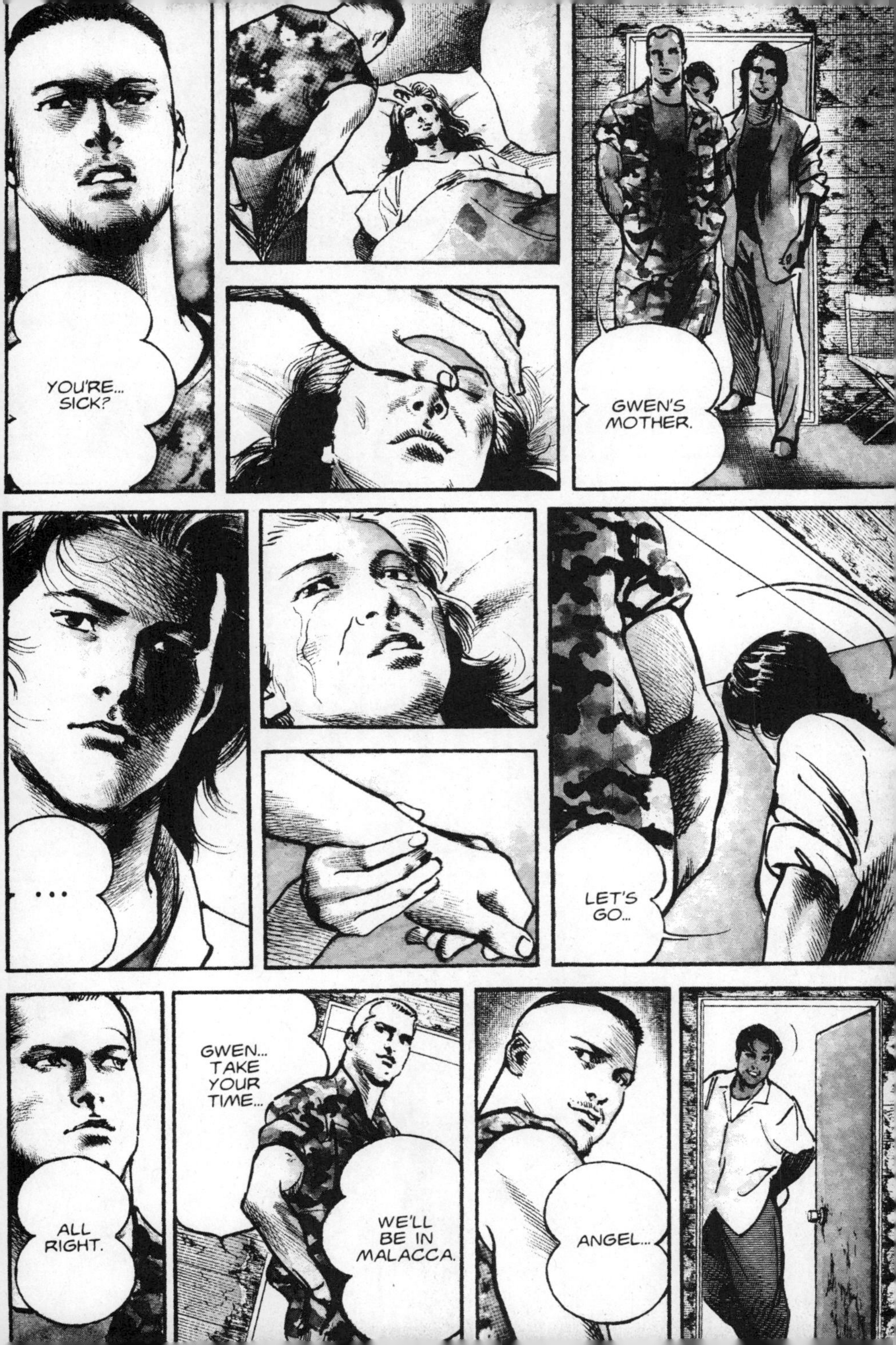
YOU'RE... SICK?
GWEN'S MOTHER.
...
LET'S GO...
ALL RIGHT.
GWEN... TAKE YOUR TIME...
WE'LL BE IN MALACCA.
ANGEL...

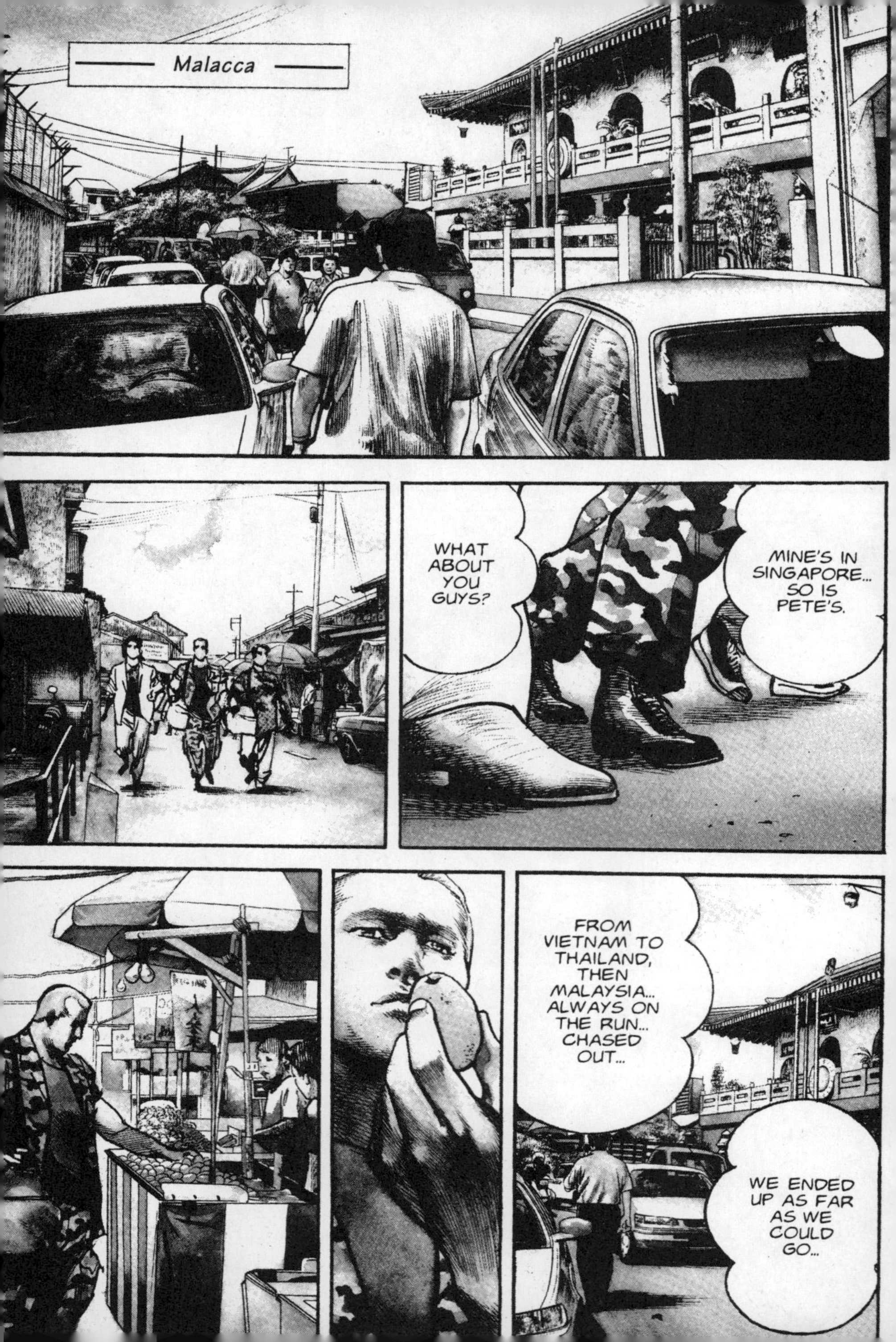
Malacca
WHAT ABOUT YOU GUYS?
MINE'S IN SINGAPORE... SO IS PETE'S.
FROM VIETNAM TO THAILAND, THEN MALAYSIA... ALWAYS ON THE RUN... CHASED OUT...
WE ENDED UP AS FAR AS WE COULD GO...

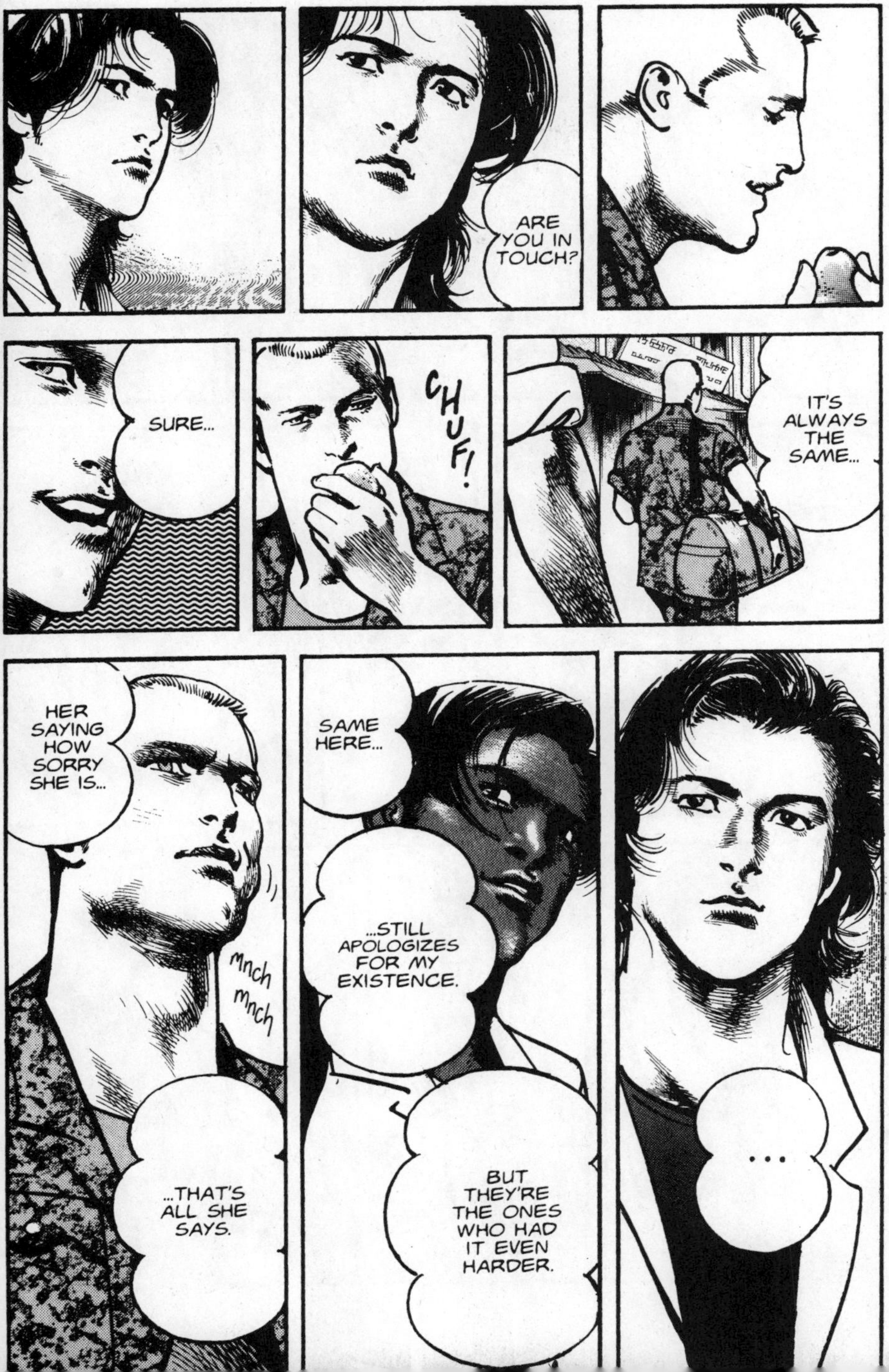
ARE YOU IN TOUCH?
SURE...
CHUF!
IT'S ALWAYS THE SAME...
HER SAYING HOW SORRY SHE IS...
mnch mnch
...THAT'S ALL SHE SAYS.
SAME HERE...
...STILL APOLOGIZES FOR MY EXISTENCE.
BUT THEY'RE THE ONES WHO HAD IT EVEN HARDER.
...

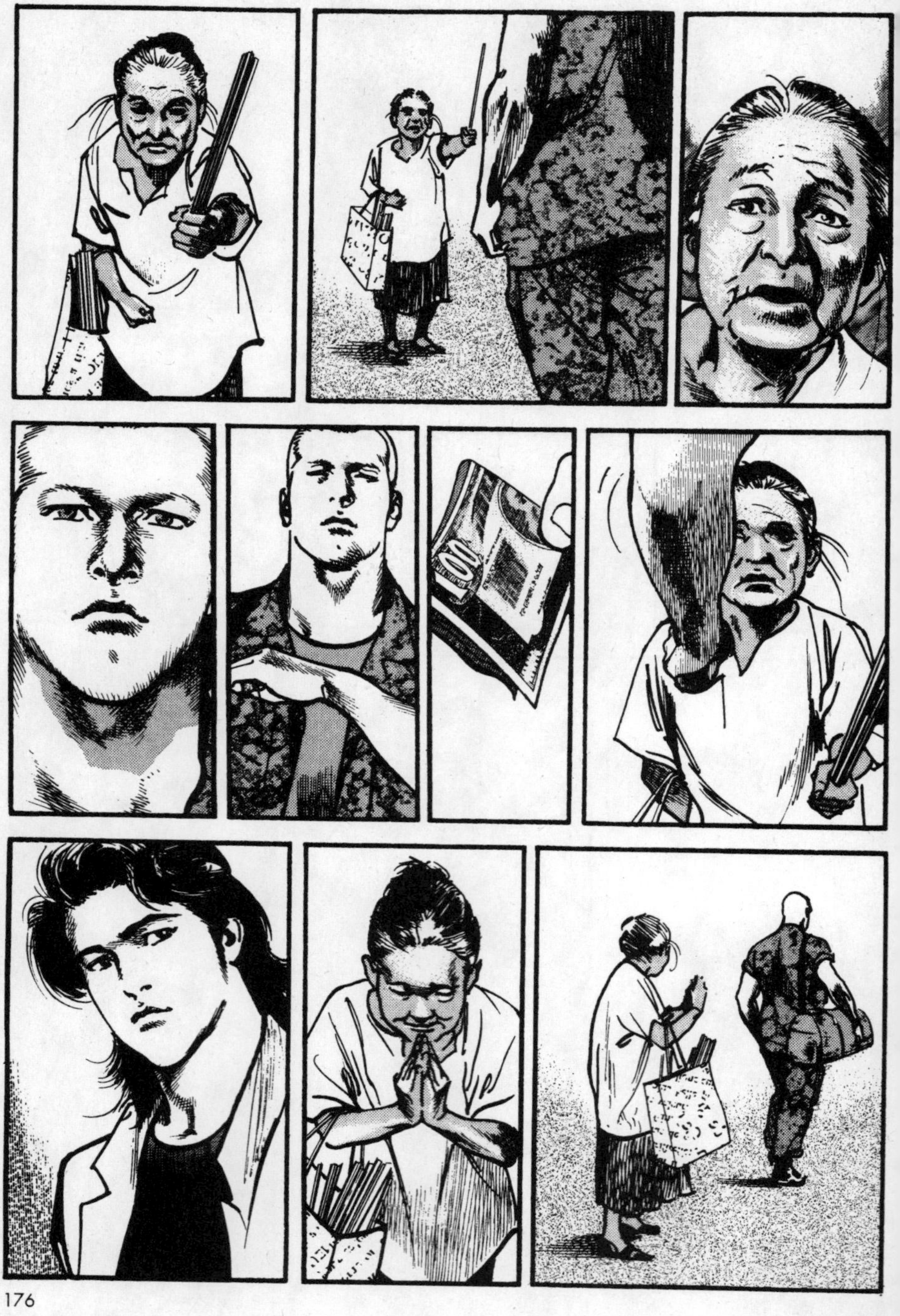

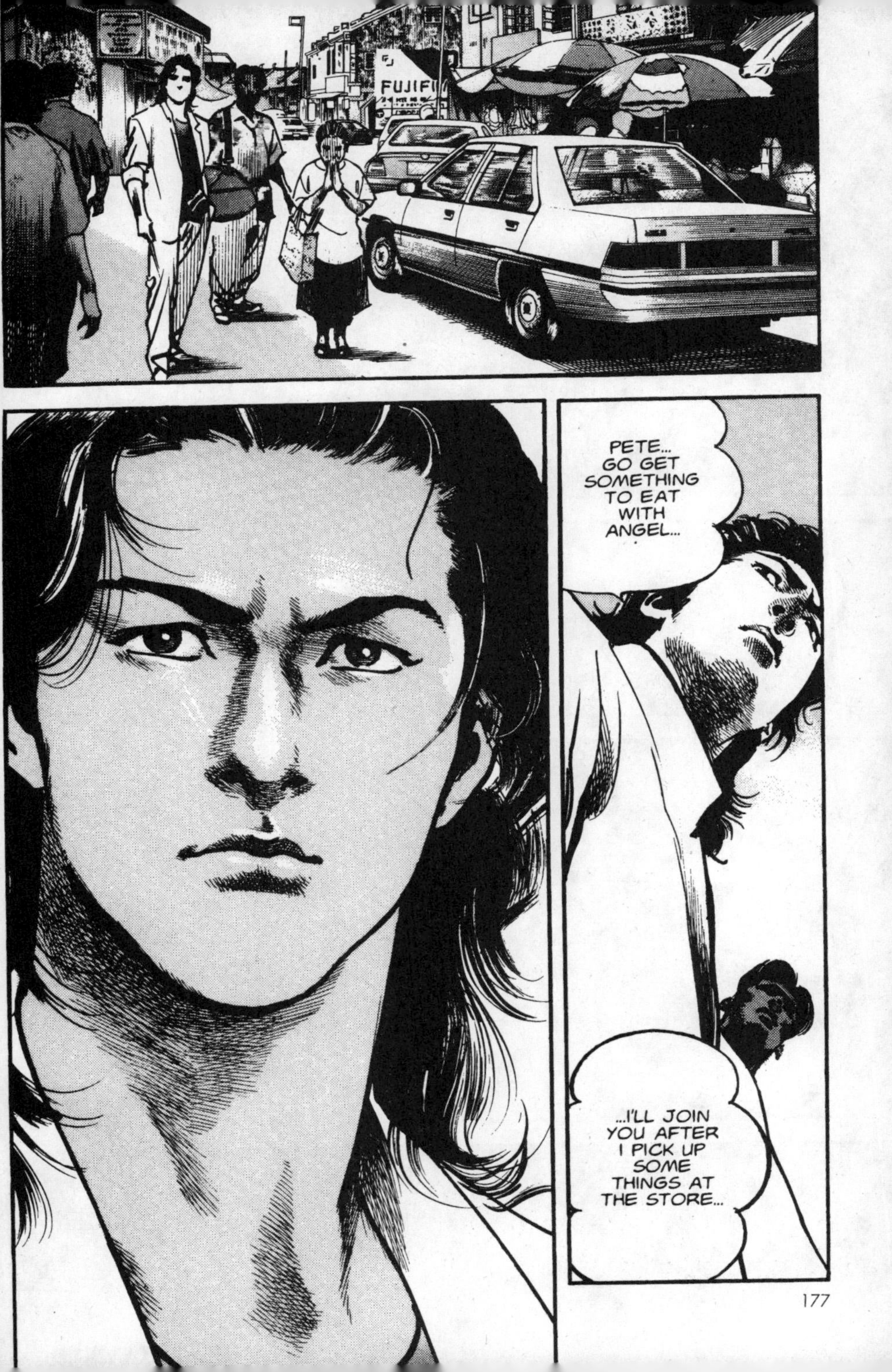
FUJIFI
PETE... GO GET SOMETHING TO EAT WITH ANGEL...
...I'LL JOIN YOU AFTER I PICK UP SOME THINGS AT THE STORE...

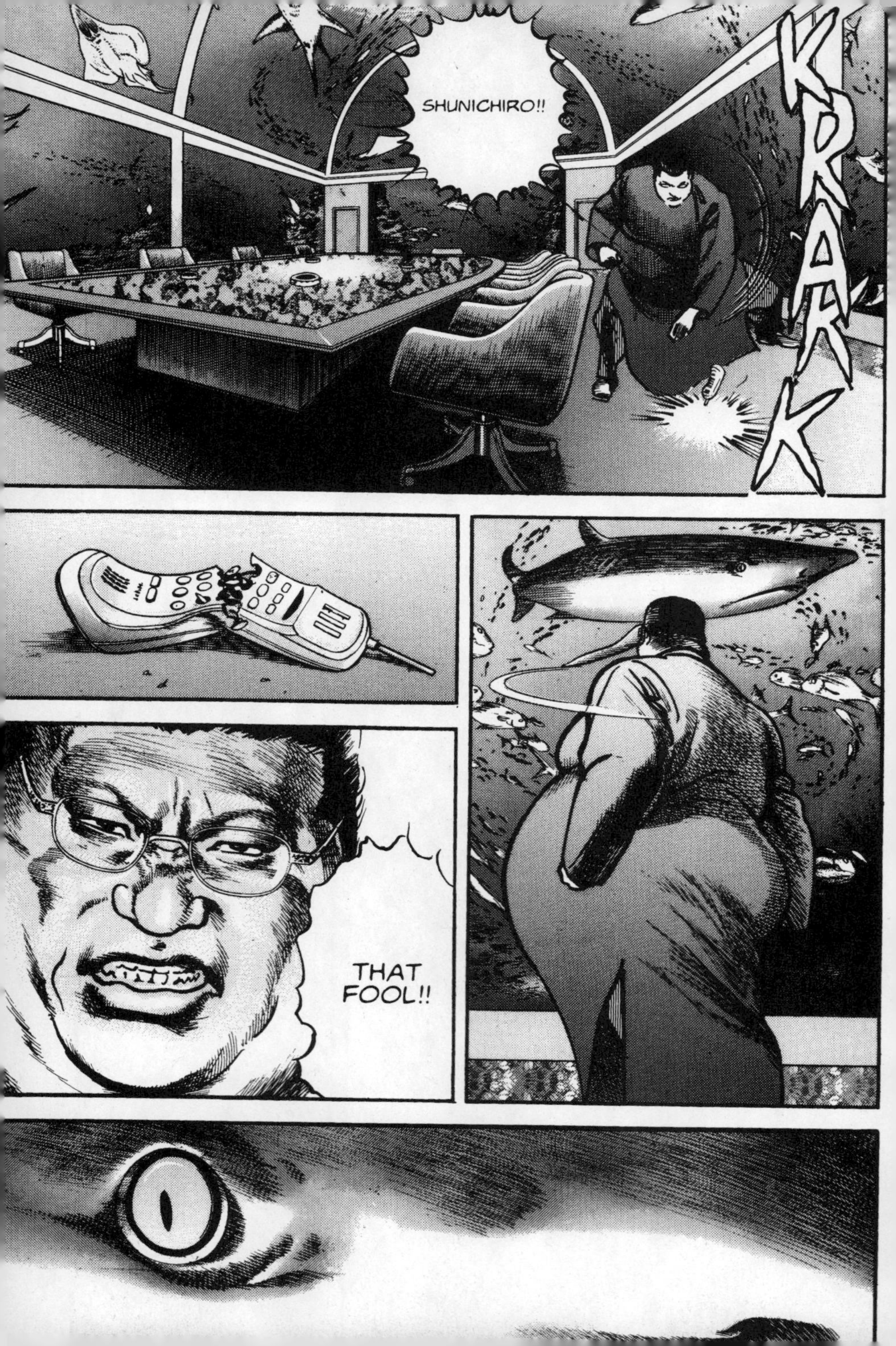
SHUNICHIRO!!
KRAKK
THAT FOOL!!

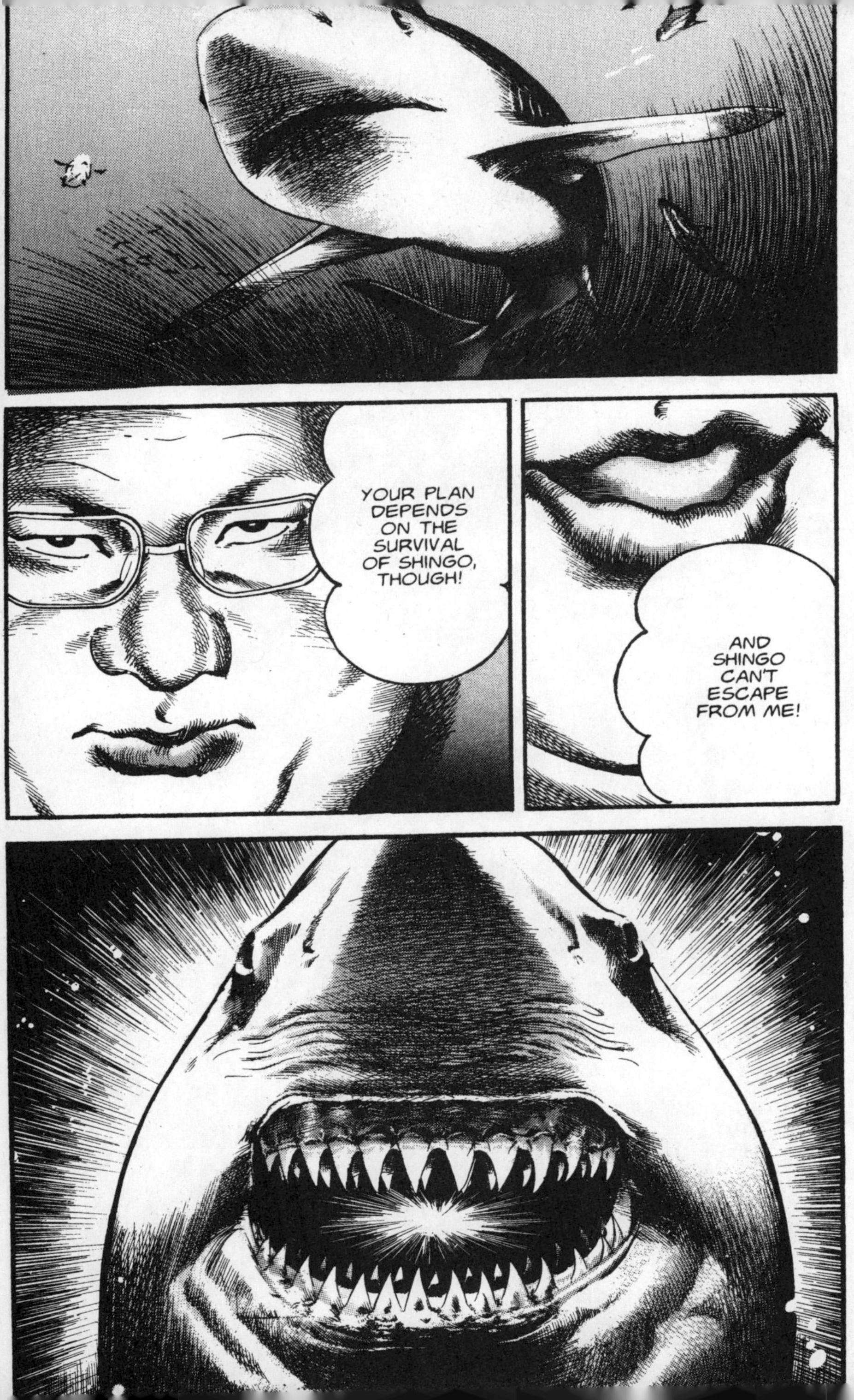
YOUR PLAN DEPENDS ON THE SURVIVAL OF SHINGO, THOUGH!
AND SHINGO CAN'T ESCAPE FROM ME!

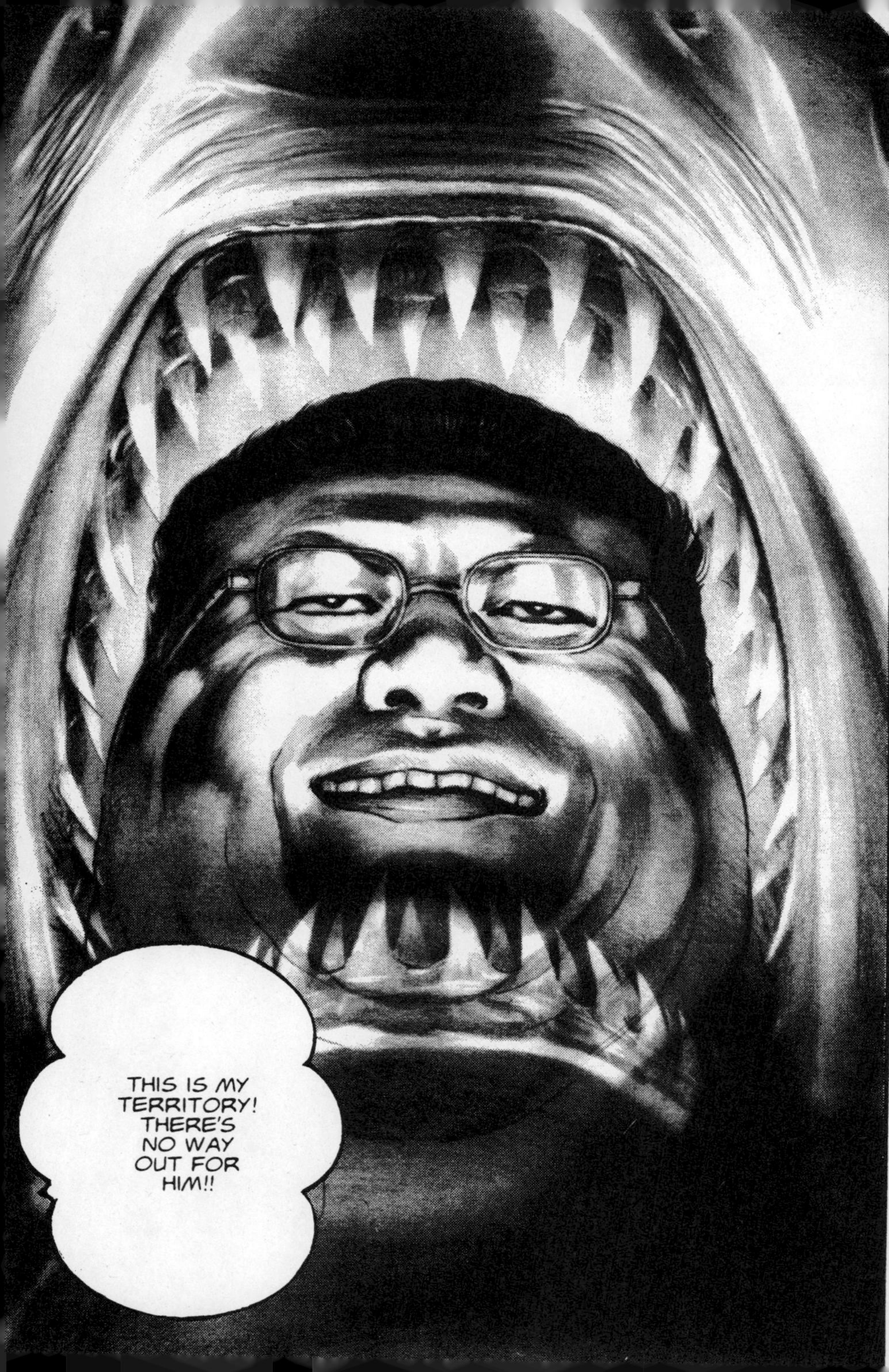
THIS IS MY TERRITORY! THERE'S NO WAY OUT FOR HIM!!

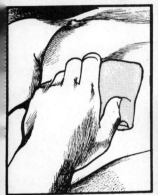

GWEN...
YOU'VE
CHANGED...

I AIN'T
THE ONLY
ONE...
ANGEL...
PETE
TOO...

WHUNK

FWAP

WHO THE—

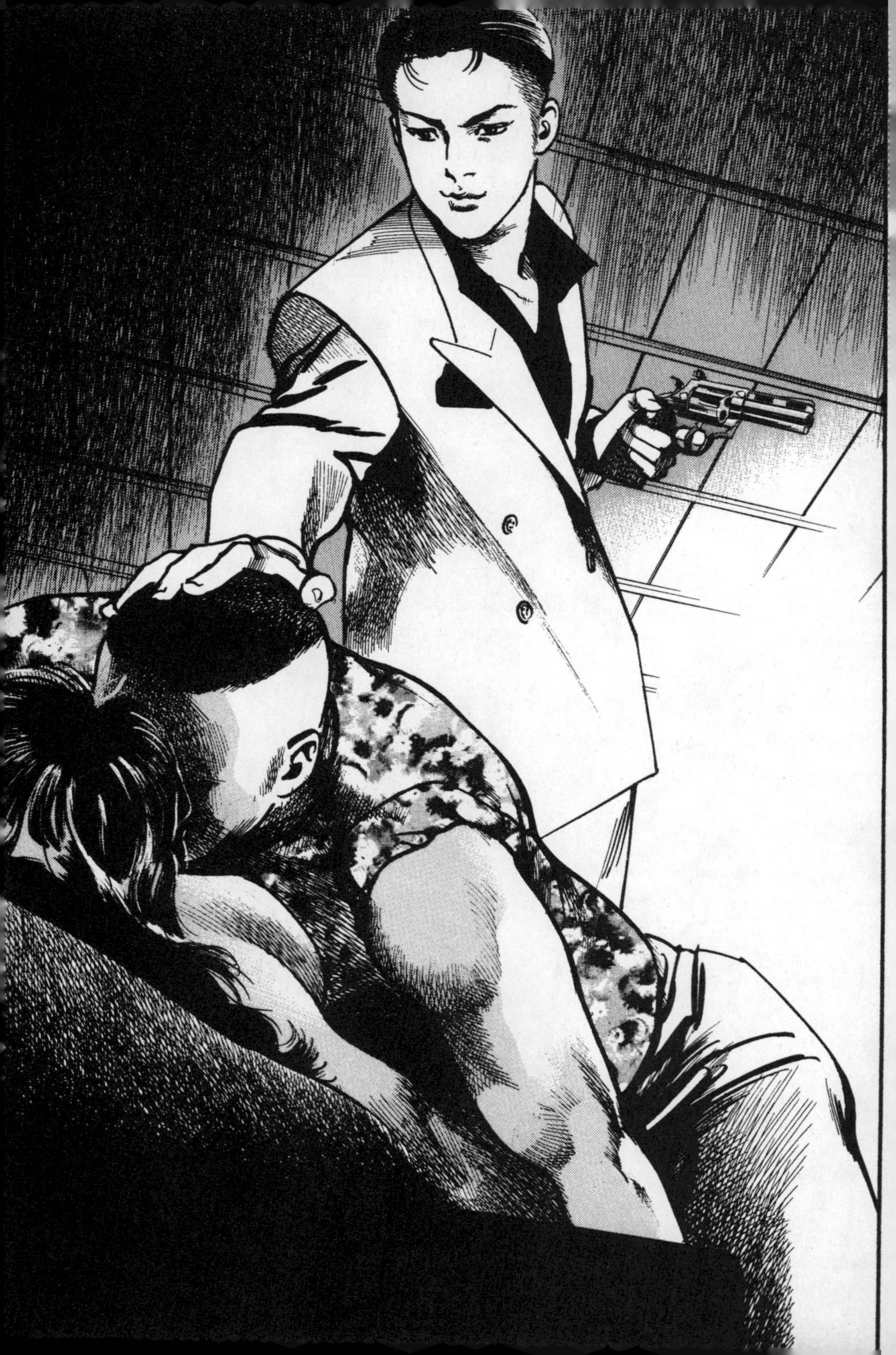

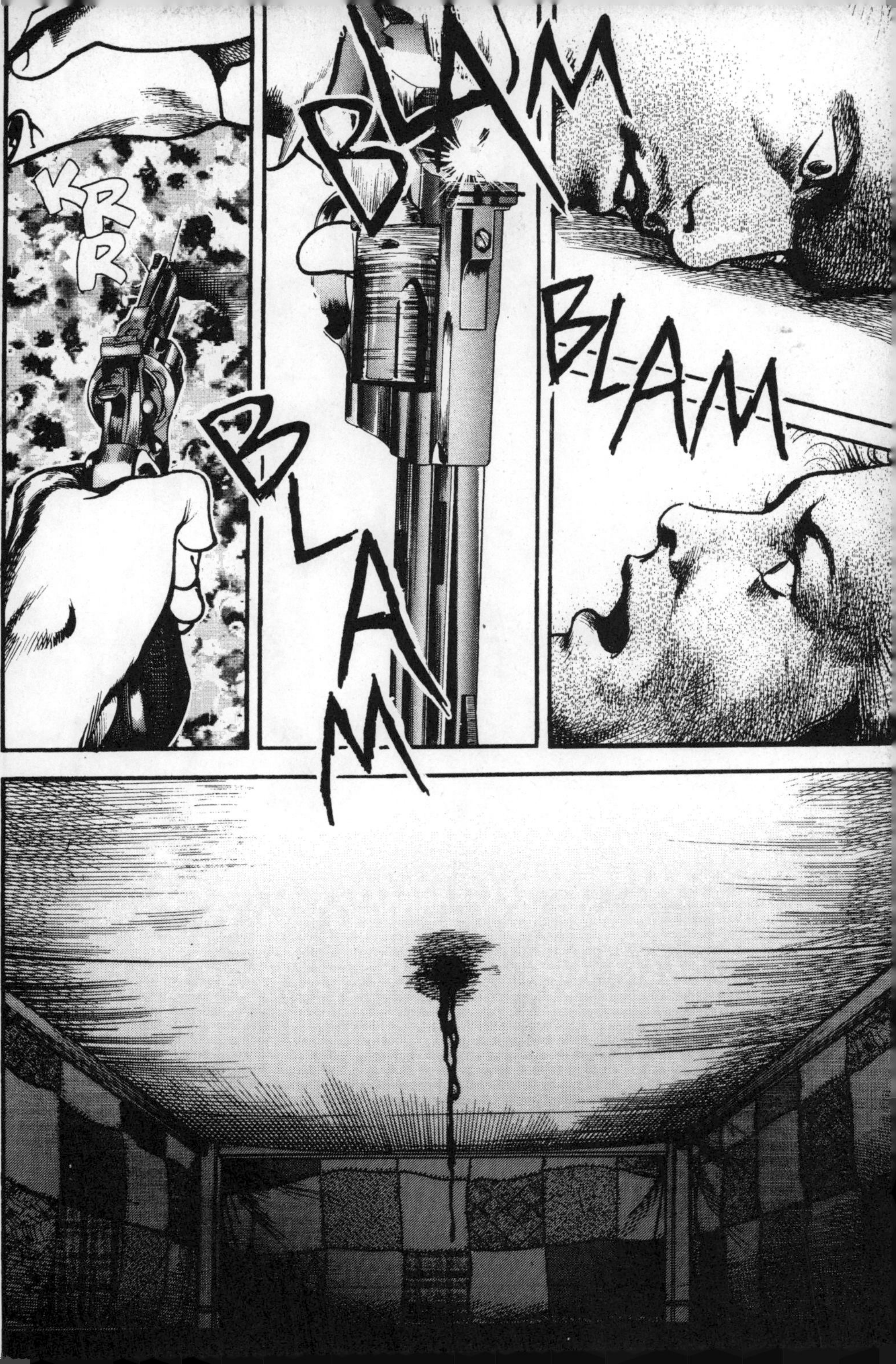
BLAM
BLAM
KRR
BLAM
BLAM

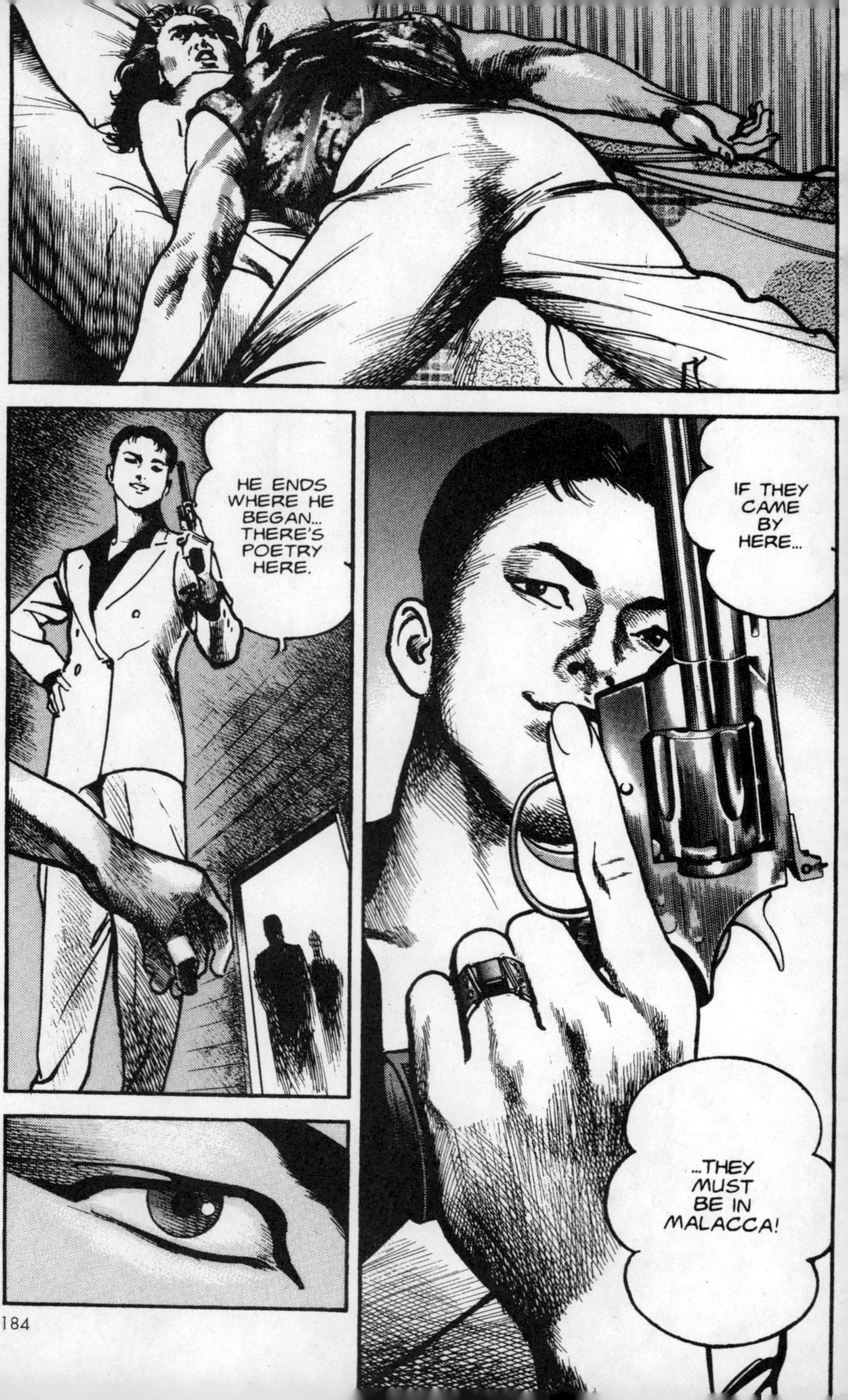
HE ENDS WHERE HE BEGAN... THERE'S POETRY HERE.
IF THEY CAME BY HERE...
...THEY MUST BE IN MALACCA!

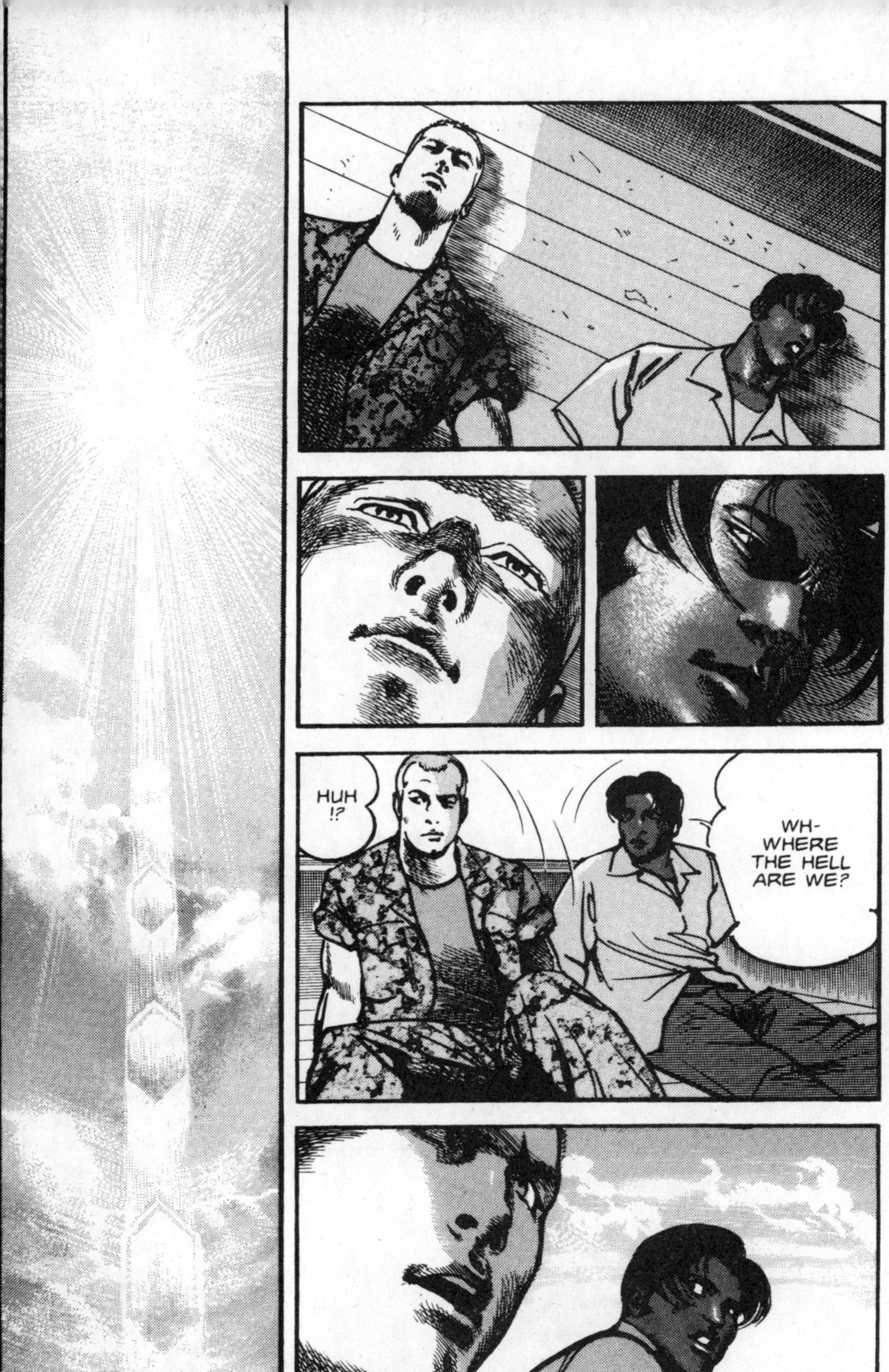
HUH !?
WH- WHERE THE HELL ARE WE?

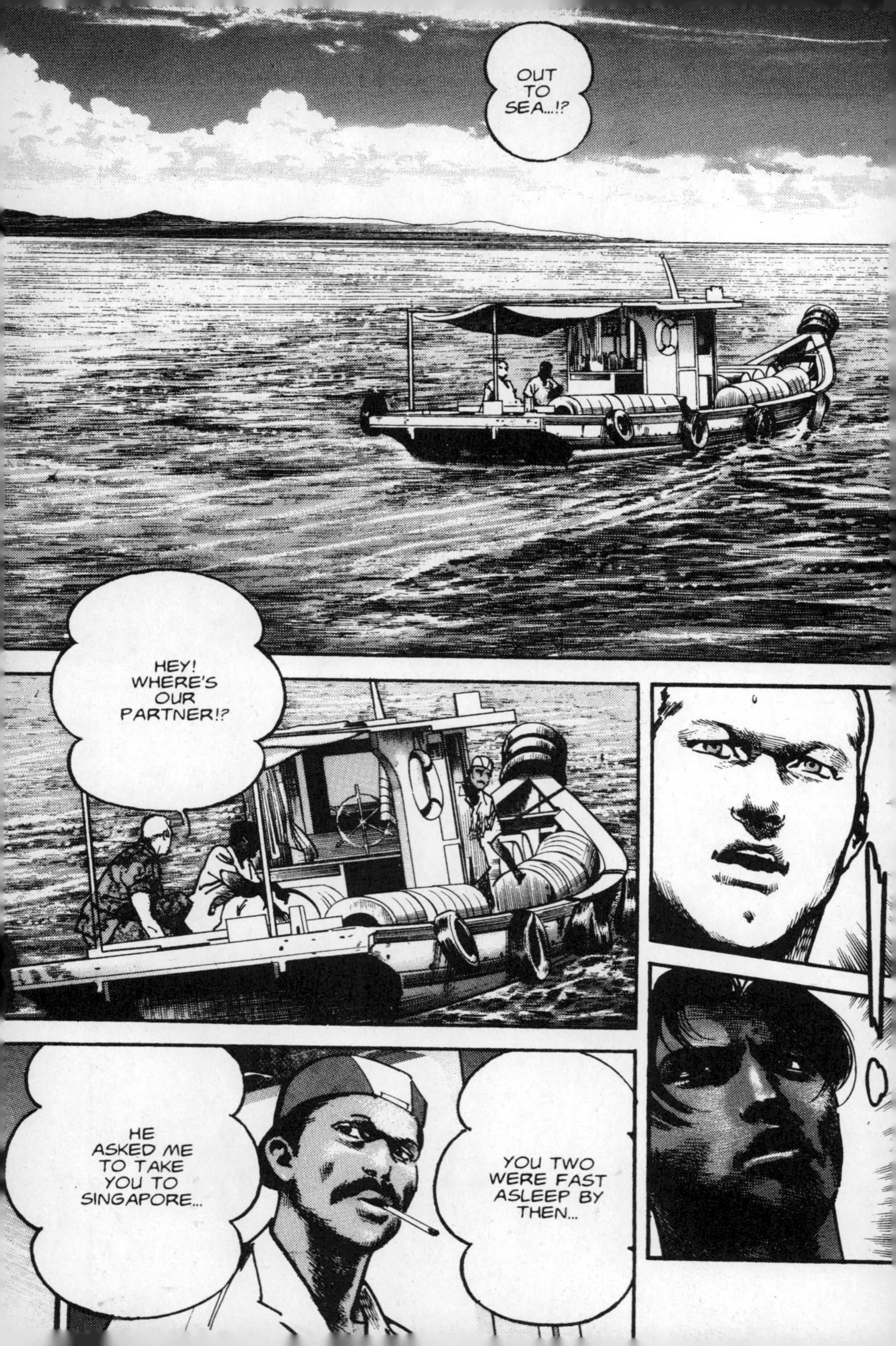
OUT TO SEA...!?
HEY! WHERE'S OUR PARTNER!?
HE ASKED ME TO TAKE YOU TO SINGAPORE...
YOU TWO WERE FAST ASLEEP BY THEN...

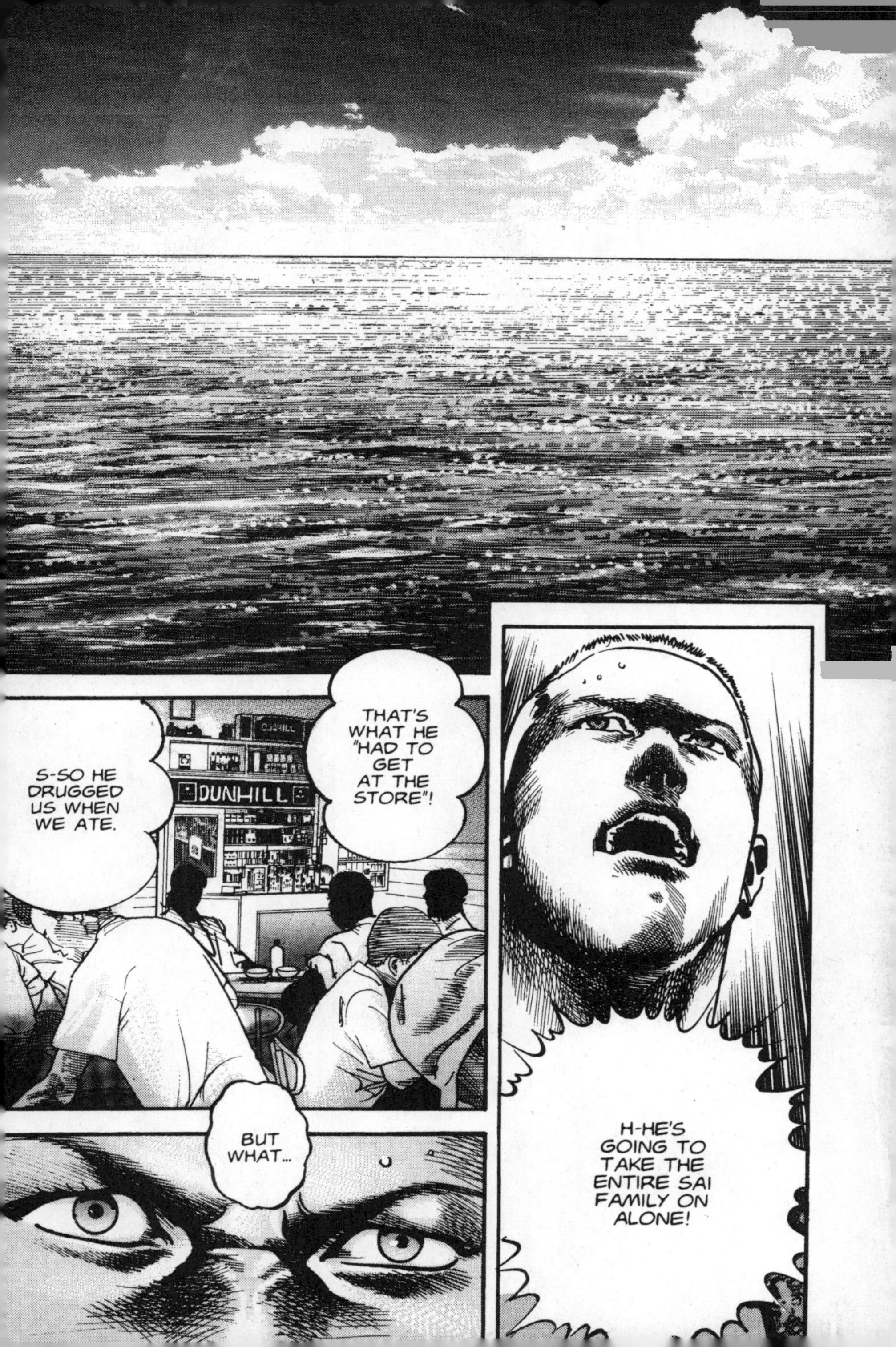
S-SO HE DRUGGED US WHEN WE ATE.
DUNHILL
THAT'S WHAT HE "HAD TO GET AT THE STORE"!
BUT WHAT...
H-HE'S GOING TO TAKE THE ENTIRE SAI FAMILY ON ALONE!

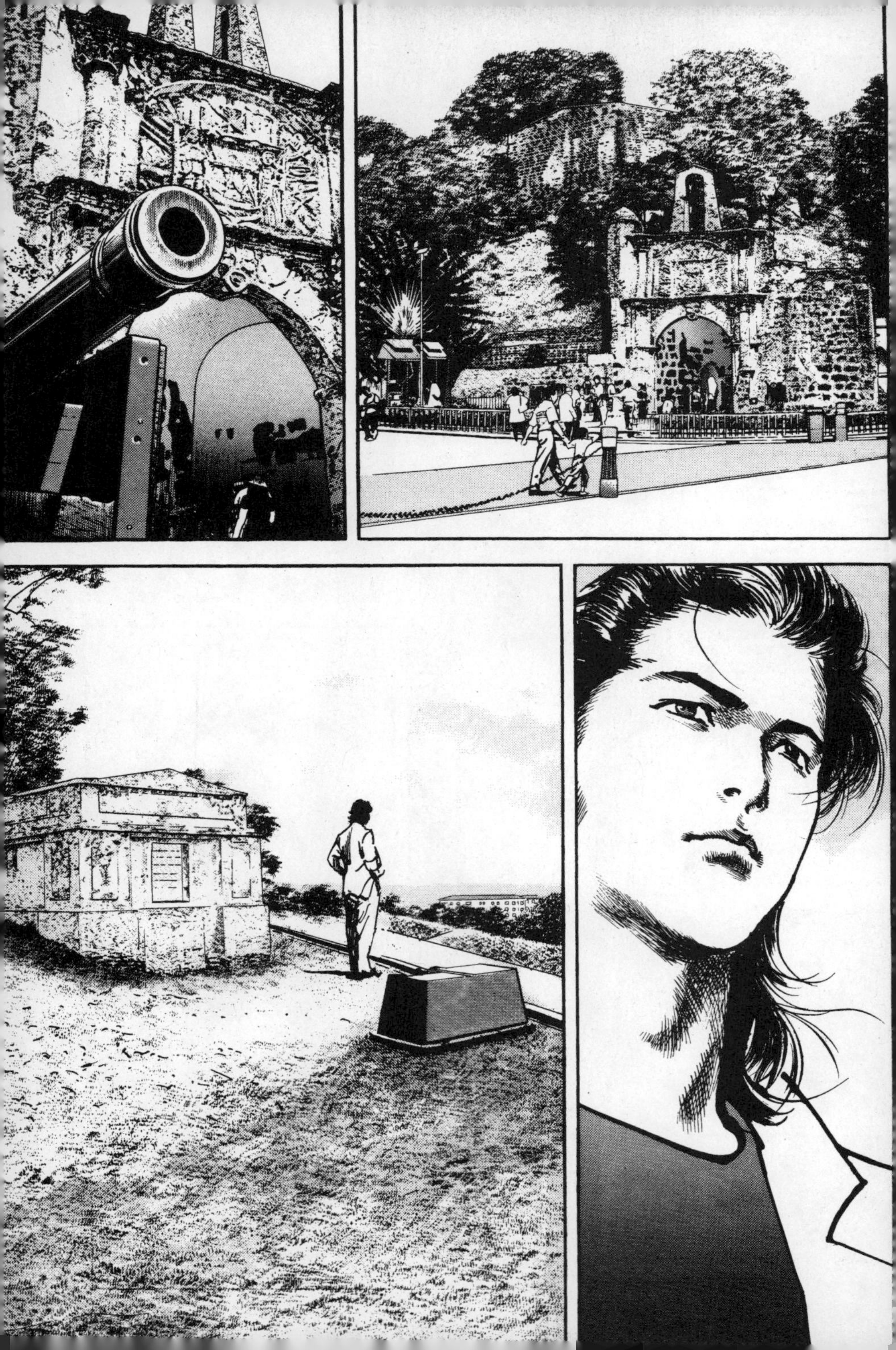

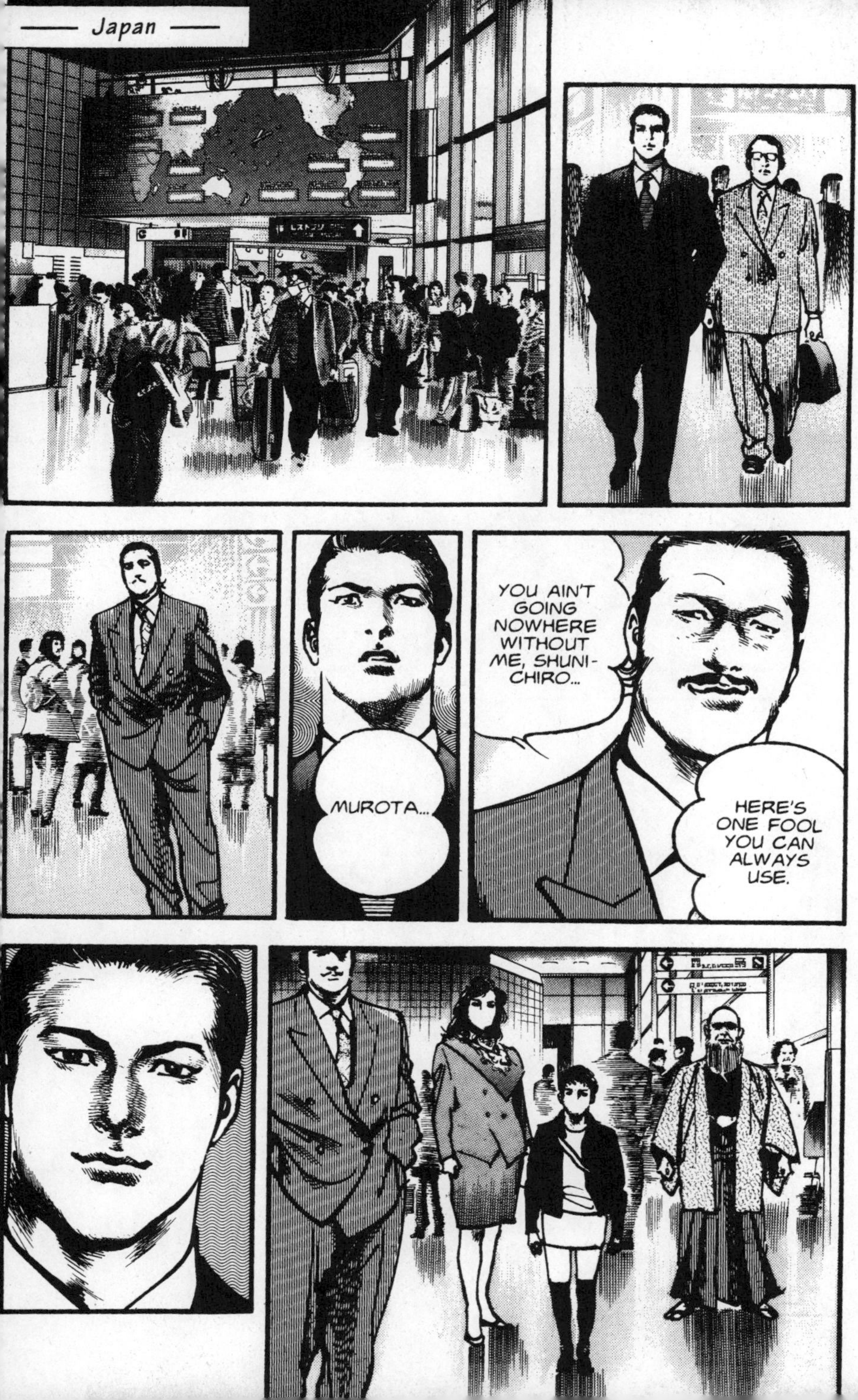
Japan
YOU AIN'T GOING NOWHERE WITHOUT ME, SHUNICHIRO...
MUROTA...
HERE'S ONE FOOL YOU CAN ALWAYS USE.

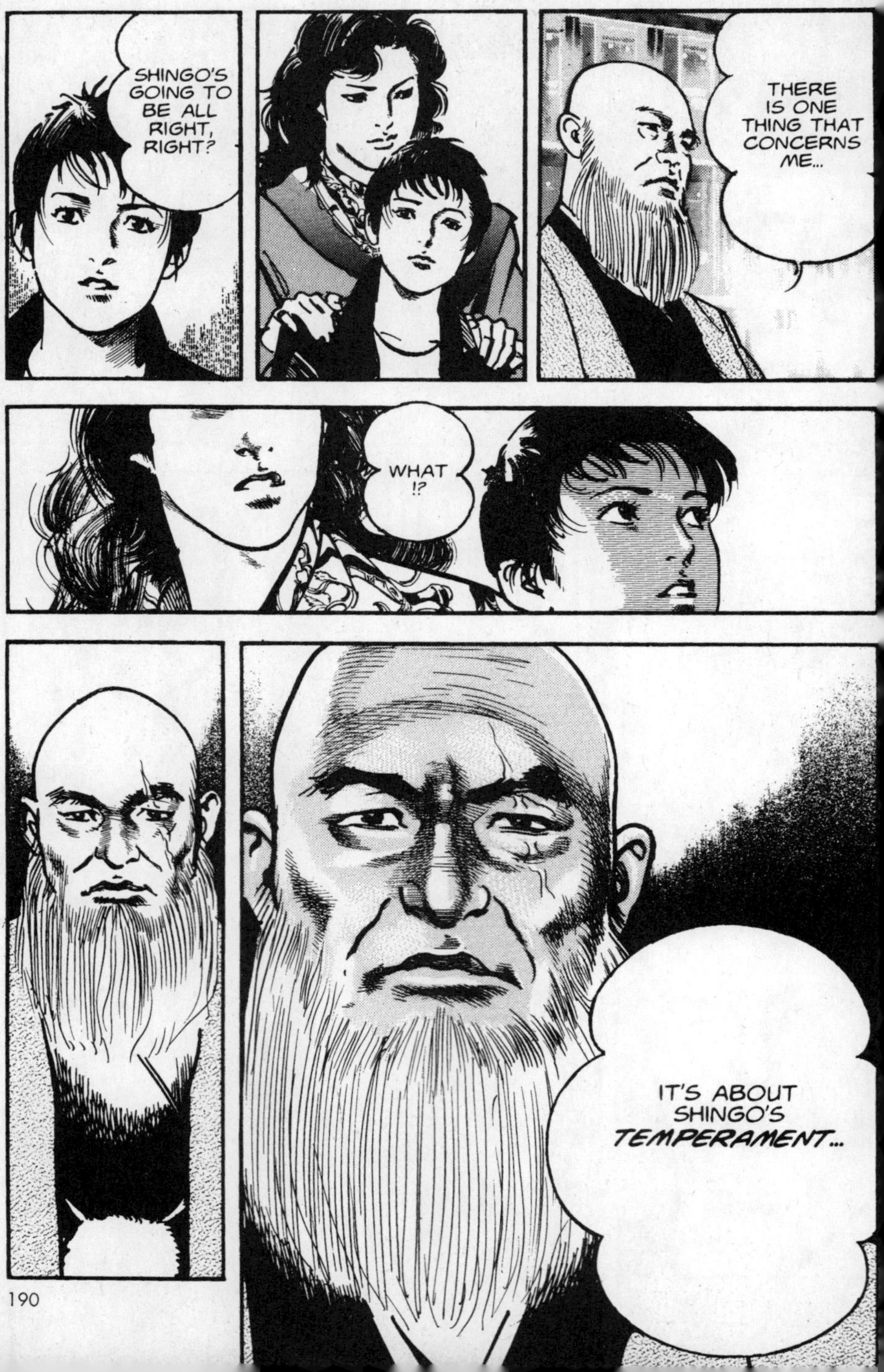
SHINGO'S GOING TO BE ALL RIGHT, RIGHT?
THERE IS ONE THING THAT CONCERNS ME...
WHAT !?
IT'S ABOUT SHINGO'S *TEMPERAMENT*...

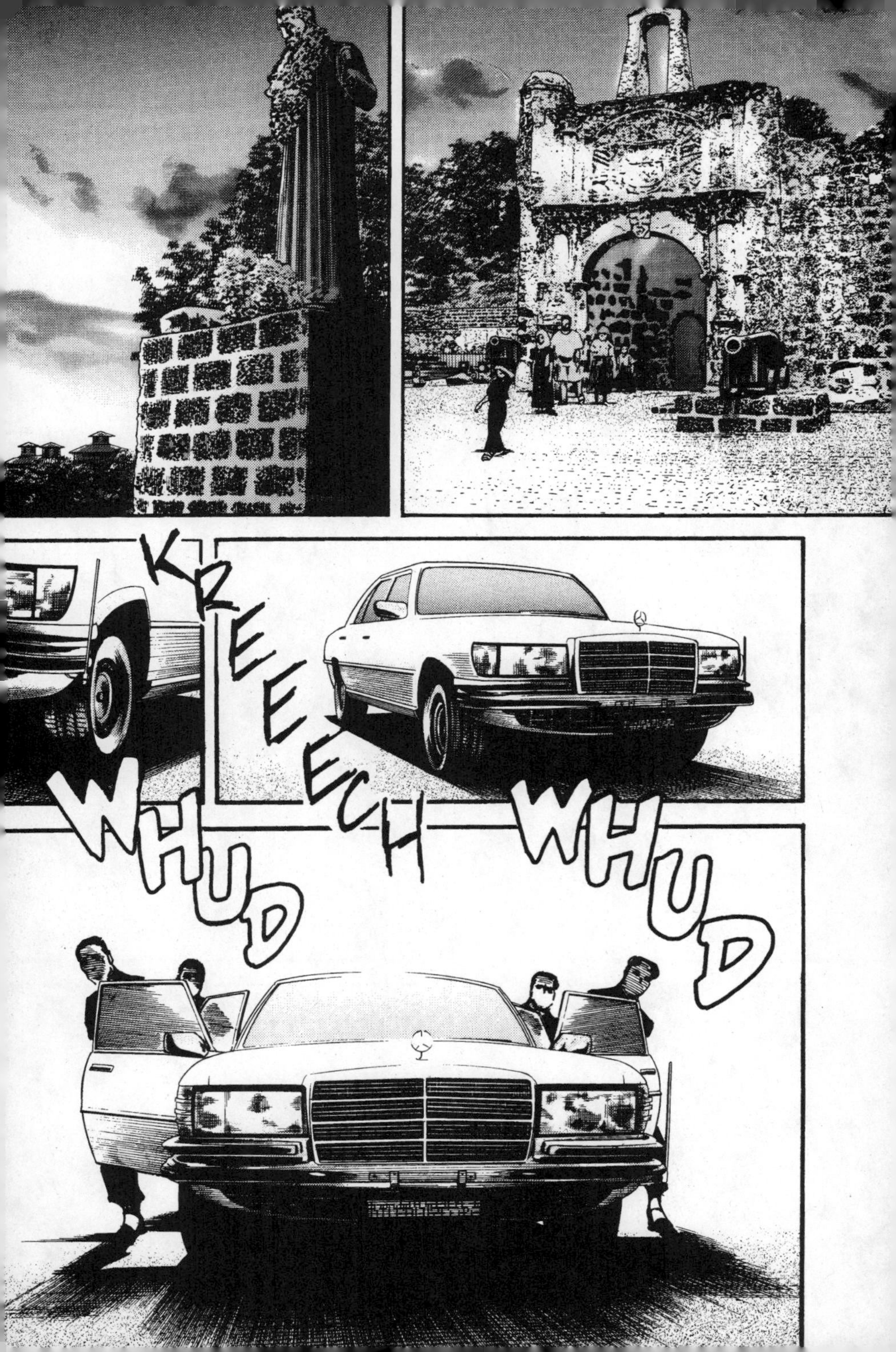
KREEEECH
WHUD
WHUD

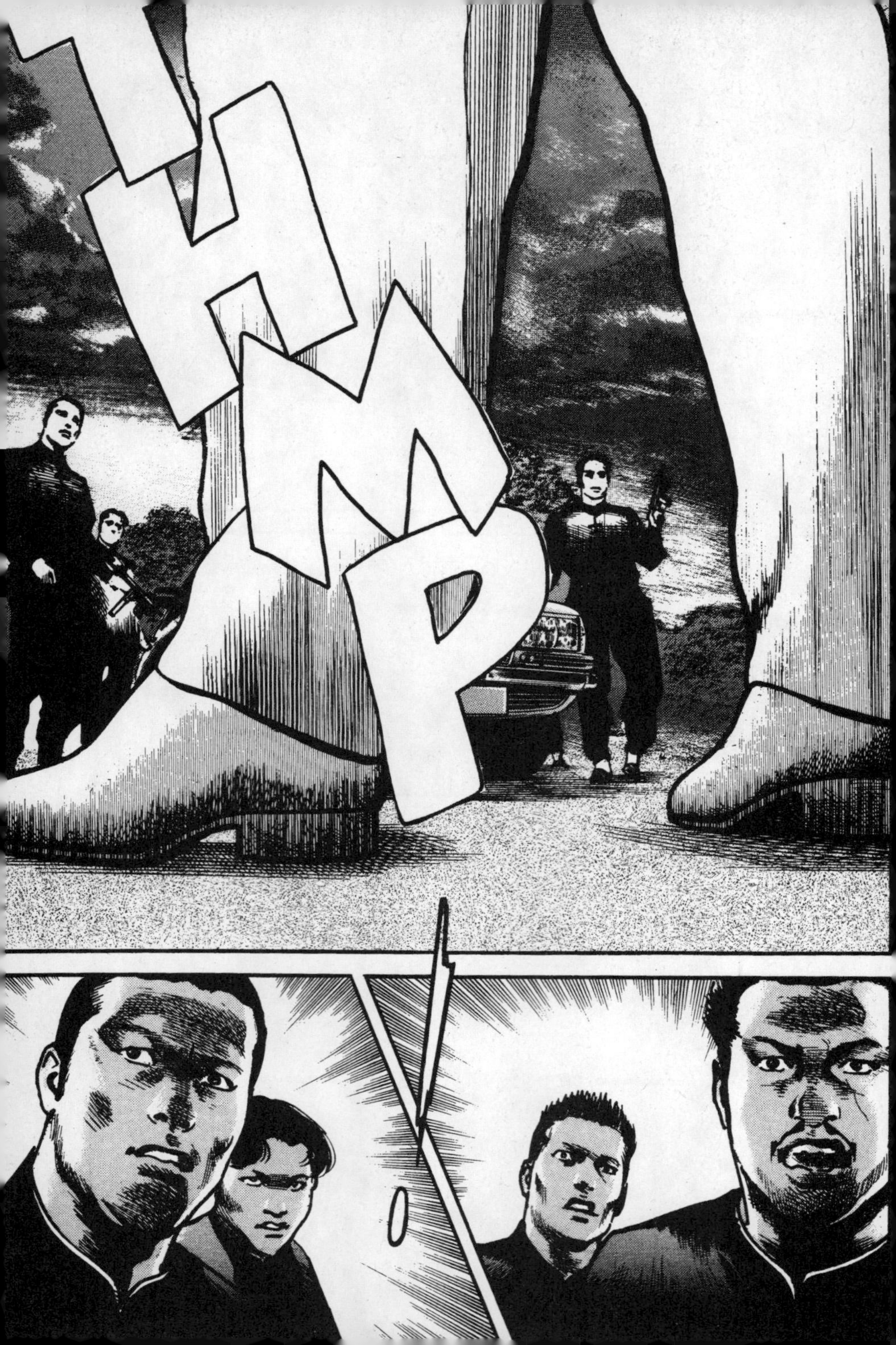
HMP
!

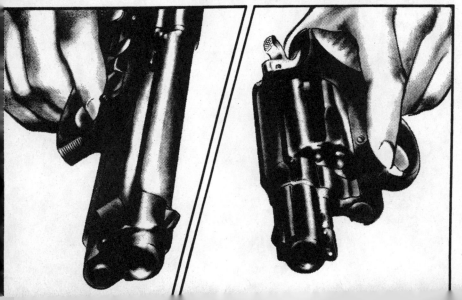

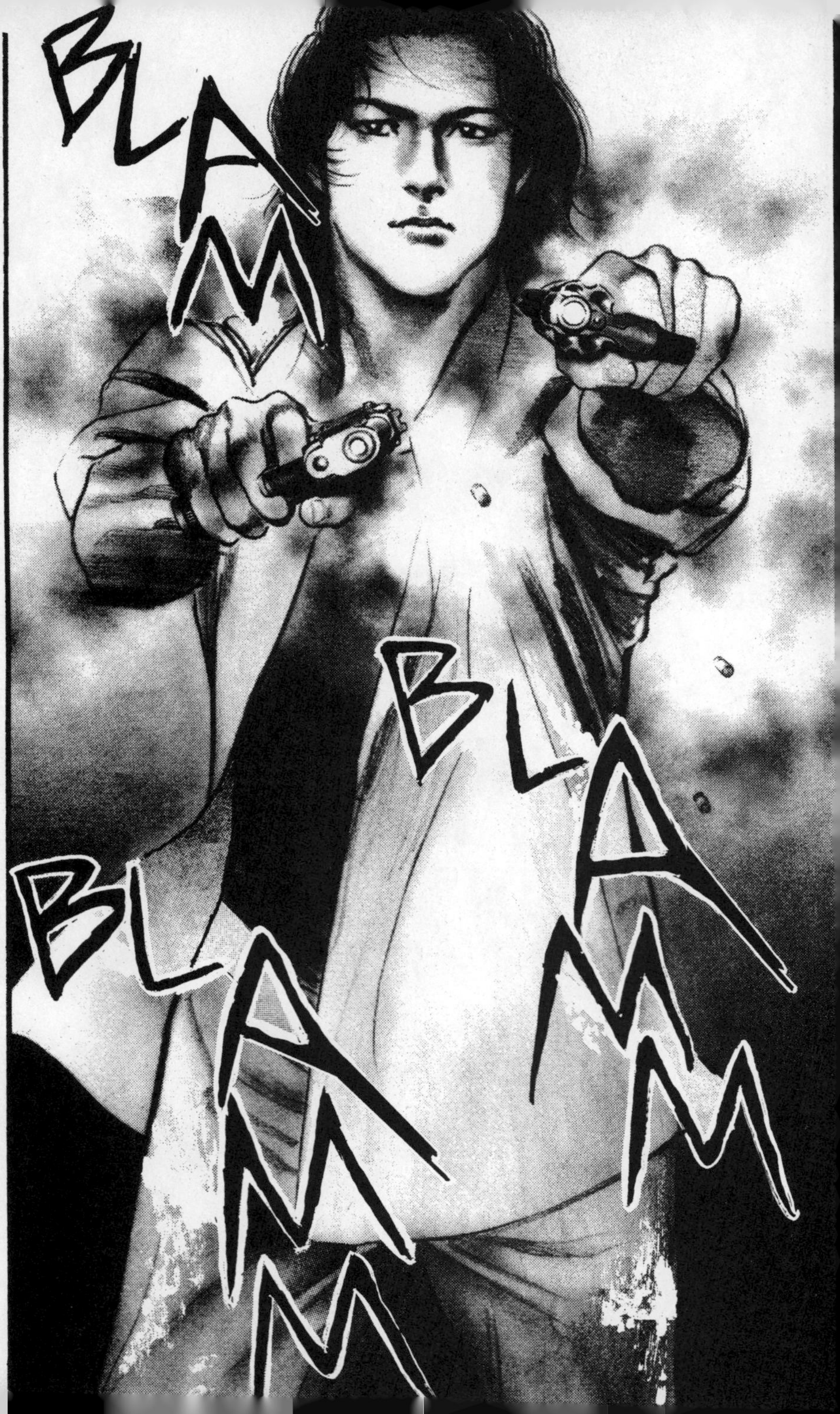
BLAM
BLAMM
BLAMMM

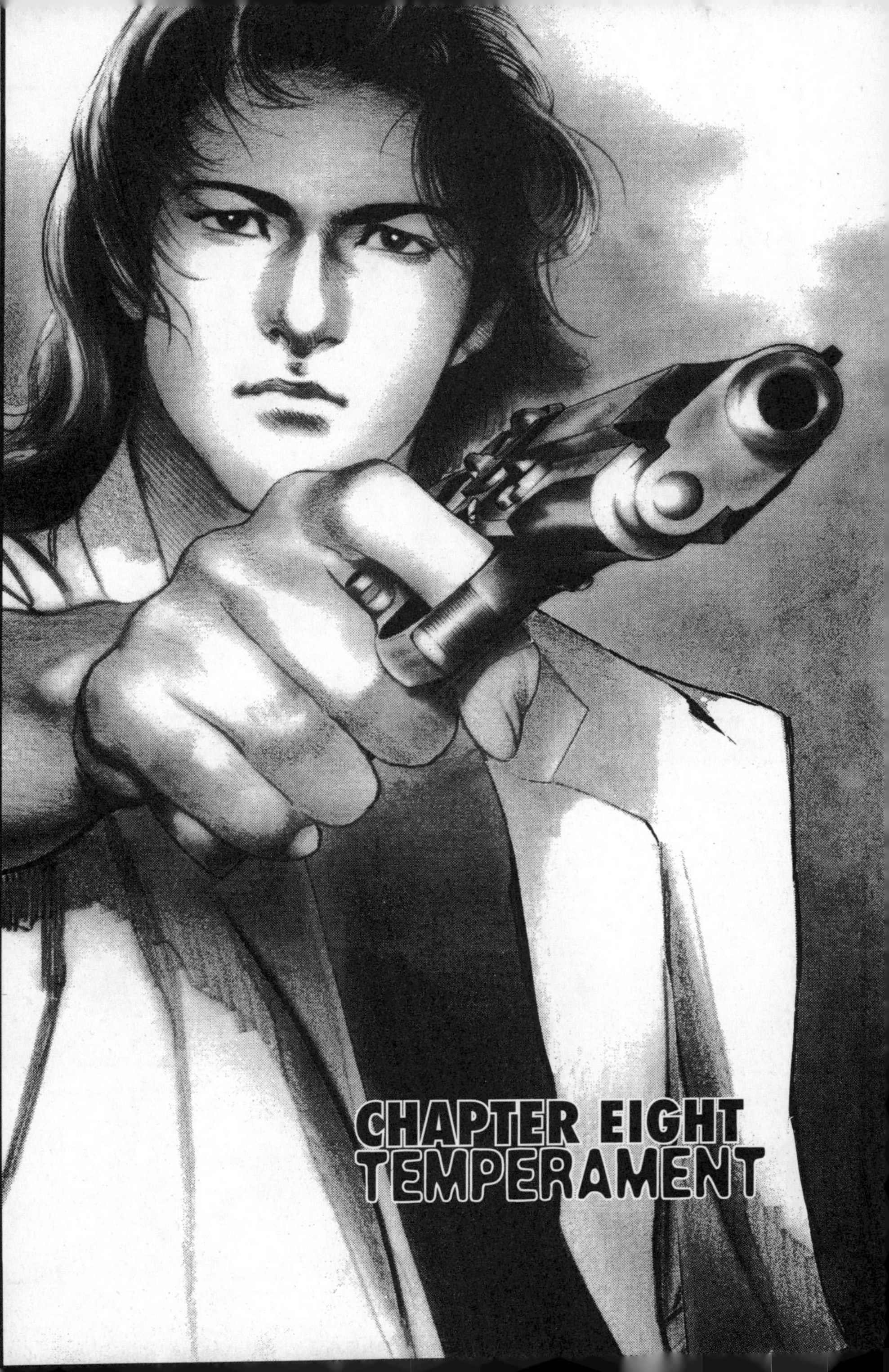
CHAPTER EIGHT
TEMPERAMENT

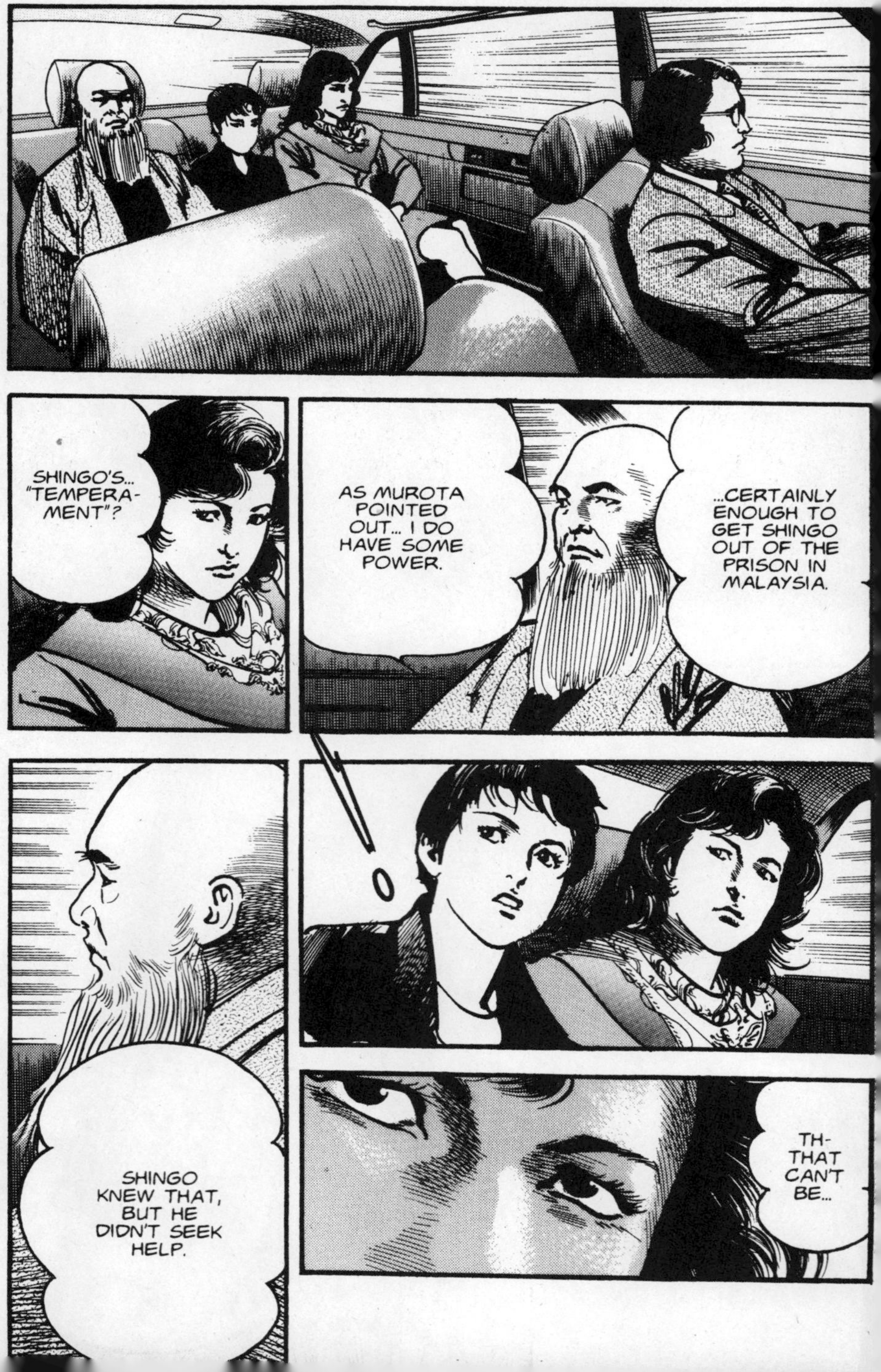
SHINGO'S... "TEMPERAMENT"?
AS MUROTA POINTED OUT... I DO HAVE SOME POWER.
...CERTAINLY ENOUGH TO GET SHINGO OUT OF THE PRISON IN MALAYSIA.
SHINGO KNEW THAT, BUT HE DIDN'T SEEK HELP.
TH- THAT CAN'T BE...

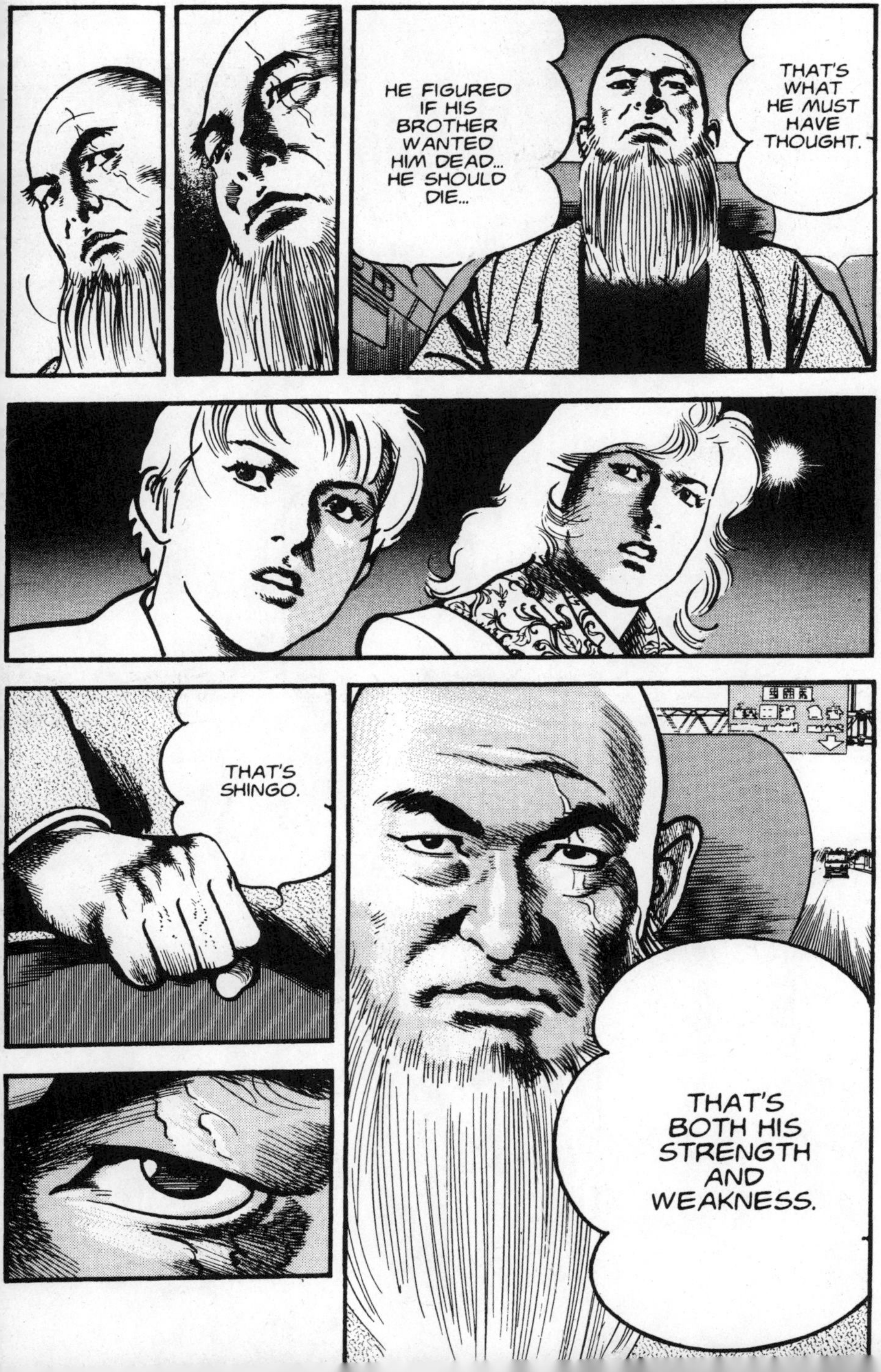
HE FIGURED IF HIS BROTHER WANTED HIM DEAD... HE SHOULD DIE...
THAT'S WHAT HE MUST HAVE THOUGHT.
THAT'S SHINGO.
THAT'S BOTH HIS STRENGTH AND WEAKNESS.

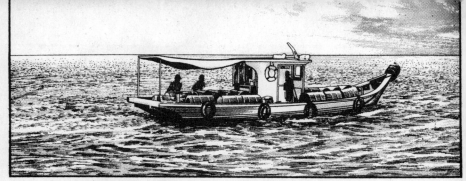

HEARING ABOUT OUR MOTHERS...

THAT BASTARD...

FWISH

HEY! WE'RE GOING BACK TO MALACCA.

B-BUT...

BLAMM

WE DIDN'T ASK YOUR OPINION!

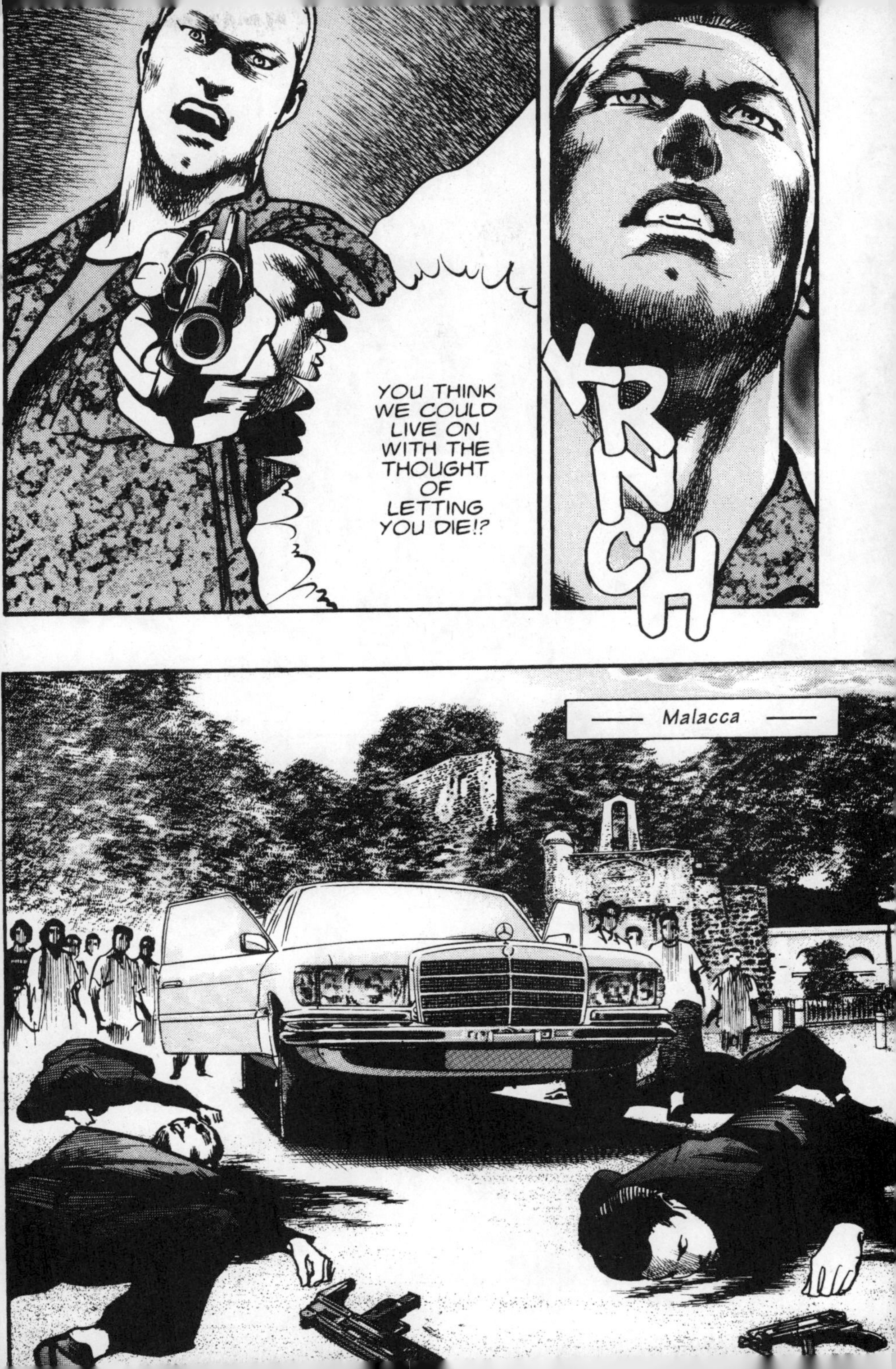
YOU THINK WE COULD LIVE ON WITH THE THOUGHT OF LETTING YOU DIE!?
KRNCH
Malacca

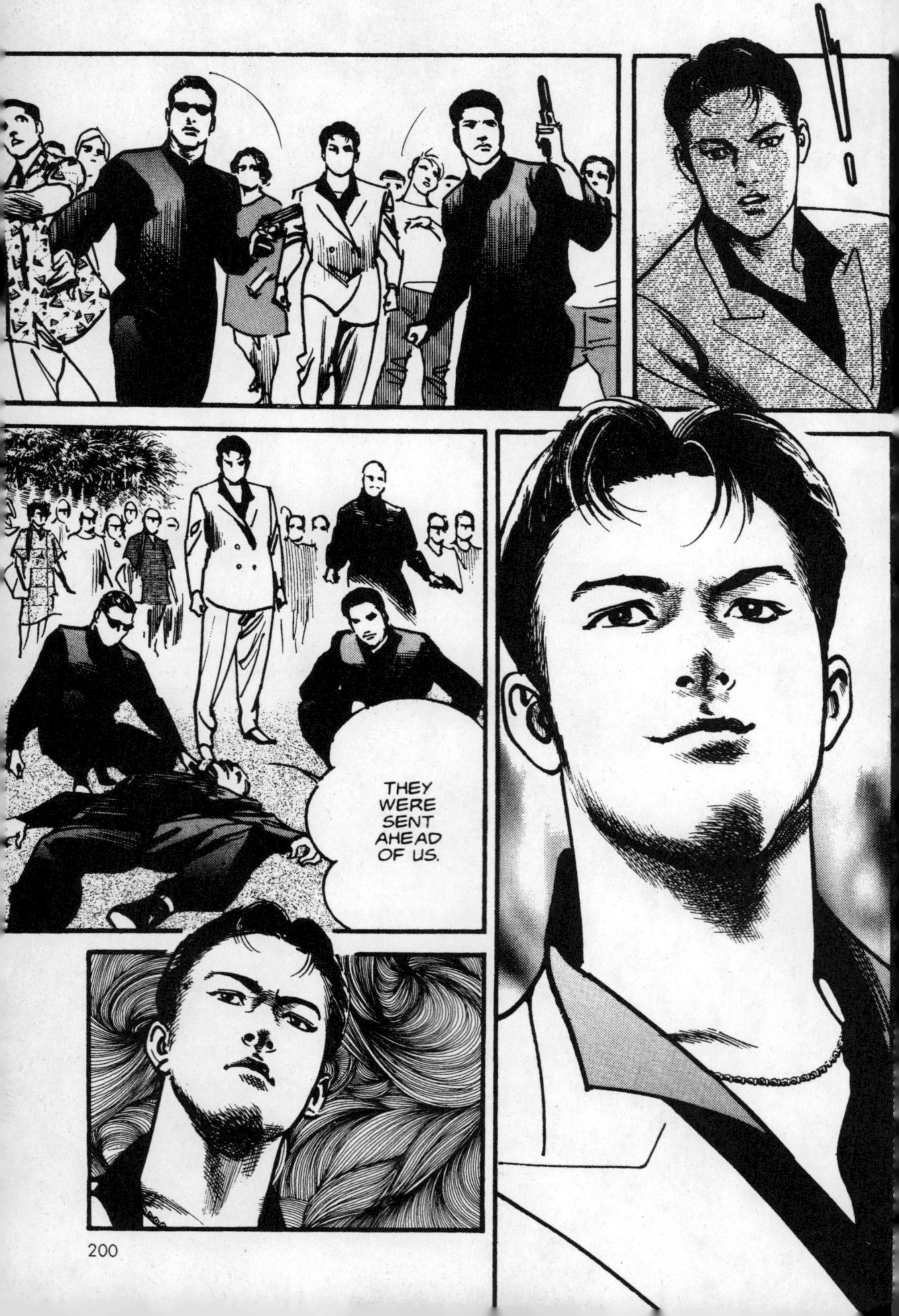
!!
THEY WERE SENT AHEAD OF US.

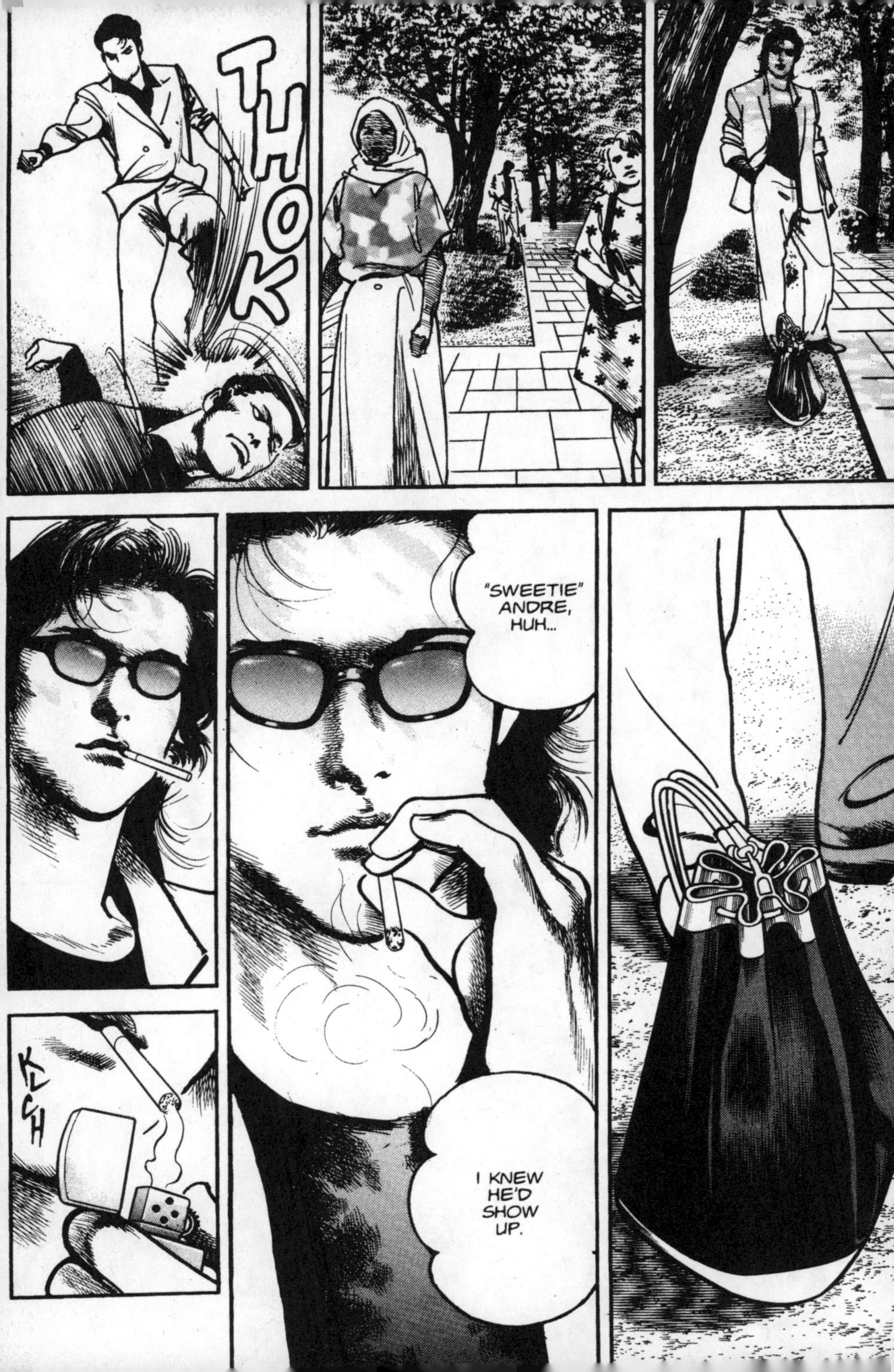
THOK
"SWEETIE" ANDRE, HUH...
KLCH
I KNEW HE'D SHOW UP.

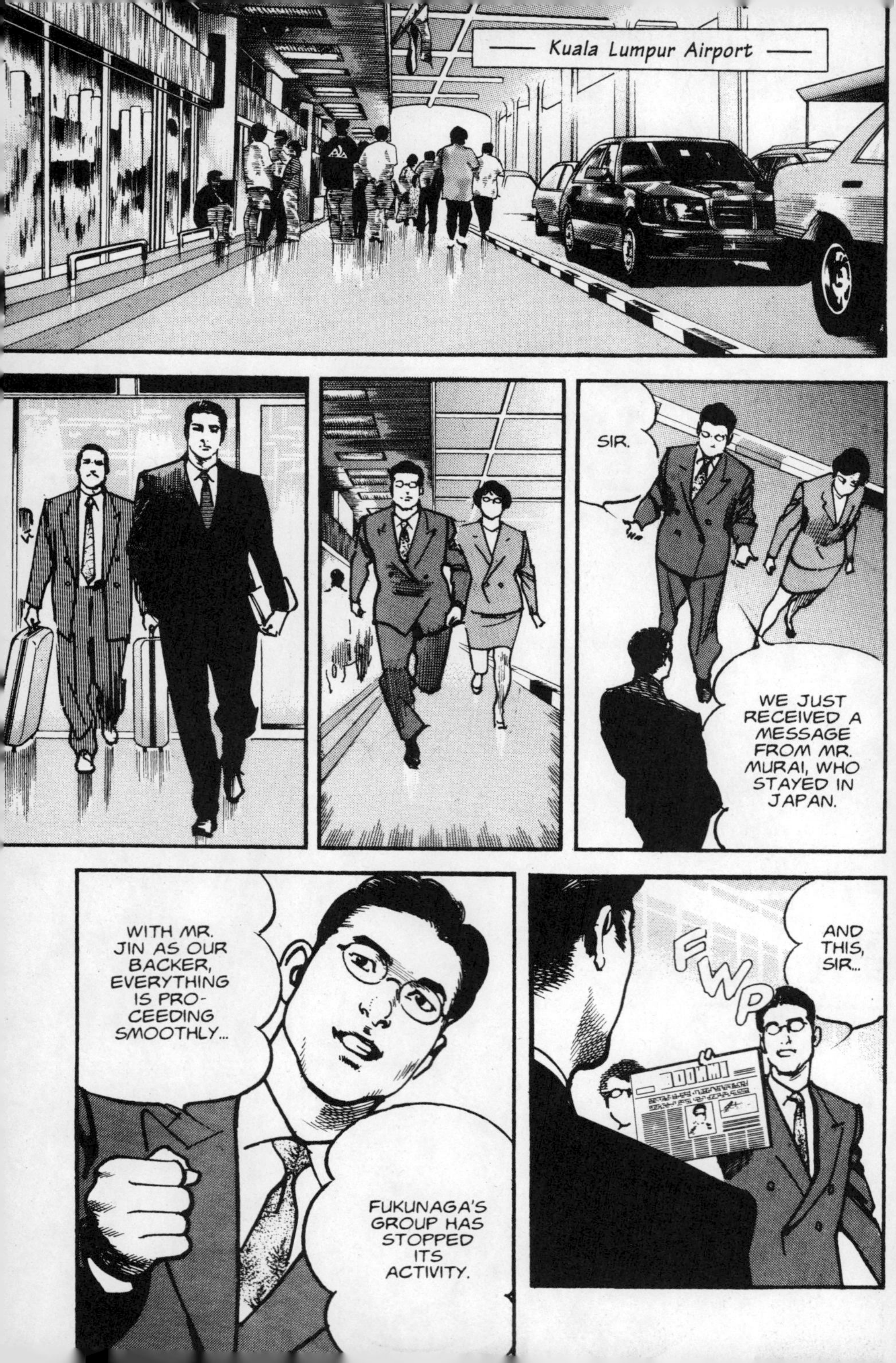

— Kuala Lumpur Airport —
SIR.
WE JUST RECEIVED A MESSAGE FROM MR. MURAI, WHO STAYED IN JAPAN.
WITH MR. JIN AS OUR BACKER, EVERYTHING IS PRO-CEEDING SMOOTHLY...
FUKUNAGA'S GROUP HAS STOPPED ITS ACTIVITY.
AND THIS, SIR...
FWP

KUSAKA CHAIRMAN STEPS DOWN

SURPRISE RESIGNATION IN FAVOR OF YOUNGER BROTHER, SHINGO

Young New Chair Of Family Corporation To Take Control As The Malaysian Oil Deal Hangs In Balance

AS INSTRUCTED, WE DISPATCHED PRESS RELEASES TO THE NEWSPAPERS, TV, AND RADIO NETWORKS.

SOME OF THE HEADLINES HAVE ALREADY HIT THE NEWSSTANDS.

LOOK, MUROTA ...IT REPORTS MY RESIGNATION.

IF SHINGO'S IN MALAYSIA HE'LL SEE THIS.

HE'LL THINK TWICE ABOUT RISKING HIS LIFE.

I JUST HOPE HE DOES...

203

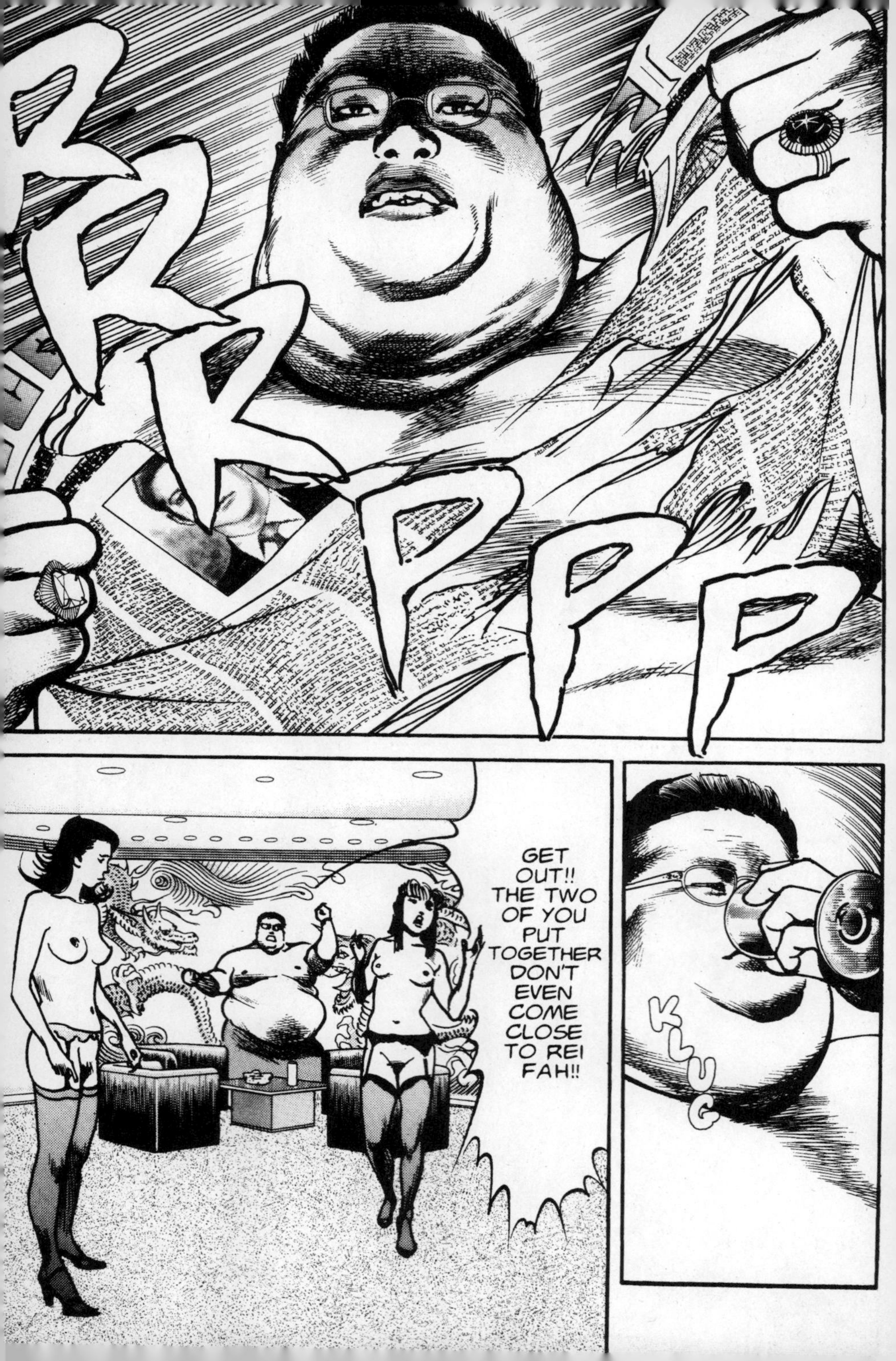
GET OUT!! THE TWO OF YOU PUT TOGETHER DON'T EVEN COME CLOSE TO REI FAH!!
KLUG

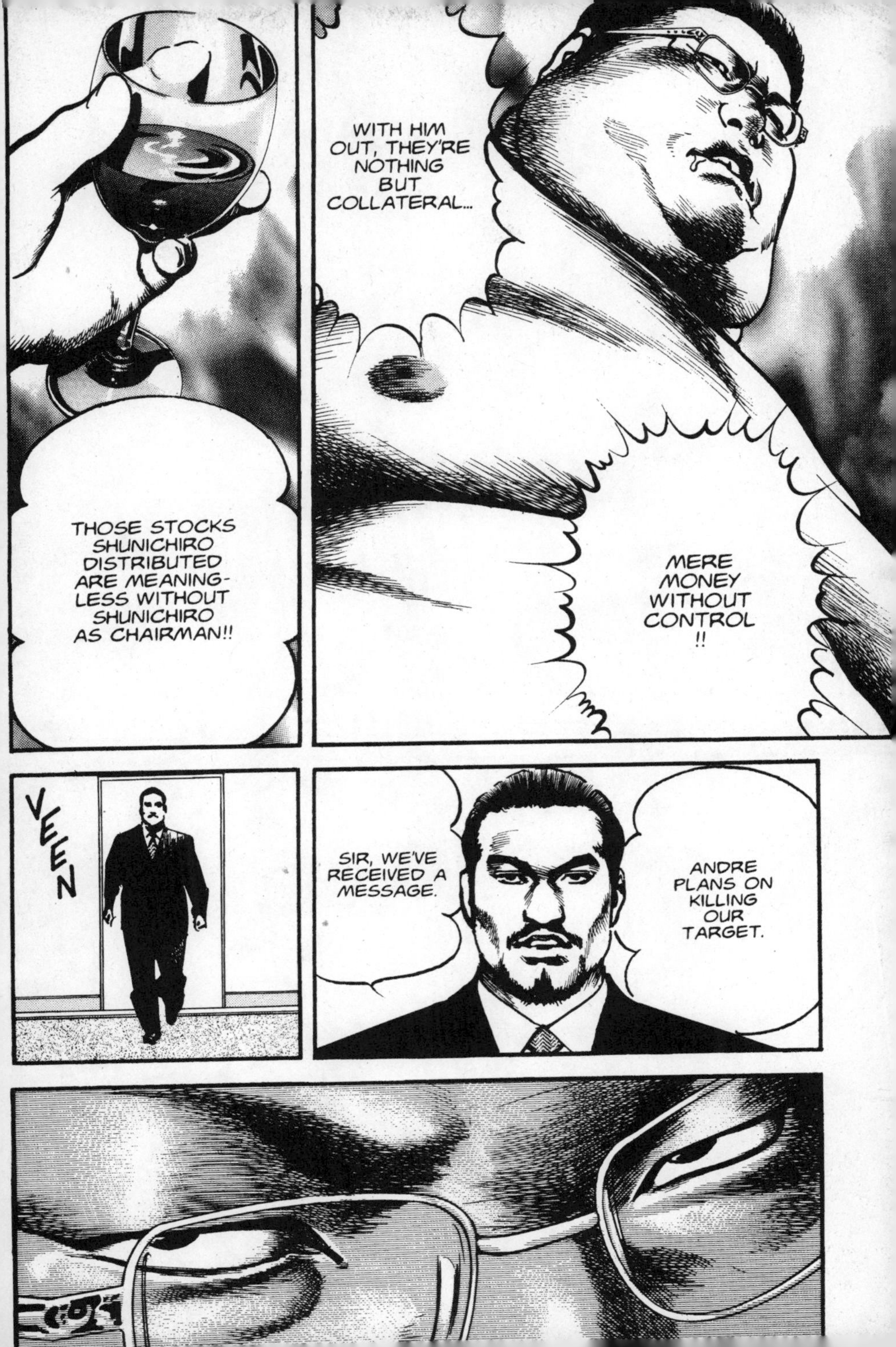
WITH HIM OUT, THEY'RE NOTHING BUT COLLATERAL...
THOSE STOCKS SHUNICHIRO DISTRIBUTED ARE MEANING-LESS WITHOUT SHUNICHIRO AS CHAIRMAN!!
MERE MONEY WITHOUT CONTROL !!
VEEN
SIR, WE'VE RECEIVED A MESSAGE.
ANDRE PLANS ON KILLING OUR TARGET.

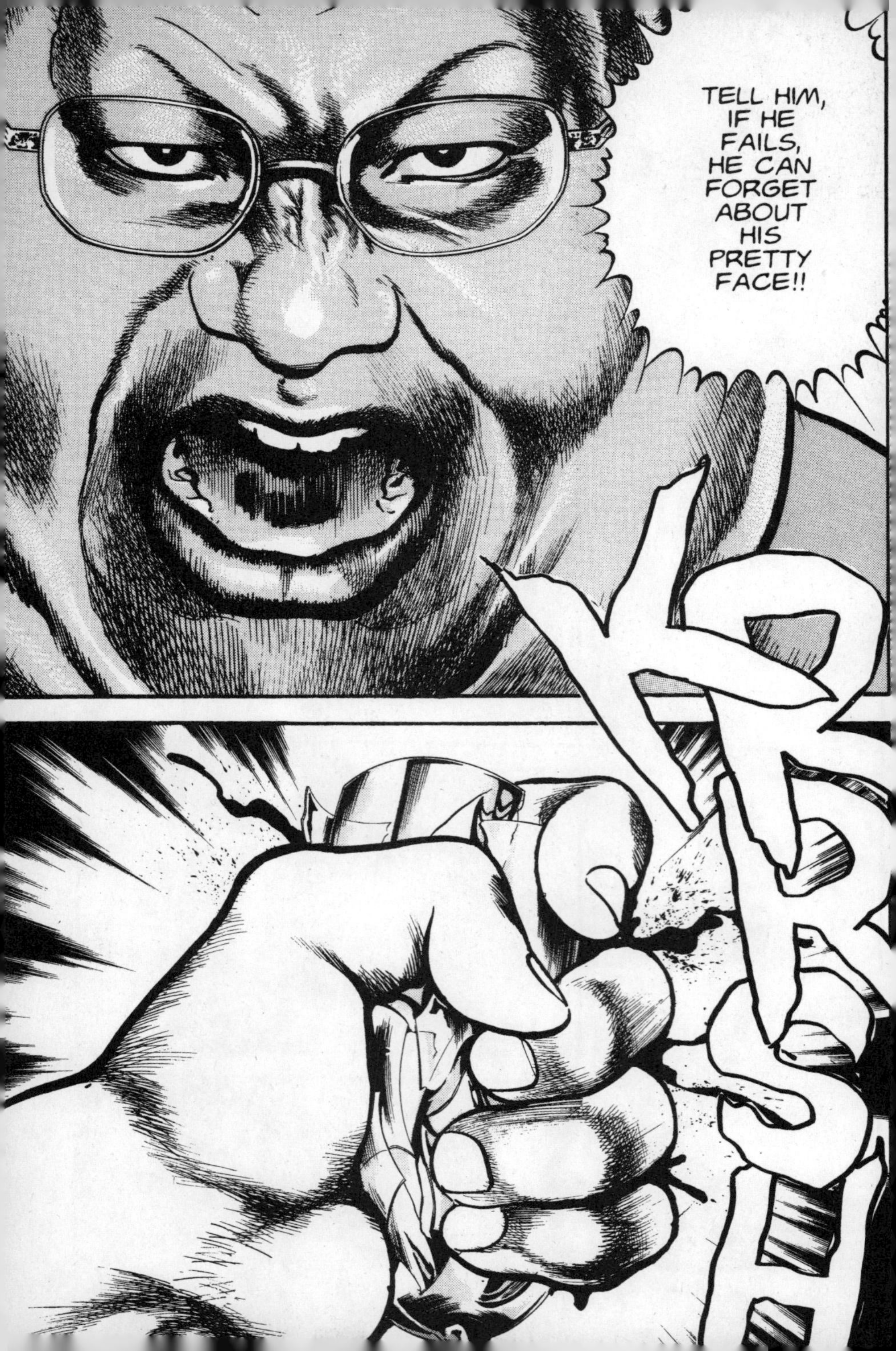
TELL HIM, IF HE FAILS, HE CAN FORGET ABOUT HIS PRETTY FACE!!

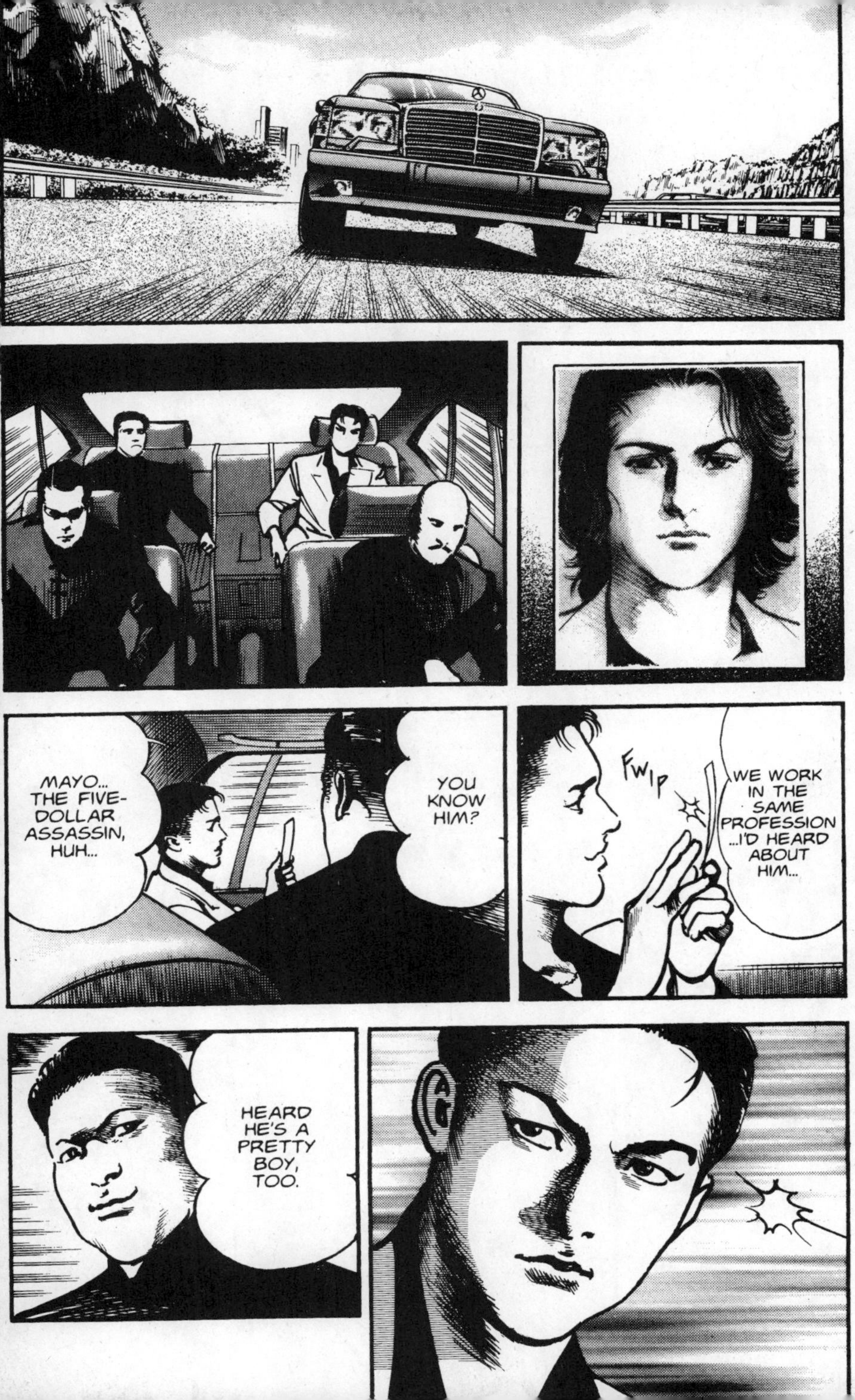

MAYO... THE FIVE-DOLLAR ASSASSIN, HUH...
YOU KNOW HIM?
FWIP
WE WORK IN THE SAME PROFESSION ...I'D HEARD ABOUT HIM...
HEARD HE'S A PRETTY BOY, TOO.

I DON'T LIKE THIS FACE...

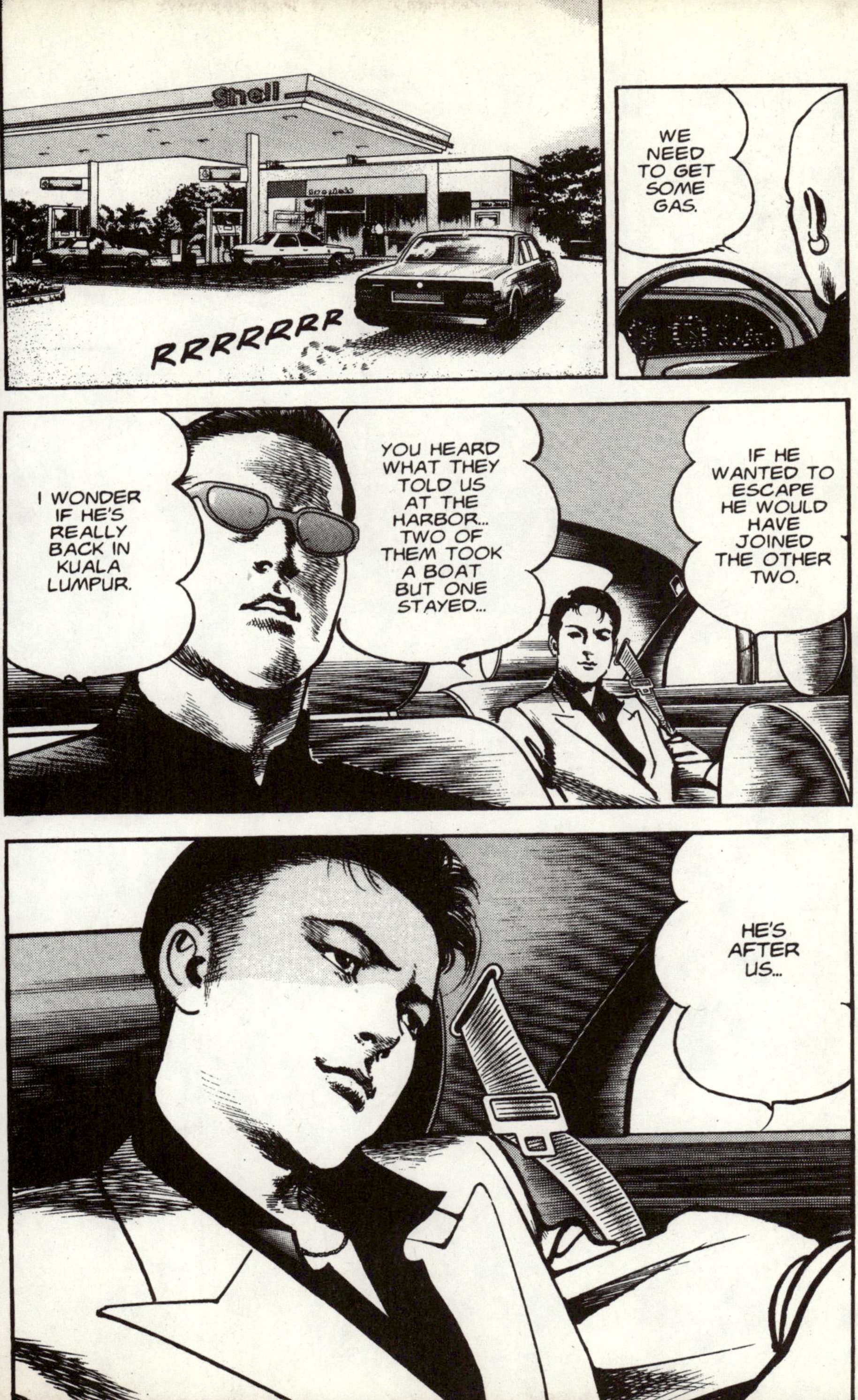
Shell
RRRRRRR
WE NEED TO GET SOME GAS.
I WONDER IF HE'S REALLY BACK IN KUALA LUMPUR.
YOU HEARD WHAT THEY TOLD US AT THE HARBOR... TWO OF THEM TOOK A BOAT BUT ONE STAYED...
IF HE WANTED TO ESCAPE HE WOULD HAVE JOINED THE OTHER TWO.
HE'S AFTER US...

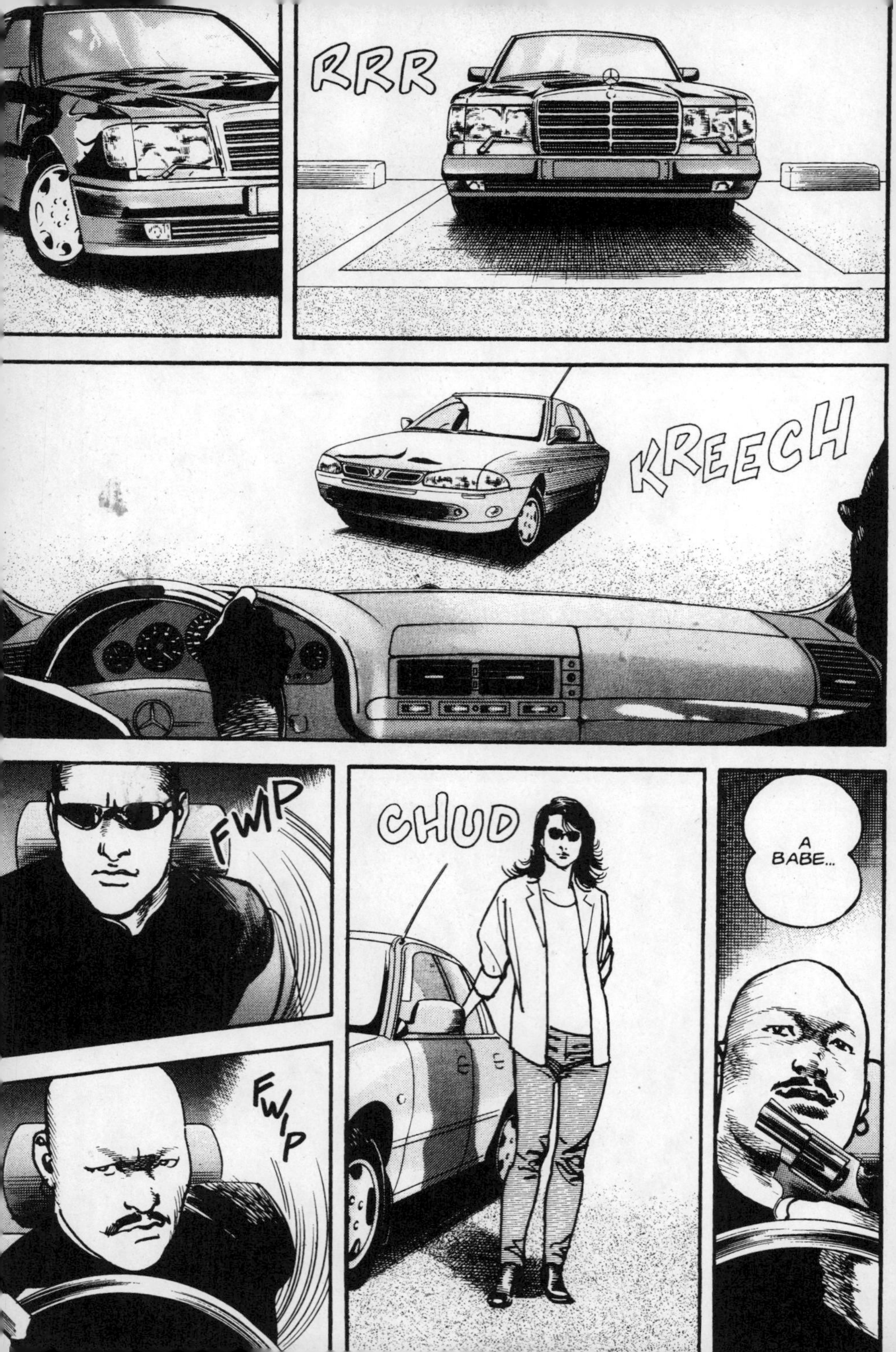
RRR
KREECH
FWIP
FWIP
CHUD
A BABE...

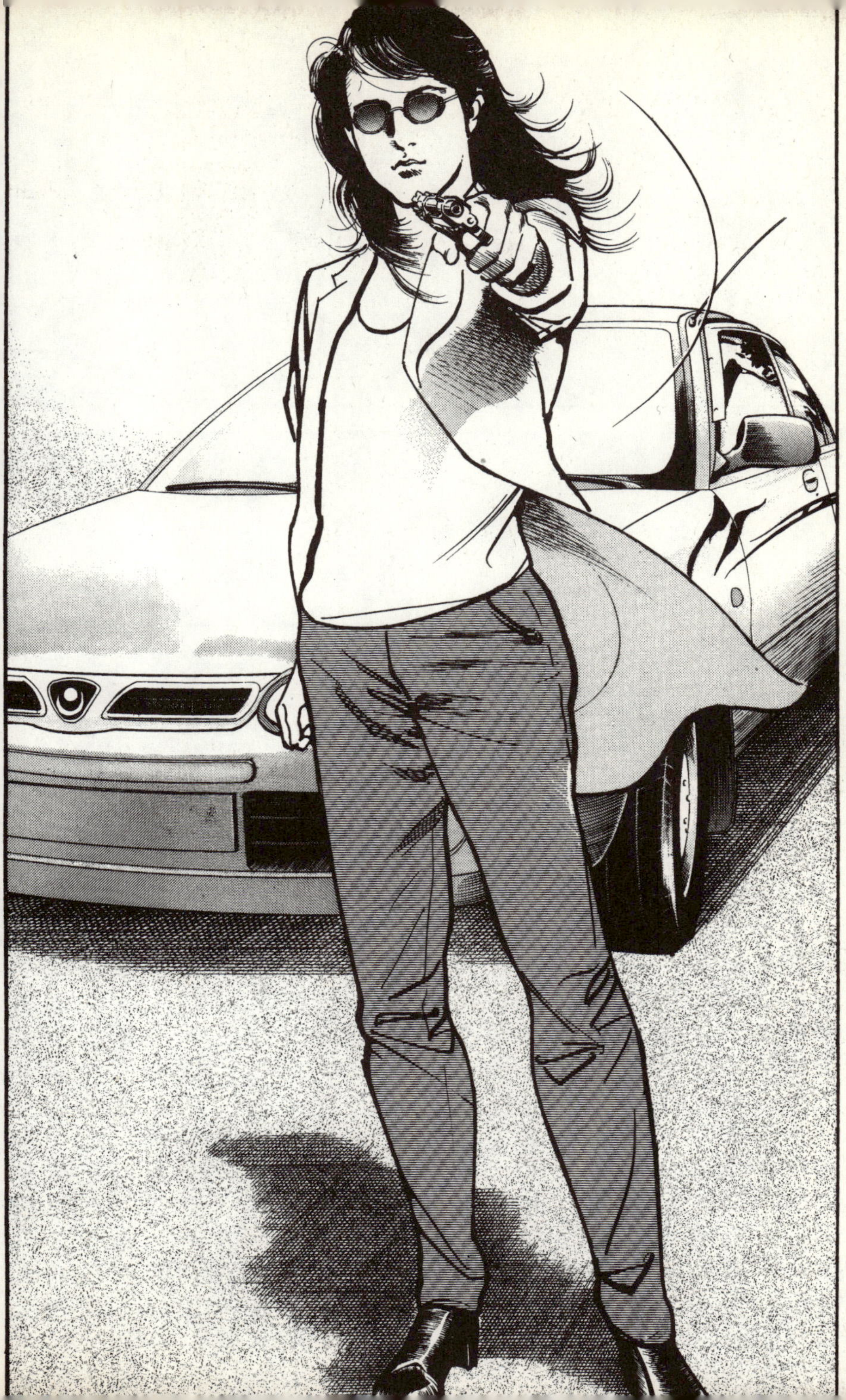

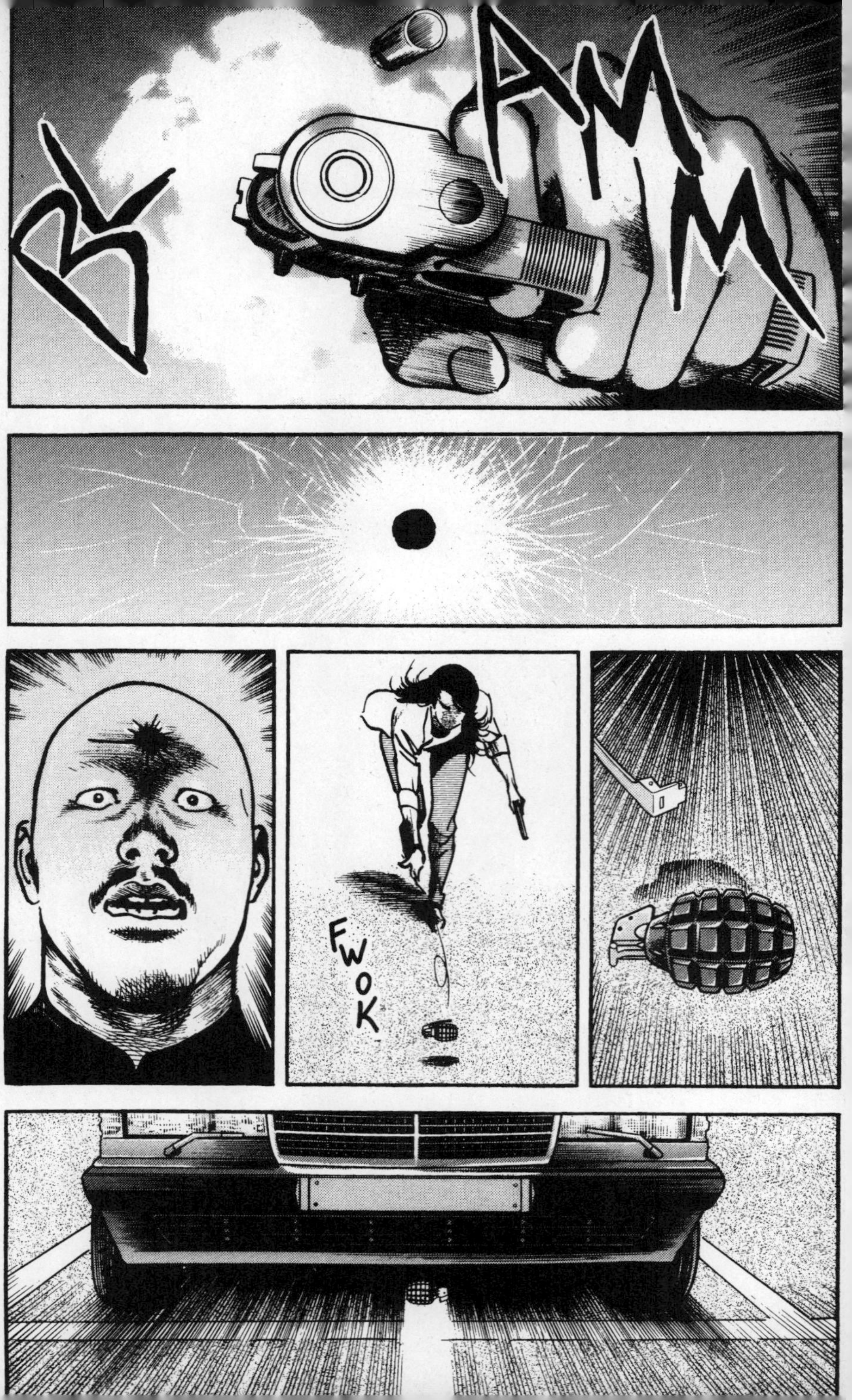
BLAM
FWOK

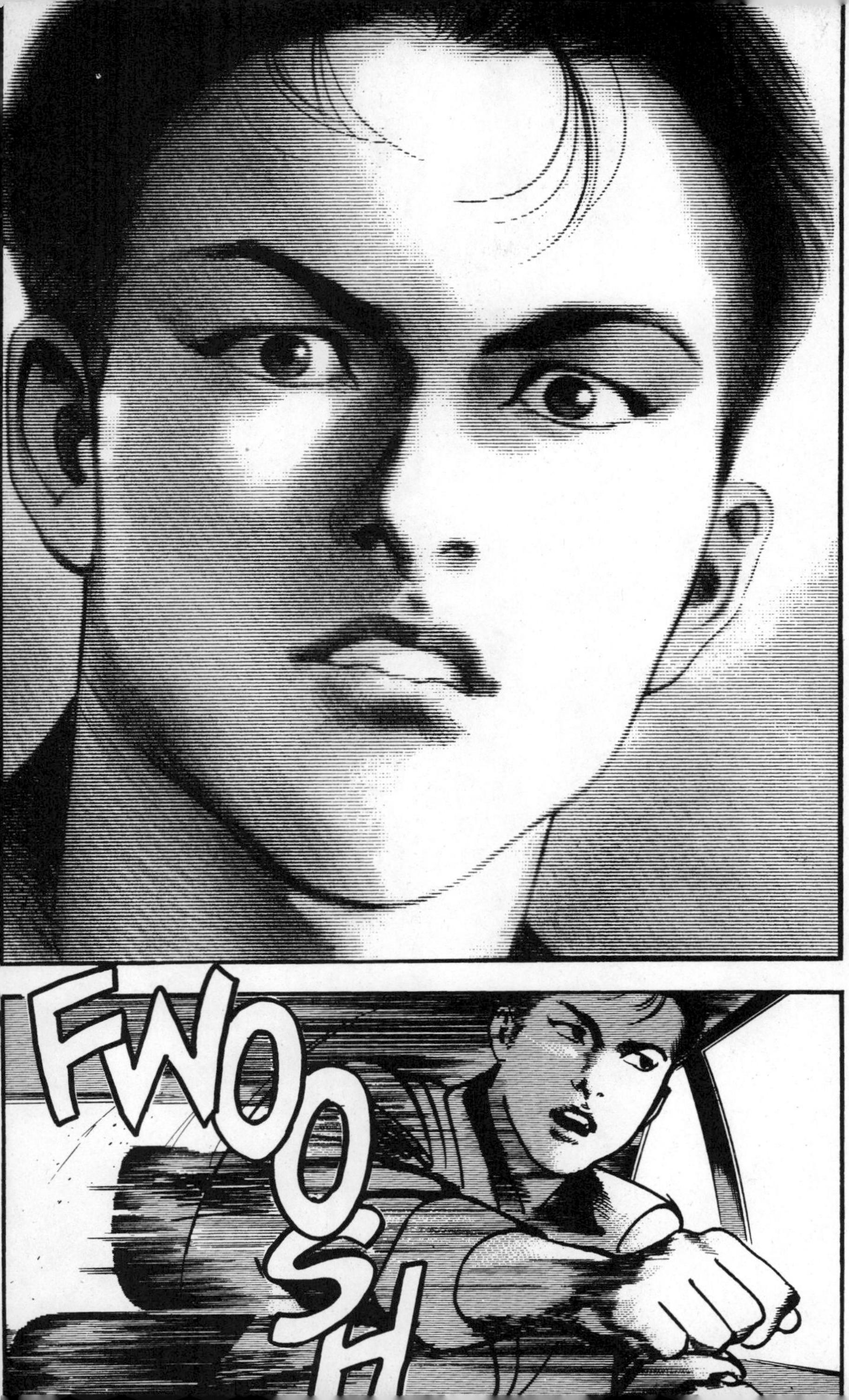
FWOOSH

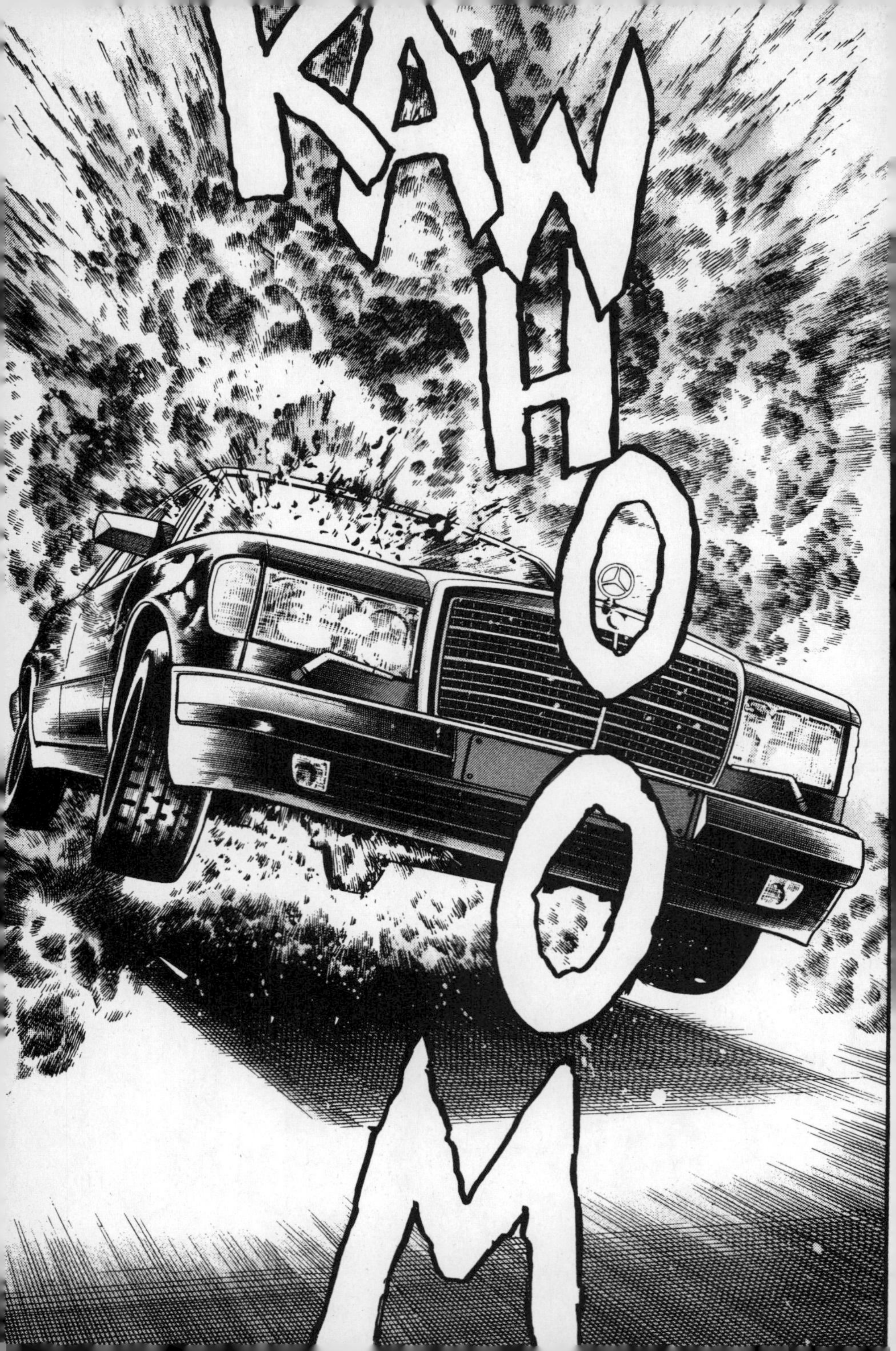
KAWHOOM

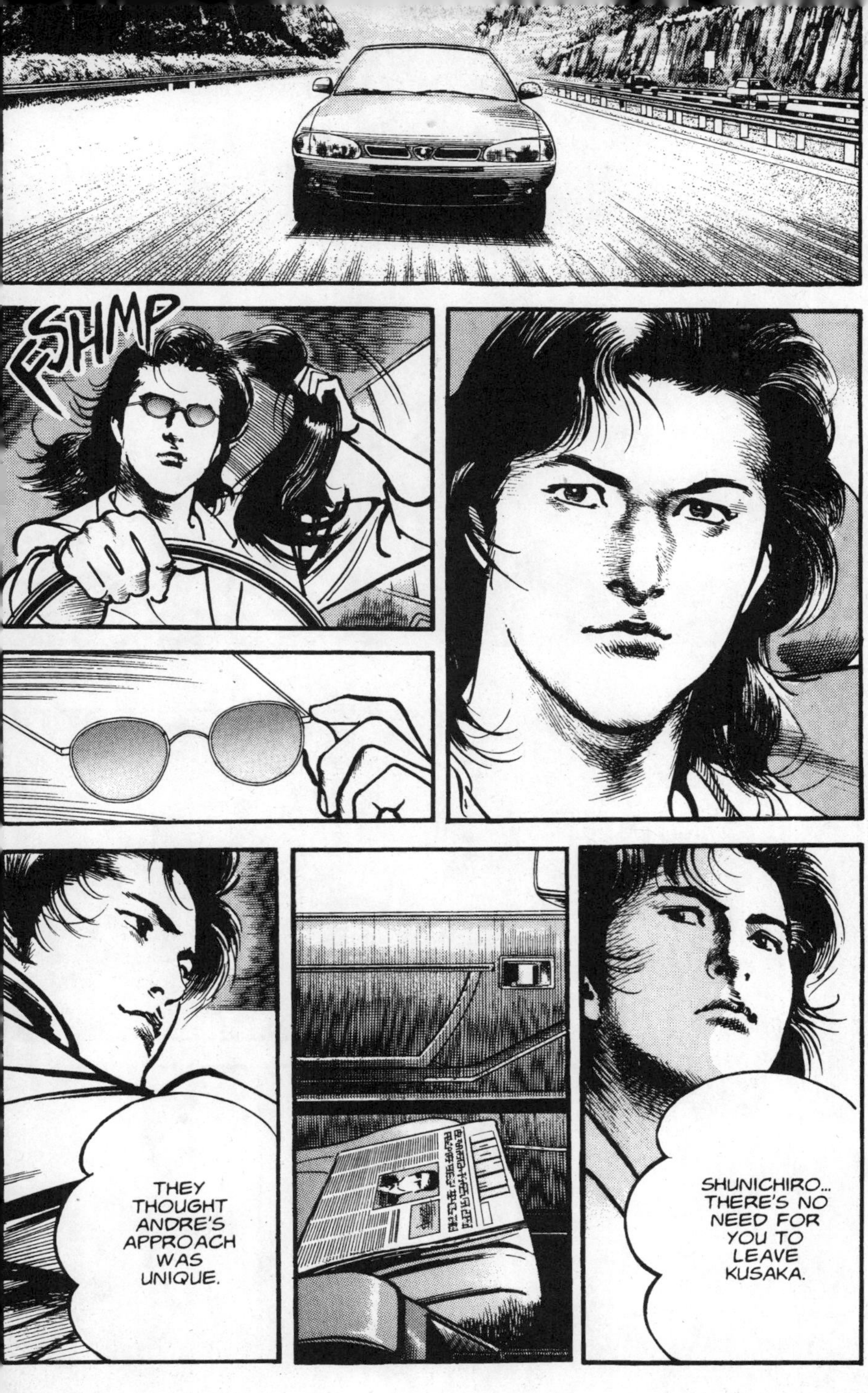
SHMP
THEY THOUGHT ANDRE'S APPROACH WAS UNIQUE.
SHUNICHIRO... THERE'S NO NEED FOR YOU TO LEAVE KUSAKA.

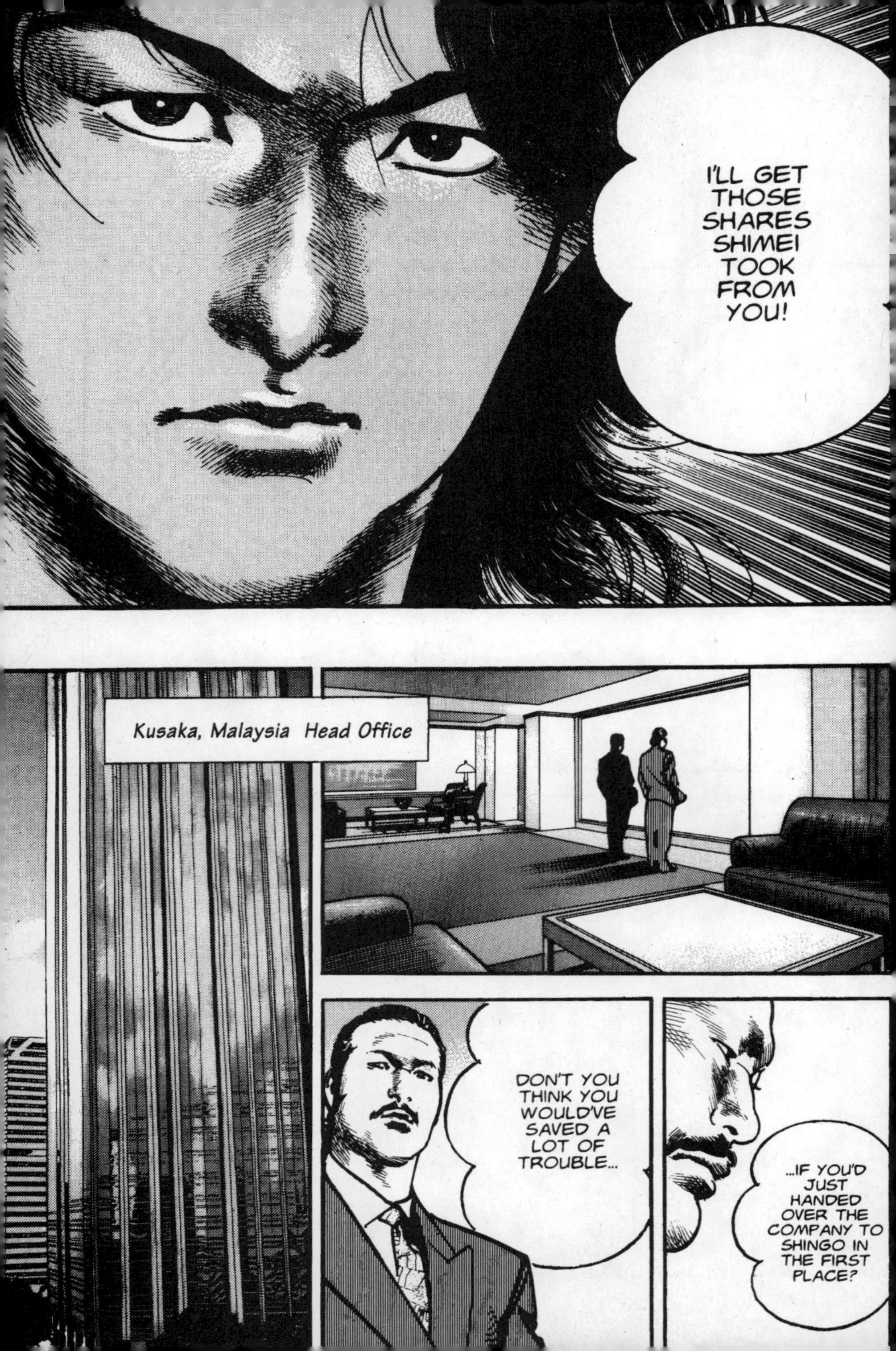
I'LL GET THOSE SHARES SHIMEI TOOK FROM YOU!
Kusaka, Malaysia Head Office
DON'T YOU THINK YOU WOULD'VE SAVED A LOT OF TROUBLE...
...IF YOU'D JUST HANDED OVER THE COMPANY TO SHINGO IN THE FIRST PLACE?

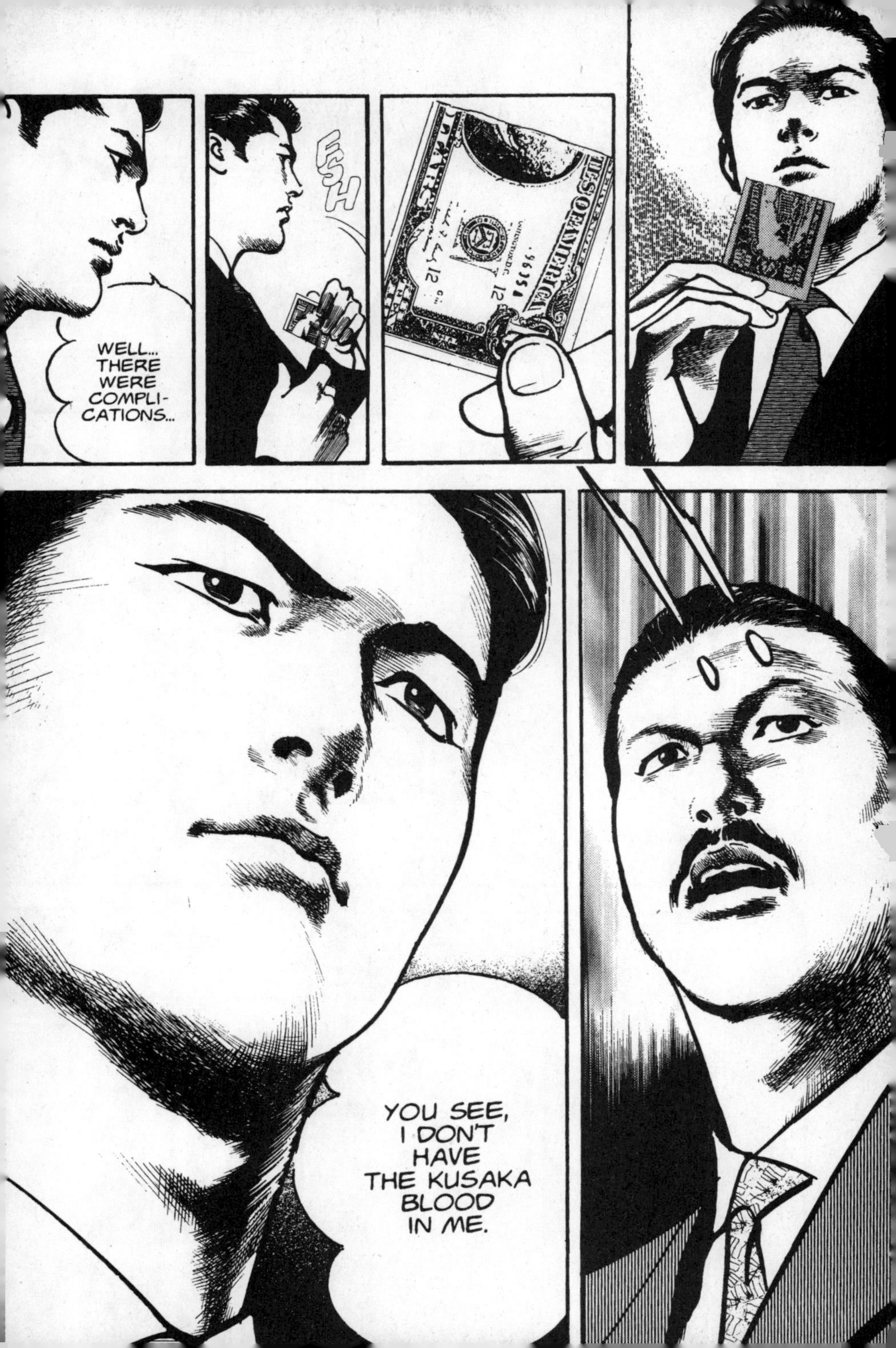
WELL... THERE WERE COMPLICATIONS...
FSH
YOU SEE, I DON'T HAVE THE KUSAKA BLOOD IN ME.

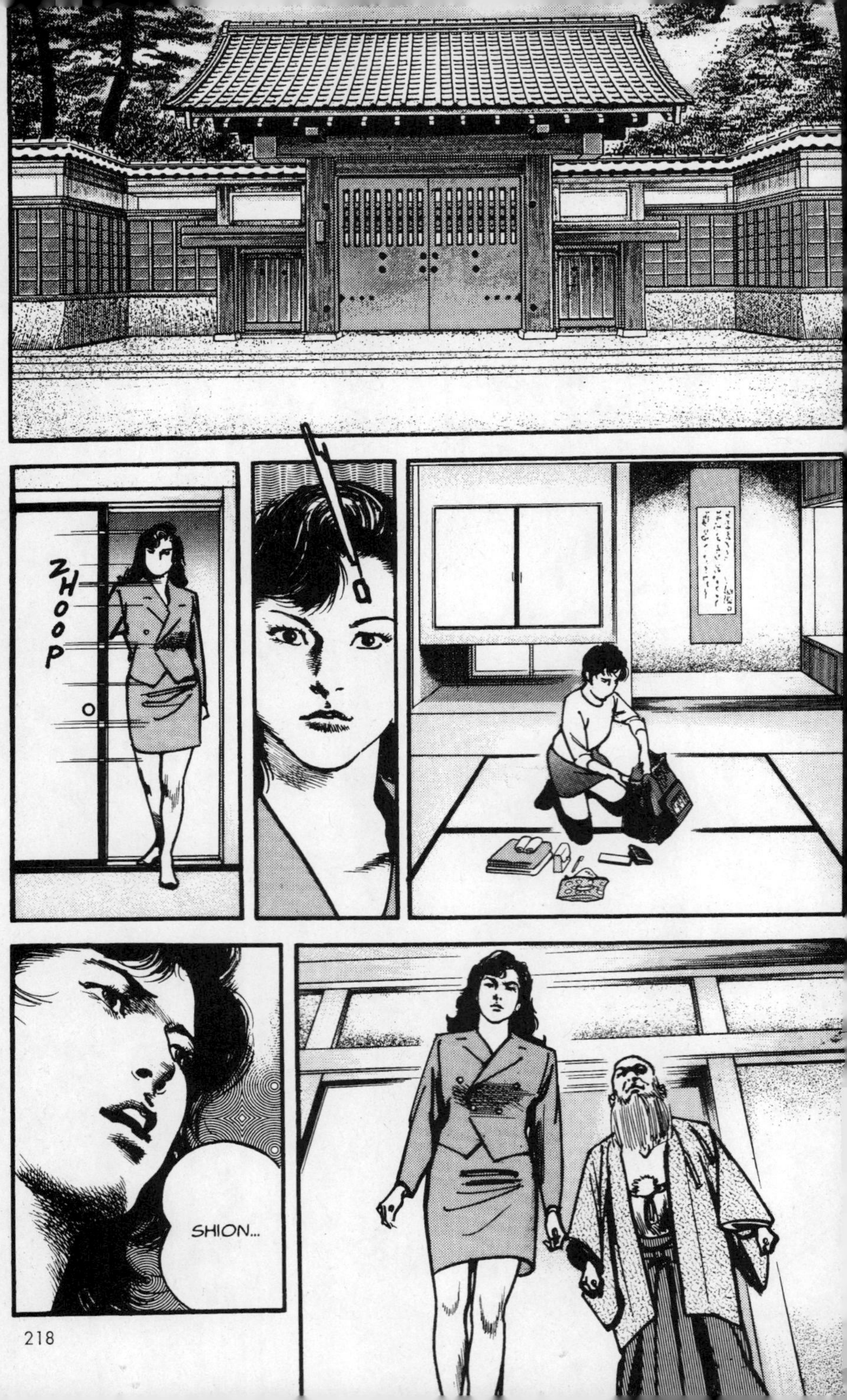
ZHOOP
SHION...

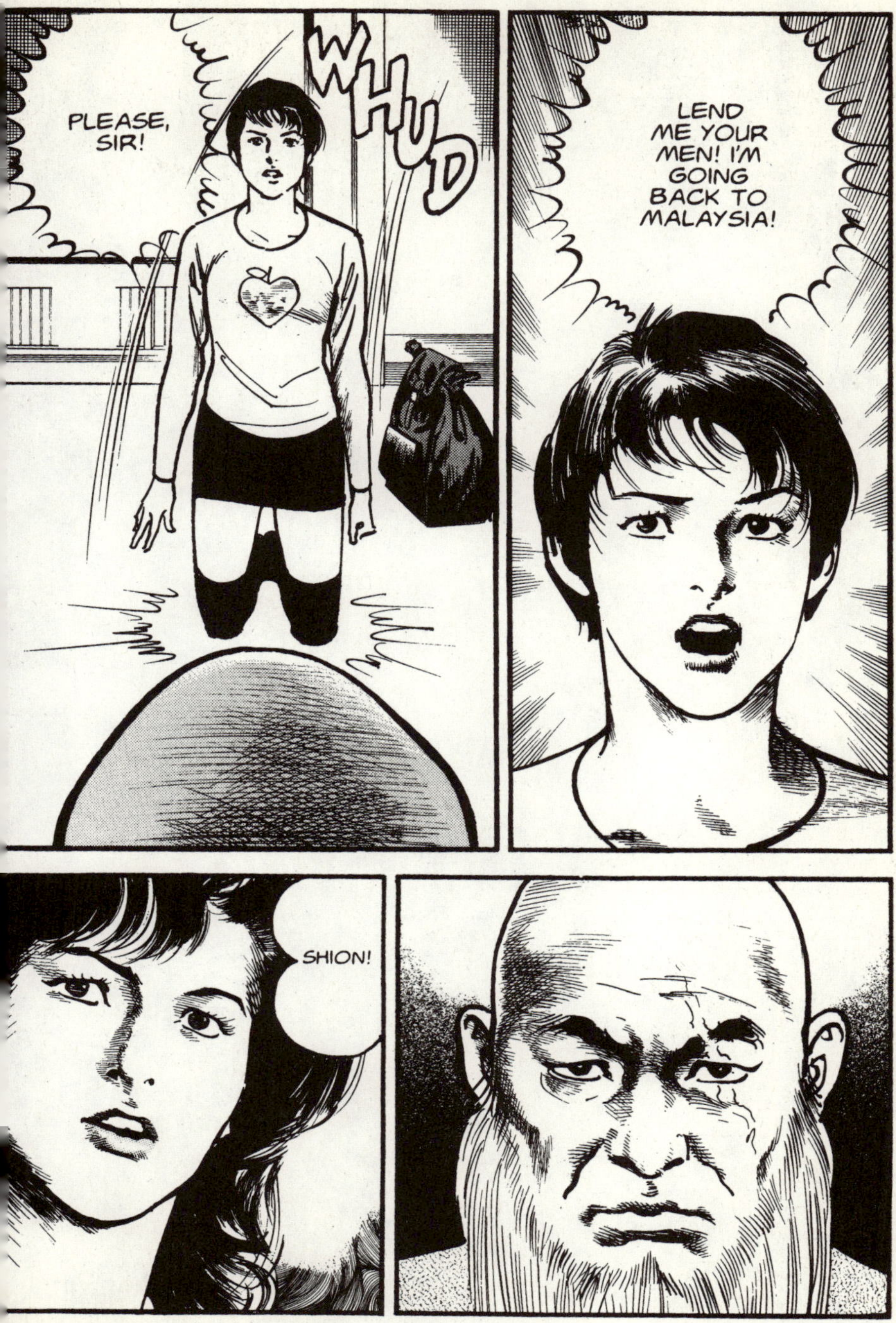
PLEASE, SIR!
WHUD
LEND ME YOUR MEN! I'M GOING BACK TO MALAYSIA!
SHION!

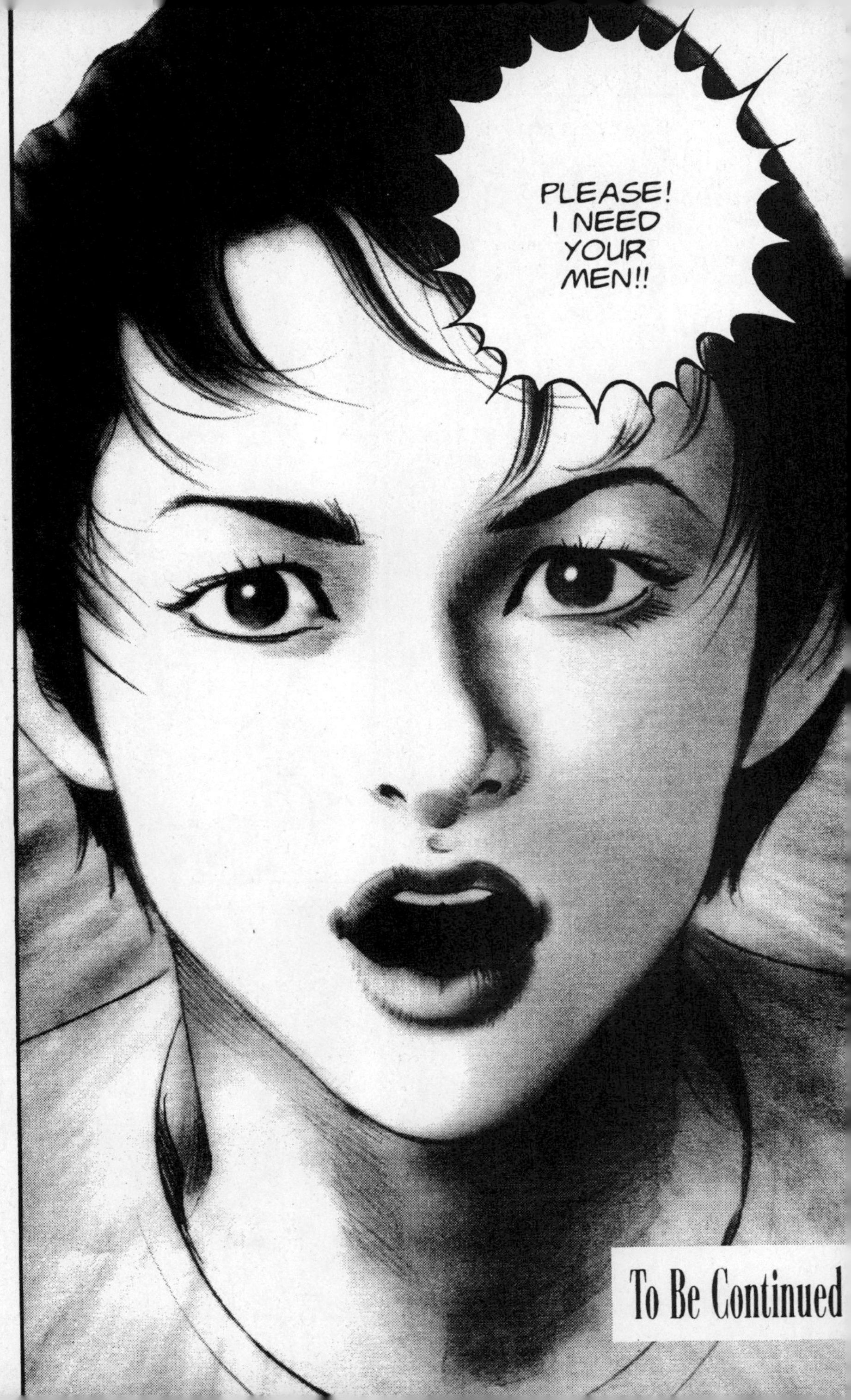
PLEASE! I NEED YOUR MEN!!
To Be Continued

HARD-HITTING POLITICS!

EAGLE: THE MAKING OF AN ASIAN-AMERICAN PRESIDENT

The monthly manga series by Kaiji Kawaguchi
The story of Kenneth Yamaoka: United States senator, Vietnam vet, and the first Japanese-American contender for the presidency.

100+ PAGES AN ISSUE!

VIZ COMICS™

Viz Comics
P.O. Box 77010
San Francisco, CA 94107
Phone: (800) 394-3042
Fax: (415) 348-8936
www.viz.com
www.j-pop.com
www.pulp-mag.com

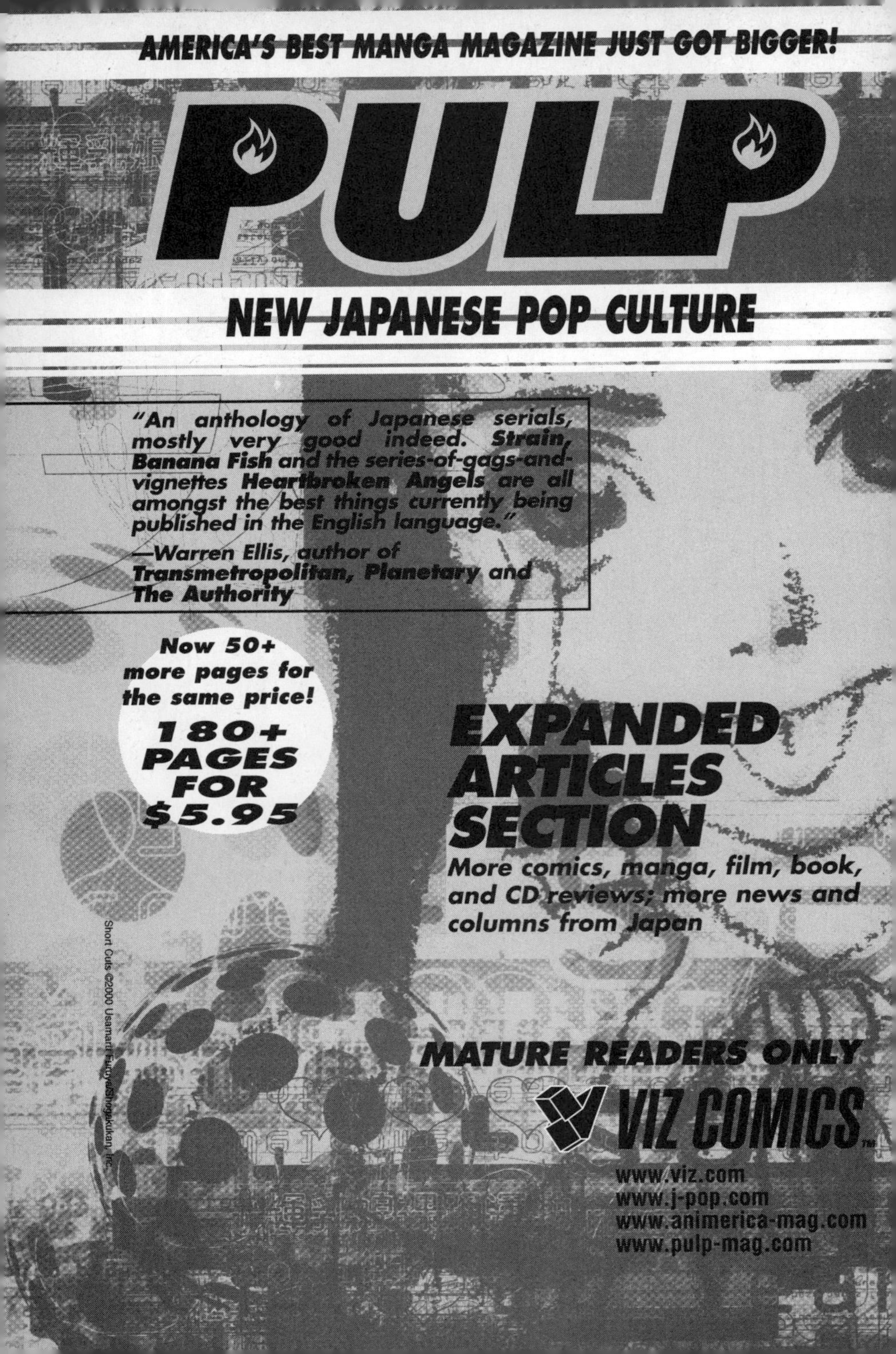
AMERICA'S BEST MANGA MAGAZINE JUST GOT BIGGER!
PULP
NEW JAPANESE POP CULTURE
"An anthology of Japanese serials, mostly very good indeed. Strain, Banana Fish and the series-of-gags-and-vignettes Heartbroken Angels are all amongst the best things currently being published in the English language."
—Warren Ellis, author of Transmetropolitan, Planetary and The Authority
Now 50+ more pages for the same price!
180+ PAGES FOR $5.95
EXPANDED ARTICLES SECTION
More comics, manga, film, book, and CD reviews; more news and columns from Japan
Short Cuts ©2000 Usamaru Furuya/Shogakukan, Inc.
MATURE READERS ONLY
VIZ COMICS™
www.viz.com
www.j-pop.com
www.animerica-mag.com
www.pulp-mag.com

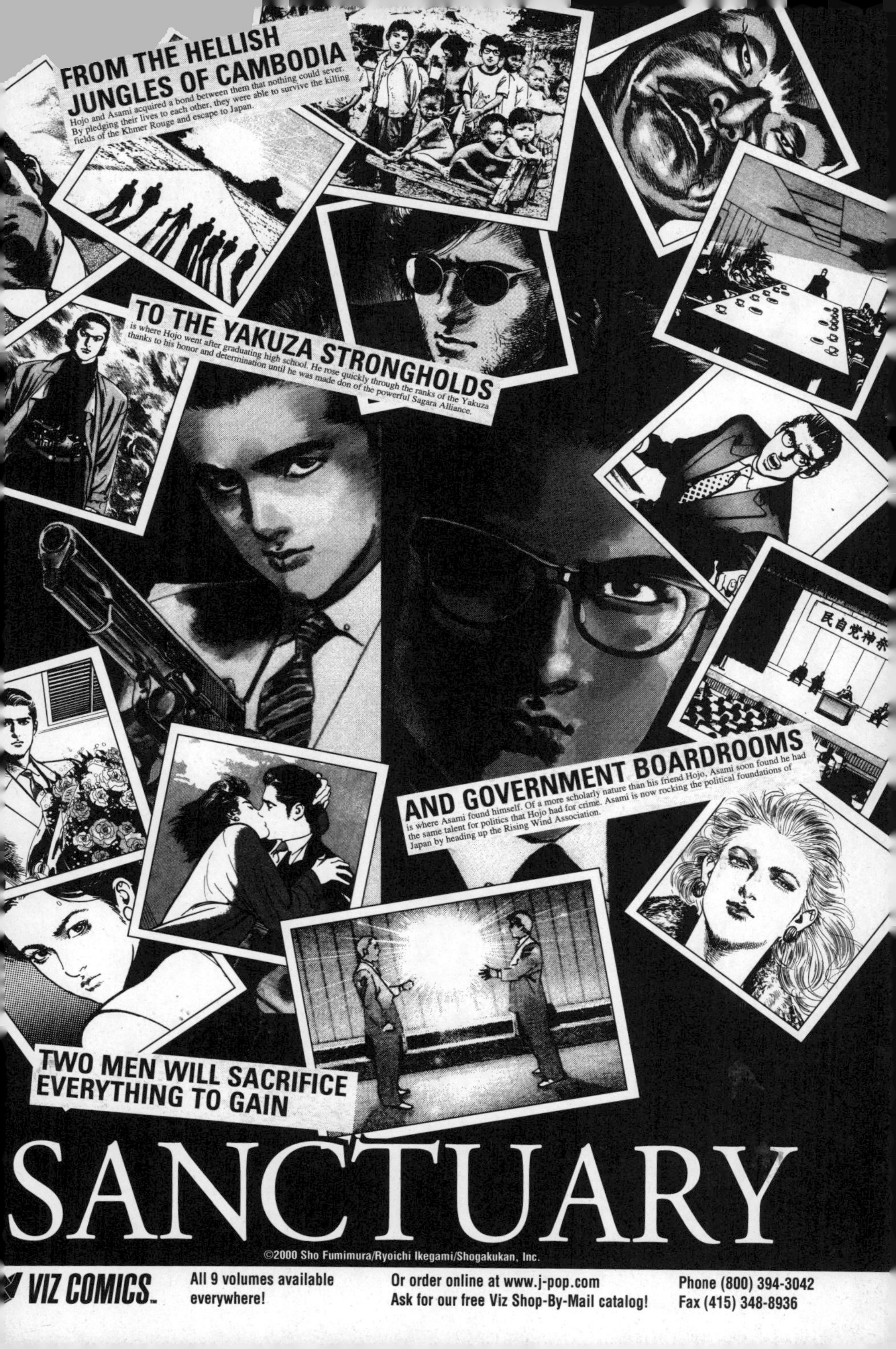
FROM THE HELLISH JUNGLES OF CAMBODIA
Hojo and Asami acquired a bond between them that nothing could sever. By pledging their lives to each other, they were able to survive the killing fields of the Khmer Rouge and escape to Japan.
TO THE YAKUZA STRONGHOLDS
is where Hojo went after graduating high school. He rose quickly through the ranks of the Yakuza thanks to his honor and determination until he was made don of the powerful Sagara Alliance.
AND GOVERNMENT BOARDROOMS
is where Asami found himself. Of a more scholarly nature than his friend Hojo, Asami soon found he had the same talent for politics that Hojo had for crime. Asami is now rocking the political foundations of Japan by heading up the Rising Wind Association.
TWO MEN WILL SACRIFICE EVERYTHING TO GAIN
SANCTUARY
©2000 Sho Fumimura/Ryoichi Ikegami/Shogakukan, Inc.
VIZ COMICS.
All 9 volumes available everywhere!
Or order online at www.j-pop.com
Ask for our free Viz Shop-By-Mail catalog!
Phone (800) 394-3042
Fax (415) 348-8936